THE TWO MEN WORE DARK SUITS, CONSERVATIVE TIES.

They were big, broad through the shoulders, and confident. Genuine, honest-to-God Men in Black. But there was something about them, something cold. They made my shoulders bunch up and the hairs on my neck stand up—hackles rising. The first guy escorted me to the sedan.

I said, "Just so we're clear: the city's vampire Mistress has the D.C. cops in her pocket, or at least enough of them in her pocket that she can order a roadblock on one of the major arteries, just to find one person."

"It would appear so," he said.

"She could have just *called* me, you know."

He glanced sidelong at me. This was a vampire we were talking about. It was all about theatrics.

P9-DJA-902

"Vaughn's clever new take on the supernatural is edgy and irreverent . . . will have readers clamoring for the next installment."

—*Romantic Times BOOKclub Magazine*

"A light touch, conversational tone, and entertaining premise . . . very appealing."

—*VOYA*

"Just when you thought nobody could put a new spin on werewolves and vampires, along comes Carrie Vaughn to prove otherwise."

—BookLoons.com

"A howling good urban-fantasy novel."

—FreshFiction.com

"Sure to be a hit . . . Don't wait for the full moon to pick up your copy!"

—RomRevToday.com

"The prose flows so smoothly . . . skillfully handled."

—Trashotron.com

*K*itty
Goes to
Washington

CARRIE VAUGHN

WARNER BOOKS

NEW YORK   BOSTON

This book is a work of fiction. Names, characters, places, and incidents are the product of the author's imagination or are used fictitiously. Any resemblance to actual events, locales, or persons, living or dead, is coincidental.

If you purchase this book without a cover you should be aware that this book may have been stolen property and reported as "unsold and destroyed" to the publisher. In such case neither the author nor the publisher has received any payment for this "stripped book."

Copyright © 2006 by Carrie Vaughn
"Kitty Meets the Band" copyright © 2006 by Carrie Vaughn. All rights reserved. No part of this book may be reproduced in any form or by any electronic or mechanical means, including information storage and retrieval systems, without permission in writing from the publisher, except by a reviewer who may quote brief passages in a review.

Cover design by Don Puckey
Book design by Stratford Publishing Services, Inc.

Warner Books
1271 Avenue of the Americas
New York, NY 10020

Printed in the United States of America

First Printing: July 2006

10 9 8 7 6 5 4 3 2 1

To Robbie

The Force will be with us, always.

Acknowledgments

I'd like to thank my beta testers: Daniel Abraham, Brian Hiebert, and Jo Anne Vaughn (a.k.a. Mom). Thanks to Sandy Karpuk for an awesome day job and for letting me use the printer; to Professor Kelly Hurley for the fascinating and useful *Dracula* discussions; to Ian Hudek for coming up with V.L.A.D.; to Jaime Levine for helping make this a much better book; to Chris Dao and the crew at Warner who've made the whole process easier; and also to my family, Max, and all the usual suspects. And of course, thank you to everyone who was so darned excited about *Kitty and The Midnight Hour*. The confidence boost really helped.

My agent, Dan Hooker, sold this book for me but passed away before he could see the finished product. My gratitude for his work on my behalf, and sadness at his loss are immense.

The Playlist

The Watchmen, "Together"

Peter Gabriel, "Games Without Frontiers"

Oingo Boingo, "No Spill Blood"

The Clash, "Know Your Rights"

Suzanne Vega, "Tombstone"

Shriekback, "Nemesis"

Pet Shop Boys, "DJ Culture"

Pink Floyd, "Us and Them"

Aqua, "Doctor Jones"

Prince, "Kiss"

Too Much Joy, "You Will"

The Clash, "(White Man) In Hammersmith Palais"

The Beatles, "Across the Universe"
(*Let It Be . . . Naked* version)

New Order, "True Faith-94"

chapter 1

"We have Beth from Tampa on the line. Hello."

"Hi, Kitty, thanks for taking my call."

"You're welcome."

"I have a question I've been wanting to ask for a long time. Do you think Dracula is still out there?"

I leaned on the arm of my chair and stared at the microphone. "Dracula. As in, the book? The character?"

Beth from Tampa sounded cheerful and earnest. "Yeah. I mean, he's got to be the best-known vampire there is. He was so powerful, I can't really believe that Van Helsing and the rest of them just finished him off."

I tried to be polite. "Actually, they did. It's just a book, Beth. Fiction. They're characters."

"But you sit there week after week telling everyone that vampires and werewolves are real. Surely a book like this must have been based on something that really happened. Maybe his name wasn't actually Dracula, but Bram Stoker must have based him on a real vampire, don't you think? Don't you wonder who that vampire was?"

Stoker may have met a real vampire, may even have

based Dracula on that vampire. But if that vampire was still around, I suspected he was in deep hiding out of embarrassment.

"Even if there is a real vampire who was Stoker's inspiration, the events of the book are sheer fabrication. I say this because *Dracula* isn't really about vampires, or vampire hunting, or the undead, or any of that. It's about a lot of *other* things: sexuality, religion, reverse imperialism, and xenophobia. But what it's *really* about is saving the world through superior office technology." I waited half a beat for that to sink in. I loved this stuff. "Think about it. They make such a big deal about their typewriters, phonographs, stenography—this was like the technothriller of its day. They end up solving everything because Mina is really great at data entry and collating. What do you think?"

"Um . . . I think that may be a stretch."

"Have you even read the book?"

"Um, no. But I've seen every movie version of it!" she ended brightly, as if that would save her.

I suppressed a growl. "All right. Which is your favorite?"

"The one with Keanu Reeves!"

"Why am I not surprised?" I clicked her off. "Moving on. Next caller, you're on the air."

"Kitty, hey! Longtime listener, first-time caller. I'm so glad you put me on."

"No problem. What's your story?"

"Well, I have sort of a question. Do you have any idea what kind of overlap there is between lycanthropes and the furry community?"

The monitor said this guy had a question about lycanthropes and alternative lifestyles. The producer screening calls was doing a good job of being vague.

I knew this topic would come up eventually. It seemed I'd avoided it for as long as I possibly could. Oh well. The folks in radioland expected honesty.

"You know, I've hosted this show for almost a year without anyone bringing up furries. Thank you for destroying that last little shred of dignity I possessed."

"You don't have to be so—"

"Look, seriously. I have absolutely no idea. They're two different things—lycanthropy is a disease. Furry-ness is a . . . a predilection. Which I suppose means it's possible to be both. And when you say furry, are you talking about the people who like cartoons with bipedal foxes, or are you talking about the people who dress up in animal suits to get it on? Maybe some of the people who call in wanting to know how to become werewolves happen to be furries and think that's the next logical step. How many of the lycanthropes that I know are furries? That's not something I generally ask people. Do you see how complicated this is?"

"Well, yeah. But I have to wonder, if someone *really* believes that they were meant to be, you know, a different species entirely—like the way some men really believe they were meant to be women and then go through a sex change operation—don't you think it's reasonable that—"

"No. No it isn't reasonable. Tell me, do *you* think that you were meant to be a different species entirely?"

He gave a deep sigh, the kind that usually preceded a dark confession, the kind of thing that was a big draw for most of my audience.

"I have this recurring dream where I'm an alpaca."

I did a little flinch, convinced I hadn't heard him correctly. "Excuse me?"

"An alpaca. I keep having these dreams where I'm an alpaca. I'm in the Andes, high in the mountains. In the next valley over are the ruins of a great Incan city. Everything is so green." He might have been describing the photos in an issue of *National Geographic*. "And the grass tastes so lovely."

Okay, that probably wasn't in *National Geographic*.

"Um . . . that's interesting."

"I'd love to travel there someday. To see the Andes for myself. Have—have you by any chance ever met any were-alpacas?"

If it weren't so sad I'd have to laugh. "No, I haven't. All the were-animals I've ever heard of are predators, so I really don't think you're likely to meet a were-alpaca."

"Oh," he said with a sigh. "Do you think maybe I was an alpaca in a past life?"

"Honestly, I don't know. I'm sorry I can't be more help. I genuinely hope you find some answers to your questions someday. I think traveling there is a great idea." Seeing the world never hurt, in my opinion. "Thanks for calling."

I had no idea where the show could possibly go after that. I hit a line at random. "Next caller, what do you want to talk about?"

"Hi, Kitty, yeah. Um, thanks. I—I think I have a problem." He was male, with a tired-sounding tenor voice. I always listened closely to the ones who seemed tired; their problems were usually doozies.

"Then let's see what we can do with it. What's wrong?"

"It all started when these two guys moved to town, a werewolf and a vampire. They're a couple, you know?"

"These are two guys. Men, right?"

"Right."

"And the problem is . . ."

"Well, nothing at this point. But then this vampire hunter started going after the vampire, I guess he'd been hired by the vampire's former human servant."

"The vampire's human servant didn't travel with him?"

"No, he dumped her to run off with the werewolf."

There couldn't possibly be more. Bracing, I said, "Then what?"

"*Another* werewolf, who used to be the alpha female mate of the werewolf before he hooked up with the vampire, showed up. She wanted to get back together with him, saying this stuff about wolves mating for life and all, but he didn't want anything to do with her, so he hired the same hunter to go after *her*—"

"This hunter, his name wasn't Cormac by any chance, was it?" I knew a vampire and werewolf hunting Cormac, and this sounded like something he might do.

"No."

Phew. "Just checking."

The story only went downhill from there. Just when I thought the last knot had been tied in the tangled web of this town's supernatural soap opera, the caller added a new one.

Finally, I was able to ask, "And what's your place in all this?"

He gave a massive sigh. "I'm the human servant of the local vampire Master. They make me deliver messages. 'Tell them they have to leave town.' 'Tell your Master we don't want to leave town!' 'Tell the hunter we'll pay him to call off the contract!' 'Tell him if he doesn't come back to me I'll kill myself!' It never ends! And all I want to know is—"

Maybe he just wanted to vent. That was what I was here for. Maybe he wouldn't ask me to sort out his drama for him. Fingers crossed. "Yes?"

"Why can't we all just get along?"

Oy. It was one of those nights. "That, my friend, is the million-dollar question. You know what? Screw 'em. They're all being selfish and putting you in the middle. Make them deliver their own messages."

"I—I can't do *that*."

"Yes you can. They've got to realize how ridiculous this all looks."

"Well, I mean, *yeah*, I've *told* them, but—"

"But what?"

"I guess I'm used to doing what I'm told."

"Then maybe you should learn to say no. When they act surprised that you've said no, tell them it's for their own good. You've basically been enabling all their snotty behavior, right?"

"Maybe . . ."

"Because if they had to start talking to each other they might actually solve some of their problems, right?"

"Or rip each other's throats out. They're not exactly human, remember."

Taking a deep breath and trying not to sound chronically frustrated, I said, "I may very well be the only person in the supernatural underworld who feels this way, but I don't think that should make a difference. Crappy behavior is still crappy behavior, and letting yourself succumb to unsavory monstrous instincts isn't a good excuse. So, stand up for yourself, okay?"

"O-okay," he said, not sounding convinced.

"Call me back and let me know how it goes."

"Thanks, Kitty."

The producer gave me a warning signal, waving from the other side of the booth window, pointing at his watch, and making a slicing motion across his throat. Um, maybe he was trying to tell me something.

I sighed, then leaned up to the mike. "I'm sorry, folks, but that looks like all the time we have this week. I want to thank you for spending the last couple of hours with me and invite you to come back next week, when I talk with the lead singer of the punk metal band Plague of Locusts, who says their bass player is possessed by a demon, and that's the secret of their success. This is *The Midnight Hour*, and I'm Kitty Norville, voice of the night."

The ON AIR sign dimmed, and the show's closing credits, which included a recording of a wolf howl—my wolf howl—as a backdrop, played. I pulled the headset off and ran my fingers through my blond hair, hoping it didn't look too squished.

The producer's name was Jim something. I forgot his last name. Rather, I didn't bother remembering. I'd be at a different radio station next week, working with a different set of people. For the better part of a year, most of the show's run, I'd broadcast out of Denver. But a month ago, I left town. Or was chased out. It depended on who you talked to.

Rather than find a new base of operations, I decided to travel. It kept me from getting into trouble with the locals, and it made me harder to find. The radio audience wouldn't know the difference. I was in Flagstaff this week.

I leaned on the doorway leading to the control booth

and smiled a thanks to Jim. Like a lot of guys stuck manning the control board over the graveyard shift, he was impossibly young, college age, maybe even an intern, or at most a junior associate producer of some kind. He was sweating. He probably hadn't expected to handle this many calls on a talk show that ran at midnight.

Most of my audience stayed up late.

He handed me a phone handset. I said into it, "Hi, Matt."

Matt had worked the board for the show when I was in Denver. These days, he coached the local crew. I couldn't do this without him.

"Hey, Kitty. It's a wrap, looks like."

"Was it okay?"

"Sounded great."

"You always say that," I said with a little bit of a whine.

"What can I say? You're consistent."

"Thanks. I think."

"Tomorrow's full moon, right? You going to be okay?"

It was nice that he remembered, even nicer that he was worried about me, but I didn't like to talk about it. He was an outsider. "Yeah, I have a good place all checked out."

"Take care of yourself, Kitty."

"Thanks."

I wrapped things up at the station and went to my hotel to sleep off the rest of the night. Locked the door, hung out the DO NOT DISTURB sign. Couldn't sleep, of course. I'd become nocturnal, doing the show. I'd gotten used to not sleeping until dawn, then waking at noon. It was even easier now that I was on my own. No one checked up on me, no one was meeting me for lunch. It was just me, the road, the show once a week. An isolated forest somewhere once a month. A lonely life.

My next evening was spoken for. Full moon nights were always spoken for.

I found the place a couple of days ago: a remote trailhead at the end of a dirt road in the interior of a state park. I could leave the car parked in a secluded turn-out behind a tree. Real wolves didn't get this far south, so I only had to worry about intruding on any local werewolves who might have marked out this territory. I spent an afternoon walking around, watching, smelling. Giving the locals a chance to see me, let them know I was here. I didn't smell anything unexpected, just the usual forest scents of deer, fox, rabbits. Good hunting here. It looked like I'd have it all to myself.

A couple of hours from midnight, I parked the car at the far end of the trailhead, where it couldn't be seen from the road. I didn't want to give any hint that I was out here. I didn't want anyone, especially not the police, to come snooping. I didn't want anyone I might hurt to come within miles of me.

I'd done this before. This was my second full moon night alone, as a rogue. The first time had been uneventful, except that I woke up hours before dawn, hours before I was ready, shivering in the cold and crying because I couldn't remember how I'd gotten to be naked in the middle of the woods. That never happened when I had other werewolves there to remind me.

My stomach felt like ice. This was never going to get easier. I used to have a pack of my own. I'd been surrounded by friends, people I could trust to protect me. A wolf wasn't meant to run on her own.

You'll be okay. You can take care of yourself.

I sat in the car, gripping the steering wheel, and squeezed

shut my eyes to keep from crying. I had acquired a voice. It was an inner monologue, like a part of my conscience. It reassured me, told me I wasn't crazy, admonished me when I was being silly, convinced me I was going to be okay when I started to doubt myself. The voice sounded like my best friend, T.J. He died protecting me, six weeks ago today. The alpha male of our pack killed him, and I had to leave Denver to keep from getting killed, too. Whenever I started to doubt, I heard T.J.'s voice telling me I was going to be okay.

His death sat strangely with me. For the first week or two, I thought I was handling it pretty well. I was thinking straight and moving on. People call that stage denial. Then on the highway, I saw a couple on a motorcycle: neither of them wore helmets, her blond hair tangled in the wind, and she clung to his leather jacket. Just like I used to ride with T.J. The hole that he'd left behind gaped open, and I had to pull off at the next exit because I was crying so hard. After that, I felt like a zombie. I went through the motions of a life that wasn't mine. This new life I had acquired felt like it had been this way forever, and like it or not, I had to adapt. I used to have an apartment, a wolf pack, and a best friend. But that life had vanished.

I locked the car, put the keys in my jeans pocket, and walked away from the parking lot, away from the trail, and into the wild. The night was clear and sharp. Every touch of air, every scent, blazed clear. The moon, swollen, bursting with light, edged above the trees on the horizon. It touched me, I could feel the light brushing my skin. Gooseflesh rose on my arms. Inside, the creature thrashed. It made me feel both drunk and nauseous. I'd think I was throwing up, but the Wolf would burst out of me instead.

I kept my breathing slow and regular. I'd let her out when I wanted her out, and not a second earlier.

The forest was silver, the trees shadows. Fallen leaves rustled as nighttime animals foraged. I ignored the noises, the awareness of the life surrounding me. I pulled off my T-shirt, felt the moonlight touch my skin.

I put my clothes in the hollow formed by a fallen tree and a boulder. The space was big enough to sleep in when I was finished. I backed away, naked, every pore tingling.

I could do this alone. I'd be safe.

I counted down from five—

One came out as a wolf's howl.

chapter 2

The animal, rabbit, squeals once, falls still. Blood fills mouth, burns like fire. This is life, joy, ecstasy, feeding by the silver light—

If turning Wolf felt like being drunk, the next day definitely felt like being hungover.

I lay in the dirt and decayed leaves, naked, missing the other wolves terribly. We always woke up together in a dog pile, so to speak. I'd always woken up with T.J. at my back. At least I remembered how I got here this time. I whined, groaned, stretched, found my clothes, brushed myself off, and got dressed. The sky was gray; the sun would rise soon. I wanted to be out of here by then.

I got to my car just as the first hikers of the morning pulled into the trailhead parking area. I must have looked a mess: hair tangled, shirt untucked, carrying sneakers in my hand. They stared. I glared at them as I climbed into my own car and drove back to the hotel for a shower.

At noon, I was driving on I-40 heading west. It seemed like a good place to be, for a while. I'd end up in Los Angeles, and that sounded like an adventure.

The middle of the desert between Flagstaff and L.A. certainly wasn't anything resembling an adventure. I played just about every CD I'd brought with me while I traveled through the land of no radio reception.

Which made it all the more surreal when my cell phone rang.

Phone reception? Out here?

I put the hands-free earpiece in and pushed the talk button.

"Hello?"

"Kitty. It's Ben."

I groaned. Ben O'Farrell was my lawyer. Sharp as a tack and vaguely disreputable. He'd agreed to represent *me*, after all.

"Happy to hear you, too."

"Ben, it's not that I don't like you, but every time you call it's bad news."

"You've been subpoenaed by the Senate."

Not one to mince words was Ben.

"Excuse me?"

"A special oversight committee of the United States Senate requests the honor of your presence at upcoming hearings regarding the Center for the Study of Paranatural Biology. I guess they think you're some kind of expert on the subject."

"What?"

"You heard me."

Yeah, I'd heard him, and as a result my brain froze.

Senate? Subpoena? Hearings? As in Joe McCarthy and the Hollywood blacklist? As in Iran-Contra?

"Kitty?"

"Is this bad? I mean, how bad is it?"

"Calm down. It isn't bad. Senate committees have hearings all the time. It's how they get information. Since they don't know anything about paranatural biology, they've called hearings."

It made sense. He even made it sound routine. I still couldn't keep the panic out of my voice. "What am I going to do?"

"You're going to go to Washington, D.C., and answer the nice senators' questions."

That was on the other side of the country. How much time did I have? Could I drive it? Fly? Did I have anything I could wear to Congress? Would they tell me the questions they wanted to ask ahead of time, as if I could study for it like it was some kind of test?

They didn't expect me to do this by myself, did they?

"Ben? You have to come with me."

Now *he* sounded panicked. "Oh, no. They're just going to ask you questions. You don't need a lawyer there."

"Come on. Please? Think of it as a vacation. It'll all go on the expense account."

"I don't have time—"

"Honestly, what do you think the odds are that I can keep out of trouble once I open my mouth? Isn't there this whole 'contempt of Congress' thing that happens when I say something that pisses them off? Would you rather be there from the start or have to fly in in the middle of things to get me out of jail for mouthing off at somebody important?"

His sigh was that of a martyr. "When you're right, you're right."

Victory! "Thanks, Ben. I really appreciate it. When do we need to be there?"

"We've got a couple weeks yet."

And here I was, going the wrong way.

"So I can drive there from Barstow in time."

"What the hell are you doing in Barstow?"

"Driving?"

Ben made an annoyed huff and hung up on me.

So. I was going to Washington, D.C.

I seemed to be living my life on the phone lately. I could go for days without having a real face-to-face conversation with anyone beyond "No, I don't want fries with that." I was turning into one of those jokers who walks around with a hands-free earpiece permanently attached to one ear. Sometimes, I just forgot it was there.

I went to L.A., did two shows, interviewed the band— no demon possessions happened in my presence, but they played a screechy death metal-sounding thing that made me wish I'd been out of my body for it. That left me a week or so to drive to the East Coast.

I was on the road when I called Dr. Paul Flemming. Flemming headed up the Center for the Study of Paranatural Biology, the focus of the Senate hearing in question. Until a month ago it had been a confidential research organization, a secret laboratory investigating a field that no one who wasn't involved believed even existed. Then Flemming held a press conference and blew the doors wide open. He thought the time was right to make the Center's work public, to officially recognize the existence of vampires, werewolves, and a dozen other things that go bump in the night. I was sure that part of why he did it was my show. People had already started to believe, and accept.

I'd been trying to talk to him. I had his phone number, but I only ever got through to voice mail. As long as I kept trying, he'd get so sick of my messages that he'd call me back eventually.

Or get a restraining order.

The phone rang. And rang. I mentally prepared another version of my message—please call back, we have to talk, I promise not to bite.

Then someone answered. "Hello?"

The car swerved; I was so surprised I almost let go of the steering wheel. "Hello? Dr. Flemming?"

There was a pause before he answered, "Kitty Norville. How nice to hear from you."

He sounded polite, like this was a friendly little chat, as if there wasn't any history between us. He wasn't going to get away with that.

"I *really* need to talk to you. You spent six months calling me anonymously, dropping mysterious hints about your work and suggesting that you want me to help you without ever giving any details, then without any warning you go public, and I have to recognize your voice off a radio broadcast of a press conference. Then silence. You don't want to talk to me. And now I've been subpoenaed to testify before a Senate committee about this can of worms you've opened. Don't get me wrong, I think it's a great can of worms. But what exactly are you trying to accomplish?"

He said, "I want the Center to keep its funding."

At last, a straight answer. I could imagine what had happened: as a secret research organization, the Center's funding was off the books, or disguised under some other innocuous category. An enterprising young congressman must have seen that there was a stream of money heading into some nebulous and possibly useless avenue and started an investigation.

Or maybe Flemming had wanted the Center to be discovered in this manner all along. Now the Senate was holding official hearings, and he'd get to show his work to the world. I just wished he'd warned me.

"So all you have to do is make sure the Center comes off looking good."

"Useful," he said. "It has to look useful. Good and useful aren't always the same thing. I'd heard that you'd been called to testify. For what it's worth, I'm sorry."

"Oh, don't be," I said lightly. "It'll be fun. I'm looking forward to it. But I'd really like to meet you beforehand and get your side of the story."

"There's nothing much to tell."

"Then humor me. I'm insanely curious." Wait for it, wait for it—"How about I interview you on the show? You could get the public behind you."

"I'm not sure that's a good idea."

Good thing I was driving across Texas—no turns and nothing to run into. Flemming had all my attention.

"This may be your only chance to tell your side of the story, why you're doing this research and why you need funding, outside of the hearings. Never underestimate the power of public opinion."

"You're persuasive."

"I try." Carry them along with sheer enthusiasm. That was the trick. I felt like a commercial.

He hesitated; I let him think about it. Then he said, "Call me again when you get to D.C."

At this point, anything that wasn't "no" was a victory. "You promise you'll actually answer the phone and not screen me with voice mail?"

"I'll answer."

"Thank you."

Mental calculation—the next show was Friday, in four days. I could reach D.C. by then. I could get Flemming on the show before the hearings started.

Time for another call, to Matt this time. "Matt? Can you see about setting up this week's show in Washington, D.C.?"

For years I hadn't left the town I lived in, much less driven across country. I didn't want to leave the place where I was comfortable and safe. It was easy to stay in one place and let my packmates, my alpha, take care of me. Easy to stagnate. Then the show started, and the boundaries became too narrow. What was supposed to happen—what happened among wild wolves, behavior that carried over to the lycanthropic variety—was that a young wolf moved up through the pecking order, testing boundaries until she challenged the leaders themselves, and if she won, she became the alpha.

I couldn't do it. I challenged and couldn't lead. I left town. I'd been essentially homeless since then. Wandering, a rogue wolf.

It wasn't so bad.

I drank coffee, which put me on edge but kept me awake and driving. Before I left Denver I'd never done this, driven for hours by myself, until the asphalt on the highway buzzed and the land whipped by in a blur. It made me feel powerful, in a way. I didn't have to listen to anyone, I could stop when I wanted, eat where I wanted, and no one second-guessed my directions.

I took the time to play tourist on the way. I stopped at random bronze historical markers, followed brown landmark highway signs down obscure two-lane highways, saw Civil War battlefields and giant plaster chickens. Maybe after the hearings I could set some kind of crazy goal and make it a publicity stunt: do the show from every state capital, a different city each week for a year. I could get the producers to pay for a trip to Hawaii. Oh, yeah.

Matt set me up at an Arlington, Virginia, radio station. I got there Friday around noon. I was cutting it close; the show aired live Friday night.

Lucky for me, Flemming had agreed to be a guest on the show.

The station's offices and broadcast center, a low brick fifties-era building with the call letters hung outside in modernist steel, were in a suburban office park overgrown with thick, leafy trees. Inside the swinging glass doors, the place was like a dozen other public and talk radio stations I'd been to: cluttered but respectable, run by sincere people who couldn't seem to find time to water the yellowing ficus plant in the corner.

A receptionist sat at a desk crowded with unsorted mail. She was on the phone. I approached, smiling in what I hoped was a friendly and unthreatening manner— at least I hoped that the dazed, vacuous smile I felt would pass for friendly. I could still feel the roar of the car tires in my tendons. She held her hand out in a "wait a minute" gesture.

"—I don't care what he told you, Grace. He's cheating on you. Yes . . . yes. See, you already know it. Who works past eleven every night? Insurance salesmen don't *have* night shifts, Grace . . . Fine, don't listen to me, but when you find someone else's black lace panties in his glove box don't come cryin' to me."

My life could be worse. I could be hosting a talk show on *normal* relationship problems.

After hanging up the phone she turned a sugary smile on me as if nothing had happened. "What can I do for you?"

Wadded up in my hand I had a piece of paper with the name of the station manager. "I'm here to see Liz Morgan."

"I think she may be out to lunch, let me check a minute." She played tag with the intercom phone system, buzzing room after room with no luck. I was about to tell her not to worry about it, that I'd go take a nap in my car until she got back.

"I don't know. I'll ask." She looked up from a rather involved conversation on one of the lines. "Can I pass along your name?"

"Kitty Norville. I should be scheduled to do a show tonight."

Raised brows told me she'd heard the name before.

She didn't take her gaze off me when she passed along the answer.

"Says she's Kitty Norville . . . that's right . . . I think so. All right, I'll send her back." She put away the handset. "Wes is the assistant manager. He said to go on back and he'll talk to you. Last door on the right." She gestured down a hallway.

I felt her watching me the whole way. Some time ago I'd stated on the air, on live national radio, that I was a werewolf. Listeners generally took that to mean a couple different things: that I was a werewolf, or that I was crazy. Or possibly that I was involved in an outrageous publicity stunt pandering to the gullible and superstitious.

Any one of them was stare-worthy.

I arrived at the last door, which stood open. Two desks and two different work spaces occupied the room, which was large enough to establish an uneasy truce between them. The man at the messier of the two stood as soon as I appeared and made his way around the furniture. He left a half-played game of solitaire on his computer.

He came at me so quickly with his hand outstretched, ready to shake, that I almost backed out of the way. He was in his twenties, with floppy hair and a grin that probably never went away. Former college cheerleader, I'd bet.

"Kitty Norville? You're Kitty Norville? I'm a big fan! Hi, I'm Wes Brady, it's great to have you here!"

"Hi," I said, letting him pump my hand. "So, um. Thanks for letting me set up shop here on such short notice."

"No problem. Looking forward to it. Come in, have a seat."

What I really wanted was to have a look at their studio, meet the engineer who'd be running the board for me, then find a hotel, shower, and supper. Wes wanted to chat. He pointed me to a chair in the corner and pulled the one from his desk over.

He said, "So. I've always wanted to ask, and now that you're here, well—"

I prepared for the interrogation.

"Where do you come up with this stuff?"

"Excuse me?"

"On your show. I mean, do you coach callers? Are they actors? Do you have plants? How scripted is it? How many writers do you have? At first I thought it was a gag, we all did. But you've kept it up for a year now, and it's great! I gotta know how you do it."

I might as well hit my head against a brick wall.

Conspiratorially, I leaned forward over the plastic arm of the retro office chair. He bent toward me, his eyes wide. Because of course I'd give away trade secrets to anyone who asked.

"Why don't you stick around tonight and find out?"

"Come on, not even a little hint?"

"Now where's the fun in that?" I stood. "Hey, it's been great meeting you, but I really should get going."

"Oh—but you just got here. I could show you around. I could—"

"Is he bothering you?"

A woman in a rumpled navy-blue suit a few years out-of-date, her black hair short and moussed, stood in the doorway, her arms crossed.

"You must be Liz Morgan," I said, hoping I sounded enthusiastic rather than relieved. "I'm Kitty Norville. My colleague should have been in touch with you."

"Yes. Nice to meet you." Thankfully, her handshake

was perfectly sedate and functional. "Wes, you have that marketing report for me yet?"

"Um, no. Not yet. Just getting to it now. Be ready in an hour. Yes, ma'am." Wes bounded to his desk and closed the solitaire game.

Liz gave me exactly the tour I wanted and answered all my questions. Even, "That Wes is a bit excitable, isn't he?"

"You should see him without his medication."

She saw me to the door and recommended a good hotel nearby.

"Thanks again," I said. "It's always kind of a crap shoot finding a station that'll even touch my show."

She shook her head, and her smile seemed long-suffering. "Kitty, we're five miles from Washington, D.C. There's nothing you can throw at us that'll compare with what I've seen come out of there."

I couldn't say I believed her. Because if she was right, I was about to get into things way over my head.

I returned to the station a couple of hours early and waited to meet Dr. Paul Flemming. I fidgeted. Ivy, the receptionist, told me all kinds of horror stories about traffic in the D.C. area, the Beltway, the unreliability of the Metro, all of it giving me hundreds of reasons to think that Flemming couldn't possibly arrive in time for the show. It was okay, I tried to convince myself. This sort of thing had happened before. I'd had guests miss their slot entirely. It was one of the joys of live radio. I just had to ad-lib. That was why the phone lines were so great.

Somebody was always willing to make an ass out of themselves on the air.

Ivy went home for the evening, so at least the horror stories stopped. Liz and Wes stuck around to watch the show. I paced in the lobby, back and forth. A bad habit. The Wolf's bad habit. I let her have it—it gave her something to do and kept her quiet. Anxiety tended to make her antsy.

Me. Made *me* antsy.

Fifteen minutes before start time, a man opened the glass door a foot and peered inside. I stopped. "Dr. Flemming?"

Straightening, he entered the lobby and nodded.

A weight lifted. "I'm Kitty, thanks for coming."

Flemming wasn't what I expected. From his voice and the way he carried on, I expected someone cool and polished, slickly governmental, with a respectable suit and regulation haircut. A player. Instead, he looked like a squirrelly academic. He wore a corduroy jacket, brown slacks, and his light brown hair looked about a month overdue for a cut. His long face was pale, except for the shadows under his eyes. He was probably in his mid-forties.

In the same calm voice I recognized from a half-dozen phone calls, he said, "You're not what I expected."

I was taken aback. "What did you expect?"

"Someone older, I think. More experienced." I wasn't sure if he intended that as a compliment or a mere statement of fact.

"You don't have to be old to have experience, Doctor." And what did he know about it? "Come on back and I'll show you the studio."

I made introductions all around. I tried to put Flemming at ease; he seemed nervous, glancing over his shoulder, studying the station staff as if filing them away in some mental classification system for later reference. I wasn't sure if that was his academic nature or his government background at work. He moved stiffly, taking the seat I offered him like he expected it to slide out from under him. The guy was probably nervous in his own living room. Maybe he *was* relaxed, and this was how he always acted.

I showed him the headphones and mike, found my own headset, and leaned back in my chair, finally in my element.

The sound guy counted down through the booth window, and the first guitar chords of the show's theme song—Creedence Clearwater Revival's "Bad Moon Rising"—cued up. It didn't matter how many different stations I did the show from, this moment always felt the same: it was mine. I had the mike, I was in control, and as long as that ON AIR sign stayed lit, I called the shots. Until something went horribly wrong, of course. I could usually get through the introduction without having a crisis.

"Good evening. This is *The Midnight Hour*, the show that isn't afraid of the dark or the creatures who live there. I'm Kitty Norville, your charming hostess.

"I have as my very special guest this evening Dr. Paul Flemming. As you may or may not know, a little over a month ago Dr. Flemming held a press conference that announced scientific recognition of what used to be considered mythical, supernatural forms of human beings. Vampires, werewolves—you know, people like me. He has an M.D. from Columbia University, a Ph.D. in epidemiology from Johns Hopkins, and for the last five years has headed up the Center for the Study of Paranatural Biology. Welcome, Dr. Flemming."

"Thank you," he said, managing to sound calm despite the anxious way he perched at the edge of his seat, like he was getting ready to run when the mortars started dropping.

"Dr. Flemming. The Center for the Study of Paranatural Biology. Am I correct in stating that this is a government-funded organization dedicated to the study of what I believe you've called alternate forms of human beings? Vampires, werewolves, et cetera?"

"Only in the simplest terms. The nature of the research was not always explicitly stated."

"You couldn't exactly put down 'Give me money for werewolves,' could you?"

"Ah, no," he said, giving me the tiniest smile.

"So this was a *secret* government research program."

"I don't know that I'd go that far. I don't want to enter the realm of conspiracy theory. The Center's findings were always available."

"But in the most obscure outlets. No attention was drawn to a potentially explosive area of research. I would have thought, as part of this research team, you'd have wanted to announce your findings a lot sooner."

"It's not so simple. You can appreciate that we risked a great amount of criticism if we drew too much attention before we were ready. We needed to have data in hand, and a good potential of public support. Otherwise we would have been relegated to the back pages of the annals of bad science."

"In your mind, this is clearly a scientific endeavor."

"Of course. The best way to approach any line of inquiry is through the scientific method."

I was quite fond of postmodern literary analysis myself, as a line of inquiry. "What drew you to the scientific study of a subject that most people are all too happy to dismiss as folklore?"

"So many legends have a seed of truth. In many cases, that seed of truth persists, even in the face of great skepticism. The existence of a real-life King Arthur for example. How many legitimate historical and archaeological investigations have been inspired by Arthurian literature? Vampire and shape-shifter legends exist all over the world, and I've always been struck by the similarities. I simply pursued the seeds of truth at their core."

I said, "I read a book once about how many vampire mythologies might have grown out of primitive burial practices and superstitions—bloated corpses bursting out of shallow graves with drops of blood on their mouths, as if they'd been feeding. That sort of thing. By the same token, some scholars traced werewolf legends to actual medical conditions marked by excessive hair growth, or psychological disorders that caused periodic animalistic, berserker-type behavior. That's where scientific inquiry into these subjects usually leads: to rationalizations. What told you that there was something real behind it all?" I was fishing for a personal anecdote. He'd had a run-in with a were-dingo as a small child and it changed him forever, or something.

"I suppose I've always appreciated a good mystery," he said.

"But there are so many other mysteries for a medical

doctor to unravel. Like a cure for cancer. Surefire weight loss on a diet of chocolate ice cream."

"Maybe I wanted to break new ground."

"Why now? Why last month's press conference? Why draw attention to your research at this point and not earlier?"

He shrugged and began obviously fidgeting—wringing his hands, adjusting his seat. I felt a little thrill—was I getting to him? Was I making him squirm? Maybe he was just shifting his position on the chair.

"Ideally, a complete report would have been published in a respected journal, making all our findings public. But this isn't always an ideal world. Members of Congress began taking an interest, and if Congress wants to ask questions, who am I to argue? I wanted everyone to be clear that this project isn't shrouded in secrecy."

Could have fooled me. In a rare show of restraint I didn't say that. I had to be nice; wouldn't do any good to totally alienate my only source of information.

"What do you ultimately hope to accomplish with the Center?"

"To expand the boundaries of knowledge. Why embark on any scientific endeavor?"

"The quest for truth."

"It's what we're all trying to accomplish, isn't it?"

"In my experience, this particular subject evokes a lot of strong emotion. People vehemently believe in the existence of vampires, or they don't. If they do, they firmly believe vampires are evil, or they're simply victims of a rare disease. Where does this emotion, these strong beliefs, fit into your investigations?"

"We approach this subject only from the standpoint of fact. What can be measured."

"So if I asked what you *believe*—"

"I think you know what I believe: I'm studying diseases that can be quantified."

This was starting to sound circular. And dull. I should have known that Flemming wouldn't be an ideal interviewee. Every time I'd ever talked to him, he'd been evasive. I'd really have to work to draw him out.

"Tell me how you felt the first time you looked a werewolf in the eyes."

Until that moment, he hadn't looked at me. That was pretty normal; there was a lot in a studio booth to distract a newcomer: dials, lights, and buttons. It was natural to look at what you spoke to. People tended to look at the foam head of the microphone.

But now he looked at me, and I looked back, brows raised, urging him on. His gaze was narrow, inquiring, studying me. Like he'd just seen me for the first time, or seen me in a new light. Like I was suddenly one of the subjects in his study, and he was holding me up against the statistics he'd collected.

It was a challenging stare. He smelled totally human, a little bit of sweat, a little bit of wool from his jacket, not a touch of supernatural about him. But I had a sudden urge to growl a warning.

"I don't see how that's relevant," he said.

"Of course it isn't relevant, but this show is supposed to be entertaining. I'm curious. How about a cold hard fact: *when* was the first time you looked a werewolf in the eyes?"

"I suppose it would have been about fifteen years ago."

"This was before you started working with the Center for the Study of Paranatural Biology?"

"Yes. I was in the middle of a pathology residency in New York. We'd gotten an anomalous blood sample from a victim of a car accident. The report from the emergency room was horrendous—crushed rib cage, collapsed lungs, ruptured organs. The man shouldn't have survived, but he did. Somehow they patched him up. I was supposed to be looking for drug intoxication, blood alcohol levels. I didn't find anything like that, but the white blood cell count was abnormal for a sample with no other sign of disease or infection. I went to see this patient in the ICU the next day, to draw another sample and check for any conditions that might have accounted for the anomaly. He wasn't there. He'd been moved out of the ICU, because two days after this terrible accident, he was sitting up, off the ventilator, off oxygen, like he'd just had a concussion or something. I remember looking at his chart, then looking up at him, my mouth open with shock. And he smiled. Almost like he wanted to burst out laughing. He seemed to be daring me to figure out what had happened. I didn't know what he was at the time, but I'll never forget that look in his eyes. He was the only one who wasn't shocked that he was still alive. I never forgot that look. It made me realize that for all my knowledge, for all my studies and abilities, there was a whole world out there that I knew nothing about."

"And the next time you saw that look"—the challenge, the call to prove one's dominance, like the one I'd just given him—"you recognized it."

"That's right."

"Did you ever find out more about him? Did he ever tell you what he was?"

"No. He checked himself out of the hospital the next day. He didn't have health insurance, so I couldn't track him. He probably didn't think he needed it."

I'd seen werewolves die. It took ripping their hearts out, tearing their heads off, or poisoning them with silver.

"You wanted to find out how he'd survived. How his wounds had healed so quickly."

"Of course."

"Is that as far as your research goes? You mentioned once the possibility of a cure."

"Every scientist who studies a disease wants to find the cure for it. But we don't even understand these diseases yet. Finding a cure may be some time off, and I don't want to raise any hopes."

"How close are you to understanding them? I've heard every kind of theory about what causes them, from viral DNA to unbalanced humors."

"That's just it, the most interesting feature of these diseases is that they don't act like diseases. Yes, they're infectious, they alter the body from its natural form. But far from causing damage or sickness, they actually make their victims stronger. In the case of vampirism, the disease grants near immortality, with relatively innocuous side effects."

He called the need to drink human blood an innocuous side effect?

He continued. "To learn the secret of how that happens would be a fantastic discovery."

"You're talking about medical applications."

He hesitated again, folding his hands on the table in front of him and visibly reining back his enthusiasm. "As

I said, I don't want to raise any hopes. We've barely begun to scratch the surface of this field of study."

I had a feeling that was all I was going to get out of him.

"Okay, I'm going to open the lines for calls now. Do you have any questions for the good doctor—"

His eyes bugged out, like I'd pulled out a gun and pointed it at him. Surely he knew I'd be taking questions from listeners.

Shaking his head, he said, "I'd rather not answer questions from the public."

Um, problem? "I'm the public," I said. "You answered my questions."

"No, not like this," he said. He put down the headset and pushed his chair away from the table. "I'm sorry."

Liz, Wes, and the sound guy stared through the booth window, helpless to stop him as he set his shoulders and rushed out of the room.

"Wait, Doctor—" I stood to go after him. Who did that bastard think he was, walking out on me? The wire trailing from my headset tugged at me. The show, I couldn't leave the show. Damn.

I settled back into my seat. I had to talk quick to cover up the silence. "I'm sorry, it looks like Dr. Flemming has urgent business elsewhere and won't be able to answer your questions. But I'm still here, and ready for the first call of the evening. Hello, Brancy from Portland . . ."

The Senate hearings were scheduled to start Monday, but I drove into D.C. proper Saturday evening. I had reservations at a hotel close to the Capitol, and within walking distance of many of the tourist attractions. I'd never been to the city. I saw no reason not to make a vacation out of this. I wanted to see the Smithsonian, dammit.

It was hard to drive and keep my eyes on the road, not craning my neck to catch a glimpse of the Lincoln Memorial. I'd checked a map; it had to be close. I didn't even know if I was looking in the right place. The sun was setting, casting a smog-tinted orange glow over the city. Sightseeing would have to wait until tomorrow it seemed.

Traffic ahead slowed. One of Ivy's notorious jams, on a Saturday no less. I was impressed. Then I spotted the flashing red and blue lights. Accident, maybe. The cars ahead crept to a stop. The trick was not to be impatient. I wasn't in a hurry. I hit the scan button on the radio, hoping to find something catchy. I could play drums on the steering wheel while I waited.

Orange reflective cones squeezed three lanes of cars into one. Up ahead, barricades blocked the road. A pair of police cars were parked on the shoulder. Four cops, flashlights in hand, were checking cars and license plates, asking the drivers questions, looking over passengers. A security checkpoint. Not surprising in these parts, I supposed. I hadn't heard anything about a terror alert or heightened security. Trust the powers-that-be not to tell anyone about a *real* threat.

My turn came to get waved through the checkpoint. A couple of uniformed cops approached the car from each side, shining their lights on the license plates, the interior, and finally at me. I rolled down the window.

"Can I see some ID?"

I had to dig in my backpack for a minute, then I showed him my driver's license. I smiled politely.

"Ma'am, could you pull over to the side of the road here?" He pointed to a spot on the shoulder beyond the barricade. He didn't give me back my license.

My stomach lurched. I suppose everyone's does when they get pulled over by the cops, no matter how innocent they are. I was pretty sure I was innocent.

"Um. What seems to be the problem, Officer?" That may have been the most cliché thing to ever come out of my mouth. In the movies, only guilty people said that.

"Just pull over and we'll get to you in a minute."

While I watched, the cops removed the barricades, cleared the cones, and worked to get traffic flowing normally again. The roadblock had served its purpose. Apparently, they'd gotten what they were looking for: me.

I refused to believe this was all for me. I really didn't consider myself a terrorist threat. There was something else going on.

I found my cell phone and brought up Ben's number. My finger poised on the call button, I watched.

A dark sedan, coming from the other direction, did a U-turn over the median, zipped across the three lanes to this side of the road, and pulled over in front of me. The driver was so smooth the move only took a minute, and the tires never squealed.

Two men climbed out, one on each side. They wore dark suits, conservative ties, and looked clean-cut and unremarkable. They seemed big, though, broad through the shoulders, and confident.

Holy cow. Genuine, honest-to-God Men In Black. This had to be a joke.

The cop handed the driver of the sedan my license and

pointed at me. Unconsciously, I shrank down in my seat, like I could melt through the floorboards.

I should have called Ben, but I waited, wanting to see where this was going to go. Surely this was all a misunderstanding.

The two Men In Black stalked toward me. Actually, they probably walked perfectly calmly and normally. To me, though, they stalked. The Wolf wanted to growl. And she wanted to get the hell out of here. I was still in the car, I could still drive—and so could the cops. I waited. Had to listen to the human half, this time.

Thinking before acting. *Good girl.* That was what T.J. would have said if he'd been here. Maybe he'd even have given me a scratch behind the ears. I felt a little better.

They stopped by my window, peered in, and looked me over. My nostrils widened; I took a breath. Human, they were normal human beings. Warm blood coursing through live veins, so they weren't vampires. No hint of lycanthropy about them, either. Lycanthropes had a sort of musky, wild scent that couldn't be covered up. They had fur just under the surface and it always showed, if you knew what to look for.

But there was something about them, something cold. They made my shoulders bunch up, and the hairs on my neck stand up—hackles rising. I gripped the steering wheel, white-knuckled. I met the driver's gaze. Couldn't show weakness.

His gaze dropped first.

He offered my license back to me. "Ms. Norville? Alette, the Mistress of the City, wishes to extend her hospitality. If you'll step out of the car, please?"

I stared in disbelief, and a wave of spent adrenaline

washed through me, making my muscles feel like rubber. The fear left with that wave, but now I was annoyed. *Severely* annoyed.

"Mistress of the City? As in vampire?" I said, and I realized what I'd sensed about them. They weren't vampires, but they had a little of the scent on them. Human servants, who spent far too much time with vampires than was healthy. They were too pale.

"Yes. She's pleased that you're visiting her city and is anxious to meet you."

"*Her* city? The U.S. capital and she's calling it *her* city?" But then, what did I expect from a vampire?

The MIB pursed his lips and took a deep breath, as if collecting himself. He was probably under orders to be polite. "Will you accept Alette's hospitality?"

"Why should I?"

"She fears for your safety. You don't know the situation among your kind here. You lack protection. She wants to keep you safe."

"How did she know I was coming?"

"It's her city."

I wondered what she thought she'd get out of keeping me safe, because she surely wouldn't offer me protection out of the kindness of her undead heart. I also wondered what exactly the situation was that would put a lone wolf like me in danger. It meant there was an alpha here who didn't like intruders on his territory.

Right now, an alpha werewolf out for blood scared me more than a vampire.

"All right," I said.

"If you'll please come with me, I'll drive you to meet her."

"What about my car?" I loved my car. We'd been across the country together. "And my hotel reservation?"

"We took the liberty of canceling your reservation. Tom will drive your car to the building. We'll keep it safe for you while you're here. Free parking in D.C., Ms. Norville. Not something to refuse lightly."

Actually, this sounded like one of those offers you weren't allowed to refuse at all.

I put my phone away and got out of the car.

The other MIB, Tom, slipped into the driver's seat as soon as I was out of the way. I looked longingly at my reliable little hatchback, like I was never going to see her again.

The first guy escorted me to the sedan.

I said, "Just so we're clear: the city's vampire Mistress has the D.C. cops in her pocket, or at least enough of them in her pocket that she can order a roadblock on one of the major arteries, just to find one person."

"It would appear so," he said.

"She could have just *called* me, you know."

He glanced sidelong at me, and I rolled my eyes. This was a vampire we were talking about. It was all about theatrics.

At least as a passenger I could look for recognizable landmarks a little more safely. After making sure Tom was following us with my car, I leaned over the dashboard and peered out the windshield, searching.

"The other guy's Tom. What's your name?" I asked.

After a pause he said, "Bradley."

Tom and Bradley. Didn't sound very sinister and Men In Black-ish.

"So, Bradley, where's the Washington Monument?"

"We're going the wrong way to see it."

I sat back and sighed, not bothering to contain my disappointment. How frustrating, to be so close to a major national landmark and not see anything.

Bradley glanced at me. Sounding amused, he said, "Give me a couple minutes and I'll swing back that way." He flicked on the blinker and made a sharp right turn.

Wait, was he being nice to me?

Back in Colorado, I could see. The sky was big, and I could look west and always see the mountains. I always knew where they were, where I was. I needed landmarks. Here, and pretty much everywhere I'd been back East, I felt vaguely claustrophobic. Thick trees grew everywhere and blocked the horizon. Even in autumn, with their leaves dried and falling, they formed walls and I could only see the sky by looking up, not out.

We turned a corner, and Bradley said amiably, in tour-guide fashion, "We now approach the famous Washington Mall. And on your right, the Washington Monument."

I pressed my face to the window. My gut gave a little jump, like it did when I saw someone famous. It was just like the pictures, but bigger. The towering obelisk was all lit up, and the lights gave it an orange cast. In the center of the vast swath of lawn that was the Mall, it stood alone in the dark.

"Wow." I watched it until we turned another corner and left it behind.

I kept track of our route. We ended up driving the opposite direction, back toward the freeway, but we veered off and continued farther west until we came to a quiet row of townhomes in the area Bradley said was Georgetown. Even in the dark I could tell it was nice, and old.

Tree-lined streets held rows of brick houses, with slatted shutters and window planters, painted doors, and fancy wrought-iron fences out front. Georgetown University was nearby. Bradley turned into an alley, then into a cobbled driveway wide enough to hold several cars. My car was already there.

I didn't get much of a sense of what I'd gotten myself into until we entered the town house, up a set of steps and through a back door.

That surprised me. Most vampires, even the heads of Families and cities, made their homes underground. It reduced the chance of them or any of their retainers suffering sunshine-related accidents. But Bradley and Tom led me into the house, through a hall, and to a parlor. This vampire held court in a room with windows—covered with heavy brocade drapes, but windows nonetheless.

The place managed to look cluttered and opulent at the same time: crammed with furniture, chaise lounges and wingback chairs, mahogany sideboard tables, end tables, and coffee tables, some with lace runners, others with lamps, both electric and oil. Curio cabinets held china collections, and a silver tea service was on display on the mantel above the fireplace. Persian rugs softened the hardwood floor. All the lamps were lit, but softly, so the room had a warm, honey-like glow. Scattered among the other decorations were pictures, small portraits, a few black and white photographs. Faces stared out of them all. I wondered who they were.

The decor didn't surprise me. Vampires lived for hundreds of years; they tended to carry their valuable collections with them. If the room reminded me of a Victorian parlor, it was probably because it was the real deal. As was its occupant.

A woman set a book down on a table and stood from an armchair that sat nearly hidden toward the back of the parlor, near a set of bookshelves. She was pale, cold, dead. No heartbeat. I couldn't guess her actual age, of course. She looked about thirty, in her prime and haughty. Her brunette hair was drawn back into a knot at the nape of her neck; her face was round, the lines of her lips hard, her gaze dark and steady. She wore a wine-colored dress suit with a short, tailored jacket and a calf-length, flowing skirt—a feminine-looking outfit that brought to mind Ingrid Bergman or Grace Kelly.

I decided she wasn't Victorian. She was older, much older. She had a gaze that looked across centuries with disdain. The present was only ever a stepping-off point for the really old ones. The oldest vampire I'd ever met was probably around three hundred years old. I couldn't be sure—it was rude to ask—but I bet this woman was older.

I had planned on being brazen. If she could disrupt my life, I could be snotty about it. But for once, I kept my mouth shut.

"Katherine Norville?" she said, an inquiring tilt to her head. She had a wonderfully melodic British accent.

"Um, Kitty. Yeah."

"I am Alette. Welcome to my city."

I still wanted to argue the *my* thing, but this woman had me cowed into silence. I didn't like the feeling.

"Bradley, Tom, any problems?"

"None, ma'am," Bradley said.

"Thank you, that will be all."

The two men actually bowed—smartly, from the waist, like trained butlers or footmen in a fairy tale. I stared after them as they left through the doorway to another part of the house.

"I do hope they treated you well."

"Yeah. Well, except for the whole getting stopped at a police roadblock thing. That was a little nerve-wracking." And this wasn't? I didn't think I could escape from her even with my claws out. What did she want with me, *really*?

"I won't apologize for that. It was necessary."

"Why?" I said. "I host a call-in radio show—my phone number is public knowledge. You could have called."

"I couldn't let you say no."

I started pacing, which required maneuvering around an expensive-looking armchair to find a straight, clear path along the edge of a rug. Alette watched me. She was elegant and regal, and I couldn't help but feel like she was indulging me this little outburst.

"You know if you try to keep me here against my will, I've got people I can call, I don't have to put up with this."

"Katherine—Kitty. If you'll please have a seat, we might discuss this in a civilized manner. I fear you're currently in danger of reverting to your other nature."

Pacing was a wolf thing. I'd been stalking back and forth, my gaze locked on her, like an animal in a cage. Obediently, I stopped and took a place on the chair she indicated. I took a deep breath and settled down. She sat nearby, at the edge of the sofa.

"I have a little better control of myself than that," I said sullenly.

"No doubt. But I am aware that I've placed you in

strange surroundings and a possibly dangerous situation. I'd best not aggravate you, hmm?"

Carefully maintaining a calm to match hers, I said, "Why did you bring me here?"

Sitting with her ankles crossed, one hand resting on the arm of the sofa, she was no less poised and dignified than standing. She might have been a duchess or something, one of those proud noblewomen in a Gainsborough portrait, draped in silk and diamonds, calmly superior.

She gave an annoyed frown. "The werewolves here are wild and ungoverned. They might see you as easy prey, or an easy target to challenge and dominate. There is no alpha to control them. You'll have enough on your mind while you're here, I didn't think you'd want to worry about that as well."

Got that right. But I was betting there was more to it. From what I gathered from stories, throughout history werewolves had either been vampires' servants or rivals. At best they came to uneasy truces when they lived near each other.

I had never seen what it looked like when there wasn't a truce. Sometimes I felt so ignorant. My old pack, my old alpha, hadn't taught me much about the wider world. With them, I'd learned how to cower. Then I'd learned how to take care of myself.

"What else?" I said. "What do you get out of it?"

She smiled for the first time, a thin and enigmatic expression. "My dear girl, this Senate hearing will be the first time in centuries that one of our kind—vampire or lycanthrope—has been summoned before a nation's government in any official capacity. You seem to have made yourself an authority on the subject."

I shook my head, wanting to laugh. "I've never claimed to be an authority—"

"Nevertheless, many people turn to you. And now, so is the government. And when you speak before the Senate you will, however indirectly, be speaking on my behalf as well."

I didn't want that kind of authority. I didn't want that responsibility. Before I could deny it, she continued.

"I've brought you here to take the measure of you. To learn whose interests you serve. Whose interests you will be serving when you speak before the Senate committee."

Which web of political entanglements was I caught up in, she meant. She wanted to know who was pulling my strings, because in her world, everybody had strings.

She wasn't going to believe me when I told her.

"I serve my own interests," I said. "I left my pack. I don't have any other associations. I'm not sure I have friends anymore. There's just me. And my show. Ratings and the bottom line. That's it."

I was sure she didn't believe me. She narrowed her gaze, maintaining a vaguely amused demeanor. Like she didn't care what I said, because she'd figure out the truth eventually. She had time.

"I suppose," she said finally, "that makes you less corruptible than many. True capitalists are extraordinarily predictable. But I've listened to your show, and there's more to you than that."

"If you've listened to my show, then you know me. Because that's all it is. I parlayed my big mouth into a career. That's all."

"You may very well be right."

I looked away, because her gaze was on me, searching,

looking for the layers to peel back. Legends said vampires could entrance you with the power of their gazes. That was how they lured their prey to them, and why some people were all too happy to bare their necks and veins to them.

I wasn't tied to anyone. I wanted to keep it that way.

She said, "If you are right, and there is nothing more to you than what I see before me, then I would be honored if you would accept my hospitality, which is, if I may be so bold, some of the finest in the city."

I would. I knew I would, probably the whole time I'd be here. Maybe because the room was nice and comfortable, and as intimidating as she was, she didn't make my hairs stand on end. Her use of the word hospitality seemed to have an Old World meaning behind it: it was more than offering a meal and bed for the night. It was a mark of pride and honor. It was an insult to refuse.

"Thank you," I said, striving for politeness though I felt ragged beside her.

Alette stood. Automatically, I stood with her, smoothing out my jeans and wondering if I should buy some nicer clothes while I was here.

"Welcome to Washington," she said and offered her hand, which I shook, a normal gesture that I accepted gratefully, even if her skin was too cold. "I've set aside a room on the second floor for you. I do hope you like it. Emma will show you to it. The kitchen is also entirely at your disposal. Tell Emma anything you need and she'll take care of it." A young woman, Emma I presumed, had appeared, called by some signal known only to her and Alette. She was fully human, bright-eyed and eager. Old World hospitality indeed. Alette had *maids*. "My only request, Kitty, is that you tell me if you plan to leave the house for any reason. I have offered you my protection and I will see the offer through."

That almost sounded like a challenge: could I get out of here without her knowing? What would she do if I tried?

And what if there really were ravening werewolves waiting to find me alone? That was a tough call.

"All right," I said noncommittally, and Alette gave me a skeptical look.

"If you'll excuse me, I have other business. Good evening to you."

She left Emma and me at the foot of a set of narrow, curving stairs outside the parlor.

"This way," Emma said, smiling, and gestured up.

Sometimes human servants were vampires in training, waiting for their masters to initiate them into true undeadness. Sometimes they were simply servants, although their brand of service usually involved a bit more than dusting the furniture. I looked around the collar of her blouse for telltale scars, signs of old bite marks. I didn't see any, but that didn't mean they weren't there, somewhere.

We reached the top of the stairs and entered a narrow hallway. More framed photographs and portraits decorated the walls. They represented different times, different eras; the hair, clothing, and demeanors of the people changed from portrait to portrait as we continued. Did Alette have some kind of obsession with collecting these images?

"Can I ask you a question?"

"Sure," Emma said. She was probably about nineteen. Hell, she might have been working her way through college.

I had to ask. "Do you know what she is?"

She smiled wryly and ducked her gaze. "My family's worked for her for generations. We followed her here from England two hundred years ago. She's been good to us." She opened a door at the end of the hall, then looked at me. "You know better than anybody, they aren't all bad."

I couldn't argue.

My duffel bag had already been brought up to the bedroom. The suite included a full bathroom, with brass handles on the sink and shower. Maybe this wasn't such a bad idea. I might even get spoiled. Emma showed me an intercom by the door, a modern amenity in the antique house. "Just ring if you need anything."

I asked for a sandwich. Then sleep. Sleep was good. Sleeping meant I wasn't wondering where the rest of Alette's vampire clan was hanging out, because human minions could only do so much and I was pretty sure she didn't rule her empire all by herself.

chapter 3

Alette wanted me to tell her if I planned on going out. Well, of *course* I planned on going out. But by the time I woke up, it was full daylight, which meant she probably wasn't around.

So I left a note. I scribbled it on a piece of notebook paper and laid it on the coffee table in the parlor.

It wasn't completely honest of me. Tom and Bradley were probably on call. Alette probably meant for me to tell one of them. I could have gotten a private chauffeured tour of the city—nice, protected, safe.

I'd put my hand on the knob of the front door when I heard footsteps trotting down the stairs behind me.

"Miss Norville!" It was Emma, her brown hair pinned up in a sloppy bun, wearing jeans and an oversized sweatshirt. The clothes made her look young. "Are you leaving?"

I took a guilty step away from the door. "Call me Kitty. I, ah, just wanted to look outside to see what the weather was like." She wasn't going to buy that. I had my backpack hitched over my shoulder. "Alette puts you to work on Sunday, does she?"

"Oh, no. She lets me use the library upstairs to study. It's my last day to catch up on homework before class tomorrow. I was just heading to the kitchen for a snack."

Wow, she really was working her way through college.

"You go to Georgetown?"

"George Washington," she said. She stayed there, leaning on the base of the banister, smiling helpfully. "Have you had breakfast? You want me to fix you something?"

"No, thanks, I'm fine." I wanted to leave. No offense or anything. I fidgeted.

The awkward pause continued. I wasn't fooling anyone. I'd even convinced myself that if I left my car in the driveway out back and used public transportation, they'd just think I was sleeping in late or something.

Finally, she sighed and said, "I can't stop you from leaving. But Alette won't be happy about it when she finds out you went out alone."

Now that didn't make me feel guilty at all. "Are you going to get in trouble if I run off?"

"No. Alette doesn't get angry, not like that. But she'll be disappointed."

And no one liked to disappoint Alette.

"It won't be long. I just want to look around. I'll be back before she even wakes up for the evening."

"Have a good time," Emma said. The statement was perfunctory rather than sincere. She swung around the corner, disappearing through the door to the kitchen in the back of the house.

I felt like a heel. I went out anyway.

D.C.'s famous Metro subway didn't run this far out, but a shuttle bus made stops between Georgetown and the nearest Metro stations. In half an hour I was in the middle of the Mall.

Then I totally, unabashedly played tourist. I couldn't see it all in a day. I probably couldn't see it all in a week, if I factored in museums. Fortunately, there were plenty of companies willing to take my money to drive me around on their tour buses and give me the spiel. The buses even dropped me off in front of just about every museum I could hope to visit. I saw the White House!

All morning and part of the afternoon, I ran around like a maniac seeing the highlights. As I did, I kept my eyes open, looking at the faces around me, wondering. But they were all tourists, round-eyed and cranky. I wasn't going to find any lycanthropes among them. Not that I could scent one across the Mall anyway. They had to be somewhere, though, and I would have liked to have spotted a friendly-looking one to buy a cup of coffee for and ask what was really going on.

I was leaving the American History Museum when my cell phone rang. I just about jumped out of my skin. I'd shoved the thing in my jeans pocket and forgotten about it.

I answered it.

"Kitty?"

"Ben? Where are you?"

"I'm at the hotel. Where are you?" The lawyer had flown into town this morning on a red-eye. We'd reserved rooms at the same hotel—the place I hadn't checked into yesterday.

"It's a long story. We should get together."

"I'm having a late lunch in my room. Can you get over here? I'll order you a steak."

"Make it rare. Thanks. See you in a few minutes."

After a few hours of walking, I fancied I knew my way around well enough that I could find the hotel by myself, and I was pleased to no end by proving myself right.

It pays to have all the escape routes mapped out ahead of time.

The hotel was a few blocks from the Capitol, within easy reach of the office complex where the committee hearing was scheduled to take place. Ben had given me his room number, so I went right up and knocked on the door. He opened it and went back to the table, where he had a room-service tray spread out, and sat to finish his own steak.

"I suppose that's going on the expense account," I said, closing the door behind me. He just smiled.

The thing about Ben was he didn't stand much on ceremony. He wore a dress shirt, untucked and unbuttoned to expose the white undershirt. He was in his thirties, rough around the edges, weathered maybe. His dirtyish blonde hair was ruffled, the hairline receding. On the bed, a briefcase sat open, a storm of papers and legal publications strewn around it. He didn't look like much, but he worked hard.

"Nice flight?" I said.

"Yeah. Great. You look like you've been running all over town."

I probably didn't look too fresh, blonde hair plastered to my face with sweat. It wasn't summer, but the city was having a balmy fall. A sticky humidity dampened the autumn air.

I hadn't even thought about the distances involved. Most tourists would probably think it was crazy, trying to cram as much as I had into that little time. But I wasn't even tired. It was one of those times when being a were-wolf had its advantages. I could run for miles.

"This place is incredible," I said. "I ran to the Air and Space Museum to see the Wright Flyer, the Natural History Museum to see the Hope Diamond and the dinosaurs, and the American History Museum to see the Star Spangled Banner. They also have Mr. Rogers' sweater, did you know that? One of them, at least, the guy must have had like a hundred. This has got to be the most culturally valuable square mile in the U.S." I'd hit the highlights in the big museums, making a sprint out of it. I didn't know when I was going to get another chance to sightsee this week.

He stared at me, wearing a mocking smirk.

"What?" I said with a whine, a little put-out.

"You actually got teary-eyed when you saw the Star Spangled Banner, didn't you? You been to Arlington Cemetery yet? You see Kennedy's grave?"

I *had* teared up. I wasn't going to admit it. "Not yet. I was going to do that tomorrow after the hearings."

"That'll push you over the edge, I bet. Bring Kleenex."

I pouted. "You don't have to make fun of me."

"Why not? You're a sentimentalist. I didn't know that before."

"So I'm a sentimentalist. So what? What does that make you?"

"A lawyer." He didn't even have to think about it. He continued straight to business. "You know who's chairing this committee you're testifying for?"

I didn't. I'd been busy with the show, the chance to interview Flemming, and traveling. I had Ben to worry about the rest, right? "No."

"You aren't going to like it."

How bad could it be? "Who is it?"

"Joseph Duke."

I groaned. Senator Joseph Duke was a witch-hunting reactionary. Literally. As in, in a world when such things were still mostly considered myth and fairy tale, Duke ardently believed in witches, vampires, werewolves, all of it, and felt it was his God-given duty to warn the world of their dangers. An earnestly religious constituency kept him in office. I'd had him on the show a few weeks ago. He'd promised to pray for my soul. It shouldn't have surprised me. He probably saw these hearings as vindication, his chance to declare to the world that he was right.

"It could be worse," I said hopefully.

"Yeah. You could be a communist werewolf." He gestured to the opposite chair. In front of it, as requested, was a mostly red steak on a plate. I sat and didn't feel much like eating.

"What's your story?" he said.

I told him. I tried to make it sound not quite so dangerous. But he gave me that frowning, *are you crazy?* look anyway.

He huffed. "The Master vampire of the city decided to make you her personal houseguest? I don't have to tell you that's creepy, do I?"

"I know. But she isn't all that bad."

"Kitty. She's a vampire."

"Yeah, and I'm a slavering werewolf. I get it."

"Listen, they've cobbled these hearings together at the last minute. I couldn't get the staff to give me a schedule of when witnesses are testifying. They're probably not going to call you tomorrow. I'm thinking they'll spend a couple days grilling Flemming. We should go and sit in, to see what kind of tone they set. Get a feel for the room, that sort of thing."

And it wouldn't hurt hearing what Flemming had to say. See if his answers to the senators were any less evasive than the ones he gave me.

"What do we know about Flemming?" I asked Ben.

"Whatever's been in the news. He's a doctor, he's been on the fringes of some pretty whacked-out research. You probably know more than I do."

"I know about his research, about his work with the Center. But I don't know anything about him. He said he did a residency in New York. Think you could track down a little history on him?"

"I'll see what I can do." He reached over to one of the piles of paper on the bed, scooped it up, and handed it to me. "Here's your mail from the last couple weeks. There's a couple of local invitations you might look at. Word seems to have got out that you were coming. You apparently got put on some media-related mailing lists."

That was it. Everybody knew I was here. Even people I didn't know about knew I was here. I supposed I ought to enjoy the attention.

"Why would people send me invitations?"

"Apparently, you have cachet," he said dryly. "You're hip."

Gah. That was almost worse than being an authority.

The invitations he mentioned were three pieces of mail that came in thick, stationery-type envelopes, cream-colored and pearl-gray. I cracked them open while I ate. One was an invitation for a cocktail party at the Washington town house of the Colorado representative from my district. Vote-pandering. I set it aside. The second was for the next installment of a lecture series sponsored by the League of Women Voters. Latent college feminist tendencies almost got the better of me on that one.

The third was a reception for the opening of a new exhibit at the Hirshhorn, the museum of modern art that was part of the Smithsonian. Attire: formal. Cultural, flashy. *Swanky.* An interesting crowd showed up to these things, I bet. It would sure beat hanging out at Alette's for the evening. I couldn't remember the last time I'd been to a real party.

I was going to have to buy a dress. And shoes. And I only had a couple of hours to do it in.

"I gotta run." I stuffed the mail in my backpack and headed for the door. "I'll see you tomorrow."

"Kitty." He stopped me, caught my gaze. He'd looked mostly at his plate until then, finishing off the last of his meal. He startled me into staring back. "I don't have to tell you to be careful, do I?"

I was a little dumbstruck. "Wow. I might start to think you really care."

"Have to protect the revenue stream," he said, quirking a smile.

I rolled my eyes and got out of there, thinking, what could possibly go wrong?

I'd never owned a little black cocktail dress. But every girl should own a little black cocktail dress before she's thirty. Now I had mine.

I returned to Alette's place just after dark, with an hour to spare before the reception. Alette met me in the foyer, like she'd been watching for me. My assurances to Emma that Alette wouldn't know I'd been gone scattered like dust.

She crossed her hands before her. "I would have preferred that you take Bradley or Tom on your outing."

Despite my best efforts, I stood there like a guilty teenager out past curfew, my backpack over one shoulder and the plastic garment bag from the department store over the other.

I shrugged, trying to turn a wince into a smile. "I didn't want to bother anyone."

Her glare told me what a poor excuse that was for flouting her hospitality.

"You've been shopping?" she said, indicating the bag.

She wasn't going to want me to go to the museum reception. She'd want me to stay all tucked up and safe, with her. But I'd been all over town today. I hadn't sensed any lycanthropes. What was more, no super-territorial werewolves had found me. That whole explanation was becoming increasingly lame.

Sneaking out while she was up and about would be a lot harder than sneaking out during daylight hours.

I wasn't going to make excuses. "Yeah. I got a dress. I have an invitation for a reception at the Hirshhorn." Earnestly, I dug in my backpack, found the invitation, and handed it to her. As if I had to prove something like that. "It sounds like fun, and it starts in an hour, and I'd really like to go."

This was ridiculous. I hadn't had to beg to go out since high school. Well, that wasn't true. I'd had to beg Carl, the alpha male of my old pack, to go out. He liked keeping his cubs under his paw, and he especially didn't want me having any fun without him. I thought I'd finished with all that when I left. When he kicked me out. I squared my shoulders and tried to seem a little bit dignified.

She examined the invitation, then me. "This dress. May I see it?"

I peeled off the plastic and held the hanger up to my shoulders. It was black silk with spaghetti straps, clingy in all the right places. The skirt was short without being trashy. I had to be able to sit down and stand up without embarrassing myself. And I found these killer strappy high heels on sale.

Alette rubbed the fabric between her fingers, stepping back to take in the whole garment. "Hm. Understated. Good lines. It will do, I suppose."

Like I needed her permission. "I'm going to get changed," I said, creeping toward the stairs.

She didn't stop me. After the first couple of steps, I ran the rest of the way.

I'd just closed the door to my room when my cell phone rang. I dug it out of my pocket, read the display—it was my mother. I'd forgotten, today was Sunday. She called every Sunday.

"Hi, Mom."

"Hi, Kitty. Where are you this week?" Her tone was laden with unspoken reprimands. She'd asked me to call her when I stopped in a new place, to let her know where I was. Since I was someplace different nearly every week, and on the road most of the time in between, it seemed kind of, well, futile to try to keep her updated on my whereabouts. I forgot, usually.

"Washington, D.C."

Her tone changed to sounding genuinely interested. "Really? That's exciting. Have you done any sightseeing?"

Thankfully, I was able to tell her yes, and we could talk about that for a minute or two. She sounded put out when I told her I hadn't been taking pictures.

"I'll send you a postcard," I said. "Look, Mom? I'm really sorry to cut you off, but I don't have time to talk right now. I've got someplace I have to be."

"Oh?" That unmistakable *Mom* question.

I relented. I felt bad for ditching her so quickly. "There's a reception at one of the art museums here. It sounded like fun."

"Are you going by yourself?"

I had no idea how she managed it, how she could ask one question and convince me she meant something entirely different. It scared me a little that we knew each other well enough that I knew exactly what she was *really* asking.

"Yes, by myself," I said with a sigh. "I haven't been here long enough to get asked out on any dates."

"Well, you know so many people all over the place, I can't keep track of it unless I ask. I worry about you, traveling alone."

This wouldn't be a good time to tell her that I was staying with a vampire. "I'm doing fine, Mom. I promise."

"All right, I believe you. Call me before you leave town, okay?"

Mental note, mental note. "I'll try to remember."

"I love you."

"Love you, too, Mom."

Finally, I was showered and dressed. I spent five minutes practicing walking in the new shoes and was ready to head downstairs.

Alette waited in the foyer at the base of the stairs. She might not have moved since I last saw her, except someone was with her now. She finished saying something to him and turned to watch me.

The one she'd been talking to, a man in a dark gray suit, stood behind her, leaning against the doorway to the parlor, his arms crossed. Not Bradley or Tom. In his mid-twenties, he was shorter, cleft-jawed, with spiky brown hair and a wry expression. He studied me slowly, pointedly dragging his gaze up my body, starting at the ankles and lingering over the interesting bits. His smile got wryer when he caught my gaze.

He smelled cold-blooded and no heartbeat sounded in his chest. Not just a vampire, but a smarmy one.

When I reached the foyer, I asked in a low voice, "Who's he?"

Alette lifted a hand to introduce him. "This is Leo. He will accompany you to the reception."

A chaperone. Great. A *vampire* chaperone? Double great.

"You know, I'm sure I'll be fine."

She gave me an arched-eyebrow look, the parental *you stay in my house you abide by my rules* kind of look.

She reached for him. Smiling, he took her hand, raised it to his lips, and kissed it lightly. Their gazes met and exchanged some long-practiced message of conspiracy. She said, "He's one of mine. You can trust him."

But I didn't trust her. I was about to suggest that I pack my bags and get a room in the hotel after all, that this wasn't going to work out. She looked me over, stepping to one side and the other to take in several angles.

Finally she said, "You really can't go out looking like

that. Wait here a moment." All business, her heels tapping on the hardwood floor, she marched out of the foyer, into the back of the house.

I tried to figure out what was wrong with me. Everything fit, everything was straight—I thought. I craned my head over my shoulder to try to see my backside. Did I have toilet paper stuck somewhere?

Leo regarded me, openly amused. "So *you're* the infamous Kitty Norville." Like Alette, he had a British accent, but his was lighter, a bit more drawling.

"Infamous? I don't know about that."

"You should be flattered. Alette doesn't bother with everyone who crosses into her territory."

"I am flattered, really," I said, scowling.

Alette returned, holding something in her hand. "It's typical," she said. "You lot spend so much time running about in the woods, you forget how to properly accessorize. Hold this."

She carried a velvet jewelry box, which she opened and handed to me. While I held it, she carefully removed the necklace within, a diamond teardrop on a gold chain. At least it looked like a diamond. Not that I knew anything about them, my trip to see the Hope Diamond that afternoon notwithstanding. It was as large as my fingernail.

I'd left my blonde hair loose. It lay in waves to my shoulders. It would start to look tangled and ratty as soon as I stepped outside, but I didn't know what else to do with it. Standing behind me, she took my hair in hand and laid it to the side, then clasped the necklace around my neck. The diamond lay an inch below the hollow of my throat, halfway between chin and neckline. Perfect.

"Now, you may be seen in public," she said, stepping around to survey me from the front.

"Not silver."

"I should think not."

I smoothed my hair back into place. "My hair, is my hair okay?"

She grasped my hands and smiled. "It looks fine, my dear."

Suddenly, I liked her. I worried a little that she was working some wily vampire trick on me. But this didn't seem like a vampire trick. This was about loaning someone a piece of jewelry. It was such an unexpectedly girly thing for a centuries-old vampire to do.

Leo offered his arm, and I stared at it like I didn't know what to do with it. I stood there long enough to feel impolite and embarrassed that I was impolite. By way of apology, I put my hand in the crook of his elbow. He smiled like a laugh was on the verge of bursting forth. I squared my shoulders and tried to muster some dignity. His arm was stiff, and I kept thinking there should have been a pulse under the skin.

Alette saw us off at the door like we were a couple of kids going to the prom. Bradley chauffeured us in the sedan, which was waiting at the curb. He stood by the open door to the backseat, and this was all getting ridiculous. Continuing with his formal actions like it was some kind of game, Leo assisted me to my seat and made a little bow before walking around to the other side of the car.

I was torn between feeling like an actress on her way to the Oscars, and the butt of someone's joke, so I kept quiet.

The Hirshhorn's main focus was modern art and sculpture. The gallery where the reception took place was stark, with white walls and a gleaming floor, lit by strategically placed track lighting. Sculptures and the odd multimedia installments stood here and there throughout the wide space, while paintings hung in scattered isolation.

The art was, for the most part, incomprehensible without referring to the notes. Whitewashed papier-mâché-looking objects projecting from the wall, spindly bits of found material built into the shape of a chair, that sort of thing. The reception was being held in honor of one of the artists, an unassuming middle-aged woman standing in a far corner of the room, surrounded by admirers. I hadn't figured out which pieces were hers, yet. Wasn't sure I wanted to, in case I was called upon to speak intelligently about them. I was more likely to say something monosyllabic like "Neat," or "Whoa," which probably wouldn't go over well.

I parked by a Jackson Pollack painting, because I recognized it. Or recognized that this particular set of splatters was by Jackson Pollack.

I looked at the art. Leo looked at everything else. His behavior was oppressively bodyguardish, though with his indifferently amused grin no one but me noticed. He appeared to be a laid-back guy whose girlfriend had dragged him along to see Culture.

"So, Leo," I said, "where you from?"

"To start? Leeds," he said. "Haven't been back in ages."

Which could have meant anything to a vampire. "A few decades? A century? Two?"

"I wouldn't want to deprive you of the mystery."

"How long have you been with Alette?"

"Isn't that the same question?"

Well, couldn't fool him, could I? "Do you miss it?"

"What? Why would I want to be there when I'm lucky enough to be here playing nanny to you?"

Sue me for trying. I turned back to the wall and pretended he wasn't there. I couldn't, very well. His presence was like a rock in a stream, a cold solid place that all the life and movement in the room flowed around, avoiding. Without any overt gesture, he managed to keep himself apart from the crowd. I caught him staring at a woman across the room. She was young, dressed in slacks and a green blouse with a plunging neckline. She held a wineglass and absentmindedly ran a finger around the rim. She laughed at something the woman next to her said; her chin tipped up, exposing a slim, clean throat.

Leo's stance was watchful, focused, and his gaze was hungry.

Vampires hunted by seduction. Youth and beauty attracted them; they in turn made themselves attractive to youth and beauty. Leo was handsome, in a rakish, English way, dressed conservatively but smartly, and more importantly richly, and he'd most likely had decades to practice his pickup lines. She'd think she was being swept off her feet, and wouldn't know what really hit her.

"You take a step in her direction, I'll run right over there and let her know that while they couldn't prove anything at the rape trial, she ought to keep her distance."

He tried to keep his smirk in place, but his glare wasn't at all amused. "No one ever accuses you of being the life of the party, do they?"

"You're never going to find out."

He stepped closer and spoke so his breath touched my bare shoulder. "Werewolf blood is quite the delicacy. You might think of giving me a try. The experience isn't as one-sided as you might imagine."

A shudder charged up my spine and my heart rate doubled. I took a step back, almost stumbling over my own feet. It was pure instinct, wolf backing into a corner and preparing for an attack, bracing for a chance to run.

Leo laughed. He'd known exactly what button to push. I closed my eyes and straightened, taking a deep breath and trying to relax. Embarrassing, certainly. This was also proof of just how close to the edge I really was, how fine the line was between the two parts of my being. A little nudge like that, and I slid right over. If he'd pushed it, I might have started Changing right there, in self-defense.

"Jerk," I muttered. "I need to use the ladies' room. I'll be back in a minute."

"Take your time, take your time," he said and pointedly turned to continue visually menacing the woman across the room. I marched away.

I didn't really have to use the bathroom. I leaned on the tile wall and pressed my hands to my cheeks, which were flushed and burning. I'd let him get to me, and I was more angry at myself than him for it. I liked to think I was better than that.

I waited until my heartbeat had slowed and I felt calm again. Checking myself in the mirror, I smoothed out my dress and nodded, satisfied. I'd just ignore him.

On the way out the door, I ran into a man exiting the men's room. I'd had my head down, not paying attention—

not as calm and collected as I'd thought. I stumbled, and he grabbed my arm to steady me.

I started to pull away and apologize, but I caught his scent, and it was wild. Fur and wilderness, open country under a full moon—not quite human. My eyes widened and my back tightened, like hackles rising.

He stared back at me, eyes also wide, his nose flaring to take in my scent. He'd sensed me just as strongly as I'd sensed him. He was tall, with a strong face, brown eyes, and dark hair.

For a moment, I tensed, ready to run, to flee what might have been a challenge; our wary gazes locked on each other. I didn't want to fight. I took a step back, but then his lips grew into a wondering smile. The expression said welcome. He didn't want to fight either.

"I don't know you. Who are you?" He had an unidentifiable accent, though his English was crisp and clear.

"Kitty," I said. "I've been looking for you. I mean, not you specifically, but—" He was a lycanthrope, but not a wolf. I couldn't identify the odd edge to his scent. "You're not wolf. What are you?"

The smile turned playful. "Jaguar."

"Really?" Awe filled my voice. That was so cool. "I had no idea."

"That's clear. My name is Luis. I work at the Brazilian embassy. You—are you visiting Washington?"

"Yes." We were just around the corner from the party. From Leo. I glanced nervously in that direction, expecting the vampire to walk in on us at any moment. I pulled Luis closer to the wall, as if that would hide us. "Luis, I was given to understand that the lycanthrope situation here is sort of unstable. Dangerous for strangers just passing through."

His brow creased. "Who said this?"

My hands wanted to clench, I was so nervous. I had so many questions, and I didn't know him at all, didn't know how he'd react, didn't know what I was getting myself into. But I was desperate for another source of information.

"Alette," I told him.

He shook his head and chuckled, but the gesture was humorless. "Alette, yes. She thinks we are rabble. Why have you spoken with her?"

I winced. "It's a long story."

"You should meet others of your kind, hear their side. I will take you there. No matter what she has told you, you will be safe."

I'd just met him. I shouldn't have trusted him, but my curiosity quickly overcame any sense of caution. And I felt something else—a warm shiver that had nothing to do with our lycanthropy. I hadn't let go of his arm. His body was close to mine, and he was *cute*.

"There's a problem. Alette sent Leo along to look after me. I don't think he'd be happy about this."

He pursed his lips, serious for a moment, and glanced over his shoulder. "It isn't a problem. Come."

He held my hand—his was warm and dry—and guided me away from the exhibit, around another corner to the service door where the catering staff passed back and forth with their trays of food and drink.

Luis said, "Some vampires have lived like nobility for so long, they forget about the servants. He won't be watching this door."

Sure enough, we traveled down a plain concrete corridor

to a fire door and emerged onto the nighttime street. No one followed us.

We walked along the Mall, which even at night hosted joggers, dog walkers, people strolling before or after a dinner out. After ten minutes or so I took off my heels and carried them. My feet tingled on the concrete sidewalk. Nighttime, and I felt like running. Full moon wasn't for another week, though. Luis glanced at me, gaze narrowed, lips in a wry smile, like he understood.

Next we rode the Metro for a few stops, ending up a mile or so north from where we started. Luis led me on for a couple more blocks before stopping.

"Here we are."

A subtle shopfront sign, silver lettering on a blue background, lit by a small exterior light, announced the Crescent. Tinted windows didn't offer much of a view of the interior.

"Upstairs is a Moroccan restaurant. Decent, a little pricey, but don't tell Ahmed I said that. We're going downstairs."

Sure enough, we bypassed the brick stairs leading up and took the set winding down to a garden-level door. "Ahmed?"

"He owns the place. You'll meet him if he's here tonight."

I heard the music before Luis opened the door. Once he did, the sound opened up with all its richness and rhythm. Live music, not a recording. A Middle Eastern drum, a string instrument of some kind, and a flute. They weren't playing an identifiable song, but rather jamming on a traditional-sounding riff. It was fast, joyous, danceable.

Once inside, I saw the trio of musicians seated on

chairs near the bar: one was white, one black, the other Arabic-looking. The whole place had an international feel to it, and I heard conversations in a few different languages. Cloth hangings decorated the walls, and while the area inside the door looked like any other bar, farther inside there weren't any chairs, but large cushions and pillows surrounding low tables. Oil lamps and candles provided light. I smelled curry and wine in the air.

A guy who couldn't possibly have been old enough to serve drinks was behind the bar, drying glasses. A few patrons sat nearby on bar stools, tapping their feet or nodding along to the music. A woman in a full skirt and peasant blouse danced—I supposed it was belly dancing, but my image of belly dancing was totally different. She was all about grace and joy of movement, not the *I Dream of Jeannie* fantasy. Her dark hair trailed in a braid that swung as she turned, and she wore a distant smile.

Another dozen people sat at the tables, watching the dancer or the musicians, talking among themselves, reclining on cushions, eating, and drinking. It was a calm, leisurely party, a nightclub of sorts, drawing people for conversation and atmosphere.

All of them were lycanthropes.

I stopped, shocked into immobility. I hadn't sensed this many lycanthropes in one place since I was with the pack. I had never seen this many in one place without them glaring at each other, stalking, picking fights, jockeying for position within the pack hierarchy. At the very least, if they weren't fighting they were cowering before the leader who kept them in line, who made peace by force. There was no leader here, not that I could see.

"Is something wrong?" Luis said.

"No, it's just—I wasn't expecting this. All of them in one place. It's overwhelming."

"You have always been alone, then?"

"I used to have a pack. But it was nothing like this."

He said, "Can I get you a drink?"

I probably needed one. "Wine. White. I think."

Two filled wineglasses in hand, Luis led me to the back half of the club, where we could sit in relative quiet. His face lit when he came to a small group gathered in a corner.

"Ahmed! You are here."

"Luis!" A large man rose to his feet more gracefully than I would have given him credit for. He displaced his friends to one side, who amiably continued their conversation without him. He managed to clap Luis on the shoulders without making him spill a drop of wine. He had a faint accent, thoroughly Americanized. "Good to see you, I was beginning to think you'd abandoned us at last."

"I've been busy."

Ahmed turned to me. He had olive features, black hair and dark stubble, a good deal of paunch without the impression of softness. It made him seem round and jovial. Over his shirt and trousers, he wore a flowing, pale-colored robe, which made him fit perfectly with the atmosphere of the place.

He was wolf. I pictured a great, grizzled old hulk of a wolf standing in his place. The image made me want to whine in terror and be on my best behavior. I suppressed an urge to inch closer to Luis and take shelter behind him.

Ahmed's gaze flashed, as if he knew exactly the effect he had on other werewolves.

"Luis, you seem to have gotten lucky tonight. Welcome, welcome!"

He offered his hand. Gratefully, I took it. I clung to normalcy when I could. He covered my hand with both of his and smiled warmly.

"Who might you be?"

"Kitty."

"Kitty. Kitty Norville? *The Midnight Hour*?"

Heaven forbid there should be more than one werewolf named Kitty loose in the world. I grinned, stupidly pleased at the recognition. "That's right."

Luis stared at me. "You're *that* Kitty? You didn't say anything."

"It didn't come up. You guys listen to the show?"

Ahmed shrugged noncommittally and Luis ducked his gaze.

"Of course I've heard it," Ahmed said. "A couple of times. But I have friends who are great fans, trust me."

I wrapped my arm around Luis's and took a glass of wine from him. The evening was looking much less bleak than it had a couple of hours ago. In fact, it was looking positively glorious.

"It's okay. I'm used to people not admitting they listen to it. Let's sit, you guys have to tell me about all this." I looked around at the room, the musicians, and the lycanthropes gathered together.

"Excellent idea!" Ahmed said.

Becoming a lycanthrope usually happened by accident, and it often didn't change the ambitions a person may have had before. The need to travel for a career, the desire to see the world, these things didn't just vanish. Lycanthropy often made them problematic, but people learned to deal with it. It was easier for some than others. Many of the other lycanthrope varieties weren't tied to packs, like werewolves typically were. But even solitary beasts had the problem of territory. Our animal instincts sometimes got the better of us, and travel meant the possibility of infringing on someone else's space, especially during full moon nights, when those instincts were most powerful. As I had quickly learned myself, the one thing a traveling lycanthrope needed more than anything was a safe place to Change and run during the full moon.

As home to the federal government, a bunch of embassies, and a couple of major universities, Washington, D.C., had a vibrant international community, and the lycanthropes were part of it. The Crescent gave them a safe place to gather.

Ahmed explained all this. "We who travel know there is no time for fighting. Death comes to us all and it is a tragedy to hasten it. We have much better things to do than continually fight over who among us is strongest. So, here we are. There are places like this in many large cities: New York, San Francisco, London, Istanbul."

If T.J. had had a place like this, if Carl had been more like Ahmed, if we could have all acted a little more *civilized*—too many ifs. I needed too many ifs to keep T.J. alive.

Ahmed pointed out a few of the patrons: Marian, the dancer, was a were-jackal from Egypt who had immigrated and was working to bring her sister over. Yutaka, near the bar, was a history student from Japan and a werefox. The musicians: two wolves and a tiger. Ahmed also mentioned a friend of his who wasn't here tonight, a professor who had defected from Russia in the seventies, who was a bear. I couldn't even picture what a were-bear would be like. The place was a zoo.

It was also a paradise, a utopia, at least to my admittedly inexperienced eyes. I heard a lot of stories from doing the show—but then, people only called me with their problems. I'd only ever heard, and lived, the worst of it. I never heard about how things worked when they were going well.

The wine made me weepy. I wiped my eyes before tears could fall. Luis handed me a clean napkin from the next table over.

"Are you all right?" he asked.

"Yeah. This is so different from anything I've known. I never thought it could be like this. Everybody's getting along. You're all so friendly."

"I'm happy we could make you welcome here."

Ahmed said, "Your experience. What's it like?"

I shook my head absently. I wasn't sure I could put it into words. "Power. Jealousy. There was an alpha, and he protected us. But he controlled us as well. I had to fight for any kind of respect, but I refused in the end. It was all fighting and death. I had to leave. Then I get here, and Alette feeds me this line about the local lycanthropes being chaotic and dangerous, that they'd try to hurt me, and it was so easy to believe her. But she lied to me."

Ahmed shook his head. "Perhaps not from her point of view. Alette mistrusts us all because there is no alpha, no one she can negotiate with or control. That is why she says we are dangerous."

"You'd give her the benefit of the doubt?"

"I've encountered many of her kind, and I think she means well, in her own way. Her worst fault is arrogance."

I had to chuckle at that, but the sound turned bitter. I wondered if it was too late to refuse Alette's hospitality. I could stay here the whole time.

The woman had stopped dancing. The musicians played slower songs now, gentle background music as they experimented with each other's sounds and harmonies. The evening seemed to be winding down; a few people were leaving, waving at friends as they left. I wasn't ready for the night to be over. I wasn't ready to leave this place.

Luis put his arm around my shoulders, a warm, comforting contact. I leaned back and nestled against him. With him on one side, and Ahmed on the other, gazing serenely over his domain, I felt like I'd rediscovered the very best part of having a pack of my own: the safety, the protection. Friends all around me who wanted to keep me warm and safe. It was how I'd felt before T.J. was killed. I didn't think I'd ever find that again.

Ahmed looked at me, his lips pursed studiously. "You know the story of Daniel, yes?"

I searched my groggy mind. I felt like a puppy napping in a friendly lap. I didn't want to have to think. "Daniel?"

"The story of Daniel and the lion's den."

"That Daniel? Sure," I said. It was a Bible story. In ancient Persia, Daniel was persecuted for his belief in God and tossed into a den of lions to be eaten. In the story, God sent angels to hold the lions' mouths closed, and he emerged from the den unscathed.

"Yes," Ahmed said. "Do you know why Daniel survived?"

"It's a story about faith. God was supposed to have protected him."

He shrugged, noncommittal. "Yes, in a way. But not

how you think. You see, Daniel saved himself. He spoke to the lions and asked them to spare him. He knew their language because he was one of them—were-lion."

My eyes widened. "The Bible doesn't say anything about that."

"Of course not—not explicitly. But it's there, if you look. This was thousands of years ago, remember. Humankind and animalkind were closer then—our years in the Garden together were not so long ago. And our kind, the lycanthropes, we were the bridge between the two. Daniel was very wise, and what he learned was his purpose. That there was a reason for him to be part lion, that God had a reason to make him that way. This is what we learn from Daniel. That we have purpose for being who we are, and what we are, though we may not always know it. Daniel is a saint to us. It's one of our greatest stories."

"I've never heard it that way before."

Ahmed sighed. "It saddens me that the tribes in this country do not tell the old tales to one another. If we gathered to tell stories and drink more, there would not be so much fighting, yes?"

"Hear hear." I raised my near-empty glass in a toast, drained it, and said, "Tell another one."

I lost track of time, lounging there on satin cushions, in Luis's arms, while Ahmed spoke of stories I knew, but had never heard like this, through the filter of my own experience: a werewolf who looked at the world through two sets of eyes, human and animal, and constantly had to bridge the gap between them. Enkidu, from the *Epic of Gilgamesh*, was a wild man who lived like a beast until he was tamed by a woman's touch. And what if he didn't just live like a beast, but *was* one, and yet found a reason to embrace civilization? There were tales that sounded like Aesop's Fables, about the kindnesses shown between humans and animals, thorns plucked from the paws of lions and the like, and Greek and Roman myths about gods and goddesses who could change form at will.

The way Ahmed told it, this wasn't a curse or a disease I'd been suffering with for the last four years. It was a gift that made me part of a long tradition of saints and heroes who slipped easily between one shape and another and made it a strength.

I wasn't ready to go so far as to feel grateful about what had happened to me. It had been an accident, a violent, bloody accident, and I didn't feel blessed. Except if I wasn't a werewolf, I wouldn't have my show and all the success it had brought me.

I was confused.

"Wait, Marian, you can't leave without saying goodbye!" Ahmed called to the dancer, who had just reached the door. "Excuse me," he said to us, then leapt to his feet and rushed over to sweep her up in a bear hug. Wolf hug. Whatever.

Luis took the opportunity to move his hand to my hip, where he settled it in an unmistakable invitation. When I tipped my face up to look at him, he was right there, looking back at me. I could feel his breath on my cheek. I craned my neck, leaned forward just a little—his lips pressed mine lightly, then drew away.

I must have flushed from scalp to toe, the way a sudden heat rose around me.

"My apartment is nearby," he said, whispering in my ear.

I felt his body stretched out behind me, the solidity of it, his warm scent, and I wanted it. I wanted him.

I pressed his hand and smiled.

We met Ahmed by the door to say goodbye, though I was self-conscious because I felt like I was glowing. Luis stood very close to me.

"Thanks for the stories," I said. "For everything." I meant the place, this shelter, the company.

"Kitty, it's a pleasure. The doors here are never locked. You're welcome anytime."

The air outside was cool; Luis and I walked arm in arm.

He had a sexy studio apartment with hardwood floors and exposed brick walls, sparse furniture and floor-length drapes. The kitchen had an island counter and looked well stocked, against expectation of the usual bachelor pad. As if he wasn't attractive enough already, he probably knew how to cook as well.

Not that I had that good a look at the place, because just like in a movie we were kissing before the door closed. He pushed me against the wall, and I wrapped one leg around his, pulling myself close to him. We couldn't get into each other fast enough. My skin was tingling, inside and out.

I suddenly realized, it wasn't enough to think back to the last time I had sex, which was long enough ago. But when was the last time I had *good* sex? That was a pathetically long time ago.

As his hand was climbing up my thigh, under my skirt, I stopped its progress, pressed it against me. I made him slow down, tasting his lips, drawing the weight and solidity of him closer. He smelled spicy, excited, simmering with sweat and hormones. I pressed my face against his neck and took a deep breath of him. He pulled the strap of my dress off my shoulder, bent his head over my bare skin, and did the same, breathing in my scent. I giggled, because I wasn't even supporting myself anymore; I was leaning into him, he was holding me, and we were breathing together.

I was going to enjoy this.

Much later, we rested together in bed, naked and glowing.

I dozed in a happy, languid haze when I noticed the mattress was vibrating with a soft, rumbling noise. I didn't think Luis was snoring; the sound was constant. It felt like one of those coin-operated massage beds in a cheap hotel. I looked up, glanced around, befuddled. The sound was coming from behind me. *Right* behind me.

I rolled over without displacing Luis's arm draped over my hip.

"Luis? Are you *purring*?"

The rumbling stopped and he sleepily mumbled, "Hmm?"

chapter 4

"Don't move. I'll get it."

Luis was already out of bed before I realized someone was knocking on the front door. The noise had a steady rhythm and was getting louder. Luis put on a robe and went to the door. "Yes?"

The answer was muffled by the barrier, but perfectly comprehensible.

"It's time for Kitty to leave now. She's had enough fun for one night."

Leo. He must have tracked me down.

It had to be getting close to dawn. Maybe I'd thought I could wait him out. As it was, he had just enough time to drag me back.

Luis looked at me. I didn't want to say anything. Leo rattled the doorknob.

"You don't have to go," Luis said. "He can't come in. *I'm* not going to invite him."

Ah, the home turf advantage. If we could stand another hour of Leo nagging at us through the door, we'd be fine.

A click and drag rattled the door—the sound of a dead

bolt sliding back. Luis moved back in time to avoid being hit as the door swung in.

Bradley stood in the doorway, holding a device that was most likely a lockpick.

Leo leaned on the wall outside, safely beyond the threshold, regarding us with an expression verging on laughter. "Fortunately, the mortal humans in Alette's employ aren't bound by that annoying little restriction."

"You're trespassing," Luis said.

"Hello, Luis. How is your band of miscreants at the Crescent these days?"

Luis stood with his hands clenched and back braced, giving the impression that he was about to pounce. Was he going to defend me in some gloriously violent manner? How romantic. It scared the daylights out of me.

"Luis, it's okay. I should probably get going."

"Why should you go with them?" He spoke over his shoulder, without shifting his gaze from the vampire.

"They're holding my car hostage," I said. Luis didn't look convinced, but he didn't say anything else. I was still in bed, holding the sheets over my chest. I glared at Leo and Bradley. "Could you close the door so I can get dressed?"

"No," Leo said. "I don't trust you. I'm not taking my eyes off you this time."

Luis started to close the door anyway, but Bradley put out his arm to block it. Bradley tried hard to brace it, leaning forward and putting his weight into it, but Luis was stronger, and slowly pushed him back. Bradley put his other hand against the door. They'd break it before Luis got it closed. They glared at each other.

"Never mind," I said. I didn't want to start a fight. Not

that I didn't think Luis couldn't handle himself. But I hated to think that I was the one who dragged him into it.

I climbed out of bed and made a point of not shrinking under Leo's gaze. Bradley was polite enough to look away, and Luis was still guarding his territory. But Leo watched me walk naked across the room to where I'd abandoned my dress on the floor. He was trying to aggravate me, which made it a little easier to ignore him. I'd run with a wolf pack; they'd seen me naked. I turned my back to him to pull the dress over my head. I found my shoes and handbag and met Luis by the door.

"Very nice," Leo said.

I said to Luis, "I had a good time. Thanks."

"Be careful with them."

"I'll watch my back." I leaned forward for a kiss and he gave it to me, gently, warmly. I closed my eyes and sighed wistfully.

"I'll see you later," he said. A statement, not a question.

I smiled. "Yeah." I lingered, thinking he might kiss me again—hoping he would.

"Finished?" Leo said. Scowling, I stepped out and Luis closed the door.

Leo and Bradley flanked me on the way out, my own personal Secret Service.

The vampire sat in the front seat of the sedan while Bradley drove.

"You're a fucking loose cannon," Leo said cheerfully over his shoulder. He crossed his arms and smirked. The sky was graying; he was cutting it close. I couldn't tell if he was anxious about it. His blasé attitude might have been an act to cover up how annoyed he really was, for all I knew.

"Thanks," I said. He rolled his eyes.

If I'd felt like a teenager on the way to her prom on the way out, Alette waiting up for me when we arrived back at her place completed the image. Bradley and Leo guided me to the parlor, where she was waiting, seated regally in her wingback armchair. At a gesture from her, they left.

Frowning, she rose. "I begin to understand why you're a wolf without a pack. Have you always been this contrary?"

"No. It took me years to develop a backbone."

"Your last pack kicked you out, did it?"

"I left."

"Leo tells me you found your way to the Crescent. What did you think of it?"

The question put me off balance. I was all ready for her to chew me out, and I was all ready to be, well, catty about it.

"I really liked it," I said. "It's been a long time since I felt like I was with friends."

"I've tried to give you that here."

Then why did I feel like a teenager being dressed down by her mother? "Leo made it difficult."

"He must find you easy to provoke."

I wasn't going to start this argument.

"Before I forget." I reached back and undid the clasp on the necklace. I hadn't taken it off all night, lest I end up a pathetic character in a de Maupassant story. I gave it back to her. "Thanks. I think it was what made Luis finally hit on me."

She narrowed her gaze. "Do I even want to know?"

"Probably not."

"We'll have to continue this tomorrow evening. I trust

you can find your way to your room? Everyone else is asleep."

I had a feeling that was a very subtle, guilt-inducing dig. "Um, yeah."

"Good morning, Kitty." She swept past me, down the corridor and away.

Morning. Sleep. Yeah. What a night.

I was bleary-eyed when I met Ben in front of the Dirksen Senate Office Building at noon.

"What the hell happened to you?" he said by way of greeting.

I peered at him through slitted, sleep-encrusted eyelids and smiled self-indulgently.

"I went out last night."

He shook his head and took a sip of coffee out of a paper cup. "I don't want to know."

I blinked, trying to focus and feeling like I was only now waking up. I *knew* this was Ben standing in front of me. The figure certainly looked like Ben, and sounded like Ben. But his suit was pressed. His shirt was buttoned. He wore a tie, and his hair lay neatly combed back from his face.

I should have known it would take the U.S. Senate to polish him up.

"What are you staring at?" he said. I could only grin sheepishly.

We went inside and managed to find the room the hearing was being held in with only a couple of wrong turns. We sat in the back of the room, which was nicer than I was expecting: blue carpet, wood-paneled walls, the desks and tables in the front made of an expensive-looking wood. The place had a formal, legal air. The chairs for the audience were padded, which was nice.

The space for observers wasn't huge, but it was filled. A lot of the people looked like reporters. They held tape recorders or notepads. A couple of TV cameras stood off to the side.

No one noticed us. I considered it one of the perks of radio that I could be well known and completely unrecognizable at the same time. The reporters focused all their attention on the front of the room: the row of senators, eight of them, each with an identifying nameplate, and Dr. Paul Flemming, sitting at a long table facing them.

Ben leaned over. "You met him. What's he like?"

"I don't know. He's kind of cagey. Nervous. Territorial."

"He looks kind of mousy."

"Yeah, that too."

C-SPAN live wasn't any more exciting than C-SPAN on TV. I paid attention anyway, waiting for McCarthy to burst out of some unassuming senator's skin and ravage the hearings with Cold War paranoia. No such luck. The proceedings were downright sedate, very Robert's Rules of Order.

Senator Duke opened the hearings after laying down the rules of how long each senator could speak and when. As Chair, he got to decide such matters.

"Because of the highly irregular nature of the subject which we have convened to discuss, and the secrecy under which the research on this subject has been conducted, the committee has opted to reserve the first two sessions for questioning the gentleman who supervised the research. Dr. Paul Flemming, welcome. You have a statement for us?"

Each witness could enter a prepared statement into the record. They tended to be dry and academic. I expected Flemming's to be doubly so.

"Five years ago, I received a grant of funds from the National Institutes of Health to conduct research into a number of previously neglected diseases. These are diseases which have for centuries been shrouded in superstition and misunderstanding—"

And so on. He might as well have been talking about cancer or eczema.

The senators' questions, when they finally started, were benign: what is the Center, where is it located, who authorized funding, from which department was funding derived, what are the goals of the Center. Flemming's answers were equally benign, repetitions of his opening statement, phrases like the ones he'd given me: the Center strives to further the boundaries of knowledge in theoretical biological research. He never even used the words vampire or lycanthrope. I squirmed, wondering when someone was going to mention the elephant in the room.

Senator Duke granted my wish.

"Dr. Flemming, I want to hear about your vampires."

Dead silence answered him. Not a pen scratched in the entire room. I leaned forward, waiting to hear what he'd say.

Finally, Flemming said, very straightforward, as if delivering a paper at a medical conference, "These are patients exhibiting certain physiological characteristics such as an amplified immune system, pronounced canines, a propensity for hemophagia, severe solar urticaria—"

"Doctor," Duke interrupted. "What are those? Hemophagia? What?"

"Consuming blood, Senator. Solar urticaria is an allergy to sunlight."

He made it sound so clinical, so mundane. But what kind of allergy caused someone to burn into a cinder?

"And what have you discovered about these so-called patients of yours, Doctor?"

Flemming hesitated a moment, then leaned closer to the microphone set before him. "I'm not sure I understand your question, Senator."

"Vampires. In your opinion, what are they?"

Flemming cleared his throat, nervousness slipping into the calm, and said cautiously, "I believe I explained previously, that vampirism is characterized by a set of physical characteristics—"

"Cut the bull, Doctor. We've all seen *Dracula*, we know the 'physical characteristics.' I want to hear about the moral characteristics, and I want to hear about why they exist."

I leaned forward, scooting to the edge of my seat, not because I would hear any better. The microphones worked great. I was waiting for the fight to break out.

"My studies don't involve the scope of your question, Senator."

"Why not?"

"Those points are irrelevant."

"With all due respect I disagree with you. Strongly."

"Senator, I'm not qualified to comment on the moral characteristics of my patients."

"Your test subjects, your patients—how do you feed them, Doctor? Whose blood do they suck out? How many of *them* turn into vampires?"

"Despite all the stories to the contrary, the condition is not transmitted by direct fluid contact—"

"And the blood?"

"Blood bank, Senator. We use pints of the most common types that the existing blood supply can spare."

"Thank you, Doctor." He said it like he'd gained some kind of victory.

"Doctor, I have some questions over the budgeting of your research—" One of the other senators on the committee, a woman named Mary Dreschler, quickly steered the discussion back to more mundane matters. A Democrat from a Midwestern state, Dreschler had run for the seat held by her late husband, who'd died suddenly in the middle of a reelection campaign. She was on her third term.

After two hours of this, the day's session was over. It was just as well it wasn't an all-day thing. If people in Congress did this sort of thing a lot, I was going to have to respect them a little more. Here I was, thinking the job was all glamour and state dinners. When Duke called the session into recess for the day, a sense of relief passed through the room, and the group sigh of exhaustion changed the air pressure.

Ben, leaning back in his chair, smirked in amusement. "If this is the tone the whole hearings are going to take, we're in for a roller coaster. I can't wait to see what Duke does with you."

"I thought you were supposed to be on my side."

"I am. It's still going to be fun to watch."

I could hear it now: *Eaten any babies lately, Ms. Norville?*

Eggs for breakfast. Does that count?

Looking purposeful, Ben gathered up his briefcase and jacket.

"Where are you off to?" I asked.

"I have some research I want to do. You don't need me for anything, do you?"

"Nope." I had some research of my own I wanted to take care of.

"Then I'll see you tomorrow." Outside the hearing room, he took off down the hallway, away from the front doors of the building.

As I turned to leave, a man with a mini digital camcorder tucked in his hand stepped into my path. I balked, startled.

"You're Kitty Norville," he said. "Aren't you?"

I wondered how he knew. I didn't include my picture with any of the publicity for the show for exactly this reason. But he might have overheard Ben talking to me. He might have pulled my file off DMV records. It could have been anything.

He wasn't tall for a guy, only a couple inches taller than my five feet six. His build was average and he dressed preppy, a brown leather coat over a sweater and khakis. But his eyes shone with a barely suppressed zeal that was unnerving, because it was focused on me.

"Who are you?"

"Roger Stockton, I'm a reporter for *Uncharted World*. Do you have a couple minutes to answer some questions?" Without waiting for an answer he hefted the camera and turned an eye to the little screen, which was no doubt showing me glaring at him.

I had to be calm. CNN was watching from down the

hall. I didn't want to do something that would get me a starring role on the six o'clock news.

"Wow. I didn't think *Uncharted World* had reporters. Aren't you guys more the urban legend and unverified amateur video footage kind of show?"

He didn't react to that, but he was probably used to getting that kind of crap from people. "What was your reaction to being subpoenaed by the oversight committee?"

"I'm sorry, I really don't have time for this." I dodged him and continued down the hallway. The guy was persistent, though. He ran after me and planted himself in front of me again, cutting me off when I tried to go around him. The hall wasn't wide enough to avoid him.

He spoke quickly. "What are your thoughts regarding the Center for the Study of Paranatural Biology and Flemming's work there?"

The shining little eye of the camera lens stayed trained on me. I had to get away from that thing. "No comment."

"Come on, you've got more of a right to an opinion on this stuff than anyone else in that room, and you can't take a minute to share your thoughts with the public? Are you going to leave it to other people to decide what tone this debate takes?"

I turned on him, my shoulders bunched, my jaw tight, my gaze burning. I only half raised my hands and took a step toward him, but his reaction was immediate and unambiguous. He stumbled back against the wall, pressing himself to it as if he could fall through it, and clutched the camera to his chest. His eyes went wide and the blood drained from his face.

He knew I was a werewolf. More importantly, he

believed it, and everything it entailed. He thought I might actually maul him, right here and now. Idiot.

"I don't want my picture on TV, especially not on *Uncharted World*. Get rid of the camera and I'll think about talking to you. But right now I'm not inclined to be nice."

I stalked away from him. And half a second later, I heard footsteps hurrying behind me.

He could *not* take a hint.

"Look, we're both in the broadcast business. Why not do a colleague a favor? Just give me a couple of quotes and I'll give your show a plug. We both win."

It didn't even help that his voice had a nervous waver to it now. I tried to ignore him, but he was right alongside me again, holding up that damned camera.

He was looking back and forth between me and the camera, so he didn't see Bradley standing in front of us, blocking the corridor. But I did.

I stopped. Stockton didn't, until Bradley grabbed his wrist and took the camera out of his hand.

"Hey!" Stockton struggled, until he looked at Bradley. First his chest, then up to his face. They couldn't have played it better if they'd been making a movie. All I had to do was sit back and watch.

"This guy bothering you?" Bradley said.

Oh, how a girl loved to hear those words from someone with Bradley's build. "I think he was just leaving. After he erases the last five minutes of footage off his camera."

Bradley let go of him, then studied the camera's controls. He started pushing buttons, and I had no doubt that in moments my face would be wiped clean from the camera's memory.

Stockton pointed a finger at him. "This is harassment."

"No, *that's* harassment," I said, nodding at the camera.

He frowned. "I don't understand why you're turning down free publicity."

"I'd like to hold on to the last bit of anonymity I have," I said. I was going to lose it soon enough when I showed up on C-SPAN.

Bradley handed back the camera. His expression was smug, so I was confident the purge had been a success.

Stockton backed away. "We'll talk again. Tomorrow."

The bodyguard and I made it out of the building without any other interruptions.

I gave a tired sigh. "I think I owe you one."

"Not to worry," he said. "It was my pleasure."

Only after a couple minutes did I realize that he'd been on his way to meet me after the hearings finished, to escort me to the car, as if I couldn't be trusted to make it to the curb without getting into trouble. Maybe I couldn't. It still annoyed me.

"Shotgun," I called as we neared the sedan in the parking garage.

He glared. He'd been heading for the rear door, preparing to be all chauffeur-y.

"I can see better out the front," I explained. He sighed in what I thought was an overly dramatic manner, but he opened the front passenger door for me.

As he pulled out of the garage and into the bright sunshine of the daytime street, I asked, "Can we make a detour? Just a tiny little stop. You can even leave the motor running."

I faced him, eyes wide and pleading. Even in broad daylight, he managed to look as foreboding as he had the night I first saw him, with his dark, nondescript suit and stony features. As we emerged into daylight, he put on a pair of sunglasses, completing the Man In Black image.

"You are an awful lot of trouble, you know that?"

"It's not on purpose, honest." The trouble I caused was almost always a direct result of speaking without thinking first. This, for example: a rational person would do whatever she could to avoid annoying Bradley. Not me. "Please? Just a tiny little errand, I promise."

"Where?"

I cringed. "The Crescent?"

"No, absolutely not!"

"I just want to run in and leave a message for Luis, that's all, I promise."

"No. No way."

"*Please?*" I wasn't above begging. "We wouldn't have to tell Alette."

"Do you really think I wouldn't tell her?"

He would, he absolutely would. For a moment, his sincerity almost made me back off. This genuine, seemingly uncoerced loyalty Alette inspired in her people was daunting. I set my elbow on the door and leaned my head on my hand.

Bradley pursed his lips, his gaze flickering at me. "She has your best interests in mind. She's only looking out for your safety."

"She thinks a wolf needs an alpha, does she? Doesn't want me running around without a leash?"

He didn't answer. As altruistic as he made Alette out to be, there was a core of truth to what I'd said. I stared out the window as we passed yet another neoclassical building. I wondered what that one was.

"All right," he said. "A minute. That's all. If you duck out on me, Alette may never let you out of the house again."

I gave him a tight-lipped smile. "All right."

He waited at the curb, with the motor running. Just so I knew the clock was ticking. I ran.

Maybe Luis would be there, maybe not. Maybe I just wanted to make sure the place was real, that I hadn't dreamed last night.

It was real. In the light of day, the silver on the sign above the restaurant part of the building sparkled. A menu was taped inside the window. I went downstairs.

The door to the lower section was propped open, letting in the slight breeze. I peeked inside. Only a few people were there, before the after work and supper crowds. A man at one of the tables in back drank coffee and read a paper, a couple was talking at the bar, and an old man sat alone at a table and chair, where the musicians had played last night. Hunkering inside a tired, stained overcoat, he stared into a tumbler that he gripped with both hands. He was a werewolf; I could tell without scenting him or sensing anything about him. He was grizzled enough, he looked the part. Wiry, steel-gray hair bristled from his liver-spotted head into thick sideburns, down his wrinkled neck, and under his ears, which were slightly pointed. I caught a glimpse of elongated canine teeth sitting just over his lower lip. His fingers were thick, ending in sharp, narrow nails. He probably terrified small children he passed on the street.

Here was someone who'd been a werewolf for a long, long time, and had spent much of that time in his wolf form. I'd heard of this, but I'd never seen it: his body was forgetting how to be human. If I hadn't known anything about werewolves, I might have looked at him and thought he was arthritic and aging badly. As it was, I expected his eyes to be golden-amber if he happened to glance up.

I somehow found my way to the bar. Bumping into it, I realized I'd been staring. I shook my head to clear it of the image of the old man.

"You're Kitty, right?" the bartender said. He was the same guy from last night, the young one. Now that I had a good look at him, I could tell that he wasn't wolf, or jaguar like Luis. I couldn't tell what the hell he was.

"Yeah, hi."

"Jack." He stuck out his hand. I gripped it. He squeezed back a little too hard, giving me a half grin as he did. Trying to prove something. He was strong—stronger than I would have expected from someone his size. But then, so was I. I let go and leaned on the counter like I hadn't noticed.

"Can I get you something?"

"No, thanks, I just wanted to leave a note for Luis." I nodded toward the old man at the table. "Who's he?"

Jack put his elbows on the bar and raised a conspiratorial brow. He whispered, "People call him the Nazi."

I blinked at him, startled.

"I don't know if he really is or not," Jack continued. "But Ahmed says he did fight in World War II, and that he is German. Who knows? He comes here every day at four, drinks his schnapps, and leaves without saying a word."

"Whether he is or he isn't, he must have some amazing stories to tell. I wonder—" And that was all I did, because the old man tipped his glass to his mouth, drained the last bit of liquid, stood, and settled his coat more firmly on his shoulders as he stalked out of the place. That was that.

I turned to Jack. "What about you? You have any good stories?"

"Me? I'm just a cub," he said, grinning. "Give me a few years."

"May your life be so dull that you don't actually collect any."

"Where's the fun in that?"

Fun? I glared at him.

I left a note for Luis. Not like I had anything to say beyond, *Hi, it's me.* It felt like high school all over again, which was kind of fun in its own way. I hadn't crushed this hard over anyone—outside of a movie screen, at least—in a long time. I felt giddy, young, and silly—and completely distracted, which meant the timing was horrible. Senate hearings were supposed to be serious, and I kept picturing Luis in bed.

Bradley got me back to Alette's house without any further ado.

Before I'd left that morning, Emma brought me an envelope, thick stationery paper with my name written on it in fancy cursive. Inside was a square of cardstock bearing a handwritten note informing me that Alette requested the pleasure of my company for dinner that evening. It felt very old-school, like something out of Emily Post.

I'd never had dinner with a vampire, and part of me dreaded finding out what that involved. The imagination ran a little wild. But if I was going to have a chance to talk to her, this was it. Maybe I could draw her out a little.

I wondered if she expected me to dress for dinner, in the Victorian tradition, silk gowns and suits in your own parlor. I'd worn slacks and a blouse for my day at the hearings, so I didn't look particularly ratty. But around

Alette, I'd feel downright drab. Then again, no matter what I wore, I'd feel drab next to Alette.

In the end, I didn't "dress for dinner." If slacks and a blouse were good enough for the U.S. Senate, they were good enough for the vampire.

I hoped Leo wouldn't be joining us.

I took a nap, washed up, and Emma brought me to a dining room in another part of the ground floor. Like the parlor, this was classically English, with wood paneling on the walls, which were hung with many paintings, rows and rows of them, landscapes and still lifes of dead birds and hunting rifles, and a few portraits of scowling old men and grim-looking ladies in opulent gowns decorated with flounces and lace. More portraits, like the ones in the parlor and the photos in the hallway upstairs. Were they old friends? Relatives?

A long table ran down the center of the room. Twenty people could have sat there easily, and for a moment I thought this was going to be like one of those comedies where two people sat at either end and had to shout at each other for the salt. But no, Alette stood by the chair at one end, and there was a place setting to her right, one chair away along the side.

"Welcome," she said. "Thank you for coming."

"Thanks for the invitation." I glanced around nervously, but Alette was alone. No Leo. I relaxed a notch. "Not that you gave me much of a choice, with Bradley keeping tabs on me all day."

She ignored the dig and indicated the chair with a graceful turn of her hand. "Please, sit."

The table only had the one place setting. By her chair, the polished mahogany surface was empty.

I should have been relieved.

She said, "I took the liberty of asking the cook to prepare your filet rare. I assume this is acceptable."

There was a time I didn't much like steak, and I preferred any meat I ate ground up and well burned on a grill. The Wolf, however, liked meat to bleed. So I ate rare steaks.

"Yeah, thanks." I gestured at the empty place on the table in front of her. "So, what are you . . ."

"I've already dined this evening."

This was going to be awkward. When one of her staff brought out a plate with the steak and tastefully arranged vegetables and set it in front of me, I half expected she'd also bring out a goblet full of thick red stuff and give it to Alette. Though it was probably just as well she wasn't going to be . . . dining . . . in front of me.

I managed to overcome a lifetime of socialization about eating in front of people who weren't and started in on the meal, which was perfect, of course. Warm, bleeding, tender, tangy. Small bites with fork and knife; *not* messily devoured. The Wolf and I compromised on these points.

"Tell me how the hearings went today."

I was supposed to be her spy, then? "I think C-SPAN was broadcasting. At least they had cameras there. You could have watched it for yourself."

She narrowed her gaze. "I was indisposed."

I shrugged, nonplussed. "You could tape it. Heck, you could probably download it off the Web." I didn't know if the old vampires even used the Internet. She probably let her minions do that.

Resting her elegant chin on her hands, she said, "I want to hear what *you* think."

Did she really want to know what I thought, or was she testing my bias?

"Flemming testified today. He's the head of the Center, and the committee has put him in the position of having to defend his project, his baby. In that respect, this could be any government research project being put under the microscope. But then there's Duke. He wants to turn it into a witch hunt. Since this is a PC world, he can't get Flemming to make a judgment call like 'vampires are evil' or 'werewolves are hellspawn.' Flemming's being very clinical about the whole thing, and I think it's pissing Duke off. I'm wondering if this isn't all his idea in the first place. He's always been on the fringe. He may see these hearings as a way to gain validation for his ideas."

"Senator Duke knows very little of the matters on which he speaks so fanatically."

"Yeah, but he's a fanatic with political clout. That makes him scary."

"The werewolf, afraid of the politician?"

I smirked. "As werewolves go, I'm a total coward. Give me a good alpha to hide behind any day."

"You just haven't found a good one, is that it?"

It was kind of like finding a good boyfriend. You kept hoping the perfect one existed, but the trial and error in the meantime could be gut-wrenching. "You're very nosy."

"It's how I learn. You have some experience with that yourself, I believe."

"Can't argue."

"What have they scheduled for tomorrow?"

"More grilling of Flemming, I think. If it's anything like today they'll end up going around in circles. This is an oversight hearing, so they could go for days, until they've heard everything they want to. They haven't even announced the whole schedule of witnesses yet. It's like the whole thing was thrown together."

"When do you testify?"

"I don't know."

"Duke will postpone your testimony until next Monday, if he can."

I paused and considered. Monday was the next full moon. Alette must have known that. Did Duke? Did he know that I'd be at my worst, the day Wolf rose so close to the surface? I didn't want to give him that much credit. "I hope not," I said simply.

She said, "What do you hope will result from these hearings?"

"I guess I just want everyone to say, 'Yeah, okay, this stuff exists.' Then I want them to leave us alone."

"What is the likelihood of that happening?"

"I don't know. The trouble is, I don't think they can both happen at the same time. I keep thinking, if the government recognizes the existence of these things, it'll want to regulate them."

"That is my fear as well. Whatever happens, that must not be allowed to come to pass. The government—Flemming, Duke, all of them—must, as you say, leave us alone."

"We may not have a choice what happens."

"Oh, there are always choices. Above all, the conclusion of these hearings must be that we are not a threat—to the public or to the government. You know very well we are not. We have regulated ourselves for centuries to ensure our secrecy, to ensure that the mortals *don't* have a reason to fear us and take action. It may be up to you to preserve that balance."

And I was one of the reasons that secrecy was coming to an end. No pressure or anything. "I don't think I have that kind of authority—"

"I think you sell yourself short. People listen to you, Kitty. You simply don't see it because you stay sheltered behind your microphone."

She was implying that it was all make-believe to me. That I didn't believe I really had an audience.

Maybe it was true. Here, for the first time, I was meeting some of my audience. I had to face them and stand up to defend all the stuff I'd been talking about on the air for the last year.

So much easier to hide behind the microphone.

"I'm only worrying about telling them the truth. I'm not going to be able to dictate what action the committee takes."

"The implications may run far wider than you think. Have you ever seen someone burned at the stake? I have."

Why was I not surprised? "It won't come to that. We've gotten past that."

"Perhaps."

Even with all the conversation, I'd managed to finish eating. The steak was good, and I'd been hungry. I tapped my fork—stainless steel, not silver, another courteous gesture from the mistress of the house—on the plate, fine china in some antique pattern. I should have been afraid of breaking it.

"Flemming's the one who's going to swing this," I said. "He's the scientist, and he's the one who depends on the committee for his livelihood. They'll listen to him."

Alette reached over and took the fork out of my hand, setting it down out of my reach. I stared at my hand, startled. I hadn't seen her coming. I hadn't had time to flinch. She said, "Are you suggesting we should be more worried about Flemming than Duke?"

"Duke is predictable. We know exactly where he stands. But Flemming? I don't know anything about him. Look, Alette. I have to be able to get out and travel around without your people hanging around me. You're worried about me and I appreciate that, but I want to look around, find out more about Flemming and his research, see if I can't follow up on a few contacts. But I can't do that with Bradley or Leo looking over my shoulder. No one would talk to me. I'm not trying to be disrespectful of your hospitality. But I can take care of myself, at least a little, and I need some freedom." I'd had precisely two days to earn her trust. I didn't know if it was enough, especially since I'd already run off once. Er, twice. But if she wanted me as an ally, she had to know she couldn't keep me on a leash and expect me to be effective.

"You aren't saying this just so you can run off with that were-jaguar from the Brazilian embassy, are you?"

I shrank back in my seat and tried to look innocent. "Maybe just a little."

She studied me, lips pursed in a wry smile. After a moment she said, "I don't suppose I could blame you for that. All right, then. But I want to hear what you learn on your investigations."

"It's a deal." The kitchen staff came to clear away the dishes, then brought dessert: chocolate mousse in a crystal goblet. My God, what had I done to deserve dessert? The maid was human. I'd only seen a small fraction of the house. I was getting nervous. "Alette, can I ask—where are the others?"

"Others?"

"I've met you and Leo. But you must have other . . ." Minions? Lackeys? ". . . companions. Vampire companions."

She suppressed a wry smile. "You're accustomed to Master vampires who surround themselves with followers, as reflections of their own importance."

Vast halls filled with pouty Eurotrash vampires—yeah, that was the image.

She said, "I'm extremely selective about who I bring into this life, this existence. It's not necessarily an easy way to be. I require pure motives. You've met no other vampires because there are none. Just the two of us. I would not tie someone to me for eternity lightly, Kitty."

Then she saw something in Leo that I didn't. She might have looked forward to spending eternity with him. I couldn't stand being in the same room with him for a minute.

chapter 5

The next day, I scoured newspapers and major news Web sites for mention of the hearings. I wanted to find out what the press was reporting. The only place that had any sort of major headline on the hearings was the Web site for *Wide World of News*: "Are Vampires Controlling the Senate?" That was so not useful. I stopped mentioning that rag entirely since they ran a "story" claiming that my show broadcast secret mind-control signals that caused teenagers to join satanic cults and run up huge debts on their parents' credit cards.

Unless they involved epic disasters or scandals surrounding major political figures, Senate committee hearings didn't normally make front page news. "Fact-Finding Hearing Gets Its Start," on page four of the *Washington Post*, was about the extent. They ran a black and white photo of Flemming at his microphone, gazing up at the committee with his sleepy eyes. They also ran a fun little sidebar titled "What Are the Facts?" defining the scientific terminology the doctor had bandied about. It all served to make the topics seem like exactly what Flemming insisted they were: diseases. Nothing more, nothing less. Nothing to be afraid of, as long as we understood it. Maybe this would turn out all right.

The next session of the hearings found me in the same place, sitting in the back of the room with Ben. Roger Stockton sat on the other side of the room from me, at the edge, where he could get a good shot of the participants with his camera. I caught him filming me a couple of times. I couldn't do anything about it without making a scene.

Flemming testified for another two hours, suffering through more questions.

Senator Deke Henderson, a Republican from Idaho, was one of those western politicians who played cowboy, to make themselves seem folksy and in touch with their roots. He wore a button-up rodeo shirt under a corduroy jacket and a big silver belt buckle. Outside the building, he'd put on the cowboy hat. He really had gotten his start in ranching, though, which gave him a hint of legitimacy. One couldn't be sure the outfit was a costume.

Henderson said, "Now that you've studied these diseases, Doctor, how close are you to finding a cure? What program would you recommend for preventing the spread of these diseases?"

Perfectly natural questions when confronted with any strange new disease. I listened closely to Flemming's answers.

He cleared his throat nervously. "As diseases go, these are quite unusual, Senator. For one, while they're life-altering, they aren't particularly destructive. In fact, they're just the opposite. They confer on the patient extraordinary resilience, immunity, rapid healing. I've studied such aspects of these conditions in detail."

"You haven't found a cure?"

"No, Senator."

"Have you even been looking?"

After a long silence, Flemming said, calmly, "I have been studying the unique characteristics of these conditions in the hopes of understanding them. For instance, if we understood the mechanics behind a vampire's longevity, or behind a werewolf's resistance to disease and injury, think of the application to medicine. I have a case history here of a patient who tested positive for the HIV virus, became infected with lycanthropy, and then all subsequent HIV tests had negative results."

Duke piped in. "You'd turn everyone into werewolves to keep them from getting AIDS? Is that what you're saying?"

"No, of course not. But I think you'll agree, the more knowledge we have about these conditions, the more power we have over them."

Duke leaned back and smiled. I couldn't see Flemming's face, which frustrated me. The two of them looked like they'd exchanged one of those all-knowing glances, like they'd just made a deal under the table in full view of everyone.

I had only assumed that the scientist and religious reactionary could never work together. I hadn't considered that they both wanted the same thing: to prove that this was real, for good or ill.

Ben and I exited into the corridor after the hearing adjourned for the day.

I leaned close, so I'd have less chance of being overheard. Especially by Stockton, who was busy cornering Flemming.

"Flemming's got to have an office somewhere in D.C. Can you find out where? I have his phone number if that helps."

He pulled a sheet of paper from the outside pocket of his briefcase and handed it to me. "Already done."

The sheet was blank letterhead with Flemming's name on it, and an address at the National Institutes of Health medical complex in Bethesda.

I beamed. "Thanks, Ben. You're the best."

"That's my job." I'd turned to leave when he said, "Wait. I found out a little more about him. He say anything to you about serving in the army?"

"Flemming was in the army?"

"Yeah. I've got a request in for a copy of his service record, I'll know more then. There's also a CIA connection."

I huffed. "You're kidding. That's just a little too outrageous to believe." I stared at the blank sheet of letterhead, like it would offer up the truth about the real Flemming.

Ben shrugged, unapologetic. "Just watch your back."

Too many questions and not enough time to look for answers. I tossed him a mock salute before jogging out of there.

I turned my cell phone back on when I left the building. Caller ID showed three missed calls, all from my mother. I thought the worst: there'd been an accident. Someone had died. Quickly, I dialed her back.

"Mom?"

"Kitty! Hi!"

"What's wrong?"

"Nothing."

I rolled my eyes and suppressed curses. "Did you call me earlier?"

"Yes, I had to ask you, your father says he saw you on C-SPAN this afternoon at those hearings they're doing on vampires. You were sitting in the audience. Now, I didn't think that could possibly be right. You weren't on C-SPAN, were you?"

I hesitated a beat. It wasn't that she was going to be angry that I was on television. No, she was going to be angry that I didn't tell her I was going to be on television so she could call all the relatives and set the timer on the VCR to record it.

"Dad watches C-SPAN?" I said.

"He was flipping channels," she said defensively.

I sighed. "Yes, he probably saw me on C-SPAN. I was in the audience."

"Well, isn't that exciting?"

"Not really. It's kind of nerve wracking. I'm supposed to testify at some point."

"You'll have to let us know when, so we can tape it."

This wasn't the school play. But I wasn't going to convince her of that. "That's cool, Mom. Look, I have someplace I need to be. I'll talk to you later, okay?"

"Okay—I'll have to call your father and tell him about this."

"Okay, Mom. Bye—"

"I love you, Kitty."

"You, too, Mom." I hung up. Why did I always feel guilty hanging up on her?

I didn't have time to track Flemming down that afternoon. I had an appointment.

At 3:55, I was at the Crescent, sitting at the table by the

bar, with a soda in front of me and a glass of schnapps in front of an empty chair. Right on schedule, the old man entered the club. He'd walked another three steps before he stopped, frozen in place, and stared at me.

I hadn't asked how long he'd been coming here. Probably since long before Jack started working here. When was the last time someone had interrupted his routine? I could almost see his thoughts working themselves out on his furrowed, anxious face as he processed this new event, this wrinkle in his life.

I nodded at the empty chair in invitation, but I didn't smile, and I didn't look directly at him. Staring might have been a challenge; smiling might have showed teeth, also a challenge. I worked on being quiet and submissive, like a good younger wolf in the pack. If his body was sliding more to the wolf half, I had to assume his mind was as well, and that those were the cues he would read.

Slowly, watching me carefully the whole time, he came to the table and took the empty seat.

"What do you want?" he said in a pronounced German accent. His voice was gravelly.

"To talk. I collect stories, sort of. I'm guessing you have some pretty good ones."

"Bah." He took a swallow from the glass. "There is nothing to talk about."

"Nothing at all?"

"You think that a pretty young thing like you will soften an old man's heart, with drink and blushing? No."

"I'm new in town," I said, soldiering on. "I came here for the first time two nights ago, and I'm just trying to learn as much as I can before I have to leave. I've been pretty sheltered until now. I was in a pack for a while. It wasn't anything like this."

"You came from a pack?" His eyebrows bunched together in curiosity.

I knew if I kept rambling long enough he'd interrupt. I nodded earnestly.

He scowled and shook his head. "The pack. Is archaic. In the old days, we needed it for protection. To defend against hunters, against rivals, against the vampires. Now? Easier to buy each other off. All the packs will go away soon, trust me."

I thought about Carl, my former alpha, running his pack into the ground to maintain his own sense of importance, and hoped he was right.

"My name's Kitty," I said.

He arched that peculiar brow at me. "A joke?"

"'Fraid not." I'd never seen much reason to change my name just because it had become a hideous irony.

He stared at me long and hard, like he was deciding whether or not to give something valuable away. Finally, he said, "Fritz."

"Nice to meet you, Fritz."

"Bah. You'll go away and in a week I won't remember you." He regarded his glass thoughtfully for a moment, then shook his head. "On second thought, you I will remember. Kitty." He snorted a brief laugh.

I had to smile. It heartened me that he could be amused by something, anything, and the icy wall around him seemed to chip a little.

He drained his glass, as he'd done the day before.

"Can I get you another one?"

He shook his head as he pushed back his chair. "Only one. Then I go. Goodbye."

"Where?" I blurted. "I mean, you obviously live in D.C. But what do you do? Where do you go?"

I'd said too much, crossed a line before earning his trust. He'd never talk to me again. He threw a glare over his shoulder and strode out the door, shrugging deeper into his coat.

Jack came over to pick up the empty glass and wipe down the table. "Good work," he said. "I've been here for a year and never heard him say more than one word."

I needed more than one word if I was going to get him to tell me his story. If I was going to convince him to tell his story on my show . . . But I was getting ahead of myself.

Then Luis walked through the door, and all such thoughts left my brain entirely. My giddy smile grew even giddier when I saw the same smile on him. He took me out for seafood, then back to his place, and Leo didn't break down the door on us this time.

The next morning, I drove to Bethesda and looked for Dr. Flemming.

The letterhead located him at the Magnuson Clinical Center, a research hospital that dated back to the fifties. I had to check in at the front gate of the campus, show ID and everything. I told them up front that I was visiting Flemming. Since the campus included several working hospitals, security was used to visitors. They gave me a pass and let me in.

Flemming's office was in the basement. I made my way from elevator to corridor, unsure of what I'd find. Fluorescent lighting glared off scuffed tile floors and off-white walls. I passed one plain beige door after another, marked with plastic nameplates, white letters indented into black backgrounds. At the ends of corridors, safety notices advised passersby about what they should do in case of emergency, red lines moving through floor plans helpfully directing them to the nearest exit. Wherever our taxpayer dollars were going, it wasn't for interior decorating.

The place smelled like a hospital, antiseptic and sickly. The vigilant attempts at cleanliness were never able to completely hide the illness, the decay, the fact that people here were hurting and unhappy. I didn't want to breathe too deeply.

I found Flemming's nameplate at the end of a little-used hallway, after passing several unmarked doors. I hadn't seen another person in the last five minutes. It seemed like he'd been relegated to the place where he'd be most out of the way.

I knocked on the door and listened. Somebody was inside. Leaning close to the door, I tried to make out the noises. A mechanical whirring sound, almost constant. Crunching paper. A paper shredder, working overtime.

And if *that* wasn't enough to make me suspicious . . .

I knocked louder and tried the doorknob. It was locked, requiring a magnetic key card to open. No sneaking in and catching the good doctor unawares, alas. I rattled the knob insistently. The paper shredder whined down and stopped. I waited to hear footsteps, heavy breathing, the sound of a gun being cocked, anything. Had Flemming—

or whoever was in there—snuck out the back? I wondered if Bradley had a lock pick that worked on card readers.

I considered: was I ready to stoop to going through Flemming's waste bin, piecing together strips of shredded documents, to find out what his research really involved and what he was hiding?

I wasn't any good at puzzles.

Then, the footsteps I'd been waiting to hear sounded, the slap of loafers on linoleum.

"Yes?" a voice said. It was Flemming.

I put on my happiest radio voice. "Hi! Is this where we sign up for tours of the lab?"

The lock clicked and the door opened a crack. Flemming stared back at me with a startled, wide-eyed expression. "You shouldn't be here."

He turned away, leaving the door open. I considered it an invitation and stepped inside.

The place was a mess. I wanted to say like a tornado had struck, but that wasn't right. The chaos had a settled look to it, as if it had accumulated over time, like sediment through the eons. Flemming must have been the kind of person who organized by piling. Papers, file folders, books, trade journals, clipboards—that was just what I saw on a cursory glance. The stacks crowded the floor around the pair of desks, lurked in corners, and blocked the bookshelves that lined the walls. Three computers, older models, hunched on the desks. If I had expected the gleaming inhumanity of a high-tech, secret government laboratory, I was disappointed. This was more like a faculty office at a poorly funded university department. A second door in the back led to who-knew-where. Probably a collection of coats and umbrellas. It had a frosted window inset into it, but the other side was dark.

The waist-high, high-volume paper shredder lurked against the back wall. Flemming returned to it, and the stack of paper on the table next to it.

"Is everything okay, Doctor?"

"I'm just cleaning up."

"In case you have to move out, is that what you're thinking?"

"Maybe."

"So, no tours of the lab today?" He'd started shredding again, and I had to speak louder to be heard over the noise.

"Ms. Norville, this isn't a good time."

"Can I come back tomorrow?"

"No."

"You don't have any hapless interns who could show me around?"

"No. There's only me."

The scene made me think Flemming wasn't just afraid of losing his funding; he was already at the end of it.

The computers were on, but the screen savers were running. I wondered if I could casually bump the desk, and get an image to flash on-screen, maybe a word-processing file with a title across the top saying, "Here's What's Really Going on in Flemming's Lab."

I took slow steps, craning my neck to read the papers on the tops of various stacks. There were graphs, charts, statistics, and articles with titles containing long, Latinate words. Without sitting down and plowing through the documents, I wasn't going to get anything out of the mess.

I really wanted to take a look at what he was shredding.

He was keeping an eye on me, watching me over his shoulder while continuing to feed pages into the shredder.

"So, um, do you think the committee would want to take a look at what you're destroying there?"

"I don't think that's any of your concern."

"Then I guess if I asked you straight up what the real purpose of your research is, you wouldn't be inclined to tell me?"

"Do you treat everyone like they're on your show?"

I hadn't really thought of it like that, but he had a point. I shrugged noncommittally.

"I've told you a dozen times, and I've told the committee: I'm doing pure science here, information-gathering research, nothing more."

"Then what was all that you told the committee about finding the secret of vampire immortality?"

He'd run out of pages to feed into the machine. The room became still, a contrast to the grinding noise of the shredder. After a pause he said, "Potential medical application. That's all. Government-funded programs like research that leads to practical applications. That's what the committee wants to hear. I had to tell them something."

"Have you done it? Found the secret of vampire immortality?"

He shook his head, and for a moment the constantly watchful tension in his face slipped. The scientist, inquisitive and talkative, overcame the paranoid government researcher. "It doesn't seem to be physiological. It's almost as if their bodies are held in stasis at a cellular level. Cellular decay simply stops. Like it's an atomic, a quantum effect, not a biological one. It seems to be outside my immediate expertise." He gave a wry smile.

"Like magic," I said.

"What?"

"Quantum physics has always seemed like magic to me. That's all."

"Ms. Norville, I'm really quite busy, and as pleasant as your company is, I don't have time to talk with you right now."

"Then when?"

He stared. "I don't know."

"Which means never."

He nodded slightly.

I stalked out of there. The door closed behind me, and I heard the sliding of a lock.

chapter **6**

The committee staffers finally put me on the docket for that afternoon. I was beginning to suffer anticipation-induced, nail-biting anxiety. I just wanted to get it over with.

Ben and I walked down the hallway to the hearing room. Fifty feet or so away, I put my hand on his arm and stopped him.

I recognized the silhouette of the man leaning against the wall outside the door. I would have noticed him in any case. He was out of place here, wearing laid-back, Midwest casual—a black T-shirt, faded jeans, biker boots—at odds with the East Coast business fashions that predominated the capital. His leather jacket hung from one hand. The building security guards let him keep his belt holster—still holding his revolver.

I knew exactly what I'd see when the man turned to face us. He was in his early thirties, with brown hair, a trimmed mustache, and a lazy frown. When he was amused, the frown turned into a smirk, which it did now. Cormac.

Somebody let Cormac in here with a gun. What happened to security? How had he snuck by them? A moment of blind panic struck. I glanced around for the nearest exit, which was behind me—I could run there in no time.

A split second of reflection reminded me that the last time I saw Cormac, I'd almost invited him into my apartment for the night. Maybe the panic wasn't entirely fear-driven. I didn't want the confusion of having Cormac around.

"What the hell?" Ben murmured, catching sight of who I stared at.

Cormac shrugged himself away from the wall, crossed his arms, and blocked the hallway in front of us. Ben matched his pose, arms crossed and face a wry mask. Ben was a couple inches shorter and a bit slimmer than the hit man, but he matched him attitude for attitude, smirk for smirk.

"What the hell are you doing here?" Cormac said to him.

With a nonchalant shrug, Ben said, "Representing my client."

The weird part of it was, Cormac was the one who referred Ben to me. By all accounts, Ben was the reason Cormac wasn't in jail. Neither of them would tell me if Cormac *ought* to be in jail.

I butted in. "What are *you* doing here?"

His eyes lit up, like this genuinely amused him. "The committee wanted someone with experience to be on hand in case things get out of control. Duke called me, hired me on as extra security. Great, isn't it?"

Security had been around the entire week. Knowing Duke and his paranoia, I had assumed they were all armed with silver bullets. That was the thing about all the "special" methods used to kill supernatural beings: a stake through the heart or a silver bullet will kill *anyone*.

I might have been mistaken. Normal security might not have changed their routine at all. Rather than arming the regular guards with silver bullets, in case the werewolf called to testify went berserk, why not call in the expert? Cormac was a professional, as he was pleased to call himself. He was a bounty hunter/hit man who specialized in lycanthropes, and brought in a few vampires on the side for fun. We'd had some run-ins. We'd even helped each other out a couple of times, once I talked him out of trying to kill me. The man scared the daylights out of me. And now he was standing here with a gun, looking at me like hunting season had just been declared open.

It seemed that Duke's paranoia knew no bounds.

"You wouldn't really shoot me, would you?" I felt my eyes go large and liquid, puppy-dog eyes. After all we'd been through, I'd like to think he wouldn't be so happy about traveling across the country for a chance to kill me.

He rolled his eyes. "Norville, if I really thought you were going to get out of control, I wouldn't have taken the job. I've seen you in action, you're okay."

I looked at Ben for a cue. His wry expression hadn't changed.

"No, I'm not going to shoot you," Cormac said with a huff. "Unless you get out of control."

"If you shoot my client, I'll sue you," Ben said, but he was smiling, like it was a joke.

"Yeah? Really?" Cormac sounded only mildly offended.

Could Ben simultaneously sue Cormac for killing me while defending Cormac against criminal charges for killing me?

I was so screwed.

Also on the docket for the day were some folklorists from Princeton who gave prepared statements about how phenomena attributed to the supernatural by primitive societies had their roots in easily explained natural occurrences. When the floor opened to questions, I was almost relieved that Duke harried them as hard as he'd harried Flemming. The senator was after everyone, it seemed. He'd cornered Flemming on vampires. He cornered the folklorists on the Bible.

"Professor, are you telling me that the Holy Scripture that tens of millions of good people in this country swear by is nothing more than a collection of folklore and old wives' tales? Is that what you're telling me? Because my constituency would respectfully disagree with you on that score."

The academics just couldn't counter that kind of argument.

Duke called one of the committee staffers over and spoke for a few moments. Then he left. The remaining senators conferred, while the audience started grumbling.

Then Senator Henderson recessed the hearing for the day. I didn't testify after all.

Anticipation produced the worst kind of anxiety. It didn't matter how nervous about a show I was beforehand, how worried I was that a guest wouldn't show, or that I'd get a call I couldn't handle, or that I was presenting a topic that would get out of control, once the show started that all went away. I was only nervous when I sat there, doing nothing, inventing terrible stories of everything that could go wrong.

The longer I sat at the hearing without doing anything,

the more nervous I got. I'd be shaking by the time I finally got up there to testify.

Cormac stayed in the back, leaning by the door, where he could keep an eye on the whole room. When the committee members left out the back and the audience was breaking up to leave, he came to our row and sat beside Ben.

"Has it been going like this the whole time?"

Ben crossed his arms and leaned back. "No. They've been totally businesslike until now. I wonder if they've lost interest."

I pouted. "That doesn't matter, they still have to let me talk. I drove all the way out here, I've been sitting here for three days—could they really not let me talk?"

"Theoretically, they can do anything they want," Ben said.

Case in point: one of Senator Duke's aides, a young man looking stiff and uncomfortable in his suit, came down the aisle toward us. I guessed he was Duke's aide—the senator had returned to the room and watched us closely from the side of the benches. The aide only glanced at Ben and me, then leaned in to whisper to Cormac.

"The senator would like a word with you, if you don't mind." He waited, then, like he expected to escort the bounty hunter that very moment.

Cormac deliberately picked himself up out of the chair, taking his time, then followed the aide to see Duke. The reason for the summons became clear at once. Duke didn't even need a microphone to be heard.

"You didn't tell me you were friendly with her!"

If Cormac answered, he kept his voice subdued, and I didn't hear him.

Duke replied, "Does conflict of interest mean anything to you?"

He apparently didn't know Cormac very well. Even I knew the answer to that one.

"You're fired! You're off security! I want you out of this building!"

With as little concern as he'd shown strolling up there, Cormac walked back, wearing a wry smile.

"So sue a guy for trying to make an easy buck," he said.

Ben asked, "Could we? Sue, I mean. Is there a breach of contract?"

"No," Cormac said, shaking his head. "I took a kill fee."

Ben hesitated, then said, "Kill fee. That's funny."

"No, it's not," I said, interrupting. "That's not funny at all."

Too bad they were both grinning. I gave a long-suffering sigh.

"Come on," Ben said. "We'd better get you out of here."

Flemming left just ahead of us. He'd tucked his brief-case under his arm, ducked his head, and strode out of the room like he was late for something. His gaze flickered over us as he passed; we were all staring at him.

"Who's that guy?" Cormac nodded after him.

"Dr. Paul Flemming," I said. "He heads the Center for the Study of Paranatural Biology. The committee spent the first two days grilling him."

"He a straight shooter?"

"Not in the least. I went to his office this morning and found him shredding a stack of documents. Just try to get a clear answer from him."

"Used to working under the radar. Going crazy now

with the spotlight on him. He looks the type." Ben nodded in agreement.

I said, "What I want to know is: what's he hiding?"

Cormac pursed his lips thoughtfully. "You really want to know? We could find out."

"How? I've tried talking to him. I even had him on the show."

Ben said, "I've pulled everything on him I could—military record, academic record. He's got this scientific veneer over everything he does. Talks a lot, uses big words, doesn't say anything."

"We could break into his office."

I hushed Cormac. "Are you out of your mind?" He was talking like this in a government building. I looked around, but no one seemed to have heard.

"You know I can do it," he said. "Especially since it looks like I'm not busy for the next couple days after all."

He could do it. I didn't know where he learned how to do things like breaking into radio stations and government buildings, but he could do it.

Cormac could probably learn more in a couple of hours of breaking-and-entering than I had in months of wheedling. He grinned, because my hesitation was all the confirmation he needed to go ahead with the plan.

"Officially, I'm not hearing any of this," Ben said. "Unofficially, be sure to wear gloves."

Cormac huffed. "I think I've just been insulted."

"I'm only saying." Ben squeezed past us to the door. "You kids have fun."

Cormac turned to me. "Where's this guy's office?"

"Bethesda. At the Magnuson Clinical Center, in the basement."

"Show up there at about four. Go inside the building, I'll be watching for you."

"Four—in the morning?" I said.

"Four this afternoon," Cormac said.

"You want to do this in broad daylight?"

"Do you trust me or not?"

If he really wanted to shoot me, he'd had half a dozen chances. And I still couldn't answer that question. I swallowed a lump in my throat. "Do I really have to be there?"

"You're the one who knows what you want to find."

Ben said to me once that Cormac wasn't a crusader. He wasn't a werewolf hunter because he hated werewolves, or had a religious beef against them like Duke. Rather, he liked to see how close he could walk to the edge without falling off. He didn't have any loyalty to the government, the people who hired him, or anyone else.

Cormac was only planning this to see if he could. For him, it was a challenge.

"All right. Four o'clock this afternoon." I sighed, hoping to still my pounding heart.

"Bring gloves," he said, then stood and walked away.

This was a bad, bad idea. I knew it in my gut. You didn't just go breaking into government buildings in the best of times, and this wasn't the best of times. But if I didn't show, Cormac might break into Flemming's office without me. If he learned anything juicy, he'd keep the information from me out of spite.

I had to go.

I drove my car from the alley around the corner and found Luis waiting outside Alette's town house. He casually leaned on the wrought-iron fence that divided the property from the sidewalk. By all appearances he looked like he was out enjoying the unseasonable sunshine, pausing during a stroll. I pulled up to the curb in front of him, parked, and got out.

He beamed at me. He had a generous smile and sparkling eyes. My stomach fluttered.

"You're a hard person to track down," he said brightly. "I hoped to find you outside the Senate building, but you were already gone."

I winced in apology. I hated the idea of him running all over town after me—then again, it was awfully flattering. "I gave you my cell number, right? You should have called."

He shrugged. "Chasing you is more fun."

Spoken like a true predator. He stepped toward me, looking like he was getting ready to pin me against the car. Part of me wanted to dodge, to keep the chase going for a little longer. But I let him put his hands on my hips and lean forward for a kiss. I held his arms and pulled him close.

I glanced over his shoulder at the windows of Alette's townhome, hoping no one was watching.

Coming up for air, I said, "You shouldn't be here."

He followed my gaze back to the building. "I'm not afraid of them. Is it too early for me to take you to dinner?"

"I'd love that. But—" I wanted to pull my hair out. I couldn't *believe* I was going to turn down Luis to go play *Mission: Impossible* with Cormac. "But I can't. I set up a meeting and I can't miss it."

"Something for your show?"

"Yeah, something like that." It wasn't an outright lie. Most everything ended up on the show eventually. But Luis looked at me sidelong, like he knew I wasn't being entirely truthful. He could probably smell it on me, or sense the twitchy nervousness through my body.

He said, "The full moon is coming soon, in just a few days. Do you know where you'll be?"

I knew the full moon was coming soon. I couldn't forget. "No. I usually scout out a place to run, but I haven't had time."

"Come with me. There's a park about an hour outside town, a few of us drive there. It's safe."

Full moon night with friends. It had been a long time since I had anyone watching my back.

"I'd really like that. Thanks."

He brought my hand to his lips and kissed it. "Then it's a date."

When one lycanthrope said to another, "run with me," it was usually a euphemism. I certainly hoped so.

"I should let you get to your meeting."

"Yes."

"Then until I catch you again." He touched my cheek, kissed me on the corner of my mouth, lingering for just a moment as if he'd draw the breath from me, then pulled back. He stepped away, grinning, and it was all I could do to keep from following him, step by hypnotized step.

He turned and continued down the street, hands tucked in his trouser pockets.

So where were all the seductive Brazilian hunks when I had time on my hands?

I picked up a visitor's badge, found my way to the Clinical Center building, and kept walking, like I was going to Flemming's office again: down the hall, around the corner to the elevators. At this point, I had no idea what I was doing. Cormac said he'd be watching for me.

It was easy for *him* to talk about sneaking into government buildings. *He* hadn't been accosted by Men In Black on his arrival in town. *He* wasn't having paranoid delusions about the hallway in the Senate building being bugged so that some security goon heard all our plans and was waiting for us to make the first move and catch us red-handed.

I clung to the wall, glancing around with wide eyes, convinced someone was following me.

I scented Cormac—his light aftershave and the faint touch of gun oil that never left him—just before he stepped around a corner and grabbed my arm. I still gasped and had to swallow back a moment of panic. *This isn't danger, I'm not in danger.* He put his hand against my back and guided me forward, so that we continued down the corridor, walking side by side, like we belonged here. He'd left his guns at home this afternoon.

We stopped by the elevators. Cormac pushed the button. No gloves, I noticed. Maybe that came later.

I leaned close and whispered, "I have to ask, aren't you worried that maybe somebody heard us? That maybe the FBI or something knows we're here and is watching us? I mean, we planned this inside a Senate office building. They probably read our lips off the video surveillance." I glanced over my shoulders. First one, then the other.

"Norville, the thing you have to understand is, the government is a big bureaucracy, and the left hand doesn't know what the right is doing most of the time. The fact that it gets anything done is a miracle. Nobody's paying attention to us. But they'll start if you keep acting like you're up to something. Stop looking around."

We didn't much look like we belonged here. Cormac was still wearing jeans and a T-shirt. I was only marginally better in slacks and a knit top. But he acted like we belonged here, and that was the key. Keep quiet, don't spend too much time looking around like you needed directions, and know where you're going.

The elevator opened, we stepped inside, after letting the few occupants exit: a couple of people in white lab coats, a woman holding a flower arrangement. She was dressed about like I was. Cormac was right. No one paid attention to us.

He pushed the button to send us to the basement, carrying on like we had an appointment with Flemming. By the time the doors opened to spit us out, my stomach was doing somersaults.

"We can't walk right into his office," I whispered at him, hoping I didn't sound as panicked as I felt. "What if he's there?"

"He won't be. I sent him on a wild goose chase."

"You *what*?"

He looked down his nose at me, the long-suffering stare that made me feel like an annoying younger sibling.

"I called him from a pay phone, said I knew him from the army and had information about his research, but I had to talk to him in person. I told him I was in Frederick." He pursed his lips in a wry smile. "He'll be gone for a couple of hours."

Frederick, Maryland. Some thirty-five miles away. Close enough for Flemming to think that following the lead was worthwhile, far enough away to keep him busy for a couple of hours. Flemming would be gone all afternoon, assuming he took the bait. Considering Flemming was more paranoid than I was, I could assume he had.

That was hilarious. I was beginning to think that Cormac hadn't just done this sort of thing before. I was sure he'd done it *often*.

Now, Cormac put on gloves, made of thin black leather. I followed suit, though mine were cheap knit ones I'd dug out of my car. Not nearly as cool as his. By the time we got to the door of Flemming's office, he'd pulled something out of his pocket: a card key.

"Where'd you get that?" I hissed.

"Janitor," he said. "Don't worry, I'll give it back."

Oh. My. God.

The lock clicked; the door slipped open.

I followed Cormac into the office. He closed the door smoothly behind me.

The office was dark. Cormac made no move to turn the lights on. Enough ambient light showed through the frosted window in the door to find our way around the room. My sight adjusted quickly. Quicker than Cormac's—I headed toward the paper shredder in the corner while he was still squinting.

The bin under the shredder was empty. So was the counter next to it. All those papers, gone. Of course they were, he'd spent the morning shredding them.

I started working my way through the remaining stacks

of documents piled around the desk and bookshelves. They were all medical journals, published articles, photocopies of articles, dissertations, and the like. Some of them I'd dug up on my own. At first glance, none of them offered insight into Flemming's research. It was all background and supporting documentation. The bread, not the meat at the middle of the sandwich.

Cormac went to the desk to fire up the computers. After they'd booted up, the screens coming to life, he shook his head at me. "Password protected," he said. "Hacking isn't my strong suit."

No, he was a stolen key and .45 revolver kind of guy.

I wasn't prepared for serious digging. I'd assumed—wrongly—that in all this mess I'd find *something* just lying around, even with all the shredding going on. I studied the bookshelves, hoping for a spark of inspiration. The physiology reference books butted up against the folklore encyclopedias amused me.

I sighed, on the verge of defeat. "Let's see if we can get into the next room."

The second door also had a frosted window in it, but the other side was dark. I couldn't see anything through the glass. Cormac took out his trusty stolen card key, slid it through the reader, and popped the door open. The door swung away from him. He straightened and gestured me inside.

"After you."

I felt like I was stepping into an ancient Egyptian tomb. The place was so still, I could hear my blood in my ears, and it was cold with the kind of chill that seeped through stone underground. I could see well enough in the dark. The linoleum floor continued, and like the office this room had walls of shelves. It also had lab benches, sinks and faucets, and a large metallic refrigerator that hummed softly. Also, Flemming had here a good collection of the medical equipment I'd expected to find in his laboratory: racks of test tubes, beakers, Bunsen burners, and unidentifiable tabletop appliances plugged into walls. They might have been oscillators, autoclaves, the kind of things one saw on medical dramas on television, or in the dentist's office. Again, the place had more of the atmosphere of a college biology laboratory than a clandestine government research facility.

The far wall was made of glass, maybe Plexiglas. Behind it, the room continued, divided in two by a partition. I moved closer. Both extra rooms had a cot, a washbasin, and a simple toilet in the corner. The Plexiglas had doors cut into it, with handles only on the outside. The doors had narrow slots through which objects might be handed through. Like meal trays. They were cells.

Moving quietly, Cormac stepped beside me. "This is kind of fucked up."

Yeah. "Do you smell garlic?" One of the cell doors was open. I wasn't mistaken; inside, the scent of garlic grew strong. It wasn't like someone was cooking with it, or there was a chopped-up piece of it somewhere. It came from everywhere. I went to a wall, touched it, then smelled it. "Is it in the paint? Did they put garlic in the paint?"

"Check this one out," Cormac said from the next cell over. He shined a penlight over the wall, which glittered. Sparkling like silver—tiny shavings of silver, imbedded in the paint. I kept my distance.

Two cells. One for a vampire, one for a werewolf, designed to keep each of them under control using innate allergies. They looked like they'd been empty for a while.

The sheets were fresh, unwrinkled. They didn't smell occupied.

"Hands-on research, looks like," Cormac said.

Involuntary test subjects was what it looked like to me. My stomach hurt.

Cormac left the cell. "You seen enough?"

"Just a minute." I scanned the room one more time. Most of the paperwork had been moved to the office and shredded, it looked like. Nothing here but empty tables and defunct equipment.

To the side of the silver-lined cell, a clipboard hung on a nail. It looked like the kind of setup someone would use to keep medical records handy. It seemed rather forlorn and forgotten. I picked it up.

Only three sheets of paper were clipped to the board. They were charts, with a list of names. Names—jackpot. Quickly, I scanned them. First names only, maybe two dozen in all.

Halfway down the second page I read: *Fritz, 6', 210 lbs., h.s. lupus. Homo sapiens lupus*. It couldn't *possibly* be the same Fritz.

I flipped back to the first page and caught another name, one I should have noticed right away: *Leo, 5'9", 150 lbs., h.s. sanguinis*. Vampire.

Riddle wrapped in an enigma . . . I wasn't sure I wanted to know how Flemming and Leo were tied together. I was about ready to buy into any conspiracy theory that came my way.

"This is it," I murmured. "This is what I need." I took it off the clipboard and started to fold it, to take it with me.

Cormac snatched the pages out of my hand. He stalked back to the next room and the tabletop photocopier parked near the shredder. The machine was so loud, and the scanning lights so bright, I thought surely security goons would find us. Quickly, in a perfectly businesslike manner, Cormac had the three pages copied. He handed the copies to me, clipped the originals back on the board, and returned it to its nail on the wall. He closed the door to the lab and made sure it was locked.

He shut down the computers and surveyed the room. Satisfied, he nodded. "Looks good. Let's get out of here."

After making sure the door to the hallway was locked, he stripped off his gloves and shoved them in a pocket. I followed his lead, then nervously curled the papers we'd liberated.

We took one detour before leaving the building. Cormac stopped at a closet in a side corridor on the main floor. True to his word, he slipped the key card into the front tray of the janitor's cart parked there. It only took a second.

We didn't speak until we were outside, walking down the sidewalk with a dozen other anonymous pedestrians. Daylight still shone, which seemed incongruous with the darkness of Flemming's offices and our clandestine activities there.

"And that is how you break into a government office," Cormac announced at last.

"Those Watergate boys could have learned something from you, eh?"

He made a disgusted huff. "What a bunch of posers."

Supper that evening was room service at Ben's hotel. Cormac sat on the bed, plate balanced on his lap, one eye on the news channel playing on the TV, volume turned way down. He and Ben drank beers, like a couple of college buddies. Maybe that was where they'd met.

We'd debriefed Ben on our field trip. The chart from the lab lay spread across the middle of the table.

Ben nodded at it. "Is this a copy or did you just take it out of his office?"

"It's a copy."

He pursed his lips and gave a quick nod, like he was happy with that answer. "Was it worth it?"

They both looked at me. I rubbed my forehead. My brain was full. "Yeah, I think so."

Ben said, "This doesn't prove anything, you know."

"I know people on that list. At least, I think I do. If I can track them down, they'll give me someone else to talk to." I hoped.

"Will they talk to you?" Cormac said.

"I don't know."

Ben leaned back in his chair. "Kitty, I know this Flemming character is suspicious as hell. But maybe he's exactly what he appears to be: an NIH doctor, ex-army researcher, nervous because he doesn't want his funding cut. What is it you think you're going to find?"

Fritz the Nazi. I wondered what kind of questions Flemming asked him, assuming he actually talked to his subjects. I wondered if Fritz told him the stories he wouldn't tell me. What would an ex-army medical researcher want to learn from a Nazi werewolf war veteran—

"Military application," I whispered. I swallowed, trying to clear my throat, because both men had set aside their forks and beers and were staring hard at me. "He told this story about a patient in a car accident, horrible injuries, but he walked out of the hospital a week later. Flemming seemed totally . . . entranced by it. By the possibilities. He talked about it in the hearing, remember? Curing diseases, using a lycanthrope's healing abilities. Imagine having an army of soldiers who are that hard to kill."

"If he had military backing he wouldn't need to be explaining himself to Congress," Ben said.

Cormac said, "Even if he's developing military applications, is there anything wrong with that?"

"There is if he's using people," I said. "He has jail cells in his lab."

"Look, I thought you liked what this guy was doing," Ben said. "That you wanted all this out in the open. You want him shut down now?"

"Yeah, I think I do."

"Why?"

I shrugged, because it was true. I'd loved seeing this stuff in the *Washington Post*. I was enjoying the respect. But I could still smell the garlic paint in the lab. "Because he's unethical."

I hadn't finished dinner, but I couldn't eat any more. It was dark now; time to see Alette. "I won't be able to track one of these guys down until tomorrow, but I think I can find the other one tonight. I'm going to go do that."

"Need company?" Cormac said. Read: need help?

"No thanks, I'll be fine. I think." I collected the pages from Flemming's lab.

"You might want to think about making a copy of those," Ben said. "Maybe put them in a safety deposit box. Just in case."

"Or mail 'em to someone," Cormac said. "With a note

to open it if anything happens to you. If you get in trouble you can use it as a threat and not be lying."

"Or you could not do it, say you did, and use it as a threat anyway." Ben said this pointedly at Cormac, weighing the statement with significance.

Cormac gave his best shit-eating grin. "Would I do something like that?"

Ben rolled his eyes. "I'm taking the Fifth on that one."

I stared. "Uh, you two go way back, don't you?"

They exchanged a look, one of those familiar, it'd take too long to explain the inside joke looks.

"You're not going to tell me, are you?"

"You're better off not knowing," Ben said.

Now I wanted to run to the nearest Internet connection and dig up what nefarious plot these two had cooked up in the distant past. At least, I *assumed* it was the distant past.

Maybe I should get a different lawyer. Except it would take too long to explain everything to a new one.

I wanted to show the list to Alette, both to find out if she knew any of the *Homo sapiens sanguinis* represented, and to rat out Leo. Yeah, I was tattling, and it hadn't felt this good since I was eight and ratted out my twelve-year-old sister's stash of R-rated videos. If she'd only let me watch with her, she could have kept the TV in her room.

I rushed into the foyer, pausing a moment to debate whether to look in the parlor or the dining room, or find Emma or Bradley and ask them where'd she be. Think, if I were the head vampire, where would I be?

A touch brushed my shoulder. I gasped and turned,

shock frying my nerves. Leo stood behind me, calmly, as if he'd been there all evening, watching the scenery. I could have sworn he hadn't been in the foyer when I entered the house. But I hadn't sensed him approach, I hadn't seen him, or smelled him, or heard him.

"Hello, there," he said lightly. "Can I help you with something?"

I wanted to punch him. "What the hell is your problem?"

"You're so easy to rile up, can you blame a man for trying?"

"Yes, yes, I can."

"Ah. Well, then." He strolled, circling around me, blocking the exits.

He was teasing me. That was all. Provoking me, like he said. I took a deep breath, determined to calm down.

"I have a question for you," I said, trying to sound bright and unperturbed. "What do you know about Dr. Flemming?"

He shrugged. "Government researcher. What would you like me to know?"

"I've spoken with him. Your name came up." Both were true, in themselves.

"Really? What did he say about me?"

"Nothing. He's closemouthed. That's why I'm asking you."

"And I'm openmouthed, am I?" He smiled to show teeth and fang. Then his expression softened. "I might have spoken with him a time or two."

"About what?"

"This and that. About being a vampire. I was—how would you call it?—a native informant." He started pacing, hands in his trouser pockets, gaze downturned. "I'll give him this much, he knows his subject. At least, he knows enough to know where to find us, if he wants to. Then, would you believe he simply asks nicely? He proves how much he knows, and you don't feel bad about answering his questions. You become just another data point. There's nothing more to it."

I had a hard time picturing Flemming traveling the streets, finding his way to a place like the Crescent, notepad and tape recorder in hand, and asking nicely.

"What did you tell him? What's it like being a vampire?"

He looked away for a moment, his gaze distant and thoughtful. It seemed he did have another personality buried in there somewhere.

"Time almost stands still," he said. "The world seems to freeze for a moment. You're able to study every little piece of it. All the microscopic points become clear. And you move through this world like a lion on the veldt. You realize everything is yours for the taking. All you have to do is reach out and grab hold of anything you like. Anyone you like."

In the next beat of time he stood beside me. Brushing my hair aside, he breathed against my neck, a faint, warm sigh. No teeth, no threat, only a caress. I shivered, but didn't move away from him. For some reason, I didn't move away.

"Is that what you expected to hear?" he said.

I turned and glared. But he hadn't done anything. They were only words.

I knew better than anyone what a person could do with mere words.

"Is that what being a vampire is all about?" I said. "Is that why you're such an arrogant prick?"

He laughed. "An arrogant prick? Really? I suppose that's how it must appear to the rest of you. But to us, you're little more than a bit of hair floating on the breeze. We don't care what you think."

"Not all vampires are like that. I've met some who are reasonable human beings." One or two. Maybe. "That's all Flemming's doing? Collecting stories? Gathering true-life accounts?"

"I'm sure that's not *all* he's doing. He's a medical doctor, isn't he? He's probably doing some blood tests on the side. I know I would." He licked his lips.

"What if I told you Flemming has a lab with holding cells? One of them has garlic in the paint, like it was meant to subdue a vampire. What if it looked like he was holding test subjects against their wills?"

His gaze had been wandering, studying the room as if he were a fan of interior design, unconcerned. Now, he focused on me, suddenly interested. I almost took a step back. Though if I'd taken one step, I might have gone ahead and run all the way out of the room. Leo's interest was not something I wanted.

"That would be extremely dangerous and foolish of him if he had done so," he said. "Even if he could trap a vampire, he could never again release it—and survive." His lips parted and he showed his teeth, the sharp points of his fangs.

"Unless he's *really* good with a stake," I said.

"In-*deed*." That British accent could make one word take on a world of meaning.

"Ah, Kitty, you've returned." Alette, queen of her domain, strode into the foyer, smartly dressed and elegant as always, looking like she was on her way from one task to another. She acknowledged Leo with a nod and stopped before me to regard me with that prim nod that made me feel like I'd somehow fallen short of her standards, and that I would always fall short. "I expected you back some time ago. I hope your tardiness means you've had a productive afternoon?"

This was where I ponied up that information I promised her. The only question was, how much did I tell her? "I've learned that Flemming has holding cells for vampires and werewolves in his lab. I think he's been keeping test subjects against their wills."

"By test subjects you mean vampires and lycanthropes? Do you know how he could possibly hold such beings against their wills?" Her disbelief was plain in her tone.

"I don't know, but he's done it," I said, frustrated. "Here, look at this. He's been talking to people." I showed her the list, being sure to point out Leo's name on the first page.

Alette looked at him. "You've been speaking with Flemming?"

I wanted Leo to squirm like a kid who'd been caught lying. I wanted him to blush, look abashed, duck his gaze, something. He stood quietly and completely unruffled.

"Yes," he said. "I have. The good doctor's been going around collecting folktales. I talked to him on the assumption that such conversations work both ways. I've been a bit of a double agent, if you like." He flashed his devil-may-care smile.

"You didn't see fit to tell me of this?" Alette said.

"Because I didn't learn anything. Which leads me to think he isn't hiding anything." He said this pointedly to me. "He really is just an earnest scientist in danger of losing his funding."

Why didn't I buy that?

Alette did. She gave a satisfied nod and handed the pages back to me. "Have those cells been recently occupied?"

"I couldn't tell," I said. I hadn't smelled anything. "I don't think so."

"We'll continue to watch Flemming. Your vigilance should be commended, Kitty. But don't let it become paranoia."

Leo said to Alette, "My dear, you seem to be in the middle of some chore. Might I be of service to you?"

"Always, Leo." He offered her his arm, and she took the crook of his elbow. She gave me one last glance over her shoulder as they left the foyer.

I had no way of knowing who to believe. I wanted to think well of Alette, and if she trusted Leo I shouldn't question it. She'd known him longer than I had. Maybe Flemming really was harmless, and all the cloak-and-dagger shenanigans with Cormac had been a waste of time. I felt like I was working my way through a maze. I *hated* mazes.

This town was getting to me.

chapter 7

Thursday was exploitative celebrity day at the hearings.

There was me, of course. I'd been told I *might* testify today, *if* the committee had time. Ben told me not to hold my breath. I was thinking of starting a pool among the press corps to guess when I'd actually be called up.

The good senators had called in others who'd made themselves famous based on the stuff of magic and the supernatural, and the others arrived today.

Waiting in the hallway outside the hearing room, a swarm of people collected around a lone figure, a slick-looking man in his thirties who smiled amiably. At first I thought the people surrounding him were reporters, but then the man took one of the notepads, signed his name on it, and handed it back. I recognized him, then: that easygoing smile, the fashionably trimmed sandy hair, the clean features that made him instantly likable and trustworthy. Jeffrey Miles, professional psychic and channeler.

He was best known on the daytime talk show circuit, where he impressed the hosts and awed the audiences with his intimate knowledge of their friends and relatives who had "passed on." He claimed to be able to communicate with the "other side," to deliver messages and reassurances from the dead, and to reveal information that only the deceased or the audience member could have known. Classic cold readings. He appealed to the angels and Precious Moments crowd.

I leaned on the wall and smirked at the proceedings. Someone in my position—werewolf, witness to the supernatural—might have been inclined to believe in his awesome powers. Except I didn't. It was manipulative bunk, and it was people like him who made it difficult for the rest of the world to believe in people like me.

The session was set to begin, and it took security guards to clear out Miles's admirers. His geniality didn't disappear with the fans; it wasn't some mask he put on for them. He shook his head, amused, straightening his blazer as he headed toward the door.

He walked right by me without a second glance, and was through the doorway before he stopped, backed up, and turned to look at me.

"You must be Kitty Norville," he said.

"And you're Jeffrey Miles." I crossed my arms.

"You know—" He scratched his head and seemed suddenly uncomfortable. "I have a confession. I hate to admit it, but I was one of those people who thought it was all a gimmick. Your show, the werewolf thing. But you really are a werewolf, and I have this urge to apologize for doubting."

I stared, dumbfounded and speechless for maybe the third time in my entire life. The polite, socialized part of my brain scrambled to graciously accept his apology. The sarcastic part clamped down on that right away.

He was human, straight up as far as I could see, with nothing in the way of heightened senses that a lycanthrope had. I really had to know, "How can you tell?"

"Your aura is very wild. Very animal. I only see that with lycanthropes."

The sarcastic part of my brain started beating itself against a figurative brick wall to stifle the laughter.

"Well, thanks for the vote of confidence," I said. "I'm sorry I can't return it."

"Too many documented frauds?"

"Something like that."

He closed his eyes for a moment and visibly relaxed, his shoulders sagging a bit, his face going slack, like he had fallen asleep right there on his feet. I watched, intrigued. Looked like I was going to get a free show.

Then he said, "Theodore Joseph holds a strong place in your thoughts."

I grit my teeth to make sure my mouth stayed closed. He might as well have punched me in the gut. I looked away before my eyes had a chance to tear up, the way they always did when I was reminded of T.J. at an unexpected moment.

My mind raced. He could have done research. He'd have known in advance that I was going to be here, he could have looked at the police record, the one where I named T.J., there were records that Miles could have easily found—

He continued. "He says—there's nothing to forgive. Stop asking for forgiveness."

That wasn't recorded anywhere. The police didn't know T.J. was dead. I hadn't told them that part.

I hadn't ever asked T.J. for forgiveness. Not out loud—
I mean, how could I? He was dead. And it was my fault he
was dead. I was so, so sorry, and maybe all these weeks
I'd just wanted to say that. I wished I'd had a chance to
tell him that. I wished that he were here for me to tell him.

And there was Jeffrey Miles, watching me with a quiet,
sympathetic look in his eyes, wearing a grim smile.

I scrubbed my eyes with the heels of my hands, but it
didn't work. Tears fell.

"I'm sorry," he said, handing me a tissue. He had it
ready, like people burst into tears in front of him all the
time. "This isn't the time or place for this."

"No, it's okay. I asked for it, didn't I?" I chuckled half-
heartedly. "I can almost hear him sometimes. You're saying it's real?" Jeffrey Miles was for real. I felt like a
jackass.

"I think he's been watching out for you. Not a ghost,
nothing so strong as that. But he's interested."

"Where—where is he?"

"Even I don't know that. They come to me. I can't find
them. Who was he?"

"Don't you know? I thought you were psychic."

"He's not a forthcoming presence."

"Got that right. T.J. My best friend. I got him killed."

"I don't think he sees it that way."

And I knew he was right. Somehow, that nagging little
voice that I had mistaken for my conscience told me that
it wasn't my fault. It had been there the whole time,
telling me I was okay, to stop being silly. I hadn't believed
it. T.J. had wanted that last fight with Carl, not just to defend me, but because the fight between them had been

brewing for months. He'd wanted to win, but that hadn't happened. *Stop asking for forgiveness.*

After that, I wasn't sure I was ready to sit in that room for two hours, but the security guards were about to close the doors, and Jeffrey urged me inside.

Ben was already in place in the back row, his laptop open on his lap, typing away at something that may or may not have had anything to do with the hearings. I sat with him, and Jeffrey joined us.

"You okay?" Ben whispered. I nodded, waving him off.

Everyone looked back at a commotion brewing by the doors. The security guy seemed to be talking to someone who wanted in. After a moment, he opened the door and let in something of an entourage: a middle-aged man with short-cropped, steely hair, wearing a dark turtleneck and slacks, flanked by a couple of hefty bodyguard types.

All my hair stood on end and a shiver passed along my spine. Those two were werewolves, big and scary, and there was something about the way they followed the first one that was unnatural. Or un-supernatural. It was like they walked too close to him, or watched him too closely. Like Labrador retrievers with separation anxiety. Not wolf-like at all.

"Who's he?" I murmured.

Jeffrey leaned over. "That's Elijah Smith. He's a self-styled faith healer to the supernatural."

My blood chilled and the gooseflesh thickened. My shoulders stiffened, and I swallowed back a wolf-inspired growl. "I know him. I know of him. We had an encounter, sort of."

"You didn't try to join his church, did you?"

"No. This was indirectly. I met someone who tried to

leave his church. It didn't turn out well." In the end, she'd killed herself. The vampire had staked herself to get away from him.

As exploitative celebrities went, Smith was in a class by himself. Jeffrey and I were little more than entertainers, to some extent. Our hearts may have been in the right places, wanting to help people, but we were also sort of freak shows. Smith, on the other hand, professed to save people.

He called his organization the Church of the Pure Faith. Preaching the motto "Pure faith will set you free," he claimed to be able to cure vampires and lycanthropes of their conditions through his style of old-fashioned, laying-on of hands faith healing.

The so-called church had more in common with a cult. Once healed, his followers never left. They traveled with him in a caravan that crisscrossed the country, collecting true believers who were utterly loyal, like the two werewolves seemed to be. My informant had said he really could cure them: vampires could walk in sunlight, werewolves never suffered the Change. But only if they stayed with him forever. For some, the loss of freedom might not have been too high a price to pay. The trouble was, Smith didn't tell them what the price was before they signed up.

What could he tell the committee? What was the point of having *him* here?

"How the hell did they manage to get him to testify?" As far as I knew, the few police who'd tried to investigate the church hadn't been able to touch him. Nothing persuaded Smith to leave his compound, and his followers defended him like an army. Jeffrey shook his head.

Ben piped in. "Rumor has it Duke offered his church

official recognition and tax-exempt status. Then he can start collecting monetary donations."

"Can Duke do that?"

Ben said, "It really only takes an application with the IRS, but Smith may not know that. Maybe Duke can expedite the application."

Didn't that just beat all?

Jeffrey watched Smith distantly, lips pursed. After a moment he said, "I don't like him. He's dark. I don't think he's human."

I looked sharply at him. "Vampire?"

"No, I don't think so. This is different. Thicker. Would it be too melodramatic to say he looks evil?"

I was right there with him. My favorite theory about Smith at the moment was that he was some kind of spiritual vampire. Rather than feeding on blood, he consumed people's devotion, awe, and worship. He didn't cure his followers; rather, he had the power to suppress their weaknesses, the vulnerability to sunlight, the need to shapeshift. My acquaintance, a vampire named Estelle, thought she was cured, but when she left Smith's caravan, the condition returned. She burned in sunlight again. He was powerful enough to control vampires and lycanthropes, and sinister enough to use them.

I didn't know enough to guess what he was, especially if Jeffrey was right and he wasn't human.

Jeffrey testified first. He flashed me a smile and a thumbs-up before he went to the table. If he had a lawyer with him, he kept the attorney hidden. He had a prepared statement, speaking carefully and nonthreateningly about being open to strangeness in the world, to mysteries we didn't understand and might possibly fear. He stated a belief that the universe was basically good, and if we approached each new encounter with the unknown with that attitude, we would be rewarded with knowledge and understanding. It sounded a little metaphysical and New-Agey for my tastes. He'd obviously never encountered a hungry werewolf in the middle of the night. Wasn't much knowledge and understanding at the end of that meeting.

Either the television celebrity garnered more respect from the panel of senators, or Jeffrey did a better job of winning them over with his charisma and amiability. He treated them like a talk show audience, engaging them, telling jokes.

He did what Duke probably brought him here to do, which was to testify to the existence of the supernatural, at least his own little branch of it. To think, a couple months ago anyone with a rational thought in his head would have written Jeffrey off as a New Age kook at best, or a manipulative charlatan at worst. But in this context, this new frame of reference, where vampires were real, the U.S. Congress had to take him seriously. I wondered if he felt at all smug or vindicated by the turn of events, the change in attitude. He just looked calm.

I leaned forward when Elijah Smith took the stand.

Smith never left his caravan. People who wanted to join him were screened before they were let inside to meet him. He'd never spoken publicly, until now. Finally, I got to see him in the flesh.

Whatever Jeffrey saw in him that indicated he wasn't human, I didn't see it. He moved with confidence, holding himself with a somber poise. His werewolf bodyguards stayed behind, seated in the first row among the audience.

They kept their gazes focused on him, refusing to let him out of their sights.

"Heaven's Gate," Ben whispered to me. I looked at him, raising my eyebrow to invite him to explain. He said, "The suicide cult. He's got that suicidal calm thing going. Jim Jones, David Koresh, you know?"

That didn't reassure me.

He didn't have a statement, so the committee launched right in to basic questions: where did he reside, what was his profession. Smith claimed to be based in California. I'd never been able to trace him to any permanent place of residence. His caravan was nomadic. Maybe he kept a post office box somewhere.

As to profession, he answered, "Spiritual adviser."

Which was about as surreal as when Jeffrey had said "communications facilitator." For some reason no one felt they could come before the Senate and say he was a professional medium or a faith healer.

Duke said, "I understand that you serve as a spiritual adviser to a specific group of people. Could you describe them?"

"They're vampires and lycanthropes, Senator." He spoke coolly, with maybe a hint of amusement.

I'd heard him before, from a distance over a tenuous phone connection. Even then his voice had had a haunted quality, hypnotic. He drew listeners to him, like any good preacher could. There was something else, though, in the way his voice hinted at mysteries to be revealed, at the dark secrets he would tell.

In person, that sense was doubled, or more. I leaned forward, head cocked, determined to hear every word. I wished the room's ambient noises—papers rustling, people coughing—would stop.

"And how do you advise them, Reverend Smith?" Duke said. This was the most respectful Duke had been of any of the witnesses. Did he actually think Smith was a good Christian preacher?

"I help them find their way to the cure."

Henderson spoke next. "Earlier this week, Dr. Flemming testified that he'd had some difficulty discovering a cure. Are you saying you've had better luck than medical science?"

"Senator, these states of being cannot be fully explained by medical science. They have a spiritual dimension to them, and the cures lie in the spiritual realm."

That was what I'd always thought. I wondered if it would be rude of me to move chairs so I was sitting closer. I didn't want to miss anything Smith had to say.

"I'm not sure I understand you."

Senator Duke turned to his colleague. "He's saying what I've been telling you, these people are cursed, possessed, and they need to be exorcized."

"We're not living in the Dark Ages, Senator Duke." Henderson returned to his witness. "Reverend Smith?"

He said, "I believe that those afflicted may look within to purge themselves of the taint of their . . . diseases."

"Through prayer," Duke prompted.

"In a manner of speaking, yes."

Prayer, yeah. That was all I had to do, it sounded so simple. I wanted to talk to him, to learn from him, because I'd struggled all this time to find some kind of peace in this life but he made it sound so simple—

"Kitty!"

My brain rattled. I blinked, disoriented. Jeffrey was shaking my arm. He'd hissed into my ear loud enough that the people in front of us looked back.

"What? What's wrong? What happened?"

Ben was staring at me, too. "You looked like a cliché there for a minute. I think you were even drooling."

"I was *not*."

But both men watched me closely, worriedly. Despite his flippant remark, Ben's brow was furrowed. Had I fainted? Passed out? I'd just been listening to the testimony, to Smith—

That steady, haunting voice filled the room. I could feel it against my heart.

"Oh, my God," I murmured. "Is it just me? You guys don't feel it—"

Jeffrey shook his head. "Not like that, but I can see it. It's like he's on fire. It started when he spoke."

Something about his voice sounded so reasonable, so pure. It hardly mattered what he said, because what I heard was, *Here is someone I can trust*.

I put my hands against my temples, quelling the headache I suspected I was developing. "This is seriously twisted."

"I think I understand his church a little better," Jeffrey said.

"No doubt." The cure was only the start of his power, it seemed. He could draw vampires and werewolves to him just by speaking. He hardly needed to cure them, if all he wanted was a flock of devoted followers.

If he had that power over me across the room, how was I going to get close enough to learn more about him?

Did I dare bring him onto the show for an interview, and broadcast his voice across the country?

Then we were done for another day. The hearing adjourned.

Smith immediately came down the aisle between the two sets of chairs, his escort trailing him devotedly. I watched him the way a wolf watches a hunter approaching with a rifle: head down, eyes glaring, lips ready to snarl a challenge if the intruder comes too close. If Jeffrey and Ben hadn't been there, I might have followed along after him, as eager and devoted as his pets.

I wasn't anybody's pet.

As he passed by, he caught my gaze. For a half a second, his lips twitched a smile—a cold smile—and his gaze held triumph.

He knew he'd gotten to me.

Some vampires and werewolves liked to say they were top of the food chain. Stronger than mortal humans, able to hunt mortal humans.

But we might have found the thing that could top us. I had to find out what he was. If I didn't risk getting closer to him, I'd never learn.

I scrambled past Jeffrey to get to the aisle. I was too late to intercept him, but maybe I could catch up.

Ben called after me, "Kitty, what are you—"

I'd only taken a couple steps toward Smith when the werewolves turned on me. Their lips pulled back in grimaces, their shoulders tensed, bunching up as if they were preparing to cock their arms for a punch. A couple of werewolves, getting ready to rumble. A shot of panic charged through me; I couldn't take these guys and my Wolf knew it. I had to work to stand there and not look away. Not cringe and cower. *Please don't beat me up . . .*

I looked past them to Smith, who had turned to see what the disturbance was.

"Hi, Reverend Smith? I'm Kitty Norville from the talk show *The Midnight Hour*. I was wondering, could I ask you a few questions? I think my audience would be very interested in learning more about you. Maybe you could come on the show."

He stared at me for a long time, and my heart beat faster and faster, in anticipation of what he might say, and what his words would do to me. Fight or flight. I should run. I should get out of here.

"If you come to me as a supplicant, I will answer all your questions." He smiled a thin, knowing smile.

They were true words; I knew they were. If I came to him, gave myself to him, I would have no more questions—at least, no will to ask them. But I couldn't. I couldn't go to him, I couldn't do it, because I'd lose myself, and I'd fought too hard to claim myself. My own two feet stood on the floor, and I was anchored to them, and I would not let his gaze swallow me.

I looked after him as he walked away, and the retreating bodyguards blocked my view of him.

Something touched my shoulder. I gasped and pulled back.

It was Jeffrey, forehead creased with concern. "That wasn't the smartest thing you could have done."

I'd been accused of a lot of things, but flights of genius wasn't one of them, so I couldn't argue.

We had to clear the room for the next set of hearings, a different committee, a different subject. The wheels of government rolled on, no matter what little paradigm shifts were going on in my head. I lingered outside in the hallway, arms crossed, shoulders hunched in and angry.

"Can we sue him?" I said to Ben. "There's got to be something we can sue him for."

He shrugged. "I don't know. I'll look into it. I'm always game for a frivolous lawsuit."

"It's not frivolous! There's something seriously creepy about that guy. We have to figure out what he's really doing with that church of his, because I know it's just horrible. It has to be."

"If he hasn't broken any laws, then there probably isn't anything we can do."

How could we know if he'd broken any laws if we didn't even know what he was really doing? Really, he was just inviting people to an old-fashioned revival meeting, and if they wanted to stay with him, well, that was their choice, right?

I had to find out what he was. "Jeffrey, if Smith isn't human, what is he?"

"I was hoping you'd have a guess," Jeffrey said.

I humphed. "Believe it or not, you probably have more experience with that kind of stuff than I do. I mean, you can *see* that he isn't right. If we find out where he's camped, take a look, maybe you'd see . . . I don't know. *Something*."

"I'm not sure I'm willing to get close enough to try that. He's dangerous, Kitty. I can see that much about him."

"Ben?"

"Don't look at me. Somebody's got to stay behind to bail your ass out of jail when things go wrong."

That vote of confidence was staggering.

Ben said, "If you're about to do something prosecutable, I don't want to know about it until afterward. I'll see you tomorrow." He started off down the hallway, waving over his shoulder.

Jeffrey watched him go. "He's your lawyer, huh? He's . . ."

"Brusque?" I said.

"I was going to say honest. He's got a good aura."

Well, that was something, I supposed. I apparently had an honest lawyer.

I sighed. "Since I don't know where Smith's caravan is, the whole plan to go looking for him is moot anyway."

I couldn't really see me climbing into a cab, flashing a fifty at the driver, and saying, "Follow that man!" I started to ask Jeffrey if he would do an interview on the show, when Roger Stockton stepped around from behind us, where he'd been lurking, eavesdropping, and who knew what else. He still had the camera, but at least he held it down and not pointed at me.

"I know where Smith is camped," the reporter said. "And I know he isn't human."

"Then what is he?" I said, once I'd regained control of my jaw. "And how do you know?" I'd tried to catch a scent off him, but his bodyguards stayed close, and I couldn't get past their smells, the overpowering scent of werewolf that set my instincts on edge.

"I'll tell you when we get out there."

"So I just get in your car and let you drive me to God knows where?"

"Look, we all want the same thing here. We all know Smith isn't curing anyone, not for real anyway, and he's got some kind of funky voodoo—I saw what he did to you back there. We all want to expose him, and we all know that he's dangerous. This way none of us has to go it alone and we all get to break the story together."

"Are you sure you're not just after some prime Kitty Norville footage for sweeps week?"

"I wouldn't *mind* that—"

I turned away with a dismissive sigh.

"He's telling the truth, Kitty. He knows," Jeffrey said. Jeffrey, who claimed to see honesty radiating off a man.

I had a guy with second sight and a reporter from *Uncharted World* for backup. A girl could do worse, I supposed. I looked around to see if Cormac was lurking somewhere. Now *there* was backup, assuming he kept his guns pointed in someone else's direction. But wouldn't you know it, the one time I might want him around, he'd disappeared. He hadn't been near the hearings since Duke fired him.

I said to Roger, "We find the caravan, we check it out. Then what?"

"Then, we see. Sound good?"

"No. If you know what he is then you should know what he's doing, and what we should do about him."

"I can't do it alone," Roger said. "Are you in?"

Jeffrey nodded. He seemed eager, even, as if this were just another enlightening experience.

I had to be out of my mind.

chapter 8

Stockton's smugness at knowing something I didn't was stifling. I was glad Jeffrey had agreed to come along. He sat in the backseat, regarding both of us with an amused smile.

I had no idea what we were going to do when we got there. If anything I'd heard about the caravan was true, shutting it down would take the National Guard.

Maybe between Jeffrey's intuition and Stockton's camera, we could collect enough evidence to bring about some kind of criminal prosecution. It was a modest enough goal.

It was all I could hope for. We weren't exactly the Ghostbusters.

Around sunset, we left tract housing and suburbs and entered countryside, driving along a two-lane state highway. The light was failing, streaking the sky shades of orange and lighting up the clouds. The land seemed dark, shadowy. The fields around us might have been fallow farmland, or rolling pastures. Fences bounded them by the roadside, but beyond that, trees surrounded them.

Trees everywhere, rows of old growth oak or elm, wind-breaks planted a hundred or two hundred years ago. The road curved from one valley into the next, making it impossible to see what lay ahead.

I was surprised, then, when we rounded a turn skirting yet another gently rolling hill, and Stockton put on the brakes. The seat belt caught me. He pulled onto the shoulder, to where we could look over the rail fence.

Ahead, occupying the back half of a wide swath of pasture, was what looked like the back lot of a down-on-its-luck traveling circus. Maybe two-dozen old-fashioned campers hitched to beat-up pickup trucks, a few RVs, Airstreams and Winnebagos, converted vans and buses, parked in a rough circle, like pioneer wagons. Another dozen cars were scattered among them. In the center, like the hub of a wheel, the top of a large canvas tent was visible. Around the perimeter, a few figures, indistinct forms in the twilight, walked around wire fencing that enclosed the settlement. Lights flooded the area inside: lights from the campers, the trucks, floodlights inside the tent. Even a hundred yards away I could hear the generators. The place was an event, a carnival without a town to go with it, a circle of light in an otherwise shadowed world.

A dirt road, little more than two tracks worn into the soil, led from the highway, through an open gate, to Smith's caravan. A couple of other cars were parked near the gate, their motors still running.

Stockton rolled down his window and leaned out, aiming his camera at the encampment.

"How did you find out it was here?" I asked.

"One of the guys at *Uncharted World*'s been following

it. Caught up with it in DeKalb, Illinois, a couple weeks ago and tracked it here."

"Then why isn't he out here filming?"

"Because two nights ago a car with no plates forced him off the road and into a dry creek bed. He's in the hospital with four broken ribs and a smashed shoulder."

"Shit." I shook my head. "Do you see anything?" I said to the backseat. "I mean, you know. *See* anything?"

"At this distance, the floodlights muddy everything up," Jeffrey said. Then he pointed to one of the other cars, that had just turned its headlights off and shut off its engine. "Although that guy's a lycanthrope."

A man—young by his gangly figure and the way he slouched—got out, closed the door softly, and started walking along the dirt track to the caravan site.

Quickly I undid the seat belt and scrambled out of the car.

"Kitty!" Jeffrey called after me, which I ignored.

I trotted after the guy and was about to call out to get him to stop, but he heard me, or smelled me, because he turned and backed away, shoulders tense, like a wolf with hackles.

"Who are you?" he said sharply.

"My name's Kitty." I stayed put, kept my gaze turned down, my shoulders relaxed. He could smell me; he knew what I was. "I'm just curious. Why are you here?"

He let his guard down the barest notch, shrugging. "I've heard there's a guy here who can help."

"Help what?" I said, like I was ignorant or something.

He glared, his eyes narrowing, suspicious. "Help *this*. Help me be normal again."

"Ah. I'd heard the same thing."

"Then you know why I'm here."

"I've also heard that he's a fraud. That his church is really a cult. That he brainwashes people so they'll stay with him. Nobody knows what goes on in there."

"Yeah, I'd heard that, too." He hugged himself like he'd suddenly become cold.

"And you're still willing to go there?"

"What choice do I have?"

"Is it really so bad? So bad that you'd give up your freedom, your identity? Assuming the rumors are true."

"I haven't been able to hold a job for more than two weeks since it happened. I keep losing my temper. I can't—I'm not very good at controlling it."

"I'm sorry. You don't have a pack, do you?" He shook his head. He hadn't had anyone teach him how to control it.

He looked over my shoulder suddenly. Jeffrey and Roger had come up behind me. The young man took a couple steps back, then turned and ran, through the gate and toward the caravan.

"Wait!" When he didn't stop, I wasn't surprised. "Damn."

"That kid's scared to death," Jeffrey said.

"But not of *me*."

"Yeah, a little. Also of his own shadow, I think. It's funny to think of a werewolf being scared of anything."

"Oh, you'd be surprised. A lot of us spend most of our time being afraid."

"Let's go," Stockton said, gesturing toward the trees at the edges of the field, around to the side of the caravan, closer to it but still in shadow. "Before his flunkies figure out we're not here for the show."

I tipped my face up, turning my nose to the air, half

closing my eyes to keep out distractions. Then I shook my head. "Let's go to the other side. It's downwind."

We walked along the road to a place where we were mostly out of sight of the main entrance to the caravan, then climbed over the fence. Quickly we made our way to the trees, following them along the edge of the pasture down a gentle slope, toward the caravan. As we approached, the floodlights grew brighter, and the area around the encampment grew darker. For all it appeared like a carnival lot, the place was quiet. No talking, no voices, no sounds of life, like pots and pans clanking together while dinner was being prepared. By all accounts, dozens of people were living there, but I couldn't make out any obvious signs of life.

Except for the smell: I sensed a kind of ripe, college dorm-room smell, of too many people living in close proximity, and not enough housekeepers. I wrinkled my nose.

"There." Stockton pointed to a gap in the trailers. Temporary wire fencing still enclosed the area, but here was a place where we might catch a glimpse of something interesting. A spot where a corner of the main tent was staked to the ground was visible.

When a pair of burly-looking men—Smith's bodyguards from earlier today—walked past, we kept very still. They were patrolling, and they didn't stop.

His back against a tree, Stockton settled down to wait, focusing his camera on the gap looking into the caravan. Jeffrey took the next tree over as his prop. I stayed by Stockton, watching what he watched.

The ground was damp, and I was getting damp sitting on it. The air was cold, getting colder. My breath fogged.

Jeffrey hugged his jacket tighter around him. I wondered how long we could possibly sit here. Something had to happen soon. The pilgrims, including that young guy, had gathered at Smith's gate. He wouldn't leave them waiting.

I moved next to Jeffrey and whispered, "Can you contact vampires who have, you know, moved on?" I was thinking of Estelle. I was thinking she might be here and could tell us something.

"I never have. That is—none of them have ever tried to contact me. I hate to ask it, but do they even have souls?"

This came up on the show all the time, and my gut reaction said yes. How could someone like Alette *not* have a soul? But what was a soul, really? I didn't know.

I didn't answer, and he shook his head. "I'm not sensing anything like that. This whole space feels numb. Asleep, almost."

Stockton sat forward suddenly and raised his camera. "Here he comes. There."

Jeffrey and I crept over to join him. Squinting, I looked through the gap.

Smith walked past it. I only saw him for a second. But Stockton muttered, with some satisfaction, "Ha, I got you. If only I could get that on film, damn you."

I hadn't seen him do anything. He looked just like he had at the hearing, conservatively dressed, his manner calm. He moved across my field of vision, that was all.

Stockton was insane, suffering from some kind of delusion. And I'd fallen for it.

Before I had a chance to call him on it, he pulled something over his head: a locket on a chain that he'd kept hidden under his shirt.

Handing it to me, he said, "Put that on. The next time he walks by, tell me what you see."

It seemed like a simple piece of jewelry, not particularly impressive. The metal wasn't silver. Pewter, maybe. It felt heavy. The locket was a square, an inch or so on both sides, and cast with patterns of Celtic knotwork, worn with age.

I fingered the latch. "What is it?"

"Don't open it," he said. "It's got a little bit of this and that in it. Four-leaf clover, a bit of rowan. Cold iron."

Some kind of folk magic, then. Now, was it the kind of folk magic that worked, or the kind that was little more than a placebo against the nameless fears of the dark?

I put the chain over my head.

I had to give Stockton credit for being more patient than I was. He was used to waiting for his stories, and he was good at it. We had no guarantee that Smith would pass within our view again. But he did.

And he *glowed*. His skin wasn't skin anymore. It looked almost white, shimmering like mother-of-pearl. At first I thought he'd gone bald as well, but his hair had turned pale, almost translucent. He looked completely different, but I knew it was him, because he wore the same clothes, and had that same meticulous bearing. For just a moment I saw his eyes, and they were far too large, and dark as night, dark enough to fall into and never climb out again.

I almost shrieked, but Stockton grabbed my arm and pinched me to keep me quiet. Then, Smith was out of sight again. My eyes remained frozen wide open.

"Holy shit, he's an alien!" I hissed.

"Um, no." Stockton donned a not very convincing Irish

brogue. "In the Old Country they called them the Fair Folk, the Gentry, the Good People, the Hill Folk—"

"He's a *fairy*?" I couldn't decide which was more completely outrageous.

"Don't say that word, he'll hear you. Give that back." He held his hand out for the pendant. Reluctantly, I returned it. "Nobody was ever able to get close enough to confirm any suspicions until he came to testify. I'm lucky I was in the right place at the right time to see him."

I had to work to keep my voice a whisper. "You can't be serious. That's—it's all stories, folklore—"

"Pot calling the kettle black, anyone?"

Just when I thought I'd heard everything, just when I thought the last mystery had been revealed and that I couldn't be shocked anymore, something like this came along. I'd never be able to blow off another story as long as I lived. Flying monkeys? Oh, yeah, I could believe. Stockton was right. I should have known better.

Maybe I should chase a few more rainbows looking for pots of gold.

"How did you know?" I said to Stockton.

"I didn't," he said. "My grandmother gave me the locket. For protection, she said. And, well, I couldn't say no to Grandma. She sets out milk for the brownies, even in the Boston suburbs. What can I say, I believed her. But I didn't know Smith was one of them until he walked into the room this afternoon. I have to tell you, I didn't expect the charm to work like *that*."

Jeffrey said, "I didn't know what I was looking at. I can't see through the disguise, but I can see the disguise. Interesting." He sounded far too academic about it.

Theoretically, having an answer to one question—

what was he?—should have brought us closer to answering other questions. Like, what was he doing with his church? Why was he drawing vampires and lycanthropes to him, and what was he doing with them? Why would an old-style Celtic folklore *elf* do these things?

Activity within the camp increased. Smith was out of sight again, but people were gathering and filing into the tent. Based on what details I could make out from here, the people looked ordinary, commonplace. Like any fringe church community going to a service. People walked with their heads bowed, their hands clasped. I normally wouldn't see this kind of patience, this kind of humility, from these groups of people.

They almost looked tired.

I expected the guards to circle back around any minute. They didn't right away, because they remained at the other side of the caravan, by the entrance, helping to escort in the new recruits.

They might be clever enough to count the number of people come to join them, versus the number of cars parked on the road, and realize there were too many cars. We couldn't stay here all night, twiddling our thumbs.

I wanted to break up the caravan. This was a cult and Smith was using people. He had some kind of ancient power, and he was dangerous.

"You know about this stuff," I said to Stockton. "How do we break his power?"

He looked panicked for a moment. "I don't know *that* much. I know what my grandmother told me. I know a few little charms, the four-leaf clover, the iron. Maybe if we threw iron filings at him."

"Would your grandmother know what to do?" I said. "She knew the locket would work, right?"

"I don't know that she ever thought I'd actually run into one of these guys."

"Could you ask her?"

"Right now?"

"You have your phone with you, right?" Hell, I had my phone with me. *I'd* call her.

"Well yeah, but—"

"So call her." And maybe after that I could talk to her and learn where her belief came from. Did she leave milk for the brownies because her family had always done so, or did she have a more immediate reason?

Stockton pulled one of those fancy little flip phones out of his front pants pocket. I was glad to see he'd had it turned off for our escapade.

The thing lit blue when he turned it on. He searched the menu, then pressed the dial button.

He sat there, listening to the ringing, while Jeffrey and I watched. It had been such a great idea, I'd thought. But she probably wasn't even home. I was getting ready to suggest that we call it a night, leave, do some research, and have a couple of beers while we came up with a plan to confront him tomorrow.

Then Stockton said, "Yes? Hello? Gramma, it's Roger . . . Yeah, I'm fine. Everything's fine . . . What do you mean I only call you when something's wrong? No, Gramma . . . Mom and Dad are fine, as far as I know . . . I don't really remember the last time I talked to them . . ."

I was used to being the goddess of phone conversations. I wanted to grab the phone out of his hand and make his grandmother get to the point. Ask her the *right* questions. Then I imagined trying to explain to her who I was.

"I'm sorry, Gramma, I can't really talk any louder . . . I said I can't talk any louder . . . I'm sort of hiding . . . That's what I wanted to talk to you about . . . You know those stories you're always telling? About the Fair Folk . . . Yes, Gramma, I crossed myself—" He quickly did so, in good Catholic fashion. "Some friends and I seem to have come across one who's doing some not very nice things . . . What kind is he? . . . I don't know . . . Seelie or Unseelie? I don't know that either . . . No, Gramma, I *do* pay attention when you tell stories . . ."

"Unseelie are the bad guys, right?" I whispered at him. "I bet he's Unseelie."

"Neither one is very good," he said, away from the phone for a moment. "Yeah, Gramma? I'm pretty sure he's Unseelie . . . That's right, it's pretty bad . . . What would you do? Pray?" He rolled his eyes. "What about getting rid of him? Will he just go away? No . . . okay . . . okay, just a minute." He took out a mini notepad and pen, and started writing. A shopping list, it looked like. "Okay . . . Got it. Then what? Really? Is that all?"

Patience, Kitty. Back in the caravan, people had entered the tent. I couldn't see anything now, or sense anything, except that a large group of people had gathered.

"Thanks a lot, Gramma. This is just what I need. I have to go now . . . Yes, yes I'm coming for Thanksgiving this year. No, I'm not bringing Jill . . . She broke up with me six months ago, Gramma." He held the phone an inch away from his ear, closed his eyes, and gave a deep sigh. I could hear the woman's voice, slow and static-laden, but not the words.

This was ridiculous. I wanted to throttle him.

"I have to go now . . . goodbye, Gramma . . . I love you." He clicked off.

"What did she say? What do we do?" I said, forcing my hands to not grab his shirt and shake him.

"We go grocery shopping."

"What?"

"Bread, salt, some different herbs. Unless you brought any of this stuff with you?" He showed me the list he'd written: verbena, Saint-John's-wort, rowan.

"Can we even find some of this at the local supermarket?"

He shrugged. "Once we get the stuff it doesn't sound like it's that hard of a spell. We just walk around the camp, sprinkle the stuff on the ground, and poof."

"Poof?"

"Poof, he's banished back to underhill, or wherever the hell he came from."

Wherever the hell. Apt phrase, that.

"So we go to the store, get the supplies, come back, and that's that. Easy," Jeffrey said, grinning like we were planning a school prank.

Stockton put the list back in his pocket. "I think I remember seeing a convenience store a few miles back, at the last intersection. They'll have some of this stuff. She didn't say we need all of it, these are just the options. Why don't you two wait here and keep an eye on things while I go get the stuff."

"Sure," Jeffrey said without hesitation. Stockton was already turning to go.

"Wait!" I tried to keep my voice down and sound desperate at the same time.

"You have a better idea?"

"I go get the stuff and you wait here?"

"I'll be back in half an hour, I promise. Here, hang on to this." He gave me the locket charm, then ran along the shelter of the trees, back to the road.

I had a bad feeling about this. "Split up," I muttered. "We can take more damage that way. You know we're stranded here once he takes the car."

"Calm down, it'll be okay. Smith's wrapped up in whatever he's doing in there and the guards haven't spotted us. We'll stay here, keep our heads down, and be fine."

"You're entirely too pleased about all this."

"Of course I am! I've never done anything like this before. I'm usually cooped up in a TV studio or a book signing. But this—running around, investigating, *spying*. How cool is it?"

How did I get myself into these situations? "So, Jeffrey—you want to be a guest on my show?"

"Um—just what exactly would that involve?"

Inside the caravan, nothing happened. If this had been any other church's revival meeting, there would have been singing, shouting, praying. I wouldn't have minded hearing some speaking-in-tongues.

But there was nothing, except Jeffrey and me sitting in the dark and the cold, under a tree, waiting.

Enough time passed for me to think that Stockton had set us up. Somewhere, hidden cameras recorded us, and any minute now actors dressed as bogeymen would leap out of the woods, screaming and carrying on. I'd freak out, adrenaline would push me over the edge, and I'd turn

Wolf, because that was what happened when I panicked in a dangerous situation. Stockton would get it all on film and broadcast it in "A Very Special Episode of *Uncharted World*: Kitty, Unleashed." I didn't know what Jeffrey would do. Get out of the way, I hoped.

Except the caravan of the Church of the Pure Faith was parked in front of us, and I wasn't going to take my eyes off them. The bogeymen would have to wait.

Jeffrey tapped my shoulder and pointed at the road. A car pulled up—Stockton's. The headlights were off, to draw less attention to it. I hissed a sigh of relief.

A few minutes later, he rejoined us, carrying a plastic bag. "Hi. Anything happen while I was gone?"

"Nothing," I said. "They've been quiet."

"*Too* quiet," Jeffrey added happily.

Stockton pulled items out of the bag: a loaf of sliced sandwich bread, a shaker of salt, a bottle of Saint-John's-wort herbal remedy, and a pill crusher.

"I figured we'd crush the pills up and sprinkle the powder," he said. "I don't think you can get Saint-John's-wort any other way these days."

I deferred to his supposedly greater knowledge, because I didn't have any better ideas.

"Jeffrey, you take the salt. Kitty—" He handed Jeffrey the salt, and me the loaf of bread. While he took the pill crusher out of the package and dug into the Saint-John's-wort, he explained. "We start at the north end of the caravan. Just sprinkle this stuff as we go, and that's that. Which way's north?"

The moon, a little over three-quarters, was rising. That marked east. I pointed to the left. "There." It was just off from the entrance of the caravan.

Stockton exhaled a deep breath. "Right. Here we go, then."

The reporter led us. He had the bottle of pills in his jacket pocket. Two at a time, he grabbed pills from the bottle, put them in the crusher, turned the knob until it crunched, then emptied the powder out on the ground. Jeffrey followed behind him, sprinkling salt. I tore the bread into pieces and dropped them. Just call me Gretel.

Stockton was whispering. I had to listen closely to understand the words.

"Our Father, who art in Heaven, hallowed be Thy name . . ." Prayer. A bit of verbal magic to bind the spell.

We walked around the caravan, clockwise, far enough away from the wire boundary to avoid drawing attention. Even the guards had gone in to Smith's service. I crumbled bread, afraid to say anything. Jeffrey pursed his lips in a serious expression, watching Stockton and the ground ahead of us. Stockton developed a rhythm, pill-crunch-sprinkle, his lips moving constantly.

Completing the circle seemed to take forever. We moved methodically, and therefore slowly. We didn't even know if this was going to work.

Finally, we returned to the north side of the caravan. We passed the entrance, which was blocked off with chains secured with padlocks, making the place look more like a prison than a religious camp. Stockton reached the spot where the trail of bread crumbs began. I closed the circle.

". . . and deliver us from evil. Amen." He sighed and licked his lips.

Nothing happened.

"What's next?" I said, trying to keep the anxiety out of my voice.

"I don't know," Stockton said. "That was supposed to be it. I can't be sure I even did it right. I mean, who knows what other shit is in those pills."

That was it, then. We did what we could. Maybe we could go back to town, do some more research, and try again later.

"No, no. Something's happening. The light's gone all funny."

Jeffrey didn't elaborate. From my perspective, nothing had changed. Who knew what he could see?

Then, inside the caravan encampment, two figures approached the entrance. They were large, male, and stalked with long, smooth strides, predators in hunting mode— Smith's werewolf bodyguards.

"Guys?" I said, backing away. "We might want to get out of here."

The two bodyguards put their hands on the chains of the gate and hopped over, leaving the chains rattling. They continued on, right toward us.

Drawing together instinctively, we moved away quickly, stepping back, unwilling to turn away from the werewolves.

They crossed the line of the circle we'd made, then stopped.

For a moment, outside the circle marked by the bread crumbs, they stood frozen. Then one of them stumbled, as if he'd lost his balance. The other one put his hand to his head and squinted. They looked around, expressions confused, like they'd just come out of hibernation. They glanced at us, then at each other.

"Oh, my God," one of them murmured.

"Spell broken," Jeffrey said.

I moved toward them slowly—let them get a good look at me, get my scent, prove that I wasn't a danger. "Hi. Are you guys okay?"

"I don't know," said the one who'd spoken. "I—we were stuck. What happened? I'm not sure what happened."

They both looked back at the gate, their faces long and sad, nostalgic almost. The chain they'd jumped over a minute before was still swinging.

"Do you want to go back?" I said.

The other one, shorter, quieter, said, "It's not real, is it?"

"No," I said.

"Shit," he muttered, bowing his head.

Now all we had to do was get everyone else to leave the caravan and cross that line.

I wondered what would happen if Smith crossed that line.

A crowd had gathered, Smith's congregation leaving the tent and filling the space behind the gate. Dozens of them stared out with earnest, devout gazes.

At the head of the crowd stood Smith himself. Surrounded by his people, he seemed small, slight. I still had Stockton's charm in my pocket. I put it on. He appeared otherworldly, his gaze blank and inhuman. He frowned, burning. Lines seemed to form around him, tendrils that joined him to all the people around him, like tethers, leashes. Two broken lines stretched in front of him, wavering, unanchored.

One of the men, the one who'd spoken first, stepped toward Smith. I ran forward, slipping in front of him, blocking his way.

"No, don't go back. Please."

Smith called out from behind the gate. "You are keeping them from peace. I can give *you* peace."

"Kitty, don't listen to him!" Jeffrey called.

But his words hadn't affected me. I didn't have to listen to him. The charm protected me.

Jeffrey stood a few yards up the hill from me, his hands clenched, looking worried for the first time all evening. Stockton was nearby, his camera up and filming. At least we'd have a record of this, however it turned out.

I had to draw him out—without seeming like I was drawing him out. He was probably already suspicious. Of course he was.

I approached the gate. "Kitty!" Jeffrey's voice was tight with fear. I waved a hand, trying to tell him it was okay. I had a plan. I hoped.

At the line, I stopped walking and tried to look pathetic and indecisive.

One of his followers started unlocking the chain. Smith never touched the metal. Steel contained iron, which was poison to his kind.

Once the people around him had pulled the chains away, Smith moved forward. I couldn't look away; his gaze trapped mine. I tried to make it a challenge. Wolves stared when they wanted to make a challenge.

"You're curious, aren't you?" he said.

I nodded. I had to keep him moving forward.

"But you hesitate. You're afraid."

He came closer. God, I wanted to run away. Wolf wanted to run away.

He was in front of me, holding out his hand, like he wanted me to take it, so he could draw me into his world. His goblin market.

Slowly, I took a step back—a hesitating step, to encourage him to follow. I was right on the edge, he could draw me to him if only he took another step toward me, over the line.

But he stopped. When he smiled, he showed teeth.

He said, "I see your spell. I'll not cross the line."

Screw it. Screw *him*. I grabbed his shirt and pulled, yanking him forward. Across the line.

I expected him to be heavier than he was. Hauling him felt like pulling on a pillow—he was light enough to fly out of my grip. Surprise at this made me lose my balance. I fell backward, but I kept hold of his shirt, determined to bring him down, literally if need be.

I hit the ground, expecting him to fall on top of me. But he didn't, because as soon as his body crossed the invisible barrier that we'd created he caught fire. He burst like a flare, yellow and red spewing with a shrill hiss that might have been a shriek. Ash and embers fell against me, onto my face, scalding. I screamed and put my arms over my face. My hands burned, throbbing and painful. I rolled, trying to get away.

Somebody stopped me and pulled me up until I was sitting. "Are you okay?" It was Jeffrey.

My hands were red, baked and itching, like a bad sunburn. My face burned and itched, too. I hated to think what it looked like.

I lurched out of his grip and twisted all the way around to look for Smith. "Where is he? Where'd he go?"

"He's gone," Jeffrey said, laughing a little, nervously. "He just burned up."

A few black cinders lay scattered on the grass. At the

gate of the caravan, people were drifting out, stumbling, confused, shaking their heads.

"It's over," I said. I was too tired to feel any kind of victory. Yet, I couldn't help but feel like there should have been more. That had almost been easy—anticlimactic. I shouldn't have been able to finish off someone that badass all by myself.

Stockton was still filming, gripping the camera with both hands, white-knuckled. So how did you wrap up a story like this? Brush your hands off and go home?

Behind me, a groan sounded, deep, changing in tone. The tenor was familiar—a human voice, turning into a wolf's growl.

One of Smith's bodyguards was shape-shifting. And why not? How long had it been since any of these people had given in to the other side of their natures? And now the power that had controlled them was gone.

The shorter one doubled over, pulling off his shirt, ripping the sleeves as he did, and growling. As the other one watched, he backed away, but his muscles were rippling, his body melting, changing. All the lycanthropes would react to that; in moments, they'd all shift.

That didn't even begin to mention what the vampires would do, freed from Smith's control.

"Jeffrey, we have to get out of here."

He looked around, his eyes widening as he realized what was happening. "Yeah, I guess we do."

"Roger!" I shouted. "Get back to the car! Now!"

Sure enough, a woman who'd made her way out of the gate grabbed a man standing next to her, tripped him so he sprawled on the ground, straddled his back, and bared her teeth. She threw herself at his neck, biting into him. He thrashed, trying to roll and swipe at her. Claws sprouted from his hand.

Many of the others, realizing what was happening, ran flat-out into the woods, no looking back.

Helping each other, Jeffrey and I got to our feet and started running. Stockton stared out, his eyes wide and surprised. His camera was still up, still recording.

I grabbed his shirt as we passed him. "Come *on*!"

A furious snarl ripped the air behind me. A wolf could run faster on four legs than I could on two.

"Run. Just run," I said to Jeffrey, shoving him toward Stockton. I turned my back on them to face the wolf that was racing toward me.

chapter 9

He wanted the easiest prey in the area. I must have looked good. Small enough to be an easy target with enough meat to make it worthwhile.

That described me in so many ways I didn't want to think about.

He was pale, almost white, which made him glow in the moonlight. He was also big, one of the stockier wolves I'd ever seen: massive through the chest and shoulders, legs working, head low, like a battering ram. He'd plow into me and knock me over like I was nothing, then rip into me without a second thought.

But I'd survive the first few cuts. I already had lycanthropy, unlike Jeffrey and Roger. I was tough; I could take it.

Holy crap.

I dodged. At the very last possible moment I dodged and grabbed the wolf's tail. I was stronger than I looked. I kept hold of it long enough to change his momentum, to make him hesitate and look back, to pause before he adjusted the vector of his attack to where his prey had slipped.

His jaws were open, aimed at my shoulder, once again to try to shove me to the ground and hold me with his teeth. Swinging my body, I deflected his face away. Instead of locking a firm grip on my shoulder, his canines scraped down my arm. A couple of deep gouges on the bicep was better than losing a shoulder, right?

I couldn't slow down to think about how much it hurt. Jeffrey and Roger should have had enough time to get back to the car. Time to run away. I kicked the wolf's face before he could gather himself for the next attack. I had to convince him I wasn't as easy a catch as he first thought. This was a time I had to let a little bit of the Wolf into my mind. She was better at fighting than I was. Kick him, snarl at him, scare him off.

Do all that, and stay anchored to my human body as well. I didn't want to lose control of that part of myself. I didn't want to leave myself vulnerable while I shifted. And I wanted to be able to talk about this when it was finished. Assuming I was still conscious when it was finished.

The wolf hesitated. He was thinking about it. Probably because other, potentially easier prey attracted him.

"Kitty! Kitty!" A kid ran up the hill toward me—the young man I'd talked to before everything hit the fan, the one who'd just tried to join the church. "Help, I don't know what to do, you have to help me—"

"Come on." I grabbed the guy's shirt, shoved him so he was behind me, and shouted at the pale wolf. "Get out of here! Go on, get away!"

I backpedaled up the hill. "Run!" I said to the guy. "Get to the car."

I turned and followed him. I didn't dare look behind me. We hopped the fence, first the kid, then me. Jeffrey stood by the car, holding open the passenger side door. He also held a Club—the attached to the steering wheel so the car doesn't get stolen kind of Club—in his right hand, ready to swing it like it was, well, a club. Just in case something was following.

I shoved the kid into the back and piled in immediately after him. Jeffrey jumped in the front seat and slammed shut the door.

The pale wolf crashed into the door, jaws open, slobbering on the window.

Stockton was filming it.

"Roger, would you put down that camera and drive?" I shouted.

The second time the wolf charged us, causing the whole car to rock on its wheels, Stockton put the camera down and started the engine. We pulled out onto the road a second later.

My straggler curled up in his seat. Hugging himself, he shook, sweat breaking out on his face. He mumbled, "Stop it . . . stop it . . ."

He was starting to Change. It began inside, a feeling like an animal clawing its way out. It hurt more when you tried to keep it from happening. When you couldn't stop the Change from happening.

I grabbed him, taking hold of his face and making him look at me. "Keep it together, okay? Take a deep breath. Slow breath. Good, that's good. Nice and easy, keep it together." His breathing slowed; he stopped trembling. After another moment, he even relaxed a little. Some of the tension left his arms.

He closed his eyes. He wouldn't look at me.

"What's your name?"

He needed a moment to catch his breath. "Ty. It's Ty."

"Nice to meet you, Ty." He nodded quickly, nervously, keeping his head down. I moved a hand to his shoulder— a light touch to keep him anchored in his body—and sat back.

Now maybe I could catch *my* breath.

I didn't want to think about the can of worms we'd opened. In the long run, Smith being gone could only be a good thing. But all those people were homeless now, and confused. And monsters. At least we were in the middle of nowhere. They could only hurt each other. Which was bad enough.

"Kitty, you're bleeding." Jeffrey stared at me between the two front seats.

Blood covered my right arm. Just looking at it sent waves of pain riding through my shoulder.

"It's okay," I said, gritting my teeth. "It'll be fine by morning."

"The rapid healing, that's true?" Stockton said. The reporter turned his camera onto me, holding it between the front seats with one hand while steering with the other and only half watching the road. "Can I watch?"

"No." I glared until he set the thing down. I took the charm off and handed it to the front seat. Roger accepted it, pulling the chain over his head. "Roger, your grandmother got you into this, didn't she? The fairy charms, the supernatural. Working for *Uncharted World*."

He smiled wryly. "Some people think I'm on that show because I'm a crappy reporter. I could be on CNN if I wanted. Except I believe. No, I don't believe. I *know*. The supernatural—it's like any other mystery. You find enough evidence, you can prove the truth. This gig gets me closer to that." Just like Flemming. The search for truth. Stockton was just traveling a different road. "So—you sure you won't let me film you next full moon?"

"No."

"How about you, kid?"

"What?" Ty looked woozy.

"No," I said.

Stockton chuckled, entirely too amused. "Hey—where are we going?"

I found my phone in my pocket, turned it on, and hesitated, because I didn't know who I could call for help. I hated to say that my first impulse was to call Cormac. *He'd* know what to do with a couple dozen rogue vampires and werewolves rampaging the countryside. Unfortunately, his solution would involve lots of silver bullets and stakes, and we'd end up with a bunch of corpses. I was trying to avoid that.

My next idea was to call Ahmed. I didn't have a phone number for the Crescent, so I called information. They were able to get me through to the restaurant side. A cheery-sounding hostess whose voice I didn't recognize answered the phone.

"Good evening, this is the Crescent. May I help you?"

"Hi, yeah—is Ahmed there?"

"Who?"

A sinking feeling attacked my stomach. "Ahmed. The guy who owns the place."

"Oh! Just a moment. May I tell him who's calling?"

"It's Kitty."

She set the phone aside. I could hear the murmur of generic restaurant noises—voice talking, tableware clinking— in the background. The moment stretched on. I started tapping my foot. I didn't have a lot of time here.

A familiar, robust voice picked up the line. "Kitty! How are you?"

Situations like this made it so hard to answer that question. "I need some help, Ahmed. What would you do with a couple dozen vampires and lycanthropes who'd lost it and you wanted to get them under control so they didn't get hurt?"

I grit my teeth. When I said it out loud like that, this mess sounded ridiculous.

He hesitated for a long time, so that I had to listen to the restaurant white noise again. Then he said, "I would leave the area, and wait until morning to return to see what was left."

"But the vampires will die without shelter."

"That would not be my concern."

No, it wouldn't, would it? "Then what about the lycanthropes? I know you'd want to help the lycanthropes."

"If you can bring them here, to the club, I can shelter them."

"But I have no way of getting them there."

"Kitty, what have you gotten yourself into?"

I sighed. He wasn't going to be any help. He probably never even left the Crescent, his little domain. "It's a long story. I'll have to talk to you later. Bye."

"Goodbye?" He sounded confused. I hung up anyway. That left one other option.

I called Alette to ask her if she could help. Bradley answered the phone, put me on hold, and returned to say that she could. She'd meet me at Smith's caravan in an hour.

An hour later, we drove back by the site. The police

had already arrived in squad cars, along with a sedan I recognized as the one Bradley drove, and a large, windowless van.

Stockton pulled onto the shoulder. A cop came forward and tried to wave him away. I rolled down the back window.

"I'm with Alette," I called. The cop hesitated, then let Stockton park.

While a trio of cops moved alongside the road setting out flares and obviously standing guard, Alette and Leo stood at the edge of the grassy field. A group of people approached them from the caravan. Leo held something out to them, and they moved slowly, cautiously toward him.

"Stay here, lock the doors," I said as I climbed out of the car. I didn't stick around to see if they listened to me.

I didn't get too close. I had my limits. The people drawn to Leo were thin, wan, cold—vampires. Leo held a jar of blood, open to the air, so that the smell drew them.

The vampires in Smith's caravan hadn't eaten in months, some of them. As they approached, Leo spoke softly to them. He touched their chins, their hair, and they bowed their heads and followed docilely. He led them to the van and guided them inside. Tom waited by the back door.

Bradley approached me, clearly on an intercept course to keep me from interrupting Alette and Leo.

"What's happening?" I asked, before he could chastise me or start issuing orders. "It looks like some kind of vampire hypnotism."

He said, "The ones who joined Smith aren't very old, only a few decades. Easy to control. Older vampires aren't going to go looking for a cure. If they've made it to a hundred without getting killed, it usually means they like it. But these—they're looking for guidance."

"What'll happen to them?"

"They'll stay with Alette until she can find out where they're from and send them home." He glanced back at Stockton's car. Of course the reporter had his camera pressed against the windshield, glaring out. He even leaned half on top of Jeffrey to get a better angle. "Your friends should leave."

His tone didn't allow argument. Besides, I pretty much agreed with him. This was like an accident scene, and Stockton didn't need to be broadcasting it on his show.

"I'll ask them, but Stockton's got the keys. Good luck getting him out of here." Then I had a brilliant idea. Stockton reported on the paranormal. He'd absolutely love this. I told Bradley, "Let me get the kid out and back in his own car. Then could you maybe pull the Man In Black routine on Stockton? It might just scare the crap out of him." I couldn't help it—I grinned.

"Man In Black?" Bradley's brow furrowed with distaste.

"Just be yourself when you tell him to get the hell out of here. It'll be fun." I trotted off to check on Ty.

Jeffrey unlocked the car for me. I opened the back door. Ty was sitting up, looking around, aware of his surroundings.

"Hey, Ty, you ready to go home? Can you drive?" I said.

He ran a hand through his floppy hair and nodded. "But can't I stay with you?"

I absolutely did not need that kind of responsibility. I'd run away from that kind of responsibility. I tried to let him down gently. "Walk with me, 'kay?"

I held out my hand. He took it and let me pull him from

the car. Staying close to him, I walked him to his car. "There's a club in D.C. for people like us. A guy named Ahmed runs it. He can help you, there's lots of people there who'd be happy to help you cope with this. You should go there."

He scrounged a pen and piece of paper from his glove box, and I wrote down directions to the Crescent for him. I also gave him my number.

"No more quack cures after this, right?"

"Right."

"You going to be okay?"

He nodded, a little more decisively than he had before. "Yeah. I'll check this place out. Thanks, Kitty. Thanks a lot."

I sent him on his way.

I turned around just in time to see Stockton's car back up a few feet in order to zoom a U-turn onto the road, engine revving. Arms crossed, a looming monolith of a man, Bradley stood at the edge of the pavement and watched him go.

When Stockton's car was out of sight, Bradley turned around. He wore a big grin. He said, "You're right. That was fun."

I was so sorry I'd missed it.

Leo, supervised by Alette, was still herding vampires. The scene was surreal and vaguely appalling.

"Does it bother you?" I said to Bradley. "Working for a vampire? Emma said her family has worked for her for centuries. What about yours? Or are you related to Emma?"

"Distant cousins." His smile was amused, wry. He nodded to the cops. "One of the officers there is another cousin. I never really thought about it, to tell you the truth. It's just how it's always been. If you don't grow up thinking any of this is weird, then it isn't weird. When I was a kid, my parents would take me to her place to visit. It was like having another aunt."

The lycanthropes wouldn't fry when the sun rose, but I was worried about what they might do in the meantime. Alette wasn't. She and Leo set out raw meat as bait and armed the police with silver bullets.

Wasn't exactly what I had in mind. But it turned out the silver bullets were weapons of last resort. The vampire mojo worked on the weres as well. The two vampires lulled them to sleep, let them slip back to human, then let the police take over. Many of the people had missing person files on them. Eventually, they'd make it back home.

The two vampires cleaned up the whole mess. That was why lycanthropes needed large numbers to defeat vampires in a head-to-head confrontation.

We explored the caravan while Alette's police friends put up yellow tape and marked the whole thing off as an investigation site. Under the tent, a temporary stage made of plywood and milk crates stood toward the rear, and a string of bare lightbulbs hung from tent poles, across the top. It looked harmless enough. The rest of the camp, though, was a disaster. None of the trailers had sewer hook-ups. The few available camp and chemical toilets were overused. Immortality and rapid healing didn't preclude the necessity of other bodily functions. Nothing had been cleaned, piles of trash lay discarded in the corners of RVs, in the beds of pickups. Some signs of food remained: empty cans of soup and beans, along with dirty dishes, were stacked in sinks and on counters. Mold and slime spotted them, and dozens of flies rose and scattered when we opened doors.

I could hardly breathe, the smell was so strong. I kept my hand in front of my face.

We found a few people, both lycanthropes and vampires, hiding in the closets of campers, on the floorboards in trucks and cars. They hugged themselves, shaking, crying—symptoms of withdrawal. They looked pale and thin, their hair was dull and limp. I didn't think anyone with lycanthropy could die of malnutrition, their bodies were so hardy and resistant to damage. But they didn't look good. The vampires—their bodies might not break down. But they might lose their minds. Smith was sustaining them, that was how they had survived.

I tried to draw them out, talking to them, reassuring them, but they didn't like me. My scent was unfamiliar, and they cowered, more animal than human. Some of them followed me into the open. Some of them, Leo had to come and whisper to them, work some of his vampire charm on them, until their eyelids drooped and they followed on command.

These people had been living a dozen to a trailer, no food, no showers. Smith had turned them into zombies.

Alette joined us as we finished our tour of the camp.

"This is a rather impressive coup you've accomplished, for someone who claims to have no authority," she said, frowning.

She asked me what happened, exactly what we had seen and what we had done to banish Smith. She nodded and seemed unsurprised, like she recognized what he was and had expected as much.

"I never thought it could be this bad," I said. "I thought

Smith was duping people. But he was sucking them dry. Keeping them alive so he could continue using them."

"It's what his kind do," Alette said. "What they've done for centuries, in one guise or another. The *sidhe*, the fairies, have always fed on the lives of mortal human beings. In the old days they stole infants and replaced them with changelings; they seduced young men and women; they kept mortal servants for decades. It's as if they aren't really alive themselves, so they need life nearby to sustain them. Vampires and lycanthropes have something more. They started as mortal, and became something powerful. Whatever the *sidhe* draw from living humans, they draw more of it from us. Smith created a situation where he could surround himself with their power. Because the *sidhe* have power over perception, especially over perceptions of space and time, he could make his followers believe anything. He could show them the world he wanted them to see. The stories say that food of the fairies would appear to be a feast, but turn to dust in your mouth." She gazed over the abandoned caravan with a look of sadness.

We returned to Alette's townhome near dawn. Bradley gave some excuse about finishing arrangements during daylight hours—Alette needed to rent a whole separate townhome where the vampire refugees could stay—and left me facing her in the foyer alone.

She stood, arms crossed, wearing a rust-colored dress with a tailored, silk top and flowing skirt, not at all rumpled after the evening's outing. How did she do it?

"Well. You're rather a mess," she said, regarding my singed clothing, dirt-smeared face, wounded arm, and bloodstained shirt. The observation sounded even more depressing in her neat British accent.

"Yeah," I said weakly. What else could I say?

"I do wish you had told me what you had planned. We might have been more prepared."

I really wanted to sit down, but I didn't dare use any of the antique furniture in the room in my grubby state. "There wasn't really a plan involved. We just sort of seized the moment. Look, I know I had no right to ask for your help and no reason to think that you'd give it—"

"Oh? You're saying I haven't given you any reason to believe that I would give aid in a crisis? That you believe I have no interest in what happens outside the boundaries of my personal domain? That my resources are for my own selfish use and haven't been developed precisely so that I might lend assistance in any situation where it might be needed?"

Alette was the vampire Mistress of Washington, D.C., and that probably wasn't an accident. From here, she could oversee goings-on around the world. She could make worldwide contacts. And she'd been humble enough to offer hospitality to a wandering werewolf. Hospitality, and the loan of a diamond pendant.

"I'm sorry." I looked away, smiling tiredly and feeling like a heel. Any rebellion had been completely wrung out of me tonight, and my arm still hurt.

She continued, softer in tone, kinder. "I happen to believe that immortality ought to make one more sensitive to the plight of the downtrodden, and more apt to work toward the betterment of humanity. Not less. We have the luxury of taking the long view. I know the behavior of some of my kind leaves much to be desired, but please do not judge me by their example."

Never again. "All right. I just . . . I keep wondering, asking myself . . ."

"Did you do the right thing?" I nodded. Destroying the church so abruptly might have caused more problems than it had solved. We might have found another way, if we could have lured people away instead of removing Smith all at once . . .

Alette said, "Elijah Smith drew people to him under false pretenses, removed their wills to decide whether or not to stay with him, and forced them to live in conditions that I consider to be criminal. Human law could not have remedied the problem. You did. Perhaps someone else might have done the job a bit more neatly. But as you say, you seized the moment. You shouldn't worry."

Would there ever come a time when human law could handle situations like this? I couldn't imagine the local sheriff's office with a copy of procedures on how to arrest and hold in custody an Unseelie fairy. Or a rogue were-wolf, or a rampaging vampire. We kept having to police ourselves. We had to be vigilantes, and I didn't like it. I kept claiming we could be a part of the "normal" world, of everyday society. Then shit like this happened to prove me wrong.

"Thanks. Again," I said.

"Ma'am? Shouldn't we be off?"

Leo spoke and I jumped, startled. He'd appeared in the doorway behind me, and I hadn't heard him. He grinned wickedly; he'd known exactly what he was doing.

"All right, Leo. Thank you." She passed me on her way to follow him, pausing a moment to look kindly on me. Like someone might look at a dog who'd had a run-in with a skunk. "Do try to get some sleep," she said.

She'd turned down the hall, out of my sight, when Leo took the opportunity to lean in and say, "Might also try a shower there, luv." He turned on his heel and followed his mistress.

The perfect end to the day, really.

So much for turning this trip into a working vacation. I wasn't getting any sleep. I'd need a week off to recover from all this. Preferably some place with a hot tub and room service. At least my arm had healed quickly.

I got to the Senate office building early, despite the lack of sleep. It meant I was able to catch Duke before the session started.

He was walking down the corridor, conferring with an aide, who was holding a folder open in front of him. I stood against the wall, waiting quietly and out of sight until they reached me. Then I hurried to keep pace with them. Both him and his aide looked over at me, startled.

"Senator Duke? Could I talk to you for just a minute?"

The aide turned to shield the senator, blocking my access to him. He said, "I'm sorry, the senator is much too busy right now. If you'd like to make an appointment—"

"Really, just a couple of questions, we don't even have to stop walking." I hopped to try to catch sight of Duke around his aide. "Senator? How about it?"

He looked straight ahead and didn't slow. "One question, if we can keep walking."

"Of course. Thanks." The aide glared at me, but shifted so I could walk next to Duke. "Why did you bring Elijah Smith here?"

"Because he understands my mission: to see these . . . diseases . . . eradicated. I'm sure you understand. And he's a man of the cloth, which brings a respect that these hearings are sorely in need of, wouldn't you agree?"

"A man of the cloth? Really? Of what denomination? Have you seen any kind of identification for him?"

He frowned. "I'm sure he's a good Christian preacher who teaches that faith saves."

"He wasn't what you think. He wasn't helping anyone."

"Was?" he said. He stopped and looked at me. "What do you mean, was?"

"He, uh, had to leave town suddenly."

Glaring, I thought he might start a fight with me right there. His aide's eyes widened, like he was worried, too. "What have you done?"

I stood my ground. I wasn't going to let him cow me. I had *authority*, didn't I? Yeah, right.

"You believe, Senator. I know you believe: ghosts, devils, angels, good and evil, the whole nine yards. Elijah Smith was a demon, preying on the weak and helpless. I hope you'll believe me."

His expression was cold, but his eyes held a light—a kind of fevered intensity. "If he was preying on anything, it was *your* kind. Vampires and werewolves—monsters. Hardly the weak and helpless." He gave a short laugh.

"We're all just people at heart, Senator. I wish I could make you understand that."

"That'll be for the committee to decide." He gestured to his aide and stalked down the corridor. His aide scurried to keep up with him.

I met Ben outside the Senate office building. He seemed

surprised to see me coming out the door instead of arriving via the sidewalk.

"You're up early," he said, raising an inquiring brow.

"Um, yeah. By the way, we don't have to do anything about Smith. You don't have to look into it."

He studied me closely. "What did you do?"

"Nothing," I said far too quickly. "Well, I mean, we did a spell."

"A spell?"

"We just threw some herbs and stuff around. That's all."

"It's not something you're going to end up in court over, is it?"

Not *human* court, at any rate. "No, I don't think so."

He sighed. "Just for you, I think I'm going to raise my rates. To pay for the hair loss treatments."

He was such a kidder.

We entered the meeting room and found our usual seats. Cormac hadn't shown up since Duke fired him, but Ben said he was still in town. Just in case, Ben said, but wouldn't say in case of what.

Today's session was late in starting. Time dragged. Reporters fidgeted, Senate aides hovered in the background, wringing their hands. The senators themselves shuffled papers and wouldn't raise their gazes. Testimony that should have taken just a few days had been dragged out to the end of the week. I quivered, waiting for something to break.

The audience was dwindling. Most of the reporters had drifted off to cover more interesting stories, and maybe a dozen general spectators remained. Even some of the senators on the committee hadn't bothered showing up.

As expected, Roger Stockton was there, ready to stick

it out to the very end. He looked like *he'd* been able to sleep. He invited himself into the seat next to mine. After last night he must have thought we were some kind of buddies.

Maybe we were.

He leaned close and immediately launched into questions. "So where are the aliens and what do they have to do with the vampires? Are vampires aliens?"

"Aliens?" Ben, overhearing, asked.

"A couple of really bad movies have covered that plot," I said. "Where did *you* come up with it?"

"Last night, the Man In Black with the vampires, the one keeping people away like it was some kind of UFO cover-up. You seemed pretty tight with all them—what aren't you telling me?"

I tried to smile mysteriously, which was hard to do when I really wanted to laugh. "It's not really my place to give away secrets. Honestly, though. The 'Man In Black' was just a guy. There aren't any aliens."

"That's what they all say," he said, glaring. "'It was Venus,' my ass."

Ben gave me a look that said, *What the hell are you talking about?* I gave him one back that said, *Later*.

Finally, the session started. I *still* hadn't been called. We listened to half an hour of testimony from Robert Carr, a B-grade filmmaker who'd been praised for the frightening werewolf shape-shifting effects in his movies—had he used real werewolves, by any chance? He claimed no, he had a talented CGI artist who used a morphing technique to shift images of people into images of wolves, and if his effects were more successful this was because he pictured actual wolves, instead of the unlikely broad-chested, fake-fur-covered mutant grotesques that most werewolf movies used.

I'd seen a couple of his films, and I was sure he was telling the truth and didn't use real werewolves. Though his effects *were* impressive and awfully realistic. He might have *seen* a real werewolf shape-shift. I'd have to tackle—er, approach—him after the hearings and get him to come on the show. We could talk about werewolves as metaphor in film.

I was a little put-out, though, that the committee decided to talk to the werewolf filmmaker before the actual werewolf. Okay, we were still in the entertainment industry portion of the testimony, and maybe some of the committee members didn't believe I was a werewolf. But I'd been on the schedule for three days now. Impatient didn't begin to describe it. I hadn't been able to eat more than half an English muffin for breakfast, I was so anxious.

"Thank you, Mr. Carr, that will be all." Duke straightened the papers on the table in front of him with an air of finality. "I'm afraid that's all the time we have for testimony today. We'll recess for the weekend and resume on Monday to hear from those witnesses we haven't called yet. Thank you very much."

The place burst into activity, people talking among themselves, getting up to leave, aides rushing to attend to the committee members. The other senators looked as confused as I felt; they hadn't been expecting this, either. The tension that had been there from the start didn't dissipate.

"This is weird," Stockton said. "Weren't you supposed to be up there today?"

"Yeah." I crossed my arms and pouted.

"I don't believe it." Ben flopped back against his chair with a sigh. "You see somebody's name on the docket, you expect them to get called. This isn't just annoying, it's unprofessional. They expect us to be on time, the least they could do is run an extra hour to hear everybody."

Maybe there was a reason. Was there anyone else due to be called after me? Or did Duke just want to postpone *my* testimony?

I counted forward, checking off days on the calendar I kept in my mind, confirming the day with the inner tide that felt the pull of it even if I didn't know exactly what day the full moon fell on. I stared across the room to the table where the senators were cleaning up, heading out, conversing with each other or aides. Duke glanced up and caught my eye. He set his jaw and turned away.

Alette was right. She'd called it.

"The bastard," I said. "He planned it. He planned it this way all along. He needs to drag the hearings out until Monday."

"What's Monday?"

"Full moon. He wants to make me testify the day of the full moon."

Stockton gave a low whistle. "Sneaky," he said with something like admiration. I glared at him. He may have thought we were great friends after our adventure last night, but he was doing a lousy job staying in my good graces. He was less like a war buddy and more like an annoying younger brother.

Ben said, "You make it sound like that's not good."

I shook my head, trying to call up some reserve of righteous outrage. Mostly I felt tired. "I'll be at my worst, that's all. Edgy, nervous. Itchy. He knows enough to know this. Maybe he thinks I'll lose my temper and Change right in front of them all." This put me in a foul mood.

"Can you handle it?" Ben said. "Should we put in a request to delay testimony for a day?"

The day after would be even worse than the day before. It felt like having a hangover, and I seemed to spend too much energy mentally holding the door to the Wolf's cage shut. I'd be distracted and no good.

"No, no," I said. "I mean, yeah. I can handle it. I think." I hoped. No caffeine for me that day.

I had to talk to Fritz, but it was getting late; I didn't know if I'd get to the Crescent in time to see him.

I ran from the Metro station to the club, jumped down the stairs, and grabbed the doorway to stop myself as I looked around in a panic.

I wasn't too late. He sat at his usual table, hunched over his tumbler, staring at nothing and wrapped up in his own world.

Pulling up a chair, I sat near him, close enough to whisper but far enough away to dodge if he decided to take a swing at me. I had no idea how this would play out.

He blinked at me, startled.

"What can you tell me about Dr. Paul Flemming?" I asked.

He stared, his gaze narrowing. "I do not know this name."

He could say that, but his expression told me otherwise. His lip twitched, his eyes were accusing. He looked like someone who had decided to lie.

"I saw your name on a list in his laboratory."

"I know nothing," he said, shaking his head. Quickly he drained his glass, slammed it on the table, and pushed his chair away.

"Please don't go. I just want to talk." This strange, lurking figure raised so many questions. At this point I didn't even care what he told me, just as long as he said something. A flash from the past, a story, an anecdote. The sweeping words of advice and judgment the old often seemed to have ready for the young. I didn't care. I wanted to find a crack in that wall.

He turned to me, looming over my chair, his lips curling. "I don't talk to anyone."

I met his gaze, my own anger rising. "If you don't want to talk to anyone, why do you even come here? Why not drink yourself to death in private?"

He straightened, even taking a step back, as if I had snarled at him, or took a swipe at him. Then he closed his eyes and sighed.

"Here, it smells safe. For a little while each day, I feel safe."

I resisted an urge to grab his arm, to keep him here. To try to comfort him through touch, the way I would have if we'd been part of the same pack. But we weren't a pack. He was a stranger, behind this wall he'd built to keep the world out, and I didn't know why I thought he'd talk to me. Just because I was cute or something.

"Why would you be afraid of anything?"

Slowly, a smile grew on his ragged features, pursed and sardonic. "You are young and do not understand. But if you keep on like this, you might."

He brushed his fingers across the top of my head, a

fleeting touch that was gone as soon as I'd felt it, as if a bird had landed on me and instantly taken flight again.

"You are young," he said, and walked away, settling his coat more firmly over his shoulders.

His touch tingled across my scalp long after he'd disappeared out the door.

I had a show to put on tonight, like I did every Friday. I asked Jack for a cup of coffee. Something to keep me awake for the next ten hours. I took out my notepad on the pretense of planning tonight's show—though really, the day of the show was far too late to be planning it. Good thing I'd been cornering hearing participants like Jeffrey Miles and Robert Carr and convincing them to appear on the show. The rest of it I'd have to wing. Not too different than usual, come to think of it.

"He's right, you know." Ahmed appeared. He slipped into the chair across from me. I hadn't heard him, and the whole place smelled like werewolf so my nose hadn't sensed him. He'd stalked quietly, like he was hunting. Today, he wore a woven vest over his shirt and trousers. The vest gave him that same man-of-two-worlds air that the robe had.

I didn't want to talk to him. He might not have had any obligation to help me with the mess at Smith's caravan, but he hadn't even made an effort, and I wasn't in the mood to be lectured by him now.

I just stared at him.

"There is much to fear in the world. Trouble finds you when you get too involved. That is why the Nazi keeps to himself."

"Fritz," I said. "His name's Fritz."

Ahmed had said that this was a safe place, a place with

"Neither do I! But I'm getting tired of everyone hiding things from me."

"Perhaps they do not hide things from you—they hide things out of habit. Many of us would prefer to keep this world hidden. We owe nothing to anyone. That is the secret to a contented life. Don't become indebted to anyone."

"So you build an oasis and lock out the world, is that it? It means you don't have to go out of your way to help anyone." I had to get out of here before I said something I would regret later. "I'm sorry, I'd really like to talk more, but I have to get going. I've got the show tonight."

"I'm sure I do not have to tell you to be careful." I'd been hearing that a lot lately. If it weren't for all the people telling me how much trouble I was potentially getting into, this trip would be a breeze.

"I'm being careful. There's some hell of a tale behind Fritz, and I'm just trying to find out what it is."

As I reached the door, he called out, "Hey, tonight, I'll listen to your show. I'll turn on the radio in the bar so everyone can listen."

No pressure or anything. "Thanks. That'd be cool."

Jack gave me a thumbs-up on my way out.

chapter **10**

Welcome back. If you just tuned in you're listening to *The Midnight Hour*. I'm Kitty Norville. For the last hour I have a new topic of discussion, something I'd love to get a little perspective on. I want to learn something new, and I want to be surprised. I'm going to open the line for calls, and I hope someone will shock me. The subject: the military and the supernatural. Does the military have a use for vampires, lycanthropes, any of the usual haunted folk? Are you a werewolf in the army? I want to hear from you. Know the secret behind remote sensing? Give me a call."

Considering how little time I'd spent on it, the show came together nicely. I'd taken advantage of the collection of interesting folk who'd gathered for the Senate hearings and spent the first hour of the show doing interview after interview. The trio from the Crescent played music, and Robert Carr came in and chatted about werewolves.

But for the last hour I opened the floodgates. I was sure someone out in radioland had some good stories to tell.

"Ray from Baltimore, thanks for calling."

"I can think of *plenty* of military jobs that are just perfect for vampires. Like submarine duty. I mean, you stick somebody on a sub for three months, cooped up in a tiny space with no sun. That's, like, *perfect* for vampires, you know? Or those guys who are locked up in the missile silos, the ones who get to push the button and start World War III."

That "get to" was mildly worrying to say the least. "There's still that food supply to contend with," I said. "It's always been a big limitation on anything vampires accomplish in the real world. I can't picture any navy seaman being really anxious to volunteer for the duty of 'blood supply.' Though it may be a step up from latrine duty."

"Aw, freeze a few pints, they'll be fine."

"All right, next call, please. Peter, you're on the air."

"Hi. Uh, yeah. When I joined the army, I knew this guy who washed out of basic training. We were all surprised, 'cause he was doing really well. Aced all the physicals, obstacle courses, hand-to-hand, nothing held this guy down. The drill sergeant said 'drop and give me a hundred,' and he seemed happy to do it. Never broke a sweat. But he turned up missing on a surprise inspection of the barracks one night. Then it happened again. They kicked him out for going AWOL."

"Let me guess: these were nights of the full moon."

"I don't really remember. I didn't notice at the time. But they were about a month apart. So I'm thinking, yeah."

"Do you think he would have made a good soldier, if he'd been allowed to take a leave of absence for those nights? If the army had made concessions?"

"Yeah—yeah, I think so."

"What about in the field? If his unit happens to be deployed in the middle of nowhere, during a full moon, what's he going to do?"

"Well, I don't know."

"I think it would take some advanced planning. A 'don't ask don't tell' policy probably isn't going to work. Thanks for calling, Peter. Moving on."

I checked the monitor. Then I double-checked it. Line four: Fritz from D.C. It couldn't be. It just couldn't be.

I punched it. "Hello, Fritz?"

"Yes. Kitty? Am I speaking with Kitty?" He spoke with a German accent, tired and grizzled. It was him. My Fritz.

"Yes you are, Fritz. It's me."

"Good, good. I almost did not wait, when the boy put me on hold." His conversational tone made me wonder if he realized that he was on the radio. How refreshing, though, to talk to someone like we were just two people on the phone, rather than being subjected to an attention-seeking crackpot.

"I'm glad you did wait. What would you like to talk about?" I held my breath.

His sigh carried over the line. "I have been thinking of what you said. All day I think to myself, 'Finally, here is someone who wants to listen to you, and you run away from her like a frightened boy.' Now, I think that was a mistake. So I call you. I will die soon. Think, to die of old age. Is rare for ones like us, eh? But someone should know. This story—someone should know of it."

"All right." I didn't dare say more. Let him talk, let him say what he wanted without leading him on.

"You must understand, it was war. People did things

they would not have thought possible before. Terrible things. But we were patriots, so we did them. On both sides, all of us patriots. I was very young then, and it was easy to take orders.

"The S.S. found us, people like us. I also heard rumors, that they created more, throwing recruits into the cage so the wolves would bite them. This I do not know. I was already wolf when they took me. They made us intelligence gatherers. Spies. Assassins, sometimes. As beasts, we could go anywhere, cross enemy lines with no one the wiser. Then we change back to human, do what we were sent to do, and return again. They trained us, drilled us, so we would remember what to do when we were wolves. Like trained dogs. I carried a sack in my mouth, with papers, maps, photographic film. I still remember."

"Fritz, just so I'm clear, you're talking about World War II. The S.S., the Nazi Secret Service—"

"Bah. They call me the Nazi, though they think I do not know. I am no Nazi. We had no choice, don't you see? It was a madness that took all of Germany. Now days, you do not blame the madman who commits a crime. No, you say he was insane. That was Germany."

If I stopped to think about it, my throat would go dry. I would fall speechless. I let the momentum of his story carry me forward. "Something I don't understand: you say you had no choice. But werewolves are stronger than normal humans. Even in human form, they can overpower just about anyone they come up against. Why didn't you? Why didn't you and the others rebel? It sounds like they recruited you against your will, but why did you let them take you instead of fighting them?"

"Besides the fact that it was war? You do not question

your countrymen in uniform in time of war. It isn't done. But more than that, they had silver bullets. The cages were made of silver."

My heart thudded. Flemming had a cage made of silver.

"Fritz, is there any documentation of this? I've been doing some research. The Nazi resistance to Allied occupation after World War II were called the Werewolves. Were you involved in that? You're not telling me the members of that group were literally werewolves, are you?"

"I do not remember. It was a long time ago."

It didn't matter. With the story in hand, I had to be able to find the evidence somewhere. There had to be someone else with stories like this. Flemming, for instance.

"Have you told Dr. Flemming this story? Did he ask you to tell him what you did in the war?"

"Yes, he did."

I closed my eyes and felt the air go out of me. "Did he tell you why?"

Fritz gave a snort. "He works for government, yes? It seems obvious."

"You know, I'd give quite a bit to get Flemming back on the show right about now. Fritz—how do you feel?"

"I'm not sure what you mean. I feel old. Tired. Shape-shifting with arthritis in the hands, the shoulders, it's very bad."

"I mean about what happened. What was it like? How old were you? You don't like talking about it, but do you feel better? Does it feel better to talk about it?"

"I think I should go now. I told the story you wanted. The only story anybody cares about."

"Fritz, no! What did you do after the war? Where did you go? When did you come to America? Fritz!"

"Goodbye, Kitty."

"Fritz!"

The line went dead.

Damn. Now what did I do with that? Tiredly, I spoke at the mike. "Dr. Flemming, if you're listening to this, I'd love it if you called in. I have a few questions for you."

Again, I checked the monitor, dreading what I'd find. I wasn't sure I really wanted Flemming to call. This wasn't likely to inspire him to a sudden bout of openness and sharing.

But Flemming didn't call in. None of the calls listed looked remotely interesting. Anything I said next would be the height of anticlimax.

"Right. It looks like we need to move on to the next call. Lisa from Philly, hello."

"Hi, Kitty. Do you know anything about rumors that there's a version of Gulf War Syndrome that causes vampirism? I'm asking because my brother, he's a veteran, and—"

Sometimes, I had absolutely no idea how I got myself into these discussions.

You have a lot on your mind," Luis said. He was driving me around Saturday morning in a cute, jet-black Miata convertible he'd rented for the occasion. He looked dashing, elbow propped on his door, driving one-handed, with his handsome Latin features and aviator sunglasses.

God, did he know how to romance a girl. How could I *possibly* be distracted with him sitting not a foot away from me? A hot Brazilian lycanthrope at my beck and call, looking like something out of a car commercial, and I was frowning. I shook my head, because I had no idea how to answer him.

He'd taken me to Arlington National Cemetery because I'd wanted to see it, but it had been depressing. It wasn't just the acres and acres of headstones, of graves, most of them belonging to people who had died too young, or the Kennedy graves, which were like temples, silent and beautiful. JFK's flickering eternal flame seemed a monument to crushed idealism. The graves were peaceful. But the ceremonies: the changing of the guard at the Tomb of the Unknown Soldier; a full military honors burial, with the horse-drawn caisson and twenty-one-gun salute. All these rituals of death. They seemed so desperate. Did honoring the dead comfort us, really? Did it really do anything to fill the holes our loved ones left behind?

T.J. didn't have a grave to visit. If he did, would I feel better? Less forlorn? If he had a grave, it would be in Denver, where I couldn't go, so it was all moot.

I'm sorry, T.J.

Stop it.

After the cemetery, we drove out of town to the state park where Luis spent full moon nights. He wanted me to be comfortable there. It was nice, getting out of town, leaving the smog and asphalt for a little while, smelling trees and fresh air instead.

We even had a picnic. Another car commercial moment: strawberries and white wine, types of cheeses I'd never heard of, French bread, undercooked roast beef, all spread on a checkerboard tablecloth laid on a grassy hillside.

Luis was trying to distract me. He was doing all this

to take my mind off everything I was worried about. The least I could do was pretend like it was working.

"Thanks," I said. "This is wonderful."

"Good. I had hoped you'd smile at least once today."

"I bet you're sorry you found me at the museum."

"No, of course not. I'm glad to have met you. I might wish you were not quite so busy."

He wasn't the only one.

I moved to sit closer to him, inviting him to put his arm around me, which he did. "Can I ask you a personal question?"

He chuckled and shifted his arm lower, so his hand rested suggestively on my hip. "After this week, I should hope so."

I smiled, settling comfortably in his embrace. "How did you get it? The lycanthropy."

He hesitated. His gaze looked out over my head, over the hillside. "It's complicated."

I waited, thinking he'd continue. His expression pursed, like he was trying to figure out what to say, and not succeeding. I didn't know him well enough to know if he was the kind of person who'd wanted to become a lycanthrope, who'd wanted to be bitten and transformed, or if he'd been attacked. We'd had a week of lust and little else, which meant we might as well have just met.

"Too complicated to explain?" I said.

"No," he said. "But it isn't a story I tell often."

"It was bad?" I said. "Hard to talk about? Because if you don't want to—"

"No, it wasn't, really. But as I said—it's complicated."

Now I had to hear it. I squirmed until I could look at his eyes. "What happened?"

"I forgot how much you like stories," he said. "I caught it from my sister. I thought she was hurt, I was trying to help her. She shifted in my arms. I didn't know about her, until then. Even when she bit me, I hardly knew what was happening. It was an accident, she didn't mean it. But she panicked, and I was in the way."

"Wow. That's rough. She must have felt terrible."

"Actually, when she shifted back to human and woke up, she yelled at me. Wanted to know why I couldn't mind my own business and leave her alone. By then I was sick, so she yelled about making her take care of me."

"Let me guess, older sister?"

"Yes," he said with a laugh.

"It sounds familiar."

"She was angry, but she was sorry, too, I think. She took care of me and helped me learn to live with this. Now we help each other keep our parents from finding out about it."

At least I didn't have that problem anymore. I'd never have to come up with another excuse about why I was missing a family gathering on a full moon night. "Your sister's in Brazil?"

"Yes. You know what she does? She spies on companies doing illegal logging in the rain forest and reports to the environmental groups. Sometimes I think she's a bit of a terrorist. Frightened loggers come out of the forest with stories about giant jaguars with glowing green eyes."

"She sounds like an interesting person."

"She is."

We'd been there maybe an hour when I glanced at my watch. I shouldn't even have brought it. But I did.

"Could we get back to town by four, do you think?" I said.

He put his hand on my knee. "Is there nothing I can do to convince you to stay a little longer?"

Oh, the agony. I put my hand on his and shook my head. "I'm sorry. Here you are, doing everything you can to sweep me off my feet, and I'm refusing to cooperate. I'm lucky you're still trying."

He grinned. "I love a challenge."

He leaned over to me, putting his hands on either side of me, trapping me with his arms, and moving closer— slowly, giving me plenty of time to argue and escape before he kissed me.

I didn't argue. Or escape.

I barreled into the Crescent at a quarter after four, convinced I was too late to find Fritz. Not that he'd ever speak to me again. I should have been happy with what he'd revealed last night on the show, but enough never was, was it?

My vision adjusted to the dimness of indoors. I watched Fritz's usual table, expecting his hulking form to be there, once I'd differentiated it from the shadow. I focused, squinting hard, but the table was empty.

Jack stood, elbows propped on the bar, reading a magazine. I leaned on the bar in front of him, and he looked up and broke a wide smile. "Hey! I heard your show last night. That was *cool*."

"Thanks," I said, distracted and not sounding terribly sincere. "I missed him, didn't I? Fritz already left."

"He didn't show today."

"But it's past four. He's never late. Does he not do weekends?"

"He never misses a day."

A weight settled into my gut. "Do you think he's okay? Do you have a phone number for him? Should I go check on him?"

"I don't have a clue where he lives."

This was my fault. Fritz was in trouble and it was my fault. He'd talked, he'd spilled the beans, and someone didn't like it. "Are you even a little bit worried?"

He shrugged. "Wouldn't do any good if I was."

Great, another disinterested isolationist. "Is Ahmed here?"

"I don't think so. I can call upstairs if you want, maybe he's there."

"Sure."

He hit a line on the phone behind the bar, stood there with the handset to his ear for what must have been five minutes, then shook his head. "Nothing."

"Do you think he knows where Fritz lives?"

"He might."

I asked for a pen and wrote my cell phone number on a napkin. "If he does, have him call me."

Jack tucked the napkin by the cash register. "You're really worried about him."

I smiled wryly. "Remember, it's not paranoia if they really are out to get you."

I called Flemming. Please, no voice mail, no voice mail—

"Yes?"

"Dr. Flemming? It's Kitty."

The pause was loaded with frustration. "I really don't have time—"

"Where's Fritz?"

"Who?"

"Don't give me that. He's an old werewolf, German. He said you talked to him. Where is he?"

"How should I know—"

"He always comes to . . . to this one place to have a drink. Four o'clock, every day. He didn't show up today, and I don't think it's a coincidence. He talked on my show, and someone isn't happy—"

"Why should I be that someone?"

"I don't know. But you're my only lead. You must have some idea where he might be."

"Look—yes, I know Fritz. I've spoken with him. If he called your show that's his own business, and I don't know why anyone would have had a problem with it. Not enough of a problem to take drastic action."

I wasn't thinking straight. If I didn't get anywhere with Flemming, I had nowhere else to go, no one else to ask. "I'm worried about him."

"He's a tough old man, he can take care of himself." His voice had changed; it had stopped being flat. I was getting to him.

"He's old. He's falling apart. Werewolves don't get sick, but they do get old. He doesn't have anyone looking after him, does he?"

He sighed. "I have his home address. If you'd like, I'll check on him."

"Can I meet you there?"

"Fine." He gave me the address.

I got the "Thanks" out about the same time I clicked off and ran out to the curb.

Luis was still waiting in the Miata. "Now where are we going?"

I told him the address.

He raised his brows. "You want me to take this car into that neighborhood?"

I smiled brightly. "You paid for damage coverage, didn't you?"

Long-suffering Luis rolled his eyes and put the car into gear.

I bit my lip. I was really going to have to do something nice to thank him later on tonight.

The address turned out to be a tenement building, about forty years old, in dire need of a coat of paint. Or maybe a wrecking ball. Flemming was waiting by the front door, arms crossed, looking around nervously.

His frown turned surly when we pulled up.

"I'm sure there's no need for this," he said as I hopped out of the car. Luis left the engine running.

"You're worried, too, or you wouldn't be here," I said.

"He's on the third floor."

The elevator didn't work, of course. I ran, quickly getting a full flight of stairs ahead of Flemming.

"What room?" I shouted behind me.

"Three-oh-six."

The door was unlocked. I pushed it open.

The place smelled like it hadn't been cleaned in a long time: close, sweaty, dank. Too warm, like the heat was turned up too high. The door opened into a main room. Another door led to what must have been a bedroom; a kitchen counter was visible beyond that.

Stacks of newspapers lined all the walls, folded haphazardly, as if Fritz had read them all, front page to back, and had meant to throw them out but never gotten around to it. Some of the piles leaned precariously. In the middle of the room, an old sofa sat in front of a TV set that must have been thirty years old, complete with rabbit ears wrapped in tin foil. It sat in a corner, on a beat-up end table. A static-laden evening news program was playing.

Something was wrong. Something in the air smelled very wrong—coldness, illness.

Dr. Flemming entered the room behind me, then pushed past me. I'd stopped, unable to cross the last few feet to the sofa. Flemming rushed to it, knelt by it, and felt the pulse of the man lying there.

Fritz lay slumped against one arm of the sofa, staring at the television, perfectly relaxed. His face was expressionless, his eyes blank.

Flemming sat back on his heels and sighed. "If I had to make a guess, I'd say it was a heart attack."

"So he's—he's dead."

Flemming nodded. I closed my eyes and sighed. "It couldn't be something else, something someone did to him?"

"You said it yourself. He's old. Something like this was going to happen sooner or later."

"It's just when he called last night, he almost sounded like he knew something was going to happen to him."

The phone—a rotary, for crying out loud—sat on the table next to the TV. He'd hung up and put it back before this happened.

"Maybe he did." Flemming stared at Fritz's body, like he was trying to discover something, or memorize him. "I've seen stranger things happen in medicine."

I bet he had. He claimed he wanted his research to be public, but he sure wasn't sharing. My anger, the shock of finding Fritz, was too much. Words bubbled over.

"Which is it, Flemming? Medical applications or military applications? Do you have dreams of building a werewolf army like the Nazis did?"

"No—no. That isn't what I wanted, but—"

"But what? What are you doing in that lab?"

He turned away. "I'll call the coroner."

He went to the phone by the TV and made the call. That didn't mean he wasn't going to get a shot at his own autopsy as part of his research. I didn't like the idea of Fritz falling out of official channels into some classified research hole of Flemming's devising, embalmed and pickled in a jar. Fritz had spent most of his life outside official channels. It left him in this lonely apartment, surrounded by newspapers and television, with a glass of schnapps at four P.M. for entertainment. How long would it have taken someone to find him if we hadn't come?

We returned to the street. Flemming said he'd wait for the coroner's van. There wasn't anything left for me to do, and Luis convinced me to leave with him.

As the car pulled away, I started crying.

Sunday morning, I was at Luis's apartment. I'd woken up before him, and lay awake in bed, staring at the ceiling, trying to think. Had Fritz really known his heart was about to give out?

I'd run into a wall. I didn't know what else I could learn about Flemming's research. Maybe there was nothing to learn, nothing but what Flemming had already said in the hearings. I was all worked up over nothing.

My cell phone rang. Luis shifted and mumbled, "Is that mine?"

"No." I retrieved my jeans and pulled the phone out of the pocket.

Caller ID said MOM. Her weekly Sunday call, but hours early. I sat up and pulled the blanket around me. Couldn't be naked, talking to Mom.

I answered the phone. "Hi."

"Hi, Kitty. We're having lunch at Cheryl's, so I wanted to make sure we talked before then. Is this a good time?"

As good as any. As in, not really. "It's okay, Mom."

"How is Washington? Dad's been taping the hearings—C-SPAN's been showing the whole thing, I think. I still haven't seen you in the audience, but he said he did, and he said that's not why he's taping them anyway. He thought you might want to have copies."

I had to smile. "That's cool. Thanks. I'm supposed to testify tomorrow, so tell him to have the VCR ready."

"Oh—good luck! I'm sure you'll do great."

"I just have to answer questions. It'll be fine."

Luis had propped himself on his elbow and was smirking at me.

"Have you had time to do much sightseeing? I visited there when I was in college, we got to see a session of Congress, but it was the House, I think, not the Senate, and—"

Her conversation was so ordinary. It was kind of nice. I made encouraging noises, and avoided saying anything that might make me sound frustrated or depressed. I didn't want her to worry.

Then again, she always knew when I was frustrated and depressed because I didn't say anything.

She actually brought the call to a close herself, almost before I was ready to hear her go. "We should get going. I think Cheryl's nervous about having us over, they've got the new house and I don't think she's got drapes up yet, and Jeffy's teething."

"Tell everyone I said hello."

"I will. Take care, Kitty."

"You, too, Mom. Bye."

"That sounded very suburban. Very American," Luis said, grinning unapologetically.

And there but for the . . . something . . . of lycanthropy went I. "Heard the whole thing, did you?"

"I assume Cheryl is your sister? Which means you have a nephew named Jeffy?"

"And a three-year-old niece named Nicky." He was still smirking. As if I could help it that my sister had picked names straight out of a 1950s sitcom. "Are you making fun of my normal family?"

"Not at all. Not at all." He considered thoughtfully, then added, "*Jeffy?*"

I threw a pillow at him.

After spending all weekend with Luis, I found getting myself to the Senate office building Monday morning almost impossible. I called Ben.

"Hi, Ben? What would happen if I just didn't show up today?"

"When you're scheduled to testify?"

"Yeah."

"They might send federal marshals after you."

Oh. Well then.

I had to stop by Alette's for a change of clothes before heading to the hearings. I thought I might get there before dawn, in time to see Alette, but no such luck. The sun was up when I pulled into the driveway. Tom, the other driver/ MIB, was in the kitchen. He told me that she'd just retired for the day. Briefly, I wondered what exactly that meant. Coffins in the basement?

For once, I didn't ask.

Tom offered me a cup of coffee and said, "We spent the night checking on the vampires you saved from Smith."

"Saved? That's giving me too much credit," I said, muttering into my cup.

He shrugged the comment off. "Some of them want to stay with Alette. They've never had a real place of their own—either they were by themselves or they had abusive Masters. That's why they went with Smith. It must have seemed better."

It probably had seemed better. Some frying pans made the fire look good.

"Is she going to let them? Will she take care of them?"

"Oh, probably. She likes taking care of people." His smile turned wry.

Turned out today was Tom's day off, but he offered to give me a ride to the Senate building anyway. I accepted, finished the coffee, and went to get dressed.

At the Senate building, Ben had something for me—he'd performed some legal wizardry and gotten a copy of Fritz's autopsy report. Flemming was right: heart attack. They were still waiting on some lab tests, but they were calling it a natural death. No conspiracy involved. He was just an old man who'd sensed his own end approaching and wanted to tell his story.

Maybe he'd just given up.

On Ben's advice, I dressed well for the day's session—a suit even, dark blue, with a cream blouse, conservative. He said, don't give them a chance to label me, or classify me as something different or alien. I was an expert witness, nothing more or less.

Not a spokesperson for the entire subject the hearing had been skirting around for the last week.

I'd never advertised what I looked like. I'd never done any publicity stills. When my appearance at the hearings was made public—the panel of witnesses was always made public—at least part of the reason some people were here was to check me out, maybe snap a few pictures for their audiences. I had no idea if I matched their expectations. I was probably younger than they thought I was: mid-twenties, on the thin side, blonde hair done up in a prim bun. Wide-eyed and a little scared. Absolutely not no alphas, no rivalries, and no need to fight among ourselves. But that didn't mean he wasn't in charge, watching. Or that he didn't have clear ideas of how things should be run. And according to him, you stayed safe by keeping to yourself and not getting involved.

I'd stuck my neck out too many times to take that attitude. I tried to keep from tensing up defensively. He wasn't challenging me. There was nothing wrong with what I was doing.

"He is little more than a crazy old man. He has his rituals, his drinking, because they fend off his memories. But everyone else remembers for him, and do not speak to him because of it. I tolerate him here because he is harmless. He is to be pitied for the ghosts he carries with him."

I was about ready to scream with all the double-talk and hints of what people *weren't* telling me. "What did he do? He won't tell me. You call him the Nazi, which implies so much. But I want to know, exactly what did he do?"

He shrugged. "The time and place he comes from say much, do they not?"

"You say you remember. That everyone remembers. Do you really, or have you just made something up and figured it's close enough?"

He was a German soldier from World War II. Everyone else just filled in the blanks. But did that really make him a war criminal? I'd probably never find out for sure.

Ahmed's brow furrowed in a way that was admonishing. Here it came, the *I'm older and wiser than you so sit down and shut up* speech. It was like having a pack alpha all over again.

"Kitty." He spread his hands in a gesture of offering. "I don't want to see you get in trouble."

what one would expect a werewolf to look like: some sultry, monstrous seductress, no doubt. Someone who exuded sex and danger. I'd never exuded either. More like, "Go ahead, bully me, I'm weak and vulnerable." I wasn't up to explaining to anyone, much less a Senate committee, the subtleties of werewolf pack dynamics, how for every scary dangerous werewolf that fit the stereotype, there were a dozen who would just as soon grovel on their bellies. People who imagined "monster" when they thought "werewolf" might be surprised to see me.

My problem was, I may have been a monster, but all the other monsters were so much bigger and scarier than I was.

I had a short prepared statement that Ben and I had worked on. I carried the folder with the typewritten page with me to the front of the room. The week's anxiety hadn't prepared me for this. I felt like I was walking to my execution.

Ben sat in the first row, right behind me, ready to bail me out if I needed it. I'd realized, over the last couple of months of being alone, that even though I didn't have a pack anymore, I didn't have to be alone. I *couldn't* be entirely alone. I'd built my own little pack: Ozzie and Matt at my old radio station, Ben, even my mom. I couldn't be afraid to rely on them.

Ben gave me his predator's smile, the one that I was sure made opposing attorneys cringe in the courtroom. A wolf in lawyer's clothing, if that wasn't redundant. I felt a little better.

I settled at the table facing the committee members. They were like vultures, perched behind their desks, staring down at me. I rested my hands on the table and willed them to remain still.

"Ms. Katherine Norville," Duke said. He didn't look at me, but at the papers in front of him, as if searching for an important piece of information. He took his time. "Welcome to this hearing. You have a statement you wish entered into the record?"

There was a microphone in front of me, which was comforting. Hell, it'd be no different than how I made my living week after week. I was just talking to an audience, no different than any other, laying out what I thought and not pulling punches.

"Yes, sir. Senator Duke, I'd like to thank you and the rest of the committee for inviting me here to testify. This is a rare opportunity, and a rare time, to have so much of what is held as scientific fact challenged and reevaluated. I'm privileged to be a part of the process.

"I am what Dr. Flemming would call *Homo sapiens lupus*. That is, I'm a werewolf. I'm allergic to silver, and once a month, during the night of the full moon, I suffer a temporary physical transformation. What this means for me personally: I make adjustments to my life, as anyone with a chronic, nonfatal illness must. And like most people with a chronic, nonfatal illness, I continue to live, to pursue a career, to gain emotional support from my family. It's a decent life, if I do say so myself.

"These phenomena merit discussion for the purpose of bringing them out of the shadows of folktales and nightmares, and into the light of day, so to speak. So that we might confront fear with knowledge."

And just like in an episode of the show, I waited for people to ask questions.

The first came not from Duke—I was bracing for one of the grillings he'd been giving everyone else all week—but from Senator Mary Dreschler.

"Ms. Norville, you'll pardon me for expressing a little skepticism. It's one thing to have so-called experts talk to me about this subject in the abstract. But to have someone sit here and claim to be a werewolf is a bit much to take. What proof can you give us?"

I could have shape-shifted right then and there, I supposed. But I didn't trust my other half to behave herself in this setting—cornered and surrounded by screaming would-be victims. No way.

She wore a flower pendant on a long chain over her cashmere sweater and tailored jacket.

"There's a blood test Dr. Flemming could probably perform. But for right now—Senator, is your necklace silver?"

She frowned quizzically. "Yes."

"May I see it?" I eyed the security goon off to the side. "May I approach?"

No one said anything, and Dreschler slipped the chain over her head, so I went to her place on the risers. She offered me the piece of jewelry.

I took it in my left hand, curling the chain around my fingers for maximum skin contact. My hand started itching immediately, and within seconds the itching turned into burning, like the metal was hot, right out of the furnace hot. I couldn't take it for much longer; my face bunched up into a wince, and I hissed a breath between clenched teeth.

"Here," I said, handing it back to her. I shook it away quickly, more inelegantly than I meant to, in my hurry to get it away from me. I stretched my hand, which still throbbed.

A red rash traced lines around my fingers and left a splotch on my palm, all the places where the necklace had made contact. I held it out, so all the committee members could see it.

"A silver allergy," Dreschler said. "It might happen to anyone. My sister can't wear earrings that don't have surgical steel posts."

"Trust me, this didn't happen before I was infected. I had to give up some killer jewelry because of this."

She showed a thin smile, almost in spite of herself. I went back to my seat; she didn't put the necklace back on.

Next to her, Senator Deke Henderson spoke. "What else? What other changes does this . . . condition bring on?"

"Dr. Flemming mentioned a lot of it in his testimony. It affects the senses. Smell becomes more sensitive, night vision is better. I'd have to say in my own experience it affects mood as well, things like temper and depression. I've heard some jokes about how women make better werewolves since they're used to turning into monsters once a month." That got a few nervous chuckles. "Although I can't say how much of any depression is caused by the condition, or stems from the frustration of dealing with it."

Henderson, the rancher who'd probably spoken out on the debate about reintroducing wild wolves to ranch country, said, "You just called yourself a monster, Ms. Norville. These conditions, as you call them: do they pose a threat to society?"

I had thought long and hard about how I would answer this question. I'd written out a dozen versions of my answer, practiced it, slept on it. Or didn't sleep on it. People on both sides of the issue might not be happy with what I wanted to say.

"No, sir. I don't believe they do. I could mention a dozen issues that better merit your attention if you're worried about dangers to society—highway safety and cancer research, for instance. If they—werewolves, vampires, all of it—*were* a danger, you'd have had to confront them long before now. For centuries, these groups have lived under a veil of secrecy. They haven't revealed themselves to the public, and they have taken great care to monitor themselves, to ensure that they don't become a danger to society at large, and thereby threaten that secrecy. Like any other citizen, it's in their best interests to live by society's laws. Individuals may pose a threat to other individuals—but no more so than any other person. Domestic violence, for example, poses a much greater danger to more people, I think."

The veil of secrecy was gone, now. The centuries of cultural conditioning that we lived by, as governed by the packs and the vampire Families, by gathering places like the Crescent and patriarchs like Ahmed, all of it swept away. A lot of people weren't going to like it. I didn't know what would happen next, what would come of all this. I felt like I was in the middle of the show, with no other choice but to plunge forward. I clung to the familiarity of that fatalism.

Senator Duke pointedly adjusted his microphone to draw attention to himself. My heartbeat quickened. He had not been kind to witnesses this week. I suspected he had saved the bulk of his ire for me.

He said, "Ms. Norville. As a werewolf, have you ever killed anyone?"

He'd done his research, I was sure. He had to know the answer to that.

The whole truth and nothing but the truth. "Yes, sir. I have."

The murmur of the audience sounded like the distant crash of waves. I heard pens scratching on paper. How nice, that some people still used pen and paper.

"Care to explain?" Duke drawled.

"The Denver police have a report of the incident. The situation was self-defense. He—the man I killed—was also a werewolf, and he had murdered several women. When he attacked me, I defended myself the best way I could." It may not have been the *whole* truth . . .

"Did you enjoy it? Killing him?"

"I hope I never have to do anything like that again."

"What about your other half? That demon inside of you? How did it feel?"

He was determined to turn this into a good ol' witch hunt, wasn't he? "There is no demon, sir. Just me."

"That's what you'd like us to think, with your fancy suit and lipstick—"

"Senator, I'm not wearing lipstick."

"—and the Good Book says, 'When he speaketh fair, believe him not for there is abomination in his heart'!"

"Does this mean we're moving away from the 'scientific discourse' part of the testimony?"

"Senator!" That was Henderson. Duke shut up, finally. I sighed. Henderson continued. "May we please return to the subject at hand? You're in danger of harassing the witness."

"Well past, I'd think," Ben muttered behind me.

Duke glared at Henderson, and I caught a glimpse of a long-standing rivalry, acrimonious and far beyond compromise.

"Senator Duke, do you have any further questions?"

Duke meaninglessly shuffled the papers before him. "I do. Ms. Norville, you host a weekly radio show called *The Midnight Hour*, is this correct?"

Yay, an easy one. "Yes."

"What is the purpose of this show?"

"Entertainment, primarily. Also education. On good days."

"Not conversion?"

I could hear Ben fidgeting, straightening, crossing and uncrossing his arms. He whispered, "Objection . . ." This wasn't a courtroom. He couldn't stand up and yell it.

"I'm not sure I understand you. Conversion to what?"

"You don't use your show to recruit?"

My jaw opened and it took me a second to close it and formulate a coherent sentence. "On the contrary, sir. I want to shatter any romantic illusions about these conditions that people might have picked up from late-night movies. I mean, just listen to the show."

"Ms. Norville, how many werewolves do you think are living in the United States today?"

"I have no idea."

"None at all?"

"No. There isn't exactly a space for it on the census form."

"Maybe we'll change that. If you had to make a guess, what would you say?"

I took at least a couple calls every week from people

claiming to be werewolves or some other variety of lycanthrope. Sometimes more, if the topic was werewolf-specific. I didn't believe all the claims. Assuming I was only getting a small percentage of the total—

"Really, sir, I hesitate to even make a guess," I said. I wasn't going to stick my neck out on a question like that.

"What about vampires?"

"Look at the numbers for any rare disease. They're probably comparable."

He made a show of holding one of his pages up, staring at it down his nose like he was trying to focus on something, like maybe he'd found the one question he'd almost forgotten to ask. He made a long buildup, which meant it was going to be the bombshell. Even worse than *are you recruiting*?

"On your show, you've met a lot of your kind, haven't you? You've said that most of you have packs, that you tend to congregate. So, let's say there's another werewolf in this room. You could tell us who it is?"

"I suppose."

"If, in the name of security, I needed you to tell me how to find other werewolves, could you do that?"

Um, I didn't like where this was going.

"How many werewolves do you personally know?"

I glared. "I couldn't say."

"Could you give us names? In the interests of security."

"Right now?"

He shrugged nonchalantly. "In the future, maybe."

I leaned toward the mike. "I think the next thing you're supposed to say is 'I have here a list of known werewolves working inside the U.S. government.' Isn't it?"

He frowned. "I was rather hoping you could help me make up that list."

"Oh, no. No way. You guys—I mean you, the Senate as an institution—you've been down this road before. I won't have anything to do with it."

"Ms. Norville, are you refusing to answer my question?"

"I don't think it's a reasonable question. It's an invasion of privacy, it's—"

"I could hold you in contempt of Congress."

The world had suddenly shifted to an old black and white newsreel. This sort of thing wasn't supposed to happen anymore.

Ben leaned forward to say in a low voice, "The phrase you want is 'Fifth Amendment.'"

Duke pointed at him. "Who are you? Are you influencing the witness?"

Ben stood. "I'm Benjamin O'Farrell, Your Honor. The witness's attorney. Under the Fifth Amendment to the Constitution my client refuses to answer your question on the grounds that it may be self-incriminating."

There. That showed him. I sat a little straighter.

"That's nonsense! It's not an unreasonable question! I can hold you in contempt, I can throw you in jail if I want. The moral and spiritual sanctity of this nation is at stake, and right here in the nation's capital we have the spawn of Satan himself lobbying for equal consideration! The Constitution does not apply to you!"

Everyone started talking at once. Well, not everyone. But it seemed like it. I was stunned, glaring bullets at Duke, and I managed to sputter something about showing him my birth certificate proving I was a natural-born citizen and the Constitution in fact did apply to me. Ben was on his feet, talking about suing in federal court for civil rights violations. Dreschler seemed to be in a mild panic, speaking with one of the committee staffers behind her. Henderson was yelling at Duke; Duke was still shouting quasi-religious bigoted inanities at me.

If I'd been a spectator it would have all been very exciting, I was sure.

Amid the chaos, that deeply buried part of myself was rising to the surface, clawing at the bars of the cage I kept her in, wanting to escape, wanting to *run*, on all her four legs. She knew that in a few hours she'd get to do just that, and she didn't want to wait.

I stayed seated and breathed very calmly, because that was the only way I'd keep her, the Wolf, locked away.

Dreschler reached over and unplugged Duke's microphone, right from the back. That didn't stop Duke from continuing to rant, but now his voice was faded and lost in the back of the room. At last, he realized he'd been had. It took him a surprisingly long time. He glared at Dreschler, eyes bugging and face turning scarlet.

"The committee withdraws the question," Dreschler said coolly into her own mike. "And with all due respect, Chairman, another outburst like that and the committee will vote to censure you."

Ben, moving in slow motion, returned to his seat. Someone in the back clapped a few beats that echoed in the chamber. I dared to look over my shoulder to see who it was. Roger Stockton, camera tucked under his arm.

Dreschler sighed, sounding as tired as I felt. "One last question, Ms. Norville. This committee was convened to determine if the work of the Center for the Study of Paranatural Biology warrants greater attention from the United

States Congress, and if the information made public by Dr. Flemming and the Center requires action by the federal government, or poses a threat to the American public. You've been here all week, you've heard the testimony that we have, and you have an insight that none of us understand. If you were sitting up here, what would be your conclusions?"

Was she asking me to do their job for them? Was this my chance to steer policy for the whole government? I spent a moment wishing I would sink through the floor. I hosted a cult radio show, that was all. I wasn't an expert. And a U.S. senator was expecting me to give her advice? Was treating me like some kind of authority? Once again, Alette had called it.

If I blew them off, refused to give them some advice they could use, no one would ever take me seriously again. I'd come too far to deny what I'd become.

"I suppose if I were going to turn activist, this would be my chance. Rally members of the supernatural underworld into some kind of new minority that can lobby the government for recognition and protection. But typically, such people are more interested in anonymity than activism. They just want to be left alone. And oppression hasn't been much of an issue when most people don't believe that the supernatural exists. What Dr. Flemming has done is brought these conditions out of the realm of mysticism and into the area of scientific examination. This is good, presuming that it is done for the right purposes. I worry about the Center's research precisely because its motives are unclear. And I worry that with these conditions now brought into the public eye, such oppression will start.

"I think it's too early to make sweeping decisions. But

I would ask the members of the committee to keep their minds open. I would hope that whatever publicity comes out of this, people remember that these are diseases, and the Americans who have them are still Americans."

"Thank you, Ms. Norville. That closes hearings for today. The committee has a long deliberation ahead of it. We'll hope to reconvene in the near future with our concluding statements."

Henderson and Dreschler stood and booked it out of there like they couldn't wait to be somewhere else. Duke took a moment to glare at me vindictively, like it was my fault he'd lost control of his own committee.

Whatever.

Ben put his hand on my shoulder. "You did okay. Let's get out of here."

"Norville! Kitty Norville! Can I ask you a few questions? How long have you had this condition? Tell us how it happened—did you survive an attack? Do you recommend people arm themselves with silver bullets?"

"We have no comment at this time. Thank you," Ben said.

Ben tried to hustle me out of there. We looked like a hundred scenes aired on news programs, of people leaving courtrooms or hearings. I kept my head up, trying to salvage some dignity, but my gaze was down, avoiding eye contact. Ben stayed close, partially shielding me from the cameras and reporters. He wasn't a werewolf, but right now he was my pack, and I was grateful for the protection.

"Kitty!"

I looked up at the familiar voice. Jeffrey Miles was trying to push toward me through the crowd. He must have been sitting in the back of the room. I paused to let him catch up to us.

He wasn't smiling. His normally easygoing demeanor was gone. He looked tense.

"What's wrong?" I asked.

"It's Roger. He left in a hurry right before the session ended. He seemed really anxious."

Sure enough, Roger Stockton wasn't among the throng that followed me. I'd have expected him to jump out in front of me with that damned camera.

I couldn't help it; his absence made me nervous. I shrugged to cover it up. "Maybe he had someplace to be."

"I think he's up to something," Jeffrey said. "Be careful, Kitty."

I nodded, uncertain. Why would Roger be up to something? We were buddies now, right? Someone shoved between us, and the crowd carried me away. Ben kept his hand on my elbow until we made it outside.

Bradley waited at the curb with Alette's car.

"You should let him give you a ride back to your hotel," I said.

Ben looked over his shoulder at the reporters and agreed. The car doors finally shut out the chaos.

"You're off to go all furry now, I assume," Ben said.

I couldn't think of a snide reply. "Yup."

"Be careful. I'm sure that Miles guy is right. Stockton knows what night it is. He'll probably try to follow you."

"We won't let that happen, sir," Bradley said, glancing at us in the rearview mirror.

Ben scowled. "Pardon me if I don't entirely trust a minion of the dark."

I shushed him. Fortunately, the hotel wasn't far away. We arrived before the discussion could degenerate further.

Ben got out, then leaned in before closing the door. "Just be careful. Call me when you get back."

I nodded, bewildered at his vehemence. He didn't look at all happy. I couldn't do anything about that.

"Thanks, Ben."

He closed the door, and we returned to Alette's. I needed to change into something scruffy.

Just after dusk, Bradley and Leo prepared to drive me to the Crescent. I'd meet Luis there. I didn't know why Leo had to come along. He said he wanted the air. Alette said she wanted him to make sure we weren't followed and that Luis would take good care of me. Like they'd turned into my parents who insisted on vetting the boys I dated. I was an adult, for God's sake. I tried to ignore him.

I couldn't wait. Before we even left the driveway, my foot was tapping a rapid beat on the carpeted floorboard in the backseat of the sedan. In moments, I'd be at the Crescent, with Luis and the others, away from Leo and politics and all of it. I was back in jeans and a T-shirt, my hair loose, feeling a weird and not unpleasant charge in the air. On these nights, when I could feel the full moon rising, even though it wasn't visible yet, the Wolf leapt inside of me. She turned into a kid at Christmas, giddy with anticipation, knowing her big moment was close.

I had to stay human a little while longer. I had to keep her locked in, and that was the hard part, because slowly, bit by bit, sliver by sliver, I was losing control. By midnight, I wouldn't be able to hold her in any longer.

"Lovely evening," Leo said conversationally, over the backseat. "I have to admit, I'm a little jealous. The chance to run around with a bunch of animals. I get chills just thinking about it."

It was a perfect night for running. Clear and crisp, with a touch of a breeze. Scents and sounds would carry. Morning would be cool enough to make me grateful to have others nearby, bodies contributing warmth. I rolled my shoulders, stretching, knowing what would come soon.

"You know," Leo continued in his mock-amiable tone. "I imagine you make a lovely little wolf. I'd very much like to see that."

I couldn't bring myself to care enough to tell him to shut up.

Bradley glanced at me in the rearview mirror. "Are you sure you're going to be okay?"

Him, I smiled at. "I've done this before, you know."

"Yeah, but it's a new place. New people. I just thought I'd ask."

"Thanks." I was sick of people asking if I was going to be okay. I'd made it this far, hadn't I?

I was going to be a little late. Just a few minutes. I hoped Luis would wait for me. But really, I didn't doubt that he would wait for me. Just nerves.

Leo said, "Bradley, would you mind pulling over here for just a moment? I'd like to take a look at something."

"Here?" Bradley pursed his lips, looking confused, but came to a stop at the corner, as Leo requested. "What is it?"

I wondered as well. The Crescent was only a few blocks away. I could walk there at this point.

"Don't worry, it won't take long." Leo flashed his grin at me, then lunged at Bradley.

It happened so fast the driver didn't have a chance to flinch. Leo grabbed his head and wrenched, twisting it sharply until it crunched. As a man, Leo didn't look like much. Didn't look strong enough to break a man's neck. But he was a vampire, with a strength and speed that were blinding. Bradley probably didn't even know what was happening.

I didn't even have a chance to scream.

Leo didn't pause before launching over the backseat. It should have been awkward, but he seemed to fly, leaping at me arms outstretched, pinning me. He grabbed my hands, slipped something out of his pocket, wrenched my arms back, and a second later I was locked in handcuffs, my hands behind my back. The cuffs burned, searing against my wrists like they were hot from an oven. When I pulled against them, the pain flared.

Who the hell had silver alloy handcuffs?

Leo rolled me faceup and straddled me, pinning my legs with his body, squeezing his hand on my throat. "Be a good little kitten and this will all be over soon. If you start shape-shifting, I *will* kill you. Understand?"

He wasn't actually wanting to *rape* me, was he?

I squirmed, the handcuffs seared my skin, and I whimpered.

"Oh, you poor dear." He leaned close, breathing against my cheek. I shut my eyes and turned away. I could get through this. Whatever he planned, I could get through it.

His teeth rubbed against my jawline just before a fang dug in. It felt like a pinch.

I screamed, arching my back to thrash away, not caring about him or the silver, just wanting to get away.

He held me too well, pinned against the length of the backseat, my arms immobile under me. I wasn't getting away. He licked the wound he'd made. Then, laughing, he straightened.

"My, you are high-strung, aren't you? Don't worry, as much fun as it might be, this isn't what the evening has in store for you."

Howl, claw, bite, Change, run away . . .

No. Couldn't let Wolf out, couldn't let her panic overwhelm me. Keep it together, stay in my body, my human body. I didn't doubt that Leo would kill me if I Changed.

That took all my strength. I didn't have enough left over to even tell him to fuck off.

From his jacket pocket he took out a couple of handkerchiefs. I was breathing hard, whining with every breath, frozen with panic. Bradley's face leaned against the seat, toward me, dead eyes staring at me. Dead, blank, gone. I should have seen it coming, he should have seen it coming, this shouldn't be happening—

Leo jammed one scarf into my mouth, tying it behind my head. Another went around my eyes.

Breathe, steady, stay anchored. Keep it together, that was what T.J. always said. *Good girl.*

T.J. wasn't around to rescue me this time.

chapter 11

The car door opened, closed. Then another one opened and closed. My nose and ears worked overtime, compensating for the lack of sight. Leo had left the backseat and returned to the front seat. A weight shifted. He was shoving Bradley's body out of the way.

The engine was still running. Bradley hadn't shut it off, only shifted to park. Leo put the sedan in gear, and we drove away.

I didn't count turns, knowing it wouldn't do any good because I couldn't judge the distance. We drove for what seemed a long time. We must have been leaving town. We could be going anywhere.

All I could do was keep breathing, and keep my hands still so the silver didn't burn as much.

Finally, we stopped. Car doors opened, first the front, then the back.

"Sit up," Leo said.

I couldn't. My muscles were frozen. He grabbed my shoulder and hauled me up.

"Out."

Again, I tried. Given enough time, I could have made the epic journey from the seat to outside the car on my own. But I was too slow for Leo. He dragged me out, and he was strong enough to keep me on my feet when all I wanted to do was collapse. He held me up with one hand on my arm. The other clamped on the back of my neck, guiding me.

"Walk," he said.

I stumbled. He moved too quickly, but somehow I got my feet under me. We were outdoors, out of D.C. The air was a little fresher. Where were we? Given another moment I might have figured it out by the smell of the air, but Leo was in a hurry.

A door opened, then closed behind us. We'd entered a building. Here, the air smelled antiseptic, sickly, too much disinfectant and not enough life. The floor was tile.

I knew that smell. I'd been here before. This was the NIH Clinical Center.

We rode an elevator. I tried not to think, because thinking made me scared and angry. The more emotion I felt right now, the closer Wolf came to breaking free. The moon was so close right now.

I leaned away from Leo; his grip on my neck tightened. I had to breathe, calmly and coolly. My mouth was dry. I swallowed back screams.

The elevator opened into the basement. Leo pushed me forward again. I knew how many steps we'd go, I knew which door he guided me through. Without seeing, I could have made my way around the furniture in the office.

In the next room I smelled people. I sucked in air, trying to sense them, how many, who they were.

"My God, was this really necessary?"

I knew that voice. I knew that voice better than I knew the man it belonged to. Dr. Paul Flemming.

"Could you have done it any better, then?" Leo said, annoyed. "You wanted me to bring her, you didn't say how."

Leo rattled the handcuffs—turning a key. Unlocking them. All my muscles tensed. He said he'd kill me and I almost didn't care. I just wanted to hurt him.

The burning metal fell away, but before I could turn, he shoved me forward. I scrambled to keep my balance. I stayed on my feet, and in the same moment tore off the gag and blindfold.

I stood in the werewolf holding cell of Flemming's lab. The walls sparkled silver, pressing against me. The door was locked. Slowly, I stepped toward the Plexiglas wall. *Keep it together,* I told myself. I wanted to face them as a human, to tell them what I was thinking.

Flemming's lab was full of people. At least, it seemed like it. I had to stare, studying the scene before me for a long time, because it didn't seem real. I didn't believe it. Flemming stood near my window, arms crossed, looking hunched-in and miserable, lips pursed and gaze lowered. To my right, near the wall, stood Senator Duke and one of his aides, a man I recognized from the hearings. Beyond them were three hard-core army-looking types: they wore all black, down to the combat boots, had severe crew cuts, and toted machine guns. They glared at me. Leo stood directly in front of me, grinning like this was the funniest thing he'd seen all week.

To my left, occupying the largest space of floor that was free of lab benches and equipment, was a news crew. It looked like a full-on studio job, with a large television camera, a camera operator, and a sound guy with a mike on a boom and headphones. And Roger Stockton, sans handheld video camera. Someone had given him a promotion. An equipment bag on the floor nearby bore the logo of a local network affiliate.

He stared at me, wide-eyed, like a rabbit in a trap. He trembled like prey, like he knew that if I wasn't currently behind a locked door, I'd kill him.

I started to laugh, then stopped, because the nausea wracking my stomach was about to break loose. I swallowed, and my mouth tasted like copper.

"What's going on here?" My voice cracked.

No one said anything. They'd come here to see a monster. Monsters weren't supposed to talk back.

Finally, Roger said, "Live broadcast. I sold the story to the network. It's my big break. I can take my work to the mainstream. Hey, if you'd just given me an interview, I wouldn't have agreed to this." A smile flickered, then disappeared.

"Unreal," I muttered, not aware I'd spoken aloud until I heard my voice. But why stop myself? "Fucking unbelievable. You were supposed to be for real! Searching for the truth, looking for knowledge—not in it for the fame and money! But you really are scum, aren't you? Playing like you're my friend, then selling me out the first chance you get—" My first impressions weren't *always* faulty, apparently. "What the hell are you trying to accomplish with this? What the *hell* do you think is going to happen? And *you*." I pressed my hands to the glass in front of Leo. "What are *you* getting out of this? Does Alette know you're working for them? God, of course not—you wouldn't have killed Bradley then. You're moving against Alette, aren't you?" His expression of amusement didn't waver.

Duke said with a tone of disgust, "We don't have to explain ourselves."

"It's just for the night," Flemming said softly. "You'll be free to go in the morning."

Then, I did laugh. Bitter, hysterical laughter. I shut my mouth before it could become a howl. "Are you kidding me? Do you think that makes everything all right? You're supposed to be a scientist, Flemming. You call this *science*?"

"I think he calls it public relations," Leo said. "He's a bureaucrat. Well, gentlemen, it's been lovely working with you, but I have business elsewhere." The vampire wore a sly grin on his face, looking terribly amused. "Doctor, if you'll remember our agreement?"

If anything, Flemming became more pale and uncomfortable-looking, kneading the fabric of his jacket sleeves. He looked over at the soldiers and nodded. Two of them moved toward the door and waited.

Leo tossed me a salute. "Take care of yourself, Miss Norville."

He stalked out of the room without waiting for a response. The two soldiers followed him.

Soldiers. Flemming had given the bastard backup. I had to call Alette. Would someone let me call Alette?

Senator Duke marched over to the doctor and pointed an accusing finger at the door Leo had just left through. "Dr. Flemming, I have to protest you making deals with that monster. When I agreed to help you, you said nothing about working with the likes of *that*."

"I think there's some debate about who's helping whom here, Senator. I'm giving you the evidence you want. You said you didn't want to be involved in collecting that evidence."

"You'd do well to remember you wouldn't even have a chance to save your research if it weren't for me."

"I seriously wonder about that." He kept his gaze focused on me. I felt like a bug under a microscope.

I had to move. I had to get out of here. I saw the way out—through the door, past my enemies. Had to be a way out. If I kept moving, walking long enough, far enough, I'd find a way out. Had to turn before I got too close to the wall—it felt hot, the silver would burn me.

"Kitty!"

I flinched, startled out of my manic thoughts. Flemming had uncrossed his arms and was watching me, concerned.

"You're pacing," he said.

Like a caged wolf, back and forth across the front of the cell. I hadn't even noticed.

I couldn't see the moon. I didn't have to. A cramp wrenched my body. I doubled over, hugging my stomach, gritting my teeth, and unsuccessfully stifling a groan.

"Jesus, what's wrong with her?" the cameraman said.

Flemming frowned. "She's a werewolf."

Public relations. That was the game we were playing, was it? Flemming and Duke would both win support for their causes if they could prove, once and for all, that the monsters were real. The hearings hadn't been able to do that; that was all just talk. They needed videotape. Brightly lit, clinical videotape.

I didn't have to give up the fight that easily. There was a way out. If I could keep in control for a little while longer, I could beat them. I breathed, taking a moment to center myself, to convince my body to stay human. *You'll be out soon*, I told Wolf. *Just give me the next hour or so*.

She settled. We lived by compromise, my Wolf and I. She understood that the human half had to fight this battle.

"Roger, come here. I have to talk to you." I stood near the glass wall, by the dinner tray slot. I turned my back to the others.

"Why?" He laughed nervously. "You look like you want to kill me."

"That's because I do. But I won't. Come here."

I must have sounded serious, because he obeyed. Stockton crept forward slowly, like he thought I could break out of here. I couldn't; leaning on the Plexiglas told me it was solid. The hinges on the door were strong—and painted with silver. I might be able to break through, but I'd have to throw myself against it all night and probably wouldn't be in great shape afterward.

Let the human side deal with this.

"I have a counteroffer, Roger. How'd you like to produce the first live televised episode of *The Midnight Hour*?"

His brow furrowed, confused. "What, here?"

"Yup. Look, I know Duke and Flemming aren't going to let me out of here. But if I'm going to end up on TV, I want to do it on my terms. I get my show, I get to have my say, and you get your footage. That's what you want, isn't it? Real live film of a werewolf transformation, in a brightly lit lab, no shadowy forests and night-vision cameras, and you get a front-row seat. I just want a little credit. Duke and Flemming still get to prove their points. Everybody wins."

"What, you want me to put in a phone line, take calls—"

"No, there's no time for that. I just want a mike so I can talk to the audience. A few supplies, some music, I'll carry the whole thing by myself. That's all I'm asking for, some odds and ends and billing for the show. What do you say? You owe me, Stockton." That did come out as a growl. Just a little. I grit my teeth, glared—I couldn't imagine what I looked like to him. Like a werewolf. He stepped back.

"If all I want is werewolf footage, I'll get that one way or the other," he said.

And he was right, of course. I was in a very poor bargaining position. "Then tell me what you want."

He glanced at Flemming and Duke, who were their usual stolid and frowning selves. He hesitated, his face gone stony with thought. His jovial, animated facade had disappeared. Then, he said, "I still want that interview. I'll interview you, then you can do or say whatever you want for the rest of the broadcast."

Dammit, if he asked me any questions I was likely to swear a blue streak at him. I didn't know how much self-control I could manage for the next hour—surely not enough to produce a cohesive interview. All I wanted to do was scream. But I was in no position to negotiate. I wanted a microphone, and if this was what I had to do to get it, then so be it. "Fine, okay."

He pursed his lips and nodded. "Right. We'll do it."

I thought I was going to melt with relief. The night wasn't over yet, but I'd gotten the ball back in my court. Half a ball, anyway.

I said, "Call my home radio station and talk to the executive producer, Ozzie, he'll clear up all the legal stuff." I gave him Ozzie's phone number, and recited the list of gear I thought I'd need. CD player, Creedence Clearwater Revival and whatever other CDs he could scrounge up, a copy of London's *Call of the Wild*, and—

"A rump roast?" Stockton stared at me before writing it down.

"It'll make her much happier, trust me." Let him work out that bit of phrasing on his own.

Stockton conferred with his crew, then turned back to me. "I'll be back in twenty—no, fifteen minutes. Don't start without me."

"Wouldn't think of it."

Flemming looked worried. "What do you think this will accomplish?"

I shrugged, feeling giddy. "Don't know. Don't care. It's just nice to be doing something."

I wasn't supposed to be here. I *really* wasn't supposed to be here. As in, this wasn't the way my life was supposed to go. Even just a few years ago, as a child of yuppies my life had been pretty much laid out for me: a decent degree from a decent university, a decent job—maybe in radio, but probably something nine to five, like sales. Marriage, children, tract housing on the prairie and a golden retriever playing fetch in the backyard. What all the other girls were doing.

Then the attack, and the wolf came, and nothing could ever, ever be normal again. There'd never be a golden retriever in the backyard—dogs hated me now. They could tell what I was.

Still, none of that explained how I got into these situations. Was I too young to retire? Get a nice, quiet job in accounting somewhere?

On full moon nights, keeping human form became

painful, then it became impossible. Wolf had to be free, she had to be released, and if she had to rip her way out, she would. So much easier to let it slide, let it happen.

I couldn't do that, not tonight. Had to stay human as long as I possibly could, had to be in control, know what was happening. I'd had practice at this. I sat still, kept still, breathed slowly. *Just a little while longer, girl.*

I had a couple of tricks I used to keep the Wolf at bay. Humming Bach while thinking of broccoli. My humming was becoming more frantic, and still my stomach churned. The thin line between human and beast was growing thinner. When it disappeared, I'd be gone.

I had to stay on my side of the line. I imagined the line growing thicker. I had to keep it in place.

"T.J., I wish you could help me."

I remembered him holding me, when I started to lose it. *Keep it together*, he'd whisper. *That's a girl.*

Keep it together.

The line remained drawn. I was still human. I took a deep breath, fitting into my skin a little more firmly.

Stockton returned in less than half an hour, more quickly than I expected despite his promise. He must really have been worried about missing something. He carried two big shopping bags. I pictured him running through the store, throwing things into a cart, and flinging his credit card at the poor checkout clerk.

"I talked to your producer. Ozzie, that's his name? He didn't believe me, so he said to call him back and get you on the phone."

Of course Ozzie didn't believe him, and I didn't blame him. I'd avoided TV like the plague. I was so glad I had smart friends.

"Do it," I said.

Duke, still off to the side, showed me an ugly snarl. "You can't think this will help you. The world will still see you as you really are."

"That's what I'm hoping," I muttered.

Flemming turned to Stockton. "I'm having second thoughts. I'm not sure we should go through with it."

"Oh, no," the reporter said. "You were the one who called me, you were the one who arranged this whole thing. I want my story—it's out of your hands."

"Stand aside, Doctor," Duke said. "Let the man work. She can't possibly say anything that will save her from what's coming. Let her incriminate herself."

Stockton called Ozzie on the land line—no mobile reception in the basement. He managed to get the phone cord to stretch halfway across the room, and the handset barely fit through the tray slot.

Ozzie launched right in. "Kitty, what's going on, what's wrong?"

"You'll see it soon enough," I said with a sigh. "Did Stockton bring you up to date?"

"Yeah—he says you're televising the show. But it's not Friday, we haven't announced anything—"

"Just set it up, Ozzie. Make it legal. Secure the rights, grant the license to the network, whatever you have to do."

"Are you okay?"

"No. But don't worry about me. I'll get through it." I hoped. I really, really hoped. "Call Ben O'Farrell for me, will you? Use his cell number."

"Sure. Put that reporter back on."

I handed the phone back and immediately missed Ozzie. I wished he were here.

They talked for a couple minutes, then Stockton hung up.

"Roger. Can I have that phone back for just a minute? I just want to make a call." Two—I wanted to call Alette, and I should call Ben myself while I was at it. Ben and Cormac both. Three calls. No, make that four—Mom. I should call Mom.

Stockton glanced at Flemming, who shook his head.

That was it, then.

Stockton brought the bags to the cell. "If I open the door, will I regret it?"

How far did he think I'd get if I made a run for it? "That depends. Is Mr. Black Ops over there packing silver bullets?"

We looked at the remaining soldier, who didn't twitch a muscle.

"Silver bullets?" Stockton asked.

He nodded, once, curtly. I had no doubt he was a very good shot.

"I'll stand back," I said wryly. Of course, I could let him shoot me and spare myself the next few hours.

Stockton got Flemming to unlock the door and open it a crack—just wide enough to shove in the shopping bags, before shutting and locking it again.

Well, I'd missed my chance to go out in a blaze of glory.

I went through the bags. It was a little like Christmas. He'd brought me a portable CD player with speakers and batteries, a stack of disks, a couple of books—London, Thoreau. And the meat, which I shoved in the corner for later. Couldn't think about that now, even though I could smell it through the plastic.

"You ready?" Stockton said, shoving a personal mike through the door slot.

I wasn't, but I'd have to be. I took the mike—still attached to a cord, which ran through the slot to the news team's broadcast equipment—and clipped it to my shirt. "How's that?" The sound tech gave me a thumbs-up.

I finished searching the CDs. One of them had a youthful and comparatively unaltered Michael Jackson on the cover.

I glared at Stockton. "*Thriller*? You brought me *Thriller*?"

"You know. *Thriller*." He clawed a hand at me and snarled like he was an extra in a certain music video.

The man had no tact. I tore the plastic off and put the disk on anyway. But I cued it up to "Billie Jean" and turned up the volume.

I watched out of the corner of my eye, and sure enough, by the second bar of music, the two news guys were tapping their feet. Stockton was bobbing his head a little; he probably didn't realize he was doing it. Hey, when the music said to dance, you had to dance.

Duke looked like he was fuming himself into a fit; his face was actually going red. But he couldn't do anything but stand there. His aide—who seemed old enough to remember freaking out over this album in grade school— shifted nervously. Like he *wanted* to tap his feet, but didn't dare.

Flemming's expression didn't change at all.

"Just tell me when we're on the air," I said to Stockton. He conferred with the crew's tech guy, then nodded quickly.

"We'll be in time for the ten o'clock news," he said.

I could imagine it, the regular anchor interrupting the newscast with a very special report from Roger Stockton: Kitty Norville, Exposed.

It wouldn't quite work like that. I hoped. I had maybe an hour before the Wolf took over completely. Had to make it count.

I cut off Michael and put on John Fogerty. CCR's "Bad Moon Rising" was the show's theme song on regular nights. It wouldn't have felt right without it.

Wait for it . . . wait for it . . .

"Okay, Kitty, you're on in three . . . two . . . one . . ." He pointed at me. I punched the play button. I let the guitar strum a few chords before looking out the glass wall and facing the camera.

Think happy thoughts. No different than being behind the mike. Don't think about the fact that I can't hide, that I can't be anonymous anymore. This was about revenge, about turning the tables, and to do that I had to be on top.

I smiled. "Greetings! Welcome to the first televised edition of *The Midnight Hour*, the show that isn't afraid of the dark—or the creatures who live there. I'm Kitty Norville."

The inside of the cell was lit as brightly as the outside, and the camera was at an angle. They'd made sure there wouldn't be any glare. Everyone could see me. All of me.

"If you're not familiar with *The Midnight Hour*, let me tell you what this is all about. Every Friday night for a few hours, I talk to people on the radio. I take calls, I invite guests on for interviews—politicians, writers, musicians, anyone I can convince to talk to me. What do we talk about? Nightmares: werewolves, vampires, witches, ghosts, demons, and magic. All those stories you read under the blanket with a flashlight, that kept you awake on nights when the wind rattled your bedroom window? You may not be ready to believe it, but those stories are real. And if you don't believe it now, just stick around. Because in an hour or so, I'm betting you'll change your mind. I'm a werewolf, and tonight I put my money where my mouth is." Money shot? Hoo-boy.

I turned the music down but let it keep playing. It distracted the part of my brain that was starting to gibber. "If you *are* familiar with the show, you may notice something a little different about the format. You may also notice this isn't the usual time slot. And those of you who are very astute might notice that tonight's the full moon, and you might be asking yourself, what the hell am I doing locked in a room? Those are really good questions. Let me introduce you to the people who've made this possible. Can we get the camera pointed that way for a second? Great, thanks." The cameraman obliged, pivoting the camera toward the other side of the room.

Flemming backed away, shaking his head. But he didn't have anywhere to go. The camera lens pinned him against the wall. Duke, a little more used to appearing on camera, didn't flee. But he glared bullets.

"Let's see, to your right is Dr. Paul Flemming, director of the Center for the Study of Paranatural Biology, whose laboratory I'm currently locked up in. Across the room you might recognize Senator Joseph Duke, who's heading up hearings regarding the Center for the Study of Paranatural Biology. Camera back here, please. Thanks." Keep smiling. Beauty queen smile, frozen and glittering. Oh, yeah.

"I want to add at this point that I'm here completely

against my will. You see, Flemming and Duke are both afraid that cheap talk in a special committee hearing isn't enough to convince the government or the American public that werewolves are real. They both really want to do this, because Flemming wants to keep his funding for the lab, and Duke wants to start a witch hunt. Wolf hunt. Whatever. So they arranged to tie me up with silver, lock me up, and broadcast the results live on national television. You know why they think they can get away with this? Because they don't believe I'm human."

"No, that isn't—" Flemming stepped forward, beginning some kind of protest. I glared him to silence.

"If you thought I was human you wouldn't have agreed to this. You wouldn't have this *jail*. So. I sort of made a deal to try to tell my side of the story before things get hairy. I mean, *really* hairy.

"A couple of things before we go much further. Mom, Dad, Cheryl?" If Cheryl was watching, she'd have called my parents by now. She was always telling on me. "I'd really appreciate it if you turned off the TV right now. You do not want to watch this. It'll upset you. You're probably not going to listen to me, but don't say I didn't warn you. I love you guys. And Ben, if you're watching? Just one word: lawsuit. No, make that two words: multiple lawsuits."

I rubbed my hands together. "Right. Let's get started then. Roger, come on over here."

The reporter slicked a hand over his mussed hair, smoothed the front of his shirt, and adjusted the mike he'd clipped to his collar before moving to stand by the door of the cell. We glared at each other through the Plexiglas, as if we could pretend it wasn't there.

"Also here tonight is Roger Stockton, a reporter for the

supernatural exposé show *Uncharted World*. Hello, Roger. As I recall, you insisted on conducting an interview. Is now a good time for you?"

He smirked. "As long as you're not busy."

"I'm a captive audience. Do your worst."

As much as I hated to admit it, his interview was good. I wished it had been under more comfortable circumstances. He made it a conversation, letting one answer lead into the next question, rather than rattling off a rote list of prepared questions. He didn't jump on the ends of my answers, letting me finish before talking again. He began by asking about the show, how it started, what my policies were, behind the scenes insights. He might not have been entirely pleased with my answers: I didn't say anything that I hadn't already said at the Senate hearing or on the show at one point or another.

Stockton started the wrap-up. "One last question, Kitty. Tonight, those of us here along with the audience at home are going to witness the legendary transformation of a werewolf, with your help—"

"—my completely involuntary help, I want to make that clear."

"Um, yes. Of course. Can you tell us a little about what we can expect to see?"

"Sure. Out of all the movies I've seen, Robert Carr's werewolf films like *New Tricks* and *Bloody Moon* are the closest I've seen to depicting what it's really like. That's because at the end of the transformation you see something that looks like a real, wild wolf—*Canis lupus*. The only difference is the werewolf is usually bigger because of conservation of mass. The average full-grown person weighs more than a wild wolf. What happens in between—

it's hard to explain. Bones re-form, skin grows fur, teeth change—all of it."

"Is it painful?"

"Usually. But most of the time it happens quickly. You try to make sure it goes quickly."

"How do these changes happen without killing the person? Without destroying the body completely?"

"People have been studying this, but no one has a good physical explanation for how the body changes shape without being destroyed. When all is said and done you still have to label this as the supernatural, because it goes beyond what we understand."

"Propaganda!" Fuming, Duke stormed into the camera's line of sight. His face was red and he was shouting, almost to the level of sounding incoherent. "This is a ploy by the left-wing radical media to undermine the truth of the Good Book, which tells us thou shalt not suffer a witch to live! This is what happens when you listen to the words spoken by an agent of Satan!"

Stockton stared at him, round-eyed and blinking.

"I'm not an agent of Satan," I said tiredly. Not that it would do any good.

"Time will tell! You're no more human than the beast inside of you!"

"Senator, for the last time, I have a birth certificate that proves I'm an American citizen, and you're currently violating my civil rights in a big way. Don't make me add slander to the charges I'm going to bring against you."

"Make your threats. I have great faith that the people will thank me for what I've done here tonight."

"Senator, look at this, look at this picture you're showing people: you've got me in a"—uh, probably shouldn't say that word on network TV—"a freaking cage! You're standing there slobbering like a madman, calling a reasonably cute blond an agent of Satan, and you think this makes you look like a good guy?"

"History will prove me right. When hordes of your kind overrun the homes and neighborhoods of God-fearing folk, people will know I'm right and my actions will be justified!"

Hordes? Huh? "Oh, you can just keep talking, because you're digging yourself a hell of a hole, monkey boy!"

"Kitty, maybe not so much yelling," Stockton said.

That stalled the tirade for the moment. I was breathing hard, like I'd just been in a fight. Duke and I glared at each other through the glass. Yeah, he could be a tough guy when I was locked in here. But put him in here with me . . .

I grunted as pain washed through me and ducked to hide my grimacing features. Too late. I'd run out of time. Pain burned through my nerves, down my limbs. I could feel every pore on my body. In moments, fur would sprout.

"Both of you, get away from the window," I said, my voice low and scratching. Surprised, they did so. I had to pull it together for just another minute.

I straightened and looked at the camera.

"Of all the authors I've read, Jack London gets my vote for most likely to have been a werewolf. Even if he wasn't, he spent a lot of time writing about the line between people and animals, civilization and the wild—how that line usually isn't much thicker than a hair, and how it gets blurred. He understood that space better than anyone. That's a lot of what being a werewolf is about: living in that blurred space and learning to reconcile the two sides. The other thing you learn is that a person doesn't have to look like a monster to be one. This is Kitty Norville, voice of the night. If you remember nothing else about this broadcast, please remember my voice. I'm not going to have it anymore."

T.J. had held me the very first time I shape-shifted. I imagined his arms around me now, his voice. *You'll be okay, you'll be okay—*

The Change slammed into me, fast and brutal. A flood bursting the dam. My punishment for keeping it locked in too long. I bent double, trying to pull off my shirt. I couldn't help it—I screamed, and my sight disappeared.

Hate and fear. And all she could do was watch.

The next day I watched a recording of what Stockton's camera crew broadcast. The news station had framed the video with all sorts of nifty graphics, "Special Report!" and "Live!" logos and the like. It made the whole thing seem cheaper, somehow. As I shape-shifted, I ripped out of my shirt—I went bra-less on full moon nights—and squirmed half out of my jeans and panties. Half naked, tawny fur rippling down my back, I toppled to my side, writhing. My limbs melted and re-formed, my face warped—I'd seen this happen to other people, I'd been through it myself so many times. But watching it happen to me was strange, like what I saw didn't match what I knew I'd felt. The transformation looked fluid, one form morphing into the other in a change that rippled outward from the center of the body. What I'd felt was ripping: the human form ripping apart to let the Wolf out of her cage.

In a few seconds a large, adult wolf lay on the floor of the cell, kicking her hind legs to untangle herself from the jeans still pulled halfway up. She was sand-colored, darker fur trimming her ears, spreading down her back, and tipping her tail. On her chest and under her body the fur turned light, cream-colored. She was sleek, alert, her eyes gleamed a bright amber.

She was beautiful. She was me.

Immediately, she ran. Caged, frightened, she searched for the way out, which meant running along the window, whirling at the silver-painted wall, running back and forth. Unfortunately, she covered the length of the cell in a single stride. She pivoted back and forth, staring out at her captors, like the ultra-neurotic predators in a zoo who seem hypnotized by their own movements.

A domestic dog who's angry or afraid might bark itself hoarse—as they were bred to do in their role as watchdogs. In the wild, wolves rarely bark. My Wolf was silent. The whole lab was dead silent, except for the click of her claws on the linoleum. The personal mike still lay on the floor, clipped to my discarded shirt, picking up the sound of it.

Duke dropped to his knees before the window, laughing harshly. "You see? You see what we're dealing with? You can't ignore this!" He looked at the camera and pointed at Wolf.

She shied back, startled, head low and ears pricked forward, waiting for a challenge.

Evidently expecting a slavering, howling beast slamming herself against the window in an effort to attack him, Duke frowned.

"Don't give me that," he said. "Don't play coy. You won't get anyone's sympathy. You'll *show* them what you really are. I'll make you show them!"

He scrambled to his feet and lunged at Stockton, who stood on the other side of the cell. The reporter put up his arms in a startled defense.

Eyes wide, lips snarling, Duke grabbed Stockton's arm and pulled him off balance. Then he opened the tray slot in the door and shoved the reporter's hand into it.

Stockton shouted in a panic and struggled to pull away, but Duke kept him locked in place, bracing with his entire body. Spry old guy, wasn't he?

"Go on! Bite him!" Duke shouted. "Show us what you are, what you're like! Attack him!"

Wolf's tail dropped and she backed away, putting distance between herself and the raving madman in front of her. She knew how to keep out of trouble.

With a soft whine and an air of sadness, she settled in the far corner of the cell—as close to the corner as she could get without touching the walls—lying flat and resting her muzzle on her front paws.

Duke stared, mouth open, disbelieving. Stockton took the chance to break free and pull away from the door.

Everyone stared at the wolf huddled in the corner. Frightened, she just wanted to be left alone. She didn't even go for the meat.

The broadcast cut off there. Watching a miserable wolf wasn't that exciting, the network decided.

chapter 12

I woke up shivering. The linoleum was cold. I hugged myself, but I was naked, lying curled on the floor, unable to get warm. My jeans were all the way in the middle of the floor. My shirt was torn, I couldn't tell if it was salvageable.

The door to the cell stood open.

Sighing, I gathered myself for the effort of dressing. I had to get out of here.

I'd crawled halfway across the floor when I saw Flemming outside the cell, leaning against a lab table, arms crossed, watching me.

Nothing to do but carry on. Quickly I pulled on my jeans and retrieved my shirt. It had a rip up the side, along the seam, but it would have to do. I sat on the cot to lace up my sneakers.

"So. Did you get what you wanted? Besides getting to watch a naked woman sleep for half the night." I tried to sound angry, but my voice cracked, weary to the point of failing.

He scowled and looked away. "I don't know. The network aired the live footage for an hour. They sold the footage and the news channels have been replaying the pertinent clips all night."

The pertinent clips. That meant the thirty seconds of me shape-shifting, and nothing else. None of my words, nothing of what I'd said to explain those thirty seconds. What a farce.

"Is that what you wanted? Do you even know what you wanted?"

He took a shuddering breath and turned his lips in a pained smile. It might have been the first time I'd ever seen him smile. "I wanted to change the world. I wanted to single-handedly open a whole new discipline of study. I wanted to find the . . . the cure for everything. Superimmunity. Somewhere in your biology is the secret to that. If I could just convince the people with money that it's not fiction, that I'm not . . . crazy."

"And you think kidnapping me, locking me up, and putting me on TV is the way to prove that?" I wanted to rip him to shreds. I could. Sprout a couple of claws, run a couple of strides, and be on his throat in a heartbeat. Inside, Wolf was growling. "The one thing you haven't learned is that you can't control this. No one can control this. People—werewolves, vampires, the church, the Senate, everybody—have been trying for centuries and it doesn't work. The Master vampires build their Families, take over cities, bully the lycanthropes, and play their little power games. Packs form and disintegrate, witches lay curses, charlatans make promises. The church holds its inquisitions, the Senate holds its hearings. And in the long run none of it works. This isn't nature, this isn't science, not like you think, because there's this . . . this *thing*, this ineffable part of it all, that takes it out of the realm of knowing. That's why it's called the supernatural, Flemming. It's magic."

He glared, quivering almost, like he wanted to argue but couldn't find the words. I glared back, challenging. Go ahead, start a fight.

His gaze dropped. "Primitive man thought the sun rising and setting was magic, but we know now that it isn't. It's science that they didn't understand. So is this. We *will* understand it."

"If you say so."

"Can—can I give you a ride somewhere?"

One of those moments, those noises that was laughter bubbling into despair, lodged in my throat. The nerve of him. The complete fucking nerve.

"You've done enough." I walked past him, concentrating so that I didn't launch into a run, keeping my head down. Clutching the torn edges of my shirt and hugging myself so I wouldn't be naked.

Part of my Wolf stayed with me. I could never be fully human because of it, despite all my high-toned rhetoric. But sometimes, her instincts were useful. It can be a strength, T.J. had always told me. I'd scoffed at him, because I hated that part of myself that I believed I had so little control over. Now, I used it. Wolf wouldn't collapse in a heap, sobbing, furious over what had happened and dreading what was to come. She'd stalk. Keep her head down and get out of there. If I could just keep moving I'd be okay.

I made it all the way out of the building. Someone had thoughtfully left the door unlocked for me. I kept walking. Kept moving.

I hadn't slept very long. The sky was still full dark, overcast. The air was cold and damp, like it was about to rain. I shivered. Keep moving. It'd keep me warm.

A ways down the sidewalk, where the building's drive intersected the main road, a midsized sedan parked by the curb turned on its headlights. My first thought was of Bradley. He couldn't be coming to pick me up. He was dead. I almost lost it, then. He was dead, and he shouldn't have been.

The two front doors opened and two men got out. It might have been Bradley and Tom, my Men In Black, the way I first saw them when I arrived in D.C. But no. I started to panic, backing up a couple of steps, ready to run. Then I breathed. I caught a familiar scent of gun oil and leather.

They moved to the driver's side of the car and leaned on the side of the hood, watching me. One had ruffled hair, wore a trenchcoat over slacks and a dress shirt unbuttoned at the collar. The other: biker boots, jeans, T-shirt and leather jacket, mustache over a frown. Ben and Cormac, with Ben's rental car.

Now, I wanted to start crying. I rubbed my face, and my hand was shaking.

Ben came forward, shrugged off his coat, and held it up for me, waiting to help put it on me like we were on some kind of date. Didn't say a word. He was mostly shadow, outside the reach of the headlights. I couldn't see his face.

Wolf wanted to run away, but I wanted to fall into his arms. While the two halves argued, I stayed rooted to the spot, unable to move.

He put the coat over my shoulders, adjusting it so it settled in place. The warmth from his body lingered and made me shiver harder for a moment, but I clutched the edges and held it tight around me. His hand stayed on my shoulder, and that made me shiver, too. I hated people, at that moment.

I was crying silent, frustrated tears and couldn't talk. Couldn't explain why I wanted him to go away, and why he couldn't, because I needed a friend.

"Let's get out of here," he said, pressing my shoulder to guide me to the car. I shuffled forward. He opened the back door and steered me inside, like I was a child or an invalid.

Cormac drove. He eyed me in the rearview mirror. "Anyone you want me to beat up?"

I laughed, a tight and painful sound. I gasped for a breath, thinking I might start hyperventilating. I said, "Can I get back to you on that?"

Ben sat with me in the back. "Personally, I like the sound of 'punitive damages' much better."

"That's because you get a percentage," Cormac said. Ben gave an unapologetic shrug.

I steadied my breathing. I was calming down a little. Maybe. "How bad is it?"

"How bad is what?" Ben said.

"Have the lynch mobs started? Torches and pitchforks? Repressive legislation?"

"Too early to tell," he said. "The talking heads are still mulling it over. They probably need to replay the broadcast for another twelve hours before people get really sick of it."

"Talking heads?"

"Every network. Every cable news network. I think the Sci Fi Channel is running a marathon of *The Howling*."

That wasn't going to help my cause. Wasn't anyone in the least bit offended that I'd been *kidnapped*?

"And your mother called. She wants you to call back."

"Are you *serious*?" My voice squealed. "What did she say?"

"She didn't say anything, she just called."

"Did she watch it?"

"I don't know. Call her back if you want to know."

I pressed my face to the cool glass of the window. Maybe if I slept, I'd wake up to find everything was all right. "Ben, what am I going to do?"

"I'd suggest heading to the hotel and getting some sleep."

"I mean big picture. My life, my job, the hearings—"

"Not much you can do about that right now. We'll see about pressing charges in the morning."

That would be up to Ben. I couldn't do anything. I didn't have control anymore, and I hated that. My attempt to turn their brutal exposé into my own show had been a flailing burst of desperation. Had it worked? Had it garnered any sympathy? And I wasn't talking about sympathy for the plight of soon-to-be oppressed werewolves and supernatural beings everywhere. I wanted sympathy for me personally—so that the public would skewer *them* instead of me. Selfish bitch.

This night wasn't even near over, and the ball was so far out of my court I couldn't see it anymore.

"Ben, let me borrow your phone." He handed it over.

Cormac turned a half smile. "Look at that, she really is calling her mom at four in the morning."

Except that I wasn't. I was calling Alette. I'd almost forgotten to include Leo in that skewering.

No one answered. I checked the flip phone's monitor for coverage, which was fine. It just kept ringing, and ringing.

I took a deep breath, shut the phone off, and gave it back to Ben.

I said, "One of Alette's minions helped Flemming and Duke. He's the one who got me into the cell."

"How?" Cormac said. Not offended, like I was. More like with a tone of professional curiosity.

"Silver handcuffs." Cormac nodded thoughtfully. I almost growled at him.

Ben said, "I *told* you to stay away from her—"

"She didn't have anything to do with it. It's Leo, he's working with Flemming and Duke." Which meant Alette was in trouble. But she was several hundred years old and could easily take care of herself, right? They didn't get to be that old unless they could take care of themselves.

Leo had left the festivities in Flemming's lab in a hurry. And with backup, though why he needed backup was anyone's guess. She wouldn't be looking for danger from him.

I had to get to Alette's.

"I have a hard time believing Duke, Flemming, and some vampire minion are all in bed together," Ben said.

"Duke didn't know about Leo. Flemming's been talking to him. But Duke and Flemming, they both want government attention—just for different reasons. I think they both think they can one-up the other when the time comes. It's like they're all playing chess, but each of them only sees a third of the board—a different third."

"What does the vampire get out of this?" Cormac said.

"Contacts? Influence in the government?" Leo wasn't interested in those things, not like Alette was. He wanted pure, simple power. He wanted to play games with it.

Maybe he wanted to start his own games. "He can go over Alette's head, for control of the city. Alette's got the cops, but if Leo got the military—"

We approached D.C. proper again. Cormac was taking us to the hotel. Get some sleep, Ben had said. Not likely. I'd be climbing up the walls.

"Stop the car. Let me out here."

Cormac kept driving, like I hadn't even said anything.

"Cormac, stop the car!"

He looked at Ben for a sign.

Ben said, "If he's got military backing, there's no way you can go up against him."

"Ben!" That *did* come out more like a growl. I'd shifted once tonight; didn't mean it couldn't happen again. I'd never done it twice this close together. It would hurt. I pressed the heels of my hands into my eyes. I had to keep human eyes. Keep it together.

"Kitty," Ben said, looking at me across the backseat. I had to hand it to him, standing up to a werewolf like this. I didn't know if he trusted me not to shape-shift. He only sounded a little anxious. "You can't do anything about it right now. Get some sleep, wait until morning. It's much safer going against vampires in daylight, trust me."

He was telling me what to do. Bossing me around. I might as well be in a pack again.

I wasn't going to put up with that.

We were at the hotel. Cormac slowed down to turn into the parking garage. I scooted closer to the door. Then, I pulled the handle, popped open the door, and rolled out. The car was still moving, jerking me over the pavement. I had to stumble to keep my feet, but I managed to stay standing. I launched into a run.

The tires screeched as Cormac braked, but I didn't look back. I didn't look to see if they followed me.

I must have run for three blocks before I got my bearings. By then, I was thinking I shouldn't have done it. They were only trying to help. Looking out for me, like friends should, no strings attached. Except I was paying Ben.

But what would I have done if they hadn't come to pick me up? Waited until morning and taken the Metro? Gone back for a ride from Flemming?

I had a couple of miles to get to Alette's. I could run that far, but I didn't want to go there, not right away. I put my head down, sucked in night air, and ran. A wolf on the open plains couldn't have gone much faster.

I arrived at the Crescent, pounded down the stairs and stopped at the door to catch my breath. It was closed. Hesitating, I tested it. Ahmed was true to his word. He kept the place unlocked, even on a full moon night. There probably wasn't anyone around, but I had to check.

No lights were on, but my eyesight worked fine in the dark. I saw the bar, moved quietly around tables, didn't see anyone. Let my nose work, taking in scents. The place wasn't empty. Someone was here. Something was here.

I continued on, and movement caught my eye. Past the front of the bar, where cushions on the floor replaced tables and chairs, a gliding shape drifted forward. Sleek, feline, huge. My heart pounded hard for a moment. I'd never seen a cat that big without a nice set of solid bars between us.

His face was stout, angular, more intimidating than any house cat's. His fur was tawny, and circular black smudges covered his coat.

He sat in front of me, blocking my progress, and for a

disconcerting moment he *did* look like a house cat, straight and poised, his slim tail giving a nonchalant flick.

"Luis." I fell on my knees. It smelled like him, even now. More fur than skin this time, but it was him.

He licked my cheek, his rough jaguar's tongue scratching painfully. Laughing weakly, I hugged him. His fur was soft and warm. I buried my face in the scruff of his neck. He remained patiently still.

"He waited for you."

Ahmed appeared at the back of the club, tying closed a dressing gown over bare legs and bare chest. His hair was wild. He must have just woken up. He must have waited, too. I wondered if the two of them had gone running on the Mall, when their animals took over. They could have hunted pigeons.

"You didn't have to do that," I said to the jaguar. "Either of you."

Luis stood and rubbed the length of his body against me before flopping down on the floor and licking his paws, then using them to wash his face.

Ahmed shrugged. "He was worried. I said you could take care of yourself. Then, it seemed that you couldn't. By then it was too late to do anything."

"I was shanghaied."

"So it seems." He sat next to me, lowering himself, propping himself with his hand, as if he were an old man with creaking bones. I didn't hear any bones creak.

"Ahmed, I need help."

"What do you need? I can give you a safe place to stay, to hide you."

I shook my head. "Not for me. For Alette. Leo's the one who shanghaied me, and I think she's in trouble."

He frowned. His whole expression darkened, eyes narrowing, like how a dog looks when it growls. But I couldn't back down. Couldn't flinch.

"You don't owe her anything," he said. "She offered you hospitality, then failed to protect you."

A technicality. He harkened back to the old traditional ideals of hospitality, where people had to offer shelter to travelers who would otherwise fall prey to robbers or wolves on the wild, ungoverned roads. There was something else going on here. The wolves were the ones I was asking for help.

The jaguar had fallen asleep, his lean ribs rising and falling deeply and regularly. He'd curled up beside me, his back pressed to my legs, where I sat.

I said, "If something happens to Alette, Leo will be in charge of the city's vampires. Do you want that?"

"And what if Leo was acting on her orders?"

"I don't believe that."

"You are too trusting."

"Alette's been . . . kind to me."

"And I have not?"

"It's not that. But someone has to help her."

"Please take my warning as a friend, as an elder: don't involve yourself with them. It's not your concern."

He sounded so somber, so serious, using the tone of voice a favorite high school teacher might, when he put his hand on your shoulder and urged you to think twice before hanging out with "that crowd." Almost but not quite patronizing. Utterly convinced that I couldn't take care of myself.

Not that I had a real excellent track record in taking care of myself. But I couldn't ignore my instincts.

If I hadn't been watching him, absently stroking the fur across his ribs, I wouldn't have noticed Luis begin to shift back to human. It happened slowly, gradually, the way ice melts. His limbs stretched, his torso thickened, his fur thinned. Bit by bit, piece by piece, cell by cell.

"What are you doing here, Ahmed? This place, this little empire of yours—you say this isn't a pack, that you aren't an alpha. But everyone treats you like you are. You expect to be treated that way. Maybe you rule by politeness and respect instead of brute force. You promote this ideal of a safe haven so you don't have to fight to keep your place. And it works, I'll give you that. It's the best system I've seen. But you ignore everything that happens outside your domain. And I can't do that."

If I'd given that speech to any other alpha male I'd ever met, I'd have started a fight. I'd offered a challenge to his place—at least, as subtle a challenge as his claim to the place of alpha here was subtle.

He spread his hands and gave me a respectful nod. "Of course that is your choice."

Which meant he maybe hadn't deserved my speech in the first place.

"I'm sorry, Ahmed," I said, starting to get up. He didn't say anything.

I touched the shoulder of the man lying asleep beside me. I didn't do more; I didn't want to wake him.

I'd talk to Luis later. I hoped I'd be around later.

chapter **13**

If I'd had any money with me I would have called a cab. I might have been able to borrow a couple bucks from Ahmed, but I was two blocks away from the Crescent before I thought of that. The shuttle to Georgetown didn't start for another hour. As it was, I jogged. I had to move fast, because dawn was near. I was so tired. I was numb, and barely felt my legs move.

I should have kept Ben's cell phone so I could call the cops. I should have had Ahmed call the cops. Should have, should have—this was why I sucked at politics. No planning ahead.

Leo would be there. I had no doubt Leo would be there, along with the two mortal soldiers. I didn't know what I was going to do about them.

I wondered who would tell Alette about Bradley. And where was Tom? Emma? Were they safe?

I arrived at the townhome; the inside was dark. Like all the other houses on the street, like any normal house should be at this hour.

Then I paused. I could see that the lights inside were

dark, because the drapes over the front bay window, the window to the parlor, were open. They'd never been open before.

Now, what were the odds the front door was unlocked, letting me walk right in?

Slowly, I climbed the steps and tried the door handle. Not only was it unlocked, it hadn't been closed all the way. It stood open just a hair, as if whoever had passed through here had been in a hurry.

I opened the door a crack.

"Did you hear that?" a male voice called from inside.

Wouldn't have to lock the door if you'd posted guards. My heart in my throat, I scrambled off the steps, over the wrought-iron railing, and crouched in the shadow by the wall of the house. I held my breath, even though I thought my head was going to burst. I wanted to run so badly, hear the Wolf's claws scraping on the pavement as we put distance between me and danger.

Hold the line. Keep it together.

The door opened wide above me. Someone stepped out and looked around. Dressed all in black, his face seemed ghostly in the near-light of dawn. He must have been one of the black ops guys that went with Leo. He watched for a moment, carefully scanning the street, then went back inside, closing the door firmly this time.

Leo needed someone to guard the place during daylight hours, the way Bradley and Tom had done for Alette.

The sky was lightening. I shivered and pulled my coat closer. Ben's coat. I'd forgotten I was wearing it. Now, I was glad I had it.

I had to get in there. I had to find out if Alette was okay. My heart was sinking with the growing evidence that she probably wasn't okay at all. The soldiers had to be in the foyer or front room to hear the faint squeak of the door hinges. I had to get them out of there, distract them somehow. They were obviously twitchy. Some kind of noise, then.

I suddenly felt like I was in a bad spy movie.

Some debris lay on the concrete pad of the window well where I'd been hiding: a few stones, chipped plaster, a rusted piece of metal. I picked up a handful of these items and climbed the railing back to street level.

Backing onto the sidewalk, then to the deserted street, I looked up at the townhome's second-story windows. I hadn't played any sports in school. I hadn't been at all coordinated. I wasn't sure I could do this. Desperation convinced me, however. I *had* to do this.

All the strength my supernatural Wolf gave me, I poured into that throw. Pitch it hard, focus on the window right above the bay window of the parlor. I grunted as I let the stone fly.

It hit the brick wall and rattled back to the sidewalk.

I growled at myself and tried again, quickly. It wouldn't do any good to have the soldiers come out on the front porch. I hefted the piece of metal this time and threw.

With a spine-numbing crack, the window shattered. The tinkling glass was like music.

To be on the safe side, I turned to the window above the front door and tried again. My whole body was shaking with adrenaline, but I must have had the knack of it this time. I hit the window—this one didn't shatter, but it crunched and a network of cracks laced out like a spiderweb.

This whole plan depended on them going upstairs to

see what had broken the windows. I had to hope they wouldn't come out the front door.

Did all plans feel this stupid in the middle of the execution?

I ran to the front door and opened it. Leaning in over the threshold, I took a deep breath of air and listened close. I smelled Alette's house, but with an edge. People I didn't recognize had been moving around in here. But I didn't hear anything, no breathing, no footsteps. Except overhead—it sounded like someone was running on the floor above me.

I went inside and shut the door behind me.

The place was dark, empty feeling. I didn't hear any breathing—but vampires didn't breathe.

I moved through the foyer, attempting silence, but the rubber soles of my sneakers squeaked on the hardwood.

The parlor window faced east. The room was almost light, now. Gray and faded, but still light. In another half hour, the sun would pour in.

The furniture had been shoved away to make a clear space on the floor, in front of the window. In the middle of this space, far enough back that I couldn't have seen her from the sidewalk, Alette sat on a chair. She faced the window, like she waited for the sun to rise, like she planned on watching it. Like she planned to die.

"Alette?"

She didn't move. I stepped closer and saw her hands tied behind her back, to the legs of the chair. Rope or cord alone wouldn't have been enough to hold her; there were also chains with crosses on them. Her feet were secured to the chair legs in front. A gag bound her mouth.

Crosses. Leo needed mortal humans to tie Alette up with crosses, which he couldn't touch.

"Alette." I ran to her. Inside the room, the rug squished wetly. What had happened here?

I pulled down the gag, a strip of cotton fabric. It snagged on a fang, but I got it loose.

Her gaze was wild, desperate, rapidly searching me. "Kitty, are you well? What have they done to you?"

I worked on the rest of the bindings. I started to toss the crosses away, then decided I might need them. I shoved them in a coat pocket. "Forced my national television debut. Don't worry, I'm okay. I'm not hurt." Physically . . .

"And Bradley—where's Bradley?"

Dammit. I hadn't wanted to be the one to tell her. This was terrible to think, but I'd hoped Leo had gloated. So at least she'd know.

"I'm sorry, Alette. Leo moved so fast, and he wasn't expecting it."

"No, I imagine he wasn't. It was probably quick, painless?"

"Broken neck."

"Kitty." Her hands free now, she put them on my shoulders, gripping them. Free of the crosses, she was strong, very strong, and at the moment she forgot it. She squeezed, pinching, and all I could do was brace against it, so she wouldn't topple me over. "They're my children, do you understand? My children's children, I've looked after my family all these years. I've provided for them, watched them grow and prosper. That's all I wanted for them, to prosper. Do you understand?"

I started to. Bradley was her great—dozens of great—grandson. And Tom, and Emma, who said her family had been with Alette for decades. Her contacts in the police department, in the government—also descendants. That loyalty came from ties of blood. Would the distance in relationship have made any difference in Alette's mind? I thought of all those portraits in the dining room, the photographs in the hall, in the parlor, all of them were her children. She kept pictures of her family throughout the house, like any doting mother.

"Alette, we have to hurry, they'll be back downstairs any minute." Not to mention the sun was rising right in front of her. I held her hands and tried to pull her from the chair.

"Wait a moment, Kitty—"

"Geez, did a pipe break?" I'd been kneeling on the wet carpet. My jeans were damp.

"Holy water. I'm sitting in it. I can't walk."

Her feet were bare. Not only that, they were burned, the flesh red and shining, rashlike. The red crawled up from her soles, touching every place that had gotten wet. Even if she'd been able to break free, she couldn't walk anywhere. I scented a whiff of damaged flesh.

She looked at me matter-of-factly, though the acidlike touch of holy water must have tortured her.

"Well, that's just great." I looked around, trying to think. I hadn't come this far to be defeated by a damp rug. "If they had this much of it why didn't they just throw it on you?"

"It might not have killed me."

And whoever did this wanted Alette to watch the approach of her own death, through the window, to torture her.

Glancing back at the pale sky, her face was ashen. She set her expression in a stoic mask.

I couldn't just close the drapes. They weren't open; they were gone, completely removed. I had to get her out of here. The footsteps continued upstairs, but the soldiers would be back down in moments.

"I'll carry you," I said, kneeling by the chair. I thought she'd argue, muttering about dignity with her British accent and stiff upper lip. She didn't. Silently, she put her arms around my shoulders and held on as I lifted, cradling her. She was far lighter than I expected. She felt dried up and hollow.

I had no idea where to go with her. I couldn't take her outside, not with daylight so close and no shelter handy. Frantically, I looked around.

"There's a storage space under the stairs. The door is there, it's a hidden panel."

When she pointed to it, I saw the line that marked the door. Setting her down, I wrenched open the thin plywood door, wincing at how much noise I made. Quiet, had to be quiet.

Alette leaned on me, unable to stand by herself. Together, we fell into the storage space. I pulled the door closed just as footsteps sounded on the stairs over our heads.

We lay curled together against a pile of junk, holding our breaths. At least I held my breath. We stared at the door ahead of us as if we could see what was happening outside.

Footsteps crossed the floor of the foyer and stopped at the entrance to the parlor. Another set of footsteps followed.

"Shit," a male voice said.

"Maybe she's already gone," a second voice said. "Burned up."

"There's not any ash. There should be ash. A burning smell. Something."

"You ever see one of them go in sunlight?"

After a pause, the other said, "No."

"Look, even if she found a way to escape, it's too close to dawn. She won't get far—hell, she won't even leave the house. We'll look."

"You don't suppose she turned into a bat or something, do you?"

"Uh, no."

Footsteps crossed back and forth, moved to the back of the house, returned to the stairs. They didn't come near the door to the storage space.

The closet ran the entire length of the flight of stairs, narrowing at the end. Despite this, we didn't have much room to move. In the faint light that seeped through the crack under the door, I could see that the place was crammed with boxes, cleaning equipment like brooms, mops, and buckets, old baby strollers, a high chair, a clothes rack stuffed with coats. Like any normal family's storage space. I got the feeling Alette had clung to the model of a normal family life after becoming a vampire.

I wondered how Leo fit into that.

"My hero." She looked at me and attempted a grim smile. Then, she slumped back, letting out a soft groan. If I didn't know better I'd have said she fainted.

I touched her, shook her shoulder. She was cold, stiff almost. Panicked, I almost shouted her name. I couldn't lose her now.

She touched her forehead, wincing, for all the world like a distraught lady in a Victorian novel. We needed a fainting couch.

I hissed, trying to keep my voice to a whisper, "What's wrong? What's the matter? It's the sun, isn't it? It's too close to dawn—"

"I haven't fed tonight," she said.

I stared at her, astounded. I was holding on to a starving vampire. Could I be any more stupid?

"Never mind that," she continued, trying to sit up. "Leo is still in the house. We've got to find him, I won't have him destroying what I've built here."

"You're not in any shape to go against Leo," I said, thinking of her injured feet as well as her lack of food.

"We can't stay locked up here, cowering, all day." She straightened, pulling herself out of my grip. She moved slowly, stiffly, like an arthritic old woman. "For good or ill, I must face him now. I don't expect you to come along. This is my fight. I'm the one who didn't see Leo's true colors. I don't believe it, almost two hundred years together and he picks now to stage a coup."

She wouldn't last, not in her condition. I'd seen him move against Bradley.

"Would it help?" I spoke quickly, before I lost my nerve. "If you took some of my blood, would it help you?"

"Kitty, if you're suggesting what I think you are, don't—"

"Because I'm not letting you go out there alone in your condition. And I can't take on Leo by myself. Will it help you?"

She hesitated a long, strained moment before saying, "Yes, it would."

"Then you have to."

God, my heart was pounding like a jackhammer. It overwhelmed thought. Lots of people, human servants, did this all the time. Nothing to it.

Except she was predator, and I was suddenly prey. I had an urge to defend myself. Or run. Fight or flight.

"Your wolf doesn't like the idea much, does she?" Alette said.

"No," I said, my voice wavering. "She—I—I mean, we don't much like feeling trapped. I'm sorry, it's under control, it's okay—"

She spoke, gently, soothingly. "I understand. You're being perfectly reasonable. You should be frightened of me."

"I'm not, not really." But I was. I knew what she was, intellectually I'd always known. But this was the reality, that she could devour me and I wouldn't be able to do anything about it.

But she wouldn't, she wasn't like that, she was kind. If only the last week hadn't completely eroded my faith in my ability to judge character.

"Just a little. I promise," she said. "A few seconds and it will be over. Is that all right?"

I nodded. She touched my face. She was a ghost in the pale light. "I will not betray your trust. Do you understand?"

"Yes."

"Are you left- or right-handed?"

"Right," I whispered.

She took my left hand and moved toward me, leaning so she spoke close to my ear. Her voice had a rhythm, lulling. It ran along my nerves, soothing them, coaxing them from taut panic to calm. More than calm—I felt yearning.

"Do not fear me. I would not have you come to me afraid."

She kissed my cheek, and I leaned into her. I let her

hold me in her arms, let her do anything she wanted to me, because her touch reached deep inside me, into my gut. A warmth rose there; my body clenched in anticipation.

Her breath caressed my neck. I might have moaned a little, because I felt so warm, burning up. She held me close, pulling that warmth into her.

"Rest your head, my dear." She guided my head to her shoulder. I shut my eyes and pressed my face against her.

She pushed the coat sleeve up my left arm, past the elbow. She supported the arm—I couldn't have, at that point. I felt like I was melting; I wanted to melt into her. She kissed the inside of my arm, firing all the nerves. I bit my lip, overwhelmed.

She traced a line up my forearm with her tongue, tasting and kissing. My hand closed into a fist, which she braced. Her mouth closed over my wrist, but I didn't feel anything except her attention, her caresses, her love.

The skin pinched, the bite. By then, I wanted it.

When she drew away, I felt like a veil had fallen, or that I'd woken from a dream.

I needed a cold shower. Very cold.

"It's over," she said. And it was. She straightened, pulling away from me. I didn't know where I'd been, but suddenly I was back in the closet under Alette's stairs, in the dark, wrapped in a trenchcoat. "Are you all right?"

"Um, yeah. I mean, I think . . . wow." It made sense, really. All part of that vampire seduction gambit: lure the prey to you, give it a reason to open its veins. Sure cut down on that messy struggling. "Just so you know, I'm straight. Totally straight. As an arrow."

Her voice held a smile. "So am I."

I smelled a touch of blood on her breath. My blood.

She no longer sounded tired, defeated, like she had a moment ago. She sat straight without effort, and the glint in her eye had returned. She seemed ready for battle.

Two sets of footsteps pounded across the foyer, right outside our hiding place. Alette looked out at the sound, frowning. Then, she pushed at the door.

"No—" I grabbed for her but missed. She slipped through the opening before I could reach her.

What could I do but follow?

Outside, in the foyer, she stood tall on her injured feet—except they didn't seem quite as injured. The redness seemed to have faded, just as her face now seemed flushed and lively.

Before her, two black-clad soldiers held handguns pointed at her. They clutched the guns in two-handed grips, straight-armed, sighting down the barrels.

"You don't want to do that," Alette said, her voice like honey, music, seduction, passion, all together. "You'd like to put your weapons down now."

Calmly, she looked back and forth between them. I couldn't see Alette's eyes at this moment. I didn't want to—her gaze focused intently on the soldiers. The men didn't shoot, they didn't say anything. One of them—his arms were trembling, causing the gun to waver.

"I know you're both reasonable gentlemen. You deserve a rest. You're very calm. Very quiet. That's right."

They both lowered their arms slowly, hypnotically, until they were hanging loose at their sides. After that, they didn't twitch a muscle. They didn't shiver, they didn't blink. They stood like statues, caught in Alette's gaze. Their breathing was slow and rhythmic, as if they slept, but their eyes were open. One of the guys' jaw hung open a little. He wasn't quite drooling.

Alette pulled the guns out of their hands and gingerly put the weapons in the closet. She closed the door. She left the soldiers standing motionless in the foyer.

How did vampires *do* that?

I crept past them, hardly believing they wouldn't reach out to grab me.

She went to the back of the foyer, to the hallway that led to the kitchen. "Leo will be downstairs by this hour."

Her gaze narrowed. The hunter had found her trail.

She walked confidently down the hallway, which opened to a modern, impressively furnished kitchen—stainless-steel counters, pots hanging above an island workstation. It seemed to be equipped to prepare and serve state dinners. Who was I to say it hadn't? Alette passed it all by, heading for a door on the far side, by the fridge.

She paused, hand on the doorknob, tilting her head to listen. So, that was the door to the basement, where the vampires spent their days in darkness and safety. Leo might be stretching out for a nap, thinking he was safe.

Or he might have been waiting for us, armed with machine guns.

"Alette, this isn't—"

She opened the door.

Common sense didn't play any part in her current motivation. Revenge probably had a big part in it, along with a liberal dose of blind rage. She didn't wait to see if I'd follow or not.

I followed.

The glow of soft lighting cast an aura up the carpeted stairs. Soundlessly, Alette stepped down.

The basement room was as Victorian in decoration as the rest of the house. Brocade wallpaper, plush carpet, antique lamps. It was a bedroom. No coffins, but a king-sized four-poster bed sat in the back, along with dressers and wardrobes, and a vanity table without the mirror.

Leo sat on the edge of the bed, leaning over the body of a young woman. Her brown hair lay loose over her shoulders, and her hands were folded over her stomach. She wore a college logo sweatshirt and faded jeans.

"It's Emma," I whispered.

"He used her as a hostage. That was how he overcame me. He promised to keep her safe," she said, sharp as steel, biting off the words.

Emma seemed asleep. I hoped she was just asleep.

Leo looked up. He wiped his mouth with the back of his hand—an ominous gesture, though I didn't see what he wiped away. A snarl curled his lips. He stood, clenching his hands, and took a step toward us. He faced Alette across the room.

"You're supposed to be dead," Leo said, his voice low, tight with emotion.

"I've been dead for quite some time, my dear."

I left the stairs and moved from behind her, my back hunched like hackles rising, glaring warily.

His gaze met mine and narrowed. "Flemming set you loose, did he? He's too soft for the game he's playing."

I wondered, if I got a chance to wring Leo's neck, would he tell me what that game was? I could wring it with little crosses on chains.

"You could do what you liked with me if you kept Emma safe," Alette said. "What have you done to her?"

Leo laughed. "Wouldn't you like to know?" He rounded

his shoulders like a prizefighter entering the ring. Alette seemed unaffected, standing poised and still as always.

"You sold me out, destroyed my home, my children. Why?"

Leo laughed, a sharp, bitter sound. "Why? That's simple. You are the worst waste of resources I have ever encountered. You command an empire, Alette. And what do you use it for? *Nesting*. You are an immortal goddess, and you can't seem to do anything but play the part of a stupid woman."

Wow. Not like he was from the nineteenth century or anything.

Alette didn't even flinch. In fact, a new resolve seemed to settle on her, like something inside her had hardened. "Is that so? If you felt that way, why stay with me for two centuries? That's a long time to have to cope with stupidity. I should know."

Leo's jaw dropped, like he was actually offended. I put my hand in my pocket, curling my fingers around the crosses there.

"He's only just now found allies with firepower," I said. "Tell us what Flemming gets by sending his men to work for you. You couldn't have taken over the place without their help."

He scowled. "I don't talk to animals."

"Oh, give me a break!"

"Answer the question, Leo," Alette said, cold and implacable. The "stupid woman" had commanded men for centuries with that voice. Even now, Leo couldn't break the habit.

"He gets a recruiting agent. Someone to help build his little army of the night. The Pentagon has already agreed to back his research when the NIH drops him. That's not what he wants, but he'll take what he can get. They've already given him a Special Forces unit to help run the operation."

Alette gave a sigh that managed to sound feminine and indignant at the same time. "You've sold one master and bought yourself another, do you realize that?"

"Oh, no," Leo said. "You're wrong about that. Flemming only thinks he's in charge. This goes far beyond him."

Flemming was too soft, Leo had said. The scientist looked the part of an academic, but played at military intelligence and black ops. Which was the real Flemming? And if Flemming was out of his league, as Leo suggested, then whose league were we playing in?

"How far?" I said, my voice falling to almost a whisper. "Who's calling the shots if not Flemming? Surely not you. You're a natural-born lackey."

Leo flashed his wicked, pretentious smile. "You'll never know, because you aren't leaving here alive."

He flew at us. In retrospect, he probably only launched himself, springing at us with the energy of frustration and determination. But he did it so fast, he might as well have flown.

Alette must have been expecting it, or she must have seen it, somehow able to slow the time frame down in a way that I wasn't. She was also moving at his speed. She dodged, stepping aside with efficient grace. The move might have been choreographed. They were like two fighters in a Hong Kong action flick, and I was the hapless bystander who was only trying to cross the street.

The move also left the path clear between Leo and me. I couldn't get out of his way fast enough. I could feel my feet backing up, as if I were looking at myself from outside. But my steps were slow, shaking. A whimper started in the back of my throat. Submissive, be submissive, lower than him—

He wouldn't listen to that.

I held the fist full of crosses in front of me and braced.

He didn't reach me, because Alette put her hand around his neck. She shouldn't have been able to stop him. He should have just tossed her aside and kept going. But who was I to decide what a multicentury-old vampire could and couldn't do? She didn't seem to strain, even, and Leo came up short, like he'd run into a clothesline. Her hand squeezed around his throat; her tendons flexing was the only sign of effort.

"I gave you everything," she said. "I'll take it all away."

"No." He gripped her wrist, scratching at it, trying to push her away. He was taller than she was, larger, rougher, yet she held him like he was made of cotton.

She couldn't kill him by suffocating him—vampires didn't breathe. She'd have to rip his whole head off. But she only stared at him, caught his gaze in hers, seeming to give him a chance to apologize, to beg forgiveness. To beg for his life. He began to thrash like an animal in a trap.

"No." He gasped, choking, his voice failing. "You're not my mistress, not anymore, you're not—"

From a reservoir of anger, he lashed out. Arms together, both hands making a fist, he swung around and hit her arm at the elbow. The joint bent, breaking her hold on him for a moment—long enough. He ripped away from her and punched her hard, once in the gut, once in the face. Something cracked, like bone breaking. Alette's expression didn't have time to register surprise.

She fell backward and hit the ground. Didn't move, and my belly turned cold. Leo turned on me, striking with an intent to do damage.

I still held the crosses as a shield, but Leo toppled into me anyway. He planted his hands on my shoulders and shoved, running me to the ground, pinning me to the floor. I clawed at him, the chains still laced around my fingers. The crosses pressed against his face.

He grimaced, his mouth opened wide as he hissed and shook himself to get free of them. The crosses left welts on his cheeks and neck, like allergy-driven hives, like silver did to me. Still, he didn't let up his pressure on me. I couldn't get away.

I didn't know if Alette was in any shape to help me. I was on my own.

Change, you can fight him—Pain burned through me, Wolf starting to claw her way out. The full moon still shone. I still had power. My hands were thickening. Wildly, I thrashed, arching my back, because I didn't want to do this, I didn't want to be trapped, I hated that he was making me Change. Human or Wolf, I wasn't strong enough to fight him.

He laughed, and in another quicksilver move, he grabbed my hand, the one holding the crosses, and jammed it to the floor. He managed to shift until both my hands were pinned, and his knee dug into my gut. He leaned in close, his fangs brushing my neck. Every breath I took was a growl, and he didn't care.

"I'll have you for dessert, my kitten," he said. He was in the perfect position to rip out my throat, and I couldn't do anything about it. I tried to work up enough spit to shoot at his face, since it seemed that was all I had left. My mouth had gone strangely dry, however.

"Leo." Someone new had arrived. I knew that voice.

Leo looked up, hissing in surprise. Then, something whistled. I felt the air whine above me. In the same moment, he fell back, as if jerked on a chain.

Freed, I rolled out of the way, away from Leo, and scrambled back on all fours.

Paul Flemming stood at the base of the stairs holding some kind of spear gun. He lowered it from the ready position and watched his target.

Leo crouched on his knees, staring at his own chest with blank astonishment. A foot-long wooden dowel, like an arrow, protruded from his heart. No blood poured from the wound, even though the spear must have gone all the way through his chest. It looked ludicrous somehow, like it was a stage prop glued to the front of his shirt. The fabric puckered in around it.

So, Flemming *was* good with a stake. It seemed the spot at the top of the food chain was still up for debate.

I gasped for breath, trying to pull myself back into myself, to stay human. Alette had recovered. She sat up, legs folded neatly under her, and watched Leo die. She frowned, her gaze showing sadness.

Leo gave a short laugh, or the sound might have been the start of a sob. He reached for her, then slumped onto his side, his eyes open and staring. The body turned waxen, then ashen, then began to collapse in on itself, turning to dust, the decay of the grave taking place in seconds instead of years. It took his clothes, the stake, everything with him. Everything touching him turned to dust, including a blackened oval shape on the carpet. He was gone.

I expected Alette to regain her feet gracefully, to resume her regal bearing and once again take charge. Instead, she remained on the floor, her eyes squeezed shut, gripping the fabric of her jacket over her heart, as if it hurt.

"How could I be so blind?" Her voice was thin, pained. "How could I be so . . . so *stupid*?"

Those words had been spoken by every woman who'd ever been screwed over by a boyfriend. Immortality didn't change some things, apparently.

She ran her fingers through her hair, and finally opened her eyes to stare at the pile of ash that had once been Leo. Her face puckered, like she might start crying. But she shook her head, and shook the mood away. "He fought at Waterloo, you know. When I met him, he was a shell, broken by what he'd seen there. But he could still laugh. I liked that. I gave him a reason to continue. I gave him a place in my household. Then—I gave him everything. I trusted him. I thought—"

She loved him. I wouldn't have thought it possible. Vampires seemed beyond love. What was more, she thought he'd loved her back.

A wave of fear crossed her expression. In a rush, she stood and went to the bed, sitting beside Emma. She touched the young woman's face, felt her neck, then held her hands. She stared at Emma's face for a long time, and my stomach turned into a lead weight.

"Alette, what—how is she?" I didn't want to know. If I didn't know, I didn't have to react.

"She's not dead," Alette said softly. She didn't sound pleased, though. She sounded resigned. "But—she's no longer precisely alive, either. On the third night she'll wake again as one of us."

Leo had turned her, made her a vampire. Had he seen the opportunity to possess something of Alette's and been unable to resist? I remembered his laugh when Alette asked him what he'd done to Emma. Maybe he'd done it as a joke.

"What are you going to do? What—what is she going to do?"

Alette smiled sadly. "I don't know." She leaned forward and kissed Emma's forehead. Emma didn't stir. Her face was white, bloodless.

Alette took a blanket from a trunk at the foot of the bed and spread it over Emma.

Flemming held the spear gun down by his side and slumped against the wall.

I swallowed, to make sure my throat was still human, that I still had a voice. "Why? Why are you here? Why did you do . . . that?"

"He was dangerous."

"Dangerous to whom? To you? To your research? Aren't you worried about losing your recruiting agent?"

"But would he recruit for me, or handpick the people he wanted on the inside of an elite military unit? I know he was spying on me." He glanced at Alette, then lowered his gaze. "I was being used. By everyone. Duke, Leo, the DOD—"

"Wait, what? The DOD?"

"Department of Defense. One door closes, another opens. Isn't that what people say? The military sees possibilities in my research. The NIH isn't going to continue my funding, not after this."

"Damn straight. Why did you ever go along with Duke? He's a nutcase."

"We both wanted government recognition. He wanted his control; I wanted funding that didn't come from the military. He was able to get my research a public hearing; I was able to give him his proof that the monsters are real. I thought—I believed that in the end, my science would trump his fanaticism. That Congress would take my proof and do some good with it."

Good defined as funding for his own project. That was the trouble with politics, everyone only believed their own personal idea of what was good and right. And science could become its own brand of fanaticism.

Flemming continued. "Duke misjudged public opinion. He really believes you aren't human, and that Congress could enact laws to set bounties on you, to let people hunt you to extinction, like they did with wild wolves a hundred years ago. He wanted to be a national Van Helsing, and he wanted my help to prove that he was right."

"I think you both came off looking like assholes," I said. "I think Jack London won. So the NIH cuts your funding, and the military welcomes you with open arms? You looked for military funding—Fritz gave you ideas. You don't care where the money comes from."

His voice turned harsh. "I got very good at telling the people with money exactly what they wanted to hear. Most researchers do. I told the DOD what I thought I could do, and by the time I decided that wasn't what I wanted . . . But I'm done, now. After this, I'll tell them all that I'm finished."

I wanted to wring his neck. "You can really just walk away? I don't believe you."

The expression he shot back at me was conflicted, full of hurt but also tinted with anger. His jaw clenched. The grip on his spear gun tightened, and with a pang I realized he was standing between me and the stairway.

"Kitty, that's enough." Alette rose from the bed and brushed off her skirt as if she'd just come in from a stroll. "Dr. Flemming, I suppose I ought to thank you for your timely arrival. Then again, I suppose it was the least you could do for helping to bring about this situation in the first place."

"I didn't do it for you," he said. "I'm tired of being a pawn."

"You very nearly decided that too late." She set her gaze on him, and for all that she was a slighter, slimmer figure than Leo, she radiated a menace that he hadn't been able to manage. Leo had been all about bravado.

Flemming reached to a long pouch strapped over his shoulder, which held more spears.

I thought I was going to have to break up a fight between them, but we were all startled by noises pounding on the floor above us, echoing over our heads. A door slammed open, several sets of footsteps ran, probably across the foyer.

Upstairs, in the kitchen, a male voice said, "Clear!" Another said, "The basement?"

I could fight. To the last breath, I could do it. Alette joined me in the center of the room; we stood side by side. Flemming remained at the base of the stairs, looking up.

The stairs creaked as someone made his way down, slowly and carefully. Another one followed. Two people. I took a deep breath, my nose flaring to catch a scent. Male sweat, leather jacket, an air of taut nerves and tired bodies, gun oil—

Cormac emerged from the shadow, gun raised and

ready. Ben followed a step behind him, a stake in one hand and mallet in the other. Flemming pointed his spear gun at Cormac, and for a moment the two looked like they were going to face off.

My knees turned to pudding. I thought I was going to faint. "Hi, guys," I said weakly.

Cormac wasn't going to lower his weapon until Flemming did. The hit man stared at him, expressionless, steady as a rock. Flemming's hands shook.

"Doctor, it's okay. They're okay," I said. Finally, he lowered his arms. Cormac waited an extra beat before doing the same, holstering the gun.

More pounding footsteps sounded on the stairs, and a pair of police officers emerged into the room, which was becoming crowded.

Ben looked around the room, took note of me, Alette, and the pile of ash on the floor. "You mean we went through the trouble of finding this place, calling the cops, racing here in the nick of time, and after all that we missed the fun?"

"There's still one left," Cormac said, eyeing Alette.

I moved to stand in front of her. "This is Alette. She's a good guy."

One of the cops drew his gun on Cormac. Too many people in this room had guns, and it was starting to piss me off.

"Nathan, it's all right, we don't want to start anything," Alette said. The cop lowered his gun.

Cormac rolled his eyes, a *you've got to be kidding* look.

"It's all right, Kitty," Alette said, moving to the side, like she was amused that I'd tried to protect her.

"Alette? This is Ben, my lawyer, and Cormac, my—"

My *what*? "And this is Cormac." She nodded politely. Ben and Cormac still looked ready for action: guns, stakes, crosses hanging from their belts.

"Uh, you guys do this a lot, don't you? Because you look like you do this a lot."

Ben and Cormac exchanged a look, and a curt, comradely nod. Ben sighed and finally lowered the mallet.

I had a vampire-hunting lawyer. Great.

Flemming said, "I'll leave. I don't want to cause any more trouble."

Alette crossed her arms. "No more recruiting, no more kidnapping. Yes?"

He nodded quickly, in a way that gave me no reassurance he'd even registered what she'd said. He turned to climb the stairs. Cormac blocked his way. The hit man glared at him in only the way that a man who carries guns that casually can. Just when I thought one of them might do something rash—they both still had loaded weapons—Cormac stepped aside. Flemming rushed up the stairs, pushing past the cops.

I wouldn't have minded asking him a few more questions.

"It's full day by now, isn't it? I can feel it my bones." Alette rubbed her forehead as if trying to erase the lines of weariness. She glanced at the bed in the back of the room. For a moment, she actually looked old. "Kitty, I don't know how to thank you. If you hadn't returned . . . well."

I gave a tired smile. "If there's anything else I can do to help—"

Ben interrupted. "Kitty, with all due respect, you pay me to give you advice, and right now I'm advising you to get the hell out of this house. I'll help you pack."

He'd wanted me to do that all along. I couldn't really argue anymore. But leaving felt like I was throwing all Alette's gestures of friendship back in her face. I wanted to stay—but I also wanted to feel safe. Alette's sanctum had been violated.

After the last twelve hours, I wanted to curl up into a hole and never come out again.

"It's all right," Alette said in response to my anguished frown. "You'll be safer away from here, now."

I nodded and forced a smile. When had safe stopped being the easy way out?

The pair of cops locked down the town house. Leo's two soldiers had been guided to a sofa in the parlor, where they now sprawled, sleeping it off. I sure didn't want to be around when they woke up. Flemming had disappeared utterly, and I couldn't blame him. He had no friends at that place.

Ben and I took my car to the hotel, while Cormac drove theirs. Ben carried my bags. I was still wearing my torn T-shirt and jeans. I needed a shower, badly. I needed to not remember the TV broadcast. I'd been able to forget, for the last few hours. When we got to the hotel, Ben handed me a homemade DVD and portable DVD player. Shit.

I showered first. I'd watch the video after. But the shower lasted a very long time. I had a lot of bad scents to wash off. Smells of antiseptic science, of calculated cruelty, of hate and violence. Of being beaten up, trapped in a jail cell, tied up with silver. My wrists had rashes from silver and puncture wounds from a vampire.

Eventually, I watched, mesmerized, my room-service breakfast abandoned.

Toward the end, Ben knocked at my door. I let him in.

"The committee's wrapping up this afternoon. You should go."

The Senate committee seemed incredibly far away at the moment.

"What's the press response to this?" I pointed at the screen, where my Wolf had retreated to a corner to curl up in as tight a ball as possible. "What's the media saying?" I hadn't looked at a newspaper yet. In a sudden nervous fit, I turned on the TV and flipped channels until I found something resembling news.

". . . experts verify that the video is not a fake, that what you're about to see is a real werewolf. We must warn you that the following images may be disturbing to some viewers . . ." The news show aired a choice clip: me, my back arching, shirt ripping, fur shimmering where skin ought to be.

I turned the channel. I found a morning show where the familiar, perfectly saccharine hosts interviewed a man in a suit.

The woman said, "By now everyone's seen the film. We have to ask, what does it mean? What's going to come out of this?"

"Well, we have to look at it in context of the hearings that have been going on for the last week. This brings all that information out of the realm of theory. For the first time we see the issue in stark reality, and what it means is the Senate committee is not going to be able to ignore it, or brush it off. I expect to see legislation—"

The next channel, a rather hyperbolic cable news show,

had Roger Stockton as a guest. Just the sight of him made my hackles rise. He and the regular host were chatting.

"Is there a way to tell?" the host was saying. "If you didn't already know she was a werewolf, would you have been able to tell?"

Stockton had become an infinitely assured expert. "Well, Don, I have to say, I think with experience you might be able to spot a werewolf. They've got this *aura* about them, you know?"

"So that whole thing with the monobrow is bunk—"

Oh, give me a break.

And a fourth channel. "Who is Kitty Norville? She gained some fame as the host of a cult radio talk show, and that put her in the spotlight. A spotlight that got a little too bright last night. She has been unavailable for comment, and investigators are looking into the possibility that she may still be held captive—"

"I've been getting calls nonstop. I've been blowing them off, *no comments at this time* sort of thing. Maybe you should hold a press conference."

At least that would be organized. I might be able to claim a bit of territory for myself.

"And your mom called again. You should probably call her back soon."

I went back to the first news channel. They showed a new clip, the Dirksen Senate Office Building where the hearings were being held. A crowd had gathered: protesters, curiosity seekers. The reporter wasn't saying, just that the committee was convening for a final time. Some people were waving signs that I couldn't read because the camera refused to focus on them.

Did they hate me? What was happening?

"I can't do it," I said softly, shaking my head in slow denial. "I can't face them. Face *that*."

"Why not?" He sounded tired. He'd been awake for all of the time that I had, over the course of the night. He'd earned his retainer in spades.

Why not, indeed. I wanted that hole, that safe den shut away from the world, and I wanted it badly. I knew this feeling; I hadn't felt it so strongly in years. "It's all out. Everyone saw me. Saw everything. I have nothing left, that's what it is. I—I feel like I've been raped."

He gave a frustrated huff. "Now how would you know about that?"

I almost swung at him. I had to take a deep breath, to pull that anger back inside. We were both tired and speaking too bluntly. "You do *not* want me to answer that, Ben."

His expression fell. "Look, Kitty. We're going to sue. We're going to litigate the shit out of Duke, Flemming, Stockton, everyone we can over what happened. The whole goddamn Senate if we have to. And that's after the criminal charges are filed. But for all that to happen, you can't hide. Those crowds aren't going away anytime soon, and you're going to have to face them."

I'd started crying, tears quietly making tracks down my cheeks. Everything that had happened over the last twenty-four hours seemed to hit me at once, and the stress was suffocating. Like being in the cell again, silver walls pressing down on me. But he was right. I knew he was right. I'd survived too much to cave now. So I wiped the tears away and drank down the glass of orange juice.

This couldn't possibly be worse than wrestling with a vampire.

chapter 14

I didn't want to bother with traffic and parking, so Ben and I took a taxi to the Senate office building. The crowd had grown until it clogged the street. Police directed traffic. They'd closed the street and weren't going to let us through until Ben rolled down the window and spoke a few words to one of the cops. The guy nodded, then called to one of his colleagues. The two of them cleared a path through the mass of people.

I hunched down, huddled inside my jacket, hiding. People outside were shouting. Most of it was incoherent, but I heard someone preaching, quoting the Bible in a clear, loud voice: *thou shalt not suffer a witch to live.*

A sign flashed, a placard someone waved above the crowd: a vertical acronym with the words spelled out horizontally. V.L.A.D.: Vampire League Against Discrimination.

That was a new one.

I closed my eyes. This was crazy. I should have just gone home. Mom wanted me to come home. I'd called her. I was right—she hadn't turned off the TV like I asked. But she seemed to have disassociated the images entirely. Like she'd decided that wasn't really me. All she knew, I was in trouble and she wanted me to come home, where I'd be safe. Where she assumed I'd be safe.

"Look," Ben said, pointing out the car window to the front door of the building. "The cops are watching the crowd. You'll be fine."

Fine. Right. Just dandy.

The taxi stopped, and my stomach coiled.

Ben paid the driver and said to me, "Stay there, I'll go around and get the door."

I waited. The driver stayed turned, looking at me over the back of the seat. Staring at me.

A lot of people were going to be staring at me in a minute. Better get used to it.

Then he said, "Hey—can I have your autograph?"

I gaped like a fish. "Really?"

"Yeah, sure. How else are the guys going to believe this?"

I bit my lip. Autopilot took over. "You got paper and pen?"

He pulled them off one of those notepads that stuck to the inside of the windshield. I wrote against the back of the seat. I had to think for a minute how to spell my own name.

"That show last night? That was something else. Hey, thanks a ton," he said as I handed back the paper. "And good luck out there."

"Thanks," I murmured.

Ben opened my door.

I looked up, and the crowd made a sound. Like an avalanche, it poured over me, cheering and cursing. I caught sight of two signs, quickly scribbled posterboard jobs their bearers shook wildly. One said, BURN THE HEATHENS!

The other said, WE ♥ KITTY!

God, this was going to be weird.

A barricaded path led from the curb to the front door. That didn't stop people from trying to lean over, hands stretched out, reaching for me. I forced myself not to cringe. Walk tall, chin up, eyes ahead. Ben had his arm across my back, keeping me moving, using his body as a shield. This was like something out of a movie, or a cop show, or Court TV.

"I love your show, Kitty!" someone screamed off to my right. I couldn't see who, but I flashed a smile in that direction. Cameras clicked—by the door, the press corps waited. TV cameras, photo cameras, a dozen microphones and handheld recorders reached out for me.

"Kitty! Kitty Norville! What action are you going to take against Senator Duke and Dr. Flemming? Have you spoken to the senator since last night? What are your plans? What do you think the Senate committee's response to this will be? Kitty!"

"My client has no comments at this time," Ben said. A couple of police officers stepped forward and cleared a path to the door.

If I thought it'd be calmer inside, I was wrong. People in suits packed the hallway. They looked official, carrying papers and briefcases, rushing around with purposeful expressions. Everyone who passed me stopped and did a double take.

"Where'd all the people come from?" I said.

"I think half of Congress is turning up for this. It's funny, the committee doesn't have any real power. They can just make recommendations, but it's like everyone's waiting for the word of God."

I thought people were just waiting for a clue, for an idea of which way to jump: if the authority figures decided I was dangerous, a threat to society, then people could react to that. They'd know to be afraid. But if they decided I wasn't dangerous—maybe people could let it go.

"Thanks for being here, Ben."

He smiled. "You're welcome."

The audience inside the hearing chamber was invitation only. They'd never have been able to fit everyone in, otherwise. Mostly, reporters and TV cameras crammed the place. We were late. The senators were already in place behind their authoritative tables. Senator Duke was absent, but I recognized his aide, the one from last night, standing in a corner. He refused to look in my direction.

I couldn't find Dr. Flemming among the audience, either. So, Duke, Flemming, and Stockton had all ditched. Did that make me the last one standing? Did that mean I won?

What, exactly, did I win?

Jeffrey Miles had made it into the audience. He smiled and gave me a thumbs-up. I wanted to hug him, but he was on the other side of the room.

Henderson leaned close to his microphone and cleared his throat. The general shuffling and murmuring in the room quieted as he drew attention to himself.

"I'd like to thank my esteemed colleagues in the Senate for taking an interest in this final day of oversight hearings regarding the Center for the Study of Paranatural Biology. I hope we can hold your interest. In the absence of Senator Duke, and with the consent of my fellow committee members, I'll be serving as the committee's acting Chair. This is mostly a formality, since the only activity on the day's schedule is our closing statement and recommendations. Without further ado, I'll now read those into the record.

"Due to recent events, and recent actions by a colleague, this committee decided to issue a statement regarding this hearing's subject matter as soon as possible, to reduce any confusion and to head off any speculation about what stance we will take. First off, I would like to thank all the panelists who testified for their time and their opinions. Without the testimony, formulating any response to the existence of the Center for the Study of Paranatural Biology and its research activities would have been impossible.

"This committee has already taken action in making recommendations to the full Senate about how that body should proceed. We have recommended that the Senate Committee on Ethics begin an investigation into the activities of our colleague Senator Joseph Duke, for suspicion of abusing his authority and conspiring to commit the crime of kidnapping. The full Senate may consider a censure against Senator Duke. We have recommended to the director of the National Institutes of Health that the Center for the Study of Paranatural Biology be dissolved, due to its questionable methodologies and possible unethical practices. Its research projects should continue, but under different supervision as part of the National Institute of Allergy and Infectious Diseases, according to all the regulations and guidelines set forth by the NIH. This committee sees no reason why, if the conditions under discussion really are the result of diseases, they should not be studied under the aegis of an existing disease research organization. It remains to be seen what, if any, criminal charges will result from the way in which the Center for the Study of Paranatural Biology conducted itself, especially in consequence of events leading to last night's television broadcast with which we are all no doubt familiar. I have received word that civil charges, at least, will soon be filed on behalf of Katherine Norville against the parties directly involved. At this point decisions and recommendations fall outside this committee's jurisdiction. We gladly leave such considerations to the judicial system.

"In closing, it is the committee's opinion that the victims of the diseases studied by Dr. Paul Flemming and his laboratory have lived in American society for years, unnoticed and without posing a threat. We see no reason why they should not continue to do so, and we urge all good people of reason not to fall into a state of hysteria. Thank you."

That was it. The whole thing was filed away, folded into the bureaucracy to be forgotten as quickly as possible. Which was what I'd wanted, wasn't it? It felt anticlimactic.

The exodus began, senators and their aides shuffling papers and closing briefcases, reporters sorting out their recorders, people massing toward the doors.

This was the first day Flemming had missed. I couldn't really blame him; he had a lot to answer for. And really, if I'd been able to corner him and talk to him, what would I have said? "Sucks to be you"? Maybe I just wanted to growl at him a little.

Maybe I should thank him for saving my life.

I hid away in a corner of the room and called his number. I expected it to ring a half-dozen times, then roll over to voice mail. But after the first ring, an electronic voice cut in. "The number you have dialed is no longer in service . . ."

I scanned the crowd and found the committee staffer who'd been herding witnesses all week. I maneuvered toward her as quickly as I could against the flow of the crowd, and managed to stop her before she left the room. She was in her thirties, businesslike, and her eyes bugged when she spotted me stalking toward her. I thought she was going to turn and run, like a rabbit. We all had the flight instinct, in the end.

"Hi, do you have a minute? I just have a question." I tried to sound reassuring and harmless.

She nodded and seemed to relax a little, though she still held her attaché case in front of her like a shield.

"Dr. Flemming wasn't here today," I said. "Do you know if he was supposed to be? Or where he might be if not here?" In jail, maybe? Was that too much to hope for?

Her gaze dropped to the floor, and the tension returned to her stance. She actually glanced over her shoulder, as if searching for eavesdroppers.

"He was supposed to be here," she said. "But right before the session started, I was informed that he'd be absent. That he had another commitment."

"Informed? By whom? What other commitment?"

"I know better than to ask questions about certain things, Ms. Norville. Flemming's out of your reach now." She hunched her shoulders and hurried away.

Conspiracy theory, anyone?

"Wait! Am I supposed to think that he's been sucked

into some dark, clandestine project and no one's ever going to see him again? Is there a phone number for him? I've got court papers to serve, you know!"

She didn't even look back at me.

The senators arranged a press conference inside the hearing chamber. Henderson and Dreschler answered questions, many of them regarding Duke and what his future in the Senate, if any, might be. Listening between the lines, I felt like they were saying nothing much would happen to Duke. He'd be censured, and that was about it. A slap on the wrist. They expected the other people involved to take the fall for him. Stockton and Flemming. I didn't have enough energy left for righteous indignation.

Then came my turn. After the senators left, I agreed to spend a few minutes at the podium, mainly because Ben convinced me that facing all the reporters at once was easier than running the gauntlet. If I gave some comments now, it would be easier to ignore them later on.

Ben was right. I had to face up to the reputation I'd built for myself. I had to face the consequences of that reputation.

I tried to think of it as being on the radio. The microphone reached out in front of me, and that looked familiar. If I could ignore the lights, the cameras, the rows of faces in front of me, I could pretend I was talking to my audience. As a voice on the radio, I could say anything I wanted.

I let Ben pick who would ask the questions. He was on hand to jump in and save me if I stuck my foot in my mouth.

The first question came from a middle-aged man in a turtleneck. "Ed Freeman, *New York Times*. It's been suggested that you were complicit in arranging last night's broadcast. That it was a publicity stunt to garner sympathy and publicize your show. Any comment?"

My jaw dropped. "Who suggested that? The *National Enquirer*?" Ben made an *erp*-sounding noise. Right, had to be serious. "Mr. Freeman, it's well known that despite the success of my radio show, I've never publicized my appearance. I never wanted to be recognized on the street and that hasn't changed. I was forced into that broadcast."

"Judy Lerma, the *Herald*. How much are you seeking in damages in your lawsuit against Duke and the others?"

I hadn't even thought of that. "I don't think it's been decided. I'll leave that to my attorney."

"Ms. Norville, how and when did you become a werewolf?"

I was going to have to tell that story over and over again, wasn't I? "It was about four years ago. I was a junior in college, and ended up in the wrong place at the wrong time. I was attacked and survived."

"Does that sort of thing happen often?"

"I think you're more likely to get mugged in a small town in Kansas than get attacked by a werewolf."

Then someone asked, "I hear that one of the networks has offered you your own TV show. Will you take the offer?"

I blinked. I looked at Ben. He wasn't so gauche as to shrug in front of the cameras, but his expression was noncommittal enough. He hadn't heard either. "This is the first I've heard of it," I said.

"Would you do a TV show? As the next step from radio?"

Good question. The little giddy show business side of me was jumping up and down. But another part of me still wanted that hole to hide in. Wolf was still scared, and so far she was doing a great job of keeping that fear locked down. But I had to get out of here soon, or we'd both blow up.

I offered a brave smile. "I don't know. I thought I might take a little time off to consider my options."

Ben stepped up and took hold of my arm. "That's all the time we have for questions today. Thank you."

Finally, we left, sneaking out a back door held open by a police officer. At last, I could breathe again.

Epilogue

I stayed in D.C. long enough to talk to Emma.

The third night, two days after the broadcast, I visited Alette's town house just after dusk. Tom answered the door. He looked grim and harried—he hadn't shaved, and his hair was tousled. The iron reserve of the Man In Black had slipped.

"How is everything?" I asked as he let me inside.

"A mess. We're all torn up over Bradley, Emma hasn't said a word. But Alette's holding everyone together. She's an anchor. I don't know how she does it."

"Tom? Is she here?" Striding briskly, Alette followed her voice in from the parlor. She wore a silk dress suit, and her hair was tied in a bun. I'd never have guessed the trauma her household had been through. "Kitty, I'm so glad you came."

Tom stepped out of the way, heading to the back of the house for some business of his own.

"How is she?" I said immediately, without even saying hello.

Alette smiled thinly. "I think she'll be all right. Eventually."

She led me to the parlor.

The rug had been replaced. This one had more blues than reds in it. Emma sat on an armchair, gripping a thick gray blanket tightly around herself. She stared, blank-eyed, at the curtains, which had been put back over the window. Her skin was sickly pale, and her hair limp. She smelled dead but not rotten—cold, static, unchanging, unliving. She smelled like a vampire.

Alette waited by the doorway while I pulled a chair closer to Emma. I put myself between her and the window, hoping she'd look at me.

"Hi," I said. Her gaze flickered. "How are you feeling?" Which was a stupid thing to ask. But what else could I say? I wanted to apologize.

"I'm cold," she said in a whisper. The words wavered, like she might start crying, but her expression remained blank. Numb. She pulled the blanket higher over her shoulders.

"Is there anything I can do?" I remembered what it was like, waking up and realizing that the world smelled different, that your body had become strange, as if your heart had shifted inside your chest.

She closed her eyes. "Should I do it? Should I open the curtains when morning comes?" And let the sun in. And kill herself. "Alette doesn't want me to. But she said she wouldn't stop me."

"I don't want you to either," I said, a bit shrilly. "You had this done to you, you didn't want it, and it's terrible. But it's not the end of the world. You're still you. You have to hold on to that."

She looked at me, her eyes glittering, fierce and exhausted at the same time, like she was on the edge of losing her self-control. "I feel different, like there's an empty place in me. Like my heart's gone, but there's something else there—and it feels like being drunk, a little. If I open myself to that—" She laughed, a tight, desperate sound, and covered her mouth. "I'm afraid of it."

"That's good," I said. "If you're afraid of it you won't let it swallow you up."

"I just keep thinking of all the things I can't do now," she said, shaking her head. "I can't see the sun ever again. I can't get a tan. I can't finish my degree—"

"There's always night school," I said.

"But what would be the point?"

"You tell me."

Her gaze was becoming more focused. I felt like she actually saw me now. Alette was right—she was going to be okay. She didn't really want to open the curtains.

"I'm still me," she said. I nodded. She held the blanket in a death grip—probably for more comfort than from the cold.

I stood, getting ready to leave her alone. She was curled up, staring at the arm of the chair, looking like she needed to be left alone.

"Kitty?" she said, glancing up suddenly. "Can I call you? Your show, I mean. If I need to talk."

I smiled. "I'll give you the private number."

Alette brought me to the kitchen for tea. She already had a pot made up. The kitchen seemed too bright, after the shadows of the parlor. It seemed too real, too normal.

She talked as she poured. Only one cup—she didn't drink tea. I wondered if she missed it.

"She didn't say it, but she's also upset about Bradley. We all are. I'm so glad Tom had that night off. I don't know what I'd have done if I'd lost them both. All three of them, in some ways. Emma will never be the same. She was so full of life, and to see her like this—"

"But you still have her, and Leo doesn't, for which I'm very grateful." I couldn't imagine what he'd have done with her, what she'd have done with him lording himself over her. Actually, I could imagine it, that was the problem.

"Yes," Alette said wryly.

"Something's been nagging me," I said, after taking a sip of tea. "Leo was a lackey. He couldn't move against you without help. He said something about this plot going beyond Flemming. That Flemming only thought he was in control. I've been wondering—who was Leo really taking orders from? The DOD?"

Alette frowned, her lips tightening. "Flemming was the military's contact, not Leo. Leo needed Flemming to get his military support. If Leo had ulterior motives, they served another purpose entirely. I wish I knew for certain. I wish I could give you a name. But the answers lie in shadow. There are stories that vampires tell each other, late at night, just before dawn, to frighten each other. To frighten ourselves. If vampires are truly immortal, there could be some very, very old beings in this world. They may be so old, their motives are alien to us. Some say that even the Master vampires have their Masters, and you would not want to meet them, even in bright daylight. I have kept quiet, kept myself and mine away from those who would seek such power."

People scared themselves with vampire stories. So what scared the vampires? A thing I hoped I never met. A thing that this brief mention of would haunt my mind. My hand held the teacup frozen, midway to my mouth.

"Are these beings like Elijah Smith?" I said.

Like I was afraid she would, she shook her head. "Creatures like Smith, the *sidhe*, come from another world entirely that rarely crosses paths with ours. They are isolated dangers. This has always lurked in the shadows of our world."

"What? What's always lurked?"

"Evil."

That sounded too damn simple. And yet, it opened a range of sinister possibilities in my imagination. I wasn't sure I'd ever met evil: madness, illness, ambition, confusion, arrogance, rage, yes. But evil?

"Just when I thought I was starting to figure things out," I muttered.

Alette straightened and brightened her tone. "I am confident that with Leo's failure, and Flemming's failure, we will not need to concern ourselves with such possibilities. Agreed?"

"Agreed," I whispered. That left one more question. I continued awkwardly. "I know this is a personal question, and if you don't want to say anything that's okay. But how did this happen? You becoming a vampire—is it something you wanted?"

She smiled and lowered her gaze, giving a hint of amusement. "I'll tell you the short version. I was desperate. I was poor, I had two children, and lived in a world where no one blinked at poverty. An opportunity presented itself, and I took it. I vowed that I would never leave my children, like their father did. Not even death would take me from them."

After a pause I said, "I suppose it worked."

"I have never regretted it."

Alette had very much proven herself adaptable to circumstance. The centuries would stretch on and she would still be here with her parlor, her pictures, and her children.

I fidgeted with the cup and saucer. "I should get going. I sort of have a date."

"With that jaguar fellow, I presume?"

"Um, yeah."

"Wait just a moment." She left me to fidget with my tea. When she returned, she held a small jewelry box. She offered it to me. "I'd like you to have this."

I opened it and found the diamond teardrop pendant on its gold chain. "Oh, Alette, you shouldn't—"

"It's something to remember me by. Do come and visit sometime."

She clasped my hand, kissed my cheek, and we said goodbye.

Earlier that afternoon, I'd had one last room-service lunch with Ben. Cormac had already left town, without even saying goodbye. I was simultaneously offended and relieved.

As usual, Ben ate while he worked, shuffling through papers, turning away just long enough to open the door. He'd ordered a steak for me. Rare.

I sat at the table and nodded at the current folder. "What's this?"

"The FCC wants to investigate you for indecency."

"What?"

"Apparently, somewhere between fully clothed human

and fur-covered wolf, you flashed breast on national broadcast television. They've gotten about a dozen complaints."

"You have *got* to be kidding me." Flashing the TV audience had been the last thing on my mind.

"Nope. I rewatched the video, and sure enough, it's there. You have to be pretty fast with the pause button to catch it."

I loved the idea of all the prudish reactionaries who must have taped the show, then sat there with their thumbs poised over the scan and pause buttons, searching for something to complain to the FCC about. And they're charging *me* with indecency?

"I'll tell you what—forward the complaint to Stockton. No, better—forward it to Duke."

"Already done. I think it'll be pretty easy to argue the complaint and prove you had no responsibility for the broadcast."

Damn straight. "I got a message from Stockton." He'd left it on my cell phone during the hearings, like he'd called specifically at a time he knew I'd have my phone turned off so he could leave a message without having to talk to me. He'd sounded downright obsequious: "Kitty. It's Roger. Look, I'm probably the last guy you want to hear from. You'll probably never speak to me again. But I really wish you'd call me back. I've been asked about a follow-up show. I see us laying down a commentary track on the coverage from last night, you know? It could be a big move for both of us, career-wise. I really think you have a future in television. I want to do right by you. Thanks."

That maniac. If I ever decided to make a go at television, it would be without his help. "You think you can sue him a lot?"

"Oh, yeah, about our good Mr. Stockton. Cormac did some digging on our behalf. Have a look at this." Ben handed me a manila folder out of his stack.

I opened it and started reading. There were a half-dozen pages of official-looking forms, spaces with names and dates filled in, and a few mug shots of the same person, a skinny kid with a doped-out gaze and wild hair.

It was Roger Stockton. A younger, crazier Roger Stockton.

"These are arrest reports," I said, awestruck.

"Mr. Stockton put himself through college by dealing hallucinogenic drugs. Not the usual weed, but exotic stuff: opium, peyote, frog-licking, that sort of thing. It seems he was into experimentation, looking for a higher power, saying it was all part of some religious ceremony that he and his friends were conducting. You know how it goes. The charges never stuck. He never served time. But it still makes for fascinating reading, don't you think?"

If this information was leaked, Stockton might be able to talk his way out of it and salvage his career. But until he did, his life would become very interesting.

"Revenge or blackmail?" I said.

"Blackmail? That's illegal. Persuasion, on the other hand—I'm betting Stockton would sure hate to see this stuff come out in a civil trial. He'll settle out of court, or his network will."

Politics. Playing each other to get what we wanted. Was there any way to avoid it? Couldn't we all just get along?

"This is never going to be over, is it?"

"I think your place in American pop culture is assured. You're going to end up as a question on a game show, you realize."

I might have groaned. Ben chuckled.

"Sure, go ahead and laugh. It just means job security for you."

He sat back in his chair, abandoning the paperwork for a moment. He wore a vague, amused grin. "I know what Cormac sees in you."

"What, a target?"

"Not at all. He's downright smitten."

"Huh?" Constantly making veiled threats constituted smitten? To an eight-year-old, maybe. And how many times had he come to my rescue now? Urgh . . .

"It's true. I've known him since we were kids."

"Kids? Really? How?"

"We're cousins. I probably shouldn't even be saying this—"

Cousins? Had to keep him talking. "No, please. Say this. What does Cormac see in me?"

"You're tough. Tough and whiny at the same time. It's kind of cute."

I couldn't tell if he was making fun of me or not. Time to change the subject.

"So you've always known Cormac. Was he always like that?"

"Like what?"

"Hard-nosed. Humorless."

"No, I suppose not. But you have to go back a long way to see him any different. He lost both his parents pretty young. I figure he deserves to be as humorless as he wants."

Even saying "I'm sorry" sounded lame at that point.

"You told me once that Cormac likes seeing how close to the edge he can get without falling off. What about you? Why do you hunt vampires?"

He shrugged. "I don't hunt anything, really. I just look out for my friends. That's all."

Which made him a good person to have at your back—all anyone could ask for, really. That, and an honest lawyer, all wrapped into one.

"When are you going back to Denver?"

"After I file suit in court. Though it may not come to that. I've gotten word from both Duke's office and the NIH that they're willing to settle. Duke won't want to settle, but if the Senate Ethics Committee gets involved, he may come around. There are still criminal charges pending, but this might not drag on so long."

"Thanks for doing all this. I don't even care about the money, you know. I just want a little old-fashioned revenge."

"That's the best part," he said, grinning his hawk's grin, the one that made me glad he was on my side.

Luis had tickets to a symphony concert at the Kennedy Center that night. It seemed a great way to spend my last night in town. We met up at the Crescent.

I wore a smoky gray skirt and jacket with a white camisole. Understated, until I put on the diamond Alette had given me. Then, it looked awfully mature. Sophisticated, even. Like something Alette might wear. I didn't feel like myself.

Ahmed met me at the door. He didn't say a word at first, just closed me in a big monstrous hug until I thought I might suffocate. I didn't have much hope of hugging back, so I leaned in and took a deep breath, of smoke and wine and wild. It smelled a little like a pack.

"Come back to visit, yes?" he said, gripping my shoulders. I nodded firmly. Looked like I was coming back to D.C. at some point. Jack waved at me from the bar.

I sensed Luis come in through the door behind me. I didn't even have to turn around. He stalked like a cat and his warmth reached out for me.

He touched my shoulders and kissed the back of my neck. Fire, warmth, happiness, I felt all that in his touch. Finally, Wolf's fear uncurled. Some light came into her burrow. I felt like running—from joy this time, not fear.

"Ready?"

I almost asked if we could blow off the symphony. But I nodded.

I was glad I went, glad I didn't miss seeing the Kennedy Center. The place was so beautiful, so momentous, walking into the four-story-high Hall of States with the marble walls, red carpeting, state flags hanging from the ceiling. I wanted to cry. Felt like I should have been wearing a sweeping ball gown and not a suit.

People stared at me. At us. The people who had tickets for the seat next to me in the concert hall moved. Everyone watched the news, I supposed. I wilted. I would have stuck my tail between my legs if I'd had it. I would have left, if Luis had let me. Bless him, he didn't flinch once. He walked past them all, holding my arm tucked in his, his back straight and chin up. Like a jaguar stalking through his jungle.

Staring at his shoulder, I leaned in and asked him, "How can you stand it? The way they look at us?"

He said, "I know that I could rip out their guts, and I choose not to."

We stood in the Grand Foyer at intermission. I looked down the hall, taking in the floor-to-ceiling mirrors, the windows framed with soft drapes, a thousand glittering lights in the chandeliers, the immense bust of Kennedy gazing out over what he'd inspired.

A couple walked by. The woman, young and elegant in a blue cocktail dress, brushed past me. Her hand caught mine, hanging loose at my side, and squeezed for just a moment. Then she walked away. She never looked at me.

She smelled like wolf. I stared after her, until Luis tugged at my arm.

After the concert we went up to the roof terrace. Looking southeast, I could see the Washington, Jefferson, and Lincoln Memorials lined up, lit and glowing like beacons in the night. Great men and their monuments. They weren't perfect. They made mistakes. But they changed the world. They were idealists.

Luis stood behind me, arms around me, and kissed the top of my head.

"Thank you for this," I said, my voice hushed. "For showing me this."

"You ever need to get away, take a vacation, call me. I'll show you Rio de Janeiro."

"It's a deal." Like, how about now?

"What will you do next?"

"Take time off. I don't know. Maybe I should write a book." I pictured myself going back to the show, back to the radio station. I sat in front of the microphone, opened my mouth—and nothing came out.

I had a place in mind, a small town where I'd spent a couple of weeks one summer in college. I could go rent a cabin, be philosophical, run wild in the woods.

And try to remember how to be an idealist.

BONUS READING!

Turn the page to enjoy a free short story
featuring our favorite werewolf, Kitty Norville!

Kitty Meets the Band

by Carrie Vaughn

Then, keep reading for a special
sneak preview of the next Kitty novel.

About the Author

CARRIE VAUGHN survived the nomadic childhood of the typical Air Force brat, with stops in California, Florida, North Dakota, Maryland, and Colorado. She holds a master's in English literature and collects hobbies—fencing and sewing are currently high on the list. She lives in Boulder, Colorado, and can be found on the Web at www.carrievaughn.com.

Kitty Meets the Band

WELCOME BACK, LISTENERS. For those of you just joining us, I'm Kitty Norville and this is *The Midnight Hour*. I just got a call from my scheduled guests this evening, the band Plague of Locusts, and I'm afraid they're caught in traffic and are going to be a little late, another ten minutes or so. So I'm going to take a few more calls while we're waiting for them to arrive. Our topic this evening: music and the supernatural.

"In the nineteenth century, rumor had it that the great violinist Paganini sold his soul to the devil in exchange for his amazing virtuoso abilities. Many artists are said to be inspired by the Muses. And music soothes the savage beast. What exactly is the mystical nature of music? Are all these tales mere metaphor, or is something supernatural controlling our musical impulses? I want to hear from you. Eddy from Baltimore, you're on the air."

"Hi, Kitty! Whoa, thanks for taking my call."

"No problem, Eddy. What do you have for me?"

"I want to sell my soul to the devil. If I had the chance,

I'd do it in a heartbeat. To play guitar like Hendrix—oh man, I'd do just about *anything*!"

"How about practice?"

"It's not enough. I've been practicing for *years*. All that time and I can do 'Stairway to Heaven,' and that's it. What Hendrix had? That's not natural."

"Do you think Hendrix sold his soul to the devil?"

"Wouldn't surprise me. So, Kitty—have any idea how I'd go about doing that?"

"What, selling your soul to the devil? Are you sure that's such a good idea?"

"Why not? It's not like I'm using my soul for anything else."

Oh man, talk about missing the point. "I get enough accusations from the religious Right that I'm damning people's souls, I'm not sure I want to put any more fuel on that fire. But the answer is no, I have no idea how you'd go about selling your soul to the devil. Sorry. Next call, please. Rebecca, hello."

"Kitty, hi." The woman's voice was low, vaguely desperate.

"Hello. You have a question or a story?"

"A question, I think. Like, you know when you get a song stuck in your head, and it drives you crazy, and no matter how much you try to think of something else you can't stop it from playing in your head? Right now I have 'Muskrat Love' stuck. It's been stuck there for days. It's . . . it's driving me crazy." Her voice turned ominous. If she told me she was holding a butcher knife just then, I wouldn't have been surprised.

I tried to sound as sympathetic as possible. "The Captain and Tennille version of the song, I assume?"

time. Maybe it could bring him back. If I had the chance, if I thought I could, I'd try."

I rubbed my face and pinched my nose to stop tears. This happened every now and then. I didn't know what to say. Nothing I could say would be the right thing.

"Maybe not all the stories start out as true. A lot of them start out as wishes, I think. The Orpheus myth, it takes something powerful that people can do—make music—and turns it into something powerful we wish we could do. Like bring back our loved ones. Ellen, I know this sounds trite, but I'm betting there's a part of him, part of his spirit that comes through every time you play."

"I—I think so, too. But sometimes it isn't enough. Kitty—if it had been me, I wouldn't have looked back."

"I know."

With incredibly bad timing, the studio door opened and let in a swarm of noise from the outside. The producer in the sound booth waved manically and ran out to try to stop them.

I rolled with the punches. "Ellen, thank you for calling and sharing your story. I know I'm not alone in extending my thoughts and sympathies to you. We're going to break now for station ID." I signed Ellen off, then turned to the door.

There they were, crowding into the studio, lugging their instruments. I recognized the lead singer from the band's publicity photo: a skinny punk, twenty-two years old, wearing cut-off jeans, a ragged, oversize T-shirt, and combat boots.

I jumped out of my seat to intercept him. "Rudy? Hi."

Our introduction would determine how the rest of the evening went. Was he a stuck-up, self-absorbed musician type who barely deigned to speak to lesser mortals, or was he a regular guy who just happened to sing in a band?

He smiled at me. "You're Kitty? Hi!" He had a warm expression and easy-going manner at odds with his punked-out persona. He seemed more surfer dude than anti-social rebel. I relaxed; this was going to go well. "Let me introduce everyone. There's Bucky on drums, Len's our guitarist. And Tim there's on bass."

Tim stood out from the rest of the band. The other guys *looked* like they were in a band: Len had lightning bolts shaved into his crew cut, Bucky had tattoos crawling up both arms. Tim, however, was wearing a cardigan, like he'd been zapped through time from a '50s doo-wop group.

I considered for a moment, then said, "So, he's the one who's possessed by a demon?"

"Yup!" Rudy said proudly. "I don't know how it happened, but there it is."

Tim glanced at us as he was plugging his bass into an amp. His expression didn't change. He looked like a regular guy.

I contained my skepticism. "Rudy, do you mind if we have a few words on the air while the others set up? Then I'd love to hear you play."

"That's what we're here for!"

I brought him to the mikes. Right on schedule, the producer signaled that we were about ready to get back to the show. He counted down on his fingers, four, three, two—

"Welcome back, faithful listeners. This is *The Midnight Hour* and I'm Kitty Norville. I have as my guests this evening the L.A. band Plague of Locusts. They've just released their third album, and their single, 'Under a Dull Knife,' is climbing the charts. Next month they embark on their first national concert tour. We'll hear some music later on, but right now the band's lead singer, Rudy Jones, is here to chat with us. Welcome to the show, Rudy. Thanks for joining us."

"Are you kidding? This is so cool! We're big fans."

"Wow, that's sweet. Thanks." Here was someone who knew the way to a girl's heart. I beamed at him. "My first question for you: the band's name, Plague of Locusts, references an event in the Bible, in the book of Exodus. I was wondering why you chose the name, and what you might be implying with it."

"We just thought it sounded cool," Rudy said, totally deadpan.

I stared hopefully. "Nothing about raining destruction down on the world, or getting into wrath-of-God kind of stuff?"

He shook his head. "Well, I suppose a plague of locusts is like a swarm. We're like a swarm, you know?" He considered thoughtfully. "We want our music to swarm in and overwhelm people."

"Devouring them until nothing remains?"

"Yeah!"

"Now, your bass player, Tim Kane. Rumors say that he's possessed by a demon. You want to tell me how that happened?"

"It was the weirdest thing. We were in Bucky's mom's garage—that's where we got our start, you know. A real honest-to-God garage band. So there we were, practicing, only we weren't really practicing because we were fighting. We did a lot of that at first. Bucky wanted to know why we wouldn't play any of *his* songs, Len thought *he* should stand in front, we argued about who's more old school, Sid Vicious or Joe Strummer. So we're in the middle of all this, and then Tim, he goes into this, like, seizure or something. His eyes roll back into his head and everything. He was totally foaming at the mouth! Then he starts talking, and his voice. It's *different*. Totally deep. Kind of echoey, you know? And he says, 'Stop fighting.' I mean, what are you going to do in a situation like that? We stopped fighting. Then he tells us—only it's not Tim anymore, it's like this demonic muse or something. He tells us that if we want to be a great band, if we really want to follow our dream, we have to do what he says."

Fascinated, I asked, "This wasn't a 'sell your soul to the devil at the crossroads' kind of thing? This demon muse is giving you all this advice for free?"

"Yeah, totally! Isn't that cool?"

"Totally." I agreed. "Then what happened?"

"The demon tells us his name is Morgantix, and he's from another dimension, and he always wanted to play in a band. So he picked us, and I guess he picked Tim because he's, you know, so quiet. I mean, Tim started out as a really good bass player. But since Morgantix came along, the whole band just kind of jelled. It's been great. And I figure as long as Morgantix is having a good time, he'll keep helping us."

"Wow," I said. "That's almost heartwarming."

I glanced at Tim, who was standing by himself in the performance space, bass slung over his shoulder, fingering the strings. He was terribly unassuming. I wouldn't have looked twice at him on the street. He didn't *smell* like he was possessed by a demon. Not that I had any idea what someone possessed by a demon would smell like. Of course, anyone who dressed like a '50s preppy was possessed by something unnatural.

Then again, he *was* in a band.

Tim caught my gaze and quirked a sly grin at me. Not quite demonic, but still . . .

I said, "Do you suppose we might have a few words with Morgantix? I'd love to hear his side of the story."

Rudy looked over at Tim. "How about it?"

Slowly, Tim shook his head. In a deep, gravelly voice he said, "Morgantix play, not talk."

"How about Tim?" I said to the man himself. "Can we get a few words about what it's like being possessed by a musically inclined demon?"

Tim just glared.

Alrighty, then.

"It's kind of unpredictable," Rudy said. "He's there one minute, gone the next. We never really know who's in control when we talk to Tim."

I had to admit, I was a bit awestruck. The possibilities were intriguing. Tim certainly did have this manner about him. But was it just a typical, standoffish, artistic temperament, or really something supernatural?

"I have to confess to a bit of skepticism, Rudy. Where's your proof? Except for the voice thing, do you have any hard evidence proving the existence of Morgantix?" Really, though, who would make up a name like Morgantix? Score one in their favor.

"Believe me, Kitty, we wouldn't have gotten this far with the band without a lot of help from another plane of existence."

I had to take Rudy's word for that. I moved on. "I'm going to open the line for calls now. Do you have a question for Rudy? You know the number. Paula from Austin, you're on the air."

Paula let out a *squee!* of ear-shattering proportions. "Omigod, hi! Rudy, I'm *such* a big fan, you have no idea—"

The next ten minutes pretty much went exactly like that. Plague of Locusts seemed to have a bevy of screaming teenage fans across the country, and they all called in to gush. Rudy seemed impressed and chatted with them all.

I had fifteen minutes left to the show when I cut off the calls. "Rudy? How about you and the boys play something for us?"

His eyes lit up. "Yeah! Cool!" He was way too cheerful to be a real punk. He called over to the band, seated with their instruments. "Hey guys, what should we play?"

Bucky said, "We could play, you know, *that* one. The one with the *bum bum bum* part."

Len nodded quickly. "Yeah—the *new* version."

"I don't know," Rudy said, pursing his lips thoughtfully. "We haven't ever played that one live. How about the one with the cool bit in the middle?"

"We *could* do that one," Bucky said. "But what about the *other* one?"

"That one's okay too," Rudy said.

I had no clue what they were talking about. I stared, rapt.

Then Tim said, in his rough, demonic voice, "Play the fast one."

Rudy perked up, his eyes going wide. "Dude, yeah! The fast one!"

Bucky jumped to his drums, Len stood with his guitar, and Rudy raced to his microphone. Tim watched them, calmly as ever.

All this carried over the studio mikes. I almost hated to

interrupt the entertaining exchange, but the musicians had already turned their attention to their instruments.

I leaned in to my mike. "Okay, listeners, it looks like Plague of Locusts is going to play us some music. I have no idea what the name of the piece is, but they're calling it 'the fast one.' I, for one, am intrigued."

Rudy called over, "Are you ready, Kitty?"

Ready as I'd ever be. "Go for it!"

Bucky the drummer banged out a count and the band plunged in, full speed ahead. They went straight from zero to manic in half a second. The fast one, yeah. Still, their playing was strangely compelling. Len hunched over his guitar, legs spread, head bobbing in time to the music; I thought the poor guy was going to get whiplash. Bucky did the same, his long hair flying, the entire drum set rattling. Rudy clutched his microphone stand in both hands, pressed the mike to his face, and screamed.

Tim kept up with the song, fingers dancing on the frets, bass chords rumbling. The man himself, though, remained still, intensely focused, the eye of this particular hurricane.

I couldn't say I understood any of the lyrics, and there wasn't a melody of any kind to speak of. The rhythm resembled that of a massive downpour on a tin roof. That only made Plague of Locusts the latest in a long line of anti-establishment, anti-musicality musicians. Call it what you will, the fans loved it. My phone lines lit up, listeners calling in to beg for more.

The band played two more songs, we took a few more phone calls from eager fans, and then came the end of the show. I was almost sorry we were out of time. This had been a hoot.

Rudy and the others apparently had a great time, too.

After the closing credits, Bucky and Len shook my hand enthusiastically. Rudy hugged me like we were long lost siblings. He promised we'd do this again sometime. I basked in a general feeling of success and well-being. It hardly mattered that Morgantix the demon hadn't agreed to speak to me through host body Tim. Though, I'd rather been looking forward to conducting the first live demon interview in radio.

Tim hung back as they left the studio, waiting until Rudy and the others were in the hallway, leaving the two of us alone. He had an air of calculating calm about him. I couldn't help it; he made me nervous. My heartbeat speeded up, and I eyed the exit.

"Can I tell you something?" he asked me in a regular tenor—an unassuming, undemonic voice. Morgantix has left the building . . .

"Okay."

He glanced at the floor a moment, suddenly looking sly, like he was about to tell a joke. "See, you're pretty cool, and I just have to tell somebody. Can you keep a secret?"

"Sure." Always say yes to that question. I learned the best stuff this way.

He said, "Okay, here it goes. I'm not really possessed by a demon named Morgantix."

Somehow, I was simultaneously surprised and not. "Are you possessed by any demon at all?"

"No," he said, shaking his head and smiling wryly.

It was almost disappointing.

"You could tell me anything and I'd have to believe you. I have absolutely no way of telling if you're possessed by a demon or not," I said.

"Fortunately, neither does anyone else."

"So why go around telling everyone you are? Is it some kind of publicity stunt?"

"Oh, it's not for the public. It's for them." He nodded out the hallway to his departing bandmates. "They're the most directionless, indecisive bunch of people I've ever met. I realized the only way the band was going to get anywhere was with some kind of leadership. But they don't listen to me—I'm the *quiet* one. On the other hand, a being from an alternate plane of existence? They'll listen to that. It's the only way I could get them to agree on anything."

Enthralled, I considered him. It was the kind of story that if I hadn't seen it in action, I'd never have believed it. You can't make this stuff up.

"Aren't you afraid I'll blow your secret?"

He smirked. "What's easier to believe: that I'm actually possessed by Morgantix the demon, or that I've spent the last three years fooling a trio of grown men into believing that I'm possessed by Morgantix the demon?"

"You know that's a toss up, don't you?"

He smiled a clean-cut, boyish smile and left the studio to follow the rest of the band.

Well, how about that? I chased down a story about the supernatural and found a completely mundane explanation. There's a switch from my usual prime-time drama sort of life. And it only reinforced what I'd known for some time now:

I *love* my job.

MORE KITTY!

Here is a special sneak preview of Carrie Vaughn's
next novel featuring Kitty Norville!

Coming Spring 2007

*She runs for the joy of it, because she can, her strides
stretching to cover a dozen feet every time she leaps. Her
mouth is open to taste the air, which is damp with spring,
yet warm with coming summer. The year turns, and the
swelling moon paints the night sky silver. Not yet a full
moon, a rare moment to be set free before her time, but the
other half of her being has no reason to lock her away.
She is alone, but she is free, and so she runs.*

*Catching a scent, she swerves from her path, slows to a
trot, puts her nose to the ground. Prey, fresh and warm.
Lots of it here in the wild wood. She stalks, drawing breath
with flaring nostrils, staring ahead for the least flicker of
movement. Her empty stomach turns, driving her on. The
smell makes her mouth water.*

*She has grown used to hunting alone. Must be careful,
must not take chances. Her padded feet touch the ground
lightly, ready to spring forward, to dart in one direction or
another, making no sound on the forest floor. The scent—
musky, hot fur and scat—grows strong, rocketing through
her brain. All her nerves flare. Close now, closer, creeping
on hunter's feet—*

The rabbit springs from its cover, a fallen rotted log grown over with budding shrubs. She's ready for it, without seeing it or hearing it she knows it is there, her hunter's sense filled by its presence. The moment it runs, she leaps, pins it to the ground with her claws and body, digs her teeth into its neck, clamping her jaw shut and ripping. It doesn't have time to scream. She drinks the blood pumping out of its torn and broken throat, devours its meat before the blood cools. The warmth and life of it fills her belly, lights her soul, and she pauses the slaughter to howl in victory—

My whole body flinched, like I'd been dreaming of falling and had suddenly woken up. I gasped a breath—part of me was still in the dream, still falling, and I had to tell myself that I was safe, that I wasn't about to hit the ground. My hands clutched reflexively, but didn't grab sheets or pillow. A handful of last fall's dead leaves crumbled in my grip.

Slowly, I sat up, scratched my scalp and smoothed back my tangled blonde hair. I felt the rough earth underneath me. I wasn't in bed, I wasn't in my house. I lay in a hollow scooped into the earth, covered in forest detritus, sheltered by overhanging pine trees. Thin fog was breaking up in a pale morning light. Birdsong rattled the treetops above me.

I was naked, and I could taste blood in the film covering my teeth.

Damn. I'd done it again.

See where Kitty got her start…

KITTY AND THE MIDNIGHT HOUR

By Carrie Vaughn

(0-446-61641-9)

Kitty Norville is a midnight-shift DJ for a Denver radio station—and a werewolf in the closet. Her new late-night advice show for the supernaturally disadvantaged is a raging success, but it's Kitty who can use some help. With one sexy werewolf-hunter and a few homicidal undead on her tail, Kitty may have bitten off more than she can chew . . .

Everyone Loves *Kitty*

"I relished this one. Carrie Vaughn's KITTY AND THE MID-NIGHT HOUR has enough excitement, astonishment, pathos, and victory to satisfy any reader."

> —*New York Times* bestselling author Charlaine Harris,
> author of *Dead as a Doornail*

"Fresh, hip, fantastic—Don't miss this one, you're in for a real treat!"
> —L.A. Banks, author of The Vampire Huntress
> Legends series

"You'll love this! This is vintage Anita Blake meets *The Howling*. Worth reading twice!"
> —Barb and J.C. Hendee, coauthors of *Dhampir*

Can't get enough
vampires and demons and witches?

Bitten & Smitten
by Michelle Rowen

"A charming, hilarious book!
I'm insanely jealous I didn't write it."

—MaryJanice Davidson,
author of *Undead and Unwed*

Doppelganger
by Marie Brennan

"I can't wait for her next book!"
—Rachel Caine, author of *Windfall*

Kitty and The Midnight Hour
by Carrie Vaughn

"I enjoyed this book from start to finish."
—Charlaine Harris, author of *Dead as a Doornail*

Out of the Night
by Robin T. Popp

"A stellar job of combining intriguing characterization with
gritty suspense, adding up to a major thrill ride!"
—*Romantic Times BOOKclub Magazine*

Working with the Devil
by Lilith Saintcrow

"A unique and engaging mélange."
—Jacqueline Carey, author of *Kushiel's Avatar*